What You Won't Do for Love

What You Won't Do for Love

Wendy Coakley-Thompson

KENSINGTON PUBLISHING CORP.
http://www.kensingtonbooks.com

FIC
Coakley

DAFINA BOOKS are published by

Kensington Publishing Corp.
850 Third Avenue
New York, NY 10022

Copyright © 2005 by Wendy Coakley-Thompson, Inc.

All Kensington titles, imprints, and distributed lines are available at special quantity discounts for bulk purchases for sales promotions, premiums, fund-raising, and educational or institutional use.

Special book excerpts or customized printings can also be created to fit specific needs. For details, write or phone the office of the Kensington Special Sales Manager: Kensington Publishing Corp., 850 Third Avenue, New York, NY 10022, Attn: Special Sales Department. Phone: 1-800-221-2647.

Dafina Books and the Dafina logo Reg. U.S. Pat. & TM Off.

ISBN 0-7582-0747-6

First Kensington Trade Paperback Printing: November 2005
10 9 8 7 6 5 4 3 2 1

Printed in the United States of America

Acknowledgments

So many people helped with this, my "second child." I have to give thanks to God for the talent, for aligning my universe, and for placing the most wonderful people in my orbit.

Countless booksellers showed me much love. Printing out their names would be another book. You can find them on my Smooches list, under the "Books" section of my Web site: (*www.wendycoakley-thompson.com*). Marcus Williams of Nubian Bookstore in Morrow, GA, and B's Books and More in Lithonia, GA, deserve special mention for going above and beyond. Speaking of books, *Sniper: Inside the Hunt for the Killers Who Terrorized the Nation*, by Sari Horwitz and Michael Ruane, gave me all sides of the story of the D.C.-area sniper attacks, even though I was avoiding white vans and pumping my gas behind a tarp like everyone else during those twenty-three horrible days in October 2002. I continue to pray for those who were killed and wounded and hope that all affected can heal with time.

Much props to the gang at Marino/WARE in South Plainfield, NJ, and Griffin, GA, especially Bob Booth, who I'm convinced is my guardian angel, and to Lee Harrington, for that interesting peek into the psyche of the Southern brothah.

Folks who helped me get the word out include my beautiful sorors at the Stone Mountain-Lithonia Alumnae and Henry County Alumnae chapters of Delta Sigma Theta Sorority, Incorporated, and their Delta Authors on Tour (DAOT). Shunda and Jamill Leigh of the Atlanta-based *Booking Matters* magazine were also invaluable. I would be remiss if I didn't thank writers Travis Hunter and Brandon Massey, who helped me to manage my expectations.

I love Marines! My absolute favorites are Major Ian Brasure, U.S.M.C. and Captain Waheed Khan, U.S.M.C. They schooled me on everything Marine, which helped me to lend authenticity to KL and to Decameron (a.k.a. D). Temeesha Hubbard, D.V.M., thanks for not laughing at my absurd veterinary questions. Renee Green, D.V.M., Bernard Vincellette, D.V.M., and the folks at Alexandria Animal Hospital and Veterinary Emergency, thanks for the help with my own pet issues. Thanks also to Traci-Liegh Curran. I alone take the hit for anything I got wrong.

I'd be inert without Janell Walden-Agyeman, the best agent on the planet. Thanks also to my editor, Karen Thomas, and her erstwhile assistant and fellow West Indian massive, Nicole Bruce, and customer service rep Jessica McLean.

Family is a wonderful concept. Mine inspires me everyday. My nephews DeShield Godet, Wihwaht Thompson, and Gavin Thompson helped me shape D and Devin. DeShield and Wihwaht, much love. Gavin, *sarang hae* from *kakun komo*. Wayne Bryan Russell, the littlest nephew, I love you. Chun Cha Thompson, my sister-in-law, who helped me wrap my English tongue around her native Korean, *sarang hae*.

Mummy and Hubes, who provide all manner of unflagging support, thanks for the love and for facilitating my dream. Sorors Robin and Aunt Sylvia Matthew, I owe you big for the accommodations as I embarked on 2004's *Sleeping on Your Relatives' Couch* book tour. Thanks to my uncle Kenneth Leon Thompson (1909–2003), the real "KL," for the use of the name. Hunter, my baby dog, a.k.a. Dogzilla, you made a great "Tony Braxton."

At its heart, this book is about sisters and the passions they evoke— on both ends of the spectrum. Angie Thompson, my sister, soror, and Ideal Reader, don't go changing. Anal-retentive works for you! And Christina Thompson-Russell, Soror Moonbeam, thanks for running off on tour with "Cousin" Lenny Kravitz, for providing me with a lifetime of adventures, and for your free spirit. There are no words to express the depth of my love for you both . . .

Prologue

April 1997

It was dark and cool under the cotton sheet, breeze generated by her movement playing against the film of sweat on Chaney's bare skin. She had him in her mouth . . . sucking and relaxing, ascending and descending on him, her nose hitting the dark curls between his thighs with a staccato rhythm. The deliciously musky scent of him filled her nostrils as she breathed in on one, out on two. She loved giving head . . . in general and to him in particular. He was her man, and levelheaded woman that she was in the rest of her life, in bed she would've done anything to please him.

But tonight was more of the same, lately. His explosive response, which used to be on cue like Old Faithful, was conspicuously absent. He was soft and limp as an overripened banana. And she was distracted, too, wondering how she was going to tell him why she would consider leaving him. So typical that a woman would have to choose between her man and her career. She was thinking too much—that was her problem. The intellectual in her was fast overpowering her inner sex goddess.

Apparently, Shane was thinking the same thing. He pulled back the covers and cupped her under her armpits. His skin brushed against her hard nipples, and she shuddered as he eased her up to face him. Even in the slashes of light from the street lamps outside, she could see his gleaming light eyes, hooded with the thickest lashes she'd ever seen on a man. She stared at his curly 'fro, his hawkish nose, his bee-stung mouth. Her eyes trailed down to his strong-veined neck, which gave way to broad, brown shoulders, which looked darker against the white sheets. A combination of light and gray curls dusted his ripped chest. *God, I could look at you forever!*

Chaney sat on her left hip and legs, at his side. Shane's mouth softened into a lopsided smile. It wasn't going to happen for either one of them that night. Again. *Is it me?*

She looked down, ran her hand through those chest curls, then gently shook him. She glanced at the glinting engagement ring on that hand. "You okay?" she asked softly.

"Sort of," he said, in that fucking sexy, husky English accent that made her so wet that she nearly slid off his dentist's chair the first time she'd heard it. The brother who sounded like Jude Law. The contrast was striking. "You?"

Guilt set in. How could she even *think* of leaving him? Was she being selfish, having everything she'd ever wanted and still grasping for more? She nodded, looking away.

"I've got an idea," he suggested. "Let's get some dinner."

"Dinner" usually meant their favorite place: The Blue Mountain Restaurant, with the picture window providing the theater that was Flatbush Avenue. The menu, loaded with rice and peas, plantains, and highly seasoned meats, was like crack for folks of West Indian descent, like Chaney and Shane. Bob Marley's distinct voice, backed up by a slamming rhythm section and the I-Threes, blasted as they waited in the pungently scented, packed-to-capacity anteroom for a half-hour for their usual table. A dreadlocked waiter seated them among the hodgepodge of Jamaican paraphernalia and nonmatching tables with tablecloths made of irie colors.

While Shane perused one of the menus that the waiter had given them, Chaney stared out the picture window at April in Brooklyn. The heavy coats were now a distant memory. Passersby walked a little slower than the usual brisk, New York got-shit-to-do stride. Lovers strolled hand in hand. People took their time getting off the dollar van coming from Kings Plaza Mall. Motorists actually talked to one another while filling up their rides at the gas station across the street. The doors to the West Indian takeaways, and the record shops that sold reggae mix tapes and CDs, and the Korean grocer that carried products from the islands were all open. The usually madding pace of car traffic down the avenue seemed to slow just a bit. Everyone appeared to be shaking off the clutch of winter. Chaney imagined that the noise outside was probably like music. *You ain't going to see this if you go up to Syracuse, girl!*

Chaney looked away from the window as Shane ordered the usual for both of them: the shrimp roti for her, and the curried goat and rice and peas for him, with two Ting grapefruit sodas. She knew it was shallow of her to value how he looked, but damn it, if he wasn't fine in his white long-sleeved T-shirt, tan cargo pants, and Tims.

She'd applied to grad school just as he'd come into her life. Even though he had his own practice right up the street, he used to go into the public schools and provide low-cost dental care for the children. He'd come to the school where both Chaney and her sister Anna Lisa taught, just as Chaney was realizing that she loved teaching but didn't much care for fifth-graders.

One of Chaney's composite fillings had come loose, courtesy of an extra-hard pretzel. Practically at gunpoint, she made her way down to his temporary office. She didn't want to like him, but three things proved to weaken her. Number one, that accent. The man could make the word *gingivitis* sound like some exotic position from the Kama Sutra. Number two, those hypnotic light eyes. She focused on his soothing stare behind his clear mask and tried to stop the pounding of her heart as he stuck her gums full of Novocain. Number three, the shared heritage. After he found out that her parents were from the Bahamas through making small talk, he told her about his family, and how they moved from Jamaica to London in the fifties to clean up after World War II.

She forgave him the pain as he filled the cavity in her back molar. Three weeks later, she let him fill a more intimate cavity. She was so in love that it didn't even bother her that she'd been put on the wait list at Syracuse because of the extraordinarily large pool of qualified applicants. *Fuck Syracuse!* Chaney had something of a career already. And after Shane took her to London last month and proposed to her in such a wonderfully over-the-top fashion in front of Buckingham Palace, she had the man of her dreams. If that made her less of a feminist, then the National Organization for Women could go straight to hell. He made her blissfully happy, and all else was secondary.

Or so she thought. Just like every weekday after school, yesterday she went to the front door of the house she shared with Anna Lisa, picked up the mail, and saw it. The Letter. She recognized the stationery and the crest almost immediately. *Suos cultores scientia coronat:* Latin for "Knowledge Crowns Those Who Seek Her." Syracuse University was calling Chaney Braxton to seek knowledge for this fall semester. She'd be *the* University Scholar in the Instructional Design, Development, and Evaluation department. That meant a full tuition ride for three years. And as a bonus, entrée into the Future Professoriate Fellowship program.

The Letter was still in her purse between her feet under the dinner table. She felt disloyal to him for even keeping it. Keeping it meant that she was reconsidering her promise to become Mrs. Shane Allum. And it didn't help that right then, he took her hands into his over the table. She stared down at those beautiful hands over hers. Her hands in his, and that emerald-cut diamond-and-platinum engagement ring, said it all for her.

He looked around at the crowded restaurant and rubbed his stomach. "God, where on earth is that bloody waiter? I could actually eat a horse and chase the rider!"

"I don't remember horse being on the menu, baby."

"Well, it better be a massive goat they've got cooking."

Chaney grimaced. "I still don't understand how you can eat a billy goat."

Shane scoffed. "Billy's flipping delicious! You should try it."

She gave him a naughty, downcast look. "I'd rather eat Shane," she whispered.

He turned sheepish suddenly, shifting uncomfortably in his chair. Not quite the reaction she'd expected. She looked at him quizzically. "What?" she asked. "I thought you liked it when I . . . you know . . ." she leaned in " . . . talked like that to you."

He looked everywhere in the restaurant but at her. "Honestly, Chaney, it's a little jarring," he confessed. "Having you, the fifth-grade teacher, saying those things."

Ouch! Chaney felt the heat in her cheeks. "I didn't realize," she mumbled.

His light eyes continued to scan the restaurant, like he was the secret service looking for a potential assassin. "Maybe I should've said something," he said softly.

Her mind warped back to all the times they'd been in bed recently, when he couldn't complete the mission, when they'd ended up cuddling instead of falling asleep in each other's arms after mind-blowing, deliciously intense sex like before. She leaned in closer to him across the table, her gaze pleading. "Is that why it hasn't been . . ."

He looked like he knew what she was going to ask. The hurt on his face was obvious. She stopped short. She rubbed her thumb against the back of his hand, meaning to comfort. "You've got to admit, it hasn't been magical recently, baby," she murmured.

He shrugged. "It's never going to be rockets and fireworks every time, Chaney," he said. "Plus . . ." his voice trailed off.

Chaney's heartbeats quickened as she wondered what was going to hit her. "Plus what?" she asked.

Shane continued to avoid her eyes. She waited for an answer . . . and waited . . . and waited until she finally let his hands go, slipped her finger under his chin, and made him face her. She hated what she saw in his light eyes: fear. "Plus what?" she repeated, louder. More desperate.

He looked like he wanted to say something, anything. But he didn't. Blood roared in Chaney's ears. Her stomach roiled. She swallowed hard. "Are we in trouble?" she asked.

Shane opened his mouth, and Chaney braced herself. But before he could say, a hand slapped him on his back. He broke their gaze to look up, and Chaney did the same.

She recognized him: Shane's friend, Trevor. Shane and he played soccer in Prospect Park every Saturday afternoon with the rest of the other coconuts—first worlders of West Indian descent like him—the Nigels, Trevors, Gareths, and Conrads, brothers with very English names. Trevor was tall and dark; he looked like a runway model. He also had this way of looking striking even when he dressed casually. That night, he wore low-slung jeans and a V-necked T-shirt under a sheer black Nike hoodie, and he still made an impression in the crowded restaurant. There was also a woman with him, equally tall, equally striking in a white linen shift and a thin white sweater. She had that aloof air that women have when they know they're pretty. Though Chaney thought someone should've told her to get rid of the obvious weave and equally fake hazel contact lenses that made her look demonically possessed.

Awkward surprise came down on Shane's face like a thick curtain. He stood up, and he and Trevor shook hands soul-style. "Oi!" Shane laughed, his voice trembling. "What are you doing here?"

Is he nervous? Chaney couldn't tell. All she knew was that she was going to have to wait for satisfaction. "It's a restaurant, dumb ass," Trevor laughed, his New York accent betraying only a hint of his Jamaican roots. He brought the woman forward. "I'm treating Merlene to dinner."

Merlene hugged Shane, resting her chin in the crook of his neck. She closed her eyes and sighed. "Let me hold you, *bwoy*!" she laughed in affected Jamaican patois.

Chaney watched the exchange, fuming. Shane looked back at her, his smile even tauter. *What the fuck is going on?!* Trevor ran a hand across Shane's midsection, and Shane laughed, grabbing the hand. "Who the fuck dresses you, you bum?" Trevor laughed, then finally looked over and acknowledged Chaney. "You let him leave the house like this?"

Chaney fake-smiled. Her focus was more on Merlene and her arms still around Shane. Merlene stared back, as if daring her to say something. "My influence on him isn't as strong as I thought," she said, quite pointedly. "Who's your friend?"

"My sister," Trevor said, then introduced Merlene, who gave her a half-assed hello.

"Nice to meet you," Chaney lied.

"Same," Merlene probably also lied.

Trevor and Shane exchanged a surreptitious glance, then shared it with Merlene. Chaney stared in disbelief at the three of them. *What, am I the only one not in on the joke?*

"Well," Trevor said finally. "We're meeting Conrad and Clover. They're taking a break from wedding planning."

Chaney looked at Shane. *Apparently, so are we . . .*

Everyone said their good-byes, and Shane sat down again. Chaney watched the parting couple in time to see Trevor look over his shoulder and wave to Shane. He quickly looked away, back at Chaney. She couldn't put her finger on it, but he looked unsettled, not his usual easygoing self. She didn't have time to figure out why. "Shane, what's going on?" she asked.

"What?" he asked.

"You were going to tell me something," she reminded him. "And then Trevor sashays in here with Merlene, and now all of a sudden, you're . . ." She stopped short, running the past couple of minutes in her mind. *Merlene.* Her insides squeezed painfully. "Are you seeing someone?"

The color drained slowly from his face, giving Chaney her answer. She sat back in her chair and exhaled trembling air from her lungs. But still, she wanted to hear him say it. "Are you seeing someone else, Shane?" she repeated, willing herself to be calm.

Shane sighed. "Not seeing someone," he awkwardly began, "but . . ."

"Okay, then. Did you fuck someone else outside of our relationship?"

He bit down on the inside of his lip and stared at her. Just as she couldn't stand it any longer, he confessed. "Yes."

The truth didn't bring her the satisfaction she thought it would have. She felt her right hand rubbing furiously at her chest, using the sensation of the cotton against the inside of her palm to focus her mind. Tears pricked at her lids. "Why?" she gasped.

His eyes were moist. He chewed at his thumb. "I dunno why," he mumbled. "But I love you, Chaney."

She sucked her teeth. "And nothing says that like fucking someone else, Shane. Next time, send flowers!"

The dreadlocked waiter appeared just then. Chaney was only remotely aware that he put their food and drinks in front of them with a flourish. She stared pointedly at Shane, her stomach sinking as she thought about what she'd been doing to him only hours before. "Who was she?" Chaney demanded, as soon as the waiter left.

Shane held his head in his hands. "Oh, God, Chaney," he moaned.

Chaney looked over her shoulder. Trevor and Merlene stared back from a few tables away. Chaney turned to face Shane again. "Who is it?" she commanded, her tone sounding desperate, even to her ears. "Is it Trevor's sister?"

Shane also glanced at the table over her shoulder. He looked weary, numbed. "No, it's not Trevor's sister."

"Well, who?"

He met her questioning gaze. "It's Trevor," he said.

Chaney stared at him, waiting for him to laugh and make fun of her for being so gullible for falling for his little prank. When he continued to sit before her, wilting, looking sadder and sadder, she realized that wasn't going to happen. She couldn't believe she hadn't seen the signs of infidelity: the shitty sex, the increased time with his boys—his boy Trevor in particular—his emotional distance, his nit-picking at her behavior . . . Even with the signs, though, it still didn't make sense. She rubbed harder against her blouse. "So, like, what, you're gay?" she finally asked.

Shane closed his eyes and sighed. "I think so, yes."

She blinked, and unshed tears spilled down her cheeks. "You *think*?" she laughed bitterly. "Either you like pussy, or you like ass. Those are the only two choices on the menu, Shane."

His eyes hardened. "It's not like you to be cruel."

Again with the wild, hurt laughter. "It's not like you to be gay! We're even!"

His gazed morphed into one of profound sadness. Despite his con-fession, a part of her wanted to wrap her arms around him and com-fort him, the part of her that loved him with all her heart. "I love you, Chaney, and I cheated on you," he sighed.

The other part of her that had begun to hate him wanted to reach across the small, rickety table and scratch his eyes out of his skull. "With a man!" she cried.

"Would it have been better to cheat on you with a woman? I still cheated!" He was quietly crying, tears plopping into the dark green sauce of his curried goat. "I was wrong," he acknowledged, shaking his head.

Her mind played over all the things she'd done with him sexually, all the high-risk behaviors she'd engaged in with the man she was going to marry. The man who now thought he was gay. Silent tears gave way to gasping sobs. "Please tell me that, when Trevor was fuck-ing you in the ass . . ."

Shane emphatically pointed to the breadth of his chest. "I don't get fucked," he stated.

Too much information! She stared at him with contempt. He so totally missed the point. " 'Scuse me—I'll rephrase," she said. "Please tell me you used a condom when you were fucking Trevor in the ass."

He nodded. "Of course I wore a condom," he mumbled.

Chaney picked up her purse, reached in for her hanky, and saw The Letter. She laughed as she blew her nose into the stark white cot-ton. She shook her head in disbelief. *To think that I actually thought I had a surprise for you!* Her heart ached. "I don't understand," she qui-etly wept.

Bob, Rita, and the I-Threes nearly drowned her out. "Sweetie," he said desperately, clutching for her hands, "I want to work this out."

She wrung her hands out of his grasp. "What are we going to work out, Shane?" she asked. "What, should we still get married, and me, you, and Trevor are going to set up house in the suburbs? In what parallel universe is this going to work?"

A sigh trembled from Shane's broad chest. The look in his moist eyes was one of resignation, like he, too, recognized the futility of the situation. "I don't know what to say, Chaney," he confessed. "I don't even know how to reconcile this with myself. I'm almost forty years old. I'd never even considered that I might be . . ." he swallowed hard ". . . gay. I don't know if this was a one-off thing. I have to know, Chaney. I've got to follow this through."

I can't believe this! Twenty-four hours ago, the search had been over for Chaney. She'd found the one person she'd wanted to spend the rest of her life with. In less than a day, her hopes and dreams unraveled like the paper-thin plot of a dime-store novel. There'd be no white dress, no fantastic wedding, no children, no Sundays in bed with the *New York Times* crossword, no growing old together. Not with him. Volcanic emotions rumbled in her chest cavity. "I gotta go," she gasped.

Shane's eyes widened. He grabbed her hand. "Chaney, please don't go," he begged. "I love you."

If you loved me, you wouldn't be gay! She couldn't give in to her profound grief, not in here, not give up her dignity. It was all she had left right then. She sure didn't have *him* anymore. She pushed him away. For the last time, she looked down at that fabulous emerald-cut diamond engagement ring and felt heartsick. Like it was on fire, she pulled at it, stressing out the flesh on her ring finger that had grown accustomed to having it there. The metal scraped her skin, grazed her knuckles. Finally, she got it off.

The classy thing to do would've been to put it on the table. *Fuck classy!* She pressed the ring, the symbol of his twisted love for her, into his curried goat. It gave her perverse satisfaction to hear him gasp as he looked at the expensive ring mashed into the greenish-white potatoes of the curry.

"Chaney!" he called after her as she got up and sifted through the mass of hungry West Indians for the nearest exit.

Chaney picked her way through the street traffic, instinct taking her to the tiny, bleak subway station on Lincoln Road. She dropped a token into the slot and pushed her tummy against the turnstile. The metal rod slapped against her bottom, pushing her inside the station. She fled down the concrete stairs, sadness filling her up as she willed the train to come. She had one thing to do before she gave in to her pending full-scale meltdown. She had to sign and mail The Letter.

May 1997

Devin stared around at his family, seated at the massive round table with the white linen cloth. From his seat at the table, he could see the huge red Pike Place Market signs that were such a part of Seattle. Hours ago, he'd just marched down the aisle to graduate from the University of Washington—or U-Dub—with his pre-vet degree. This was supposed to be his day, the culmination of the first leg of his journey to becoming what he wanted to be. But all he thought about and felt was the palpable tension at the table. And there was the polarizing force, all six-feet-five of him, seated facing everyone, nursing his fifth whiskey.

Devin didn't look much like his father, despite the biological fact that Kenneth Leon Rhym, whom everyone called KL, had given Devin twenty-three of his chromosomes. Aside from the height, Devin was more like his mother in facial features and temperament. He had her flat head, her slanted eyes, though his father's influence made them a little rounder and Westernized. His father had also added some cocoa to his mom's yellow to produce a smooth brown that Devin had only seen on himself. He did rock that curly afro, though, that was probably the only sign to outsiders that he was, in fact, a brothah.

His father was a stranger to him. He'd almost forgotten what his father looked like. KL's visits to Seattle were nonexistent, and Devin used to spend his summers in Korea with his mother's extended family, this freakishly tall hybrid that practically dwarfed them. Devin did remember that imposing air, though. Even though his father was not in uniform, KL was still the embodiment of a Marine Corps colonel: buzz cut, ramrod-straight shoulders, authoritative gait, and touchable testosterone. What the Marines didn't give him in confidence, years as a JAG prosecutor more than filled the breach. No wonder everyone at the table looked like they were seconds away from shitting a pickle in that fancy restaurant.

Chauncey, a lawyer, Devin's older brother and KL's son with First Wife, sat with his arm protectively around his wife Renee, also a lawyer, who was pregnant with their second child. She fawned over the first child, Jeffrey, who sat next to her in his high chair, playing with a fistful of mashed potatoes and salmon. He was probably a future lawyer. Chauncey, too, shifted uncomfortably in his chair, like this was the last place he wanted to be. Devin couldn't blame him. He and his older brother were strangers, which could have been attributed to more than the yawning chasm of a seventeen-year age gap between them.

Eric, Devin's second brother and KL's son with Second Wife, looked irritated. His desire to pack it in was less subtle, displeasure making his light eyes crinkle at the corners. Irritation compounded by his white girlfriend, Marlene, rambling on about nothing in particular. Nerves, Devin guessed, being surrounded by this motley crew of a family. Devin thought he and Eric would have had something in common; Eric, with his red-tinged slack curls and his light eyes, looked as impure as Devin did. Unfortunately, Eric saw Devin as the enemy in his attempts to jockey for KL's affections, attempts that went as far as Eric going to law school to be like his father. And he seemed to blame Devin for the fact that KL left his mother for Devin's.

That left him, Devin, son of Third Wife, Kim-Chin, who sat at his right. His mother who defied convention and left her pussy hound of a husband, took her child, and moved three thousand miles away so they could have a life away from KL and his rules that applied to everyone but him, and his obsessive, militaristic quest for perfection. Kim-Chin, KL's uppity war bride who made a life for herself and Devin with her own job teaching Korean to Seattle businessmen, and later, with Bill Charles, who showed Devin that real men could be gentle . . . with the animals in his practice . . . with the wounded woman who he later married . . . with her abandoned son.

Kim-Chin, who, despite the stand she took for independence eight years ago, looked like she was about to cry at any second under KL's caustic glare. Even Bill, who was so even-tempered as to seem inert sometimes, seemed keyed up, like some of the skittish animals that Devin encountered in his practice.

A young waiter in a blindingly white shirt, black slacks, suspenders, and a black tie appeared with a leather-bound check cover that Devin knew, on instinct, held the bill for this majorly expensive drama that masqueraded as a family dinner. The waiter slapped on an obsequious grin. Casting a sweeping glance around the table, he asked, "How are we doing here?"

KL gulped from his whiskey glass. " 'We're' doing just dandy," he declared, boring an optical hole through the poor kid who was probably just doing this to get through college, like Devin had to, because his father refused to pay for anything but a pre-law major.

The barb washed off the waiter's back. He probably had his share of unruly, no-tip-leaving customers. "Good!" he laughed, shaking the leather-bound check cover. "I'll just leave this here, then."

Both KL and Bill grabbed for the check cover before it could hit the table. Bill won—most likely, Devin guessed, because of the twenty-plus more years KL carried. Bill took the check cover and sat back down in his chair. He didn't seem to gloat, and Devin loved him even more for that. "I'll get this," Bill said, gray eyes twinkling. "Your money's no good here, Ken."

Devin had never heard anyone call his dad "Ken." It was always "KL," or "Colonel," or "Mr. Rhym," or "Dad."

Bill took out a platinum card, and the waiter, practically salivating, took everything and went away. KL simmered, and everyone else avoided each other's eyes until Marlene took up the champagne bottle in the bucket nearest to her, got up, and circled the table, topping off everyone's champagne glasses. "Why don't we propose a toast to the graduate?" she chirped.

Eric looked at her disapprovingly. "Only if he wants one," he snapped.

"Why wouldn't he want one?" Renee asked. "After law school, I spent the first month in a bottle, celebrating!"

Jeffrey, the baby in the high chair, cackled and clapped his chubby hands, spewing mashed potatoes every which way.

Renee winked at Devin as Marlene came up behind him and filled up his champagne flute. Devin gave his brothers credit; they sure could pick good women. *Like our father.*

"Who's going to make the toast?" Marlene innocently asked.

Kim-Chin shyly held up her glass. Devin could always tell what his mother was feeling; her face betrayed her every emotion. Today, it was unvarnished pride. "I remember when Devin born," she said in her still-halting English. "He bring me joy. When I young and first come to this country, I know nobody. Just my son. My baby son. He bring me joy then. He bring me joy today."

It all came flooding back to Devin, his mother's unflagging care for him, her frustrating attempts to navigate Arlington when her English was so poor, her late-night tears, her heated arguments with his father after he'd come home smelling like some other woman. The only thing that would comfort her was hugs from him. His eyes misted as he got up and practically gobbled her up in his massive arm span. He buried his face in the crook of her neck. "*Omma*," he whispered. "*Sarang hae yo.*" *I love you.*

"*Sarang hae*, Devin," Kim-Chin said.

They both sat down, trying to compose themselves. Bill slipped a protective arm around Kim-Chin, squeezed her close, and dropped a quick kiss in the crown of her pixie cut. Devin saw his father's hooded eyes narrow further. Clearly, KL wasn't pleased about the PDA between his ex-wife and Second Husband. Bill, unsuspecting, turned to KL. "You want to take this one, Ken?" he asked.

Devin, too, looked hopefully over at his father. Would he take an open opportunity to say something nice about him, even though KL hardly knew him? "Naw, you go ahead," KL said. "I'll go last."

Devin's heart sank. He looked away, lest he punk out and begin sobbing like he did all those times that KL promised he'd come out to visit him for the summer, only to renege.

Bill looked over at Devin with those kind gray eyes. Devin remembered the first time he'd met Bill, how he'd wanted to hate him for taking his mother away from him . . . until Bill trained those twinkling gray eyes on him. Devin was instantly won over. "Devin," Bill sighed. "Until I met your mother and you, the most important thing in my life was my practice and my career. Wasn't the most demonstrative of fellas. Probably the tight-ass in me. Probably why I spent my life around animals, not people."

He laughed, and Devin joined in. "Yeah, you were a little bit puckered there, Bill," Devin agreed.

Bill gave him a look, like he was getting fresh. But Devin knew he didn't mean any harm. Devin knew that Bill would never take a strap to him, like KL had when he lived under the same roof with his father. Bill's school of parenting was the noncorporal kind: lengthy lectures, discussions, deprivation of favorite things, looks of unhidden disappointment. Sometimes, Devin wished that Bill would hit him and get it over with. "But," Bill said pointedly, with a broad, white smile, "before I could even grasp what the responsibility of instant fatherhood would involve, you thawed my heart, kiddo. I couldn't imagine my life without ya. I hope I never find out what that's like. I love you like you were my own flesh and blood."

Bill stood and raised his glass. He blinked, and a tear rolled down his cheek. "To Devin Subin Leon," he said. "This is only the beginning, son. You're going to do great things."

Devin didn't even raise his glass and drink. He couldn't. He got up and gave Bill a tight hug. *That's what every son should hear from his father.* "Thanks, Bill," he said into the wet spot he created on Bill's shoulder.

Bill patted Devin's broad back. "No problem, big guy," Bill returned with characteristic reserve.

They sat, and Bill sipped at his champagne, as if the display of emotion had drained him like a chunk of kryptonite. All eyes at the table now focused on KL, like everyone was wondering what he would say that would top Bill. The suspense was killing Devin. Just what could an absentee father say about a son he hardly knew? KL looked like he was thinking up something witty to say, too, like he was preparing closing arguments that would sink a defendant in military court. Finally, through the pea-soup-thick fog of suspense, Chauncey said, "Pops. Your turn."

KL pushed the champagne flute aside, clutched his whiskey glass, and stood, unfolding himself to his full height. He looked down at Devin, and Devin's heart skipped a beat. At that second, Devin regressed to a five-year-old, ten seconds from quaking under the gaze of a man from whom he so desperately wanted endorsement. KL then did something that Devin did not expect: he actually smiled. Devin was immediately sucked in. "What can I say, son?" KL began.

Say anything, Dad. Anything to let me know you approve . . .

"Devin Subin Leon, my third and last born," KL continued, then took a sloppy sip of his whiskey. "I admit that I wasn't the best father, the most present father for you, son. That wasn't my fault . . ." his gaze darted to Kim-Chin for a second, then darted back to Devin, ". . . but that's the way things turned out. I hope that now, I'll be able to get to know the man that you've become. I think that, once you've started law school, like your brothers, we'll be able to spend hours talking about the cases you're working on. It's a rite of passage for us Rhym men . . . me, your brothers . . . we'll all welcome you to the family business, son!"

Devin's face fell. Typical of his father, making assumptions that his life was already preplanned. Kim-Chin looked away, and Bill, puzzled, glanced over at Devin. "Umm . . . Dad," Devin began, wondering if he still had the courage to go his own way in the face of KL's almost certain eruption. "Dad, I just got accepted to the veterinary medicine program at Washington State University. I start in September."

"With a full scholarship and everything," Bill said proudly. "He's going to make an excellent vet. He's been working with me at the office. He's gifted."

"I know he's gifted; he's MY son!" KL roared.

Everyone at the table started at the sound of his booming voice. After a second's delay, Jeffrey, the baby, let out a scared cry. Some restaurant patrons glanced over at the multiracial table to see what on earth was going on. Renee took Jeffrey out of the high chair and held him close to her ample breasts filling with milk for the second one in the oven.

"Dad, I told you that I wasn't interested in going to law school," Devin reminded him, harkening back to five years ago, when he was just looking at colleges. "That's why you cut me off, remember?"

"Obviously, you didn't learn your lesson," KL declared. "I thought this shit was just some rebellious phase you were going through."

"With all the respect that is due in this awkward situation, Ken, you don't reach the top ten of your class in one of the toughest veterinary programs in the nation with rebellion as your sole motivation," Bill said, quiet but firm nonetheless.

KL strafed Bill with his gaze, but Bill stood strong. "Duly noted, Bill," KL said, with the appropriate snotty emphasis on Bill's name, "but Devin is my child . . . a black child at that. I was raised in the segregated South. I know firsthand that the only defense a black man has in this racist country is an intricate knowledge of the law so that he can arm himself for battle with vanilla motherfuckers like you!"

Devin felt sick to the stomach. He stared incredulously at his childish father. *This "vanilla motherfucker" clothed me, and fed me, and drove me to swim meets and basketball games; where the fuck were you?* "This was my choice," he declared. "It's what I want to do with *my* life."

Eric reached up, grabbing his father's elbow. "Dad," he cautioned.

KL snatched his arm away. "No, son, I'm not going to be quiet! Your brother wants to waste his life playing with doggies and kitties when we live in a world where brothahs get murdered for stupid shit like whistling at white women."

Bill was steadily losing his cool. "How can you draw a parallel between those unfortunate incidents and your son wanting to pursue his dream?"

"How could you not?" KL countered.

"He wants to step out of his father's shadow and be his own man."

"So, he steps out of my shadow and into yours? His white daddy?!"

Immediately, Devin got it. In his father's eyes, Devin's rejection of a career in law was a rejection of him as a father. And Bill got it, too. He looked hurt. "Every day, I'm reminded that I'm only the stepfather of this wonderful kid, Ken," he said softly. "I'm the last person who's a threat to you."

The waiter, looking appropriately perturbed, came over with the leather check cover, which he handed to Bill. He then bravely turned to KL. "Sir, your tone," he said in a soft, clinical voice. "Some of our customers have expressed alarm."

KL looked around and saw everything from displeasure to outright fear from restaurant patrons and the people at his table. Resigned, he slowly eased back down into his chair and shook his head, like he couldn't believe Devin was defying him, and Devin was getting support from everyone around. KL handed the glass to the waiter. "Fill that," he ordered, then fished into his pocket for *his* platinum card. "Charge it."

"Of course, Mr. . . . ." the waiter looked at the card " . . . 'Rhyme.' "

Years of having people fuck up his name set KL off even further, if that were possible. "It's pronounced like 'Rim,' as in 'Fill the glass to the rim, won't you?' "

Reluctantly, the waiter took the glass and disappeared into the scenery. Devin looked at his father, who looked so battle-worn and defeated all of a sudden. And his extreme displeasure with Devin was the cause of that.

The waiter returned with the whiskey, and KL signed for it. The only sound at the table was Jeffrey's cries slowly ebbing to a fitful whine. Finally, Kim-Chin spoke. "KL, you concern with Devin being smart, or being big-time lawyer," she said softly. "That don't make him a man. All I care, he have good heart. That's how I measure a man. My son is a man. Shame you not see."

KL threw back the whiskey, swallowing the amber liquid in two gulps. Then he looked at Devin. The pain in his dark eyes cut Devin to the quick. "Son, you disappoint me," he declared. "There's a price for this. You just don't know it yet."

Devin felt all the blood leave his face. Suddenly, all of his accomplishments in his young life meant absolutely nothing. Because his father didn't co-sign them.

KL struggled to his feet. Eric and Chauncey rose to help him, but KL pushed them away. They returned to their respective positions beside their women, who were sufficiently ashamed at the spectacle they'd just witnessed.

Devin would carry that moment with him for years . . . watching his father's broad, straight back as he headed for the exit and hearing those words. *Son, you disappoint me . . .*

One

Both Chaney and the uniformed female Delta Airlines Logistics staffer peered critically into the extra-large beige plastic crate. Two huge brown eyes stared intelligently back, then, from behind the black metal bars, appeared to give the gray Washington National Delta office and its blue carpet the once-over. Chaney hiked up her slacks that were about a minute from being too small, stooped, and looked closer into the cage. She put her hand up against the black bars. Almost instinctively, a wet pink nose met the flesh of her open palm. Even though she'd never been a dog person, Chaney smiled. But then, she instantly hardened her heart. She didn't want to get too attached . . . just in case this was a huge mistake.

Chaney looked up at the Delta staffer, complete with clipboard, pen, and a sheaf of carbon papers, all awaiting Chaney's signature. "Does that look like a golden retriever to you?" Chaney asked.

The staffer gave a jaded shrug, like she had better things to do. Being from New York herself, Chaney was quite familiar with that shrug. She'd used it herself when circumstances didn't allow you to overtly tell someone to fuck off. "What do I know from dogs?" the staffer sighed.

Chaney tore herself away from those patient brown eyes and stood up. The eyes followed her. First of all, the dog was a leviathan, all legs and tail, a tail which thumped the plastic and shook the whole cage when its owner wagged it. Secondly, its fur was short, not the typically long hair that draped a golden retriever. There was no draping here. The dog's hair was so short that she could indeed see that it was a male, complete with a full, dangling nut sack. And the dog wasn't even golden; he was more like a honey-yellow color. Chaney sighed. *Daisy.* She was the older sister; why didn't she act like one?

The staffer flipped back reams and reams of carbon paper on her clipboard. Suddenly, her faded gray eyes came to life. "Here's the Interstate and International Certificate of Health Examination for Small Animals," she said, scanning it. She looked up from the form and at Chaney. "You're Chaney Braxton, Suffolk Court, Alexandria?"

Chaney hovered over her shoulder, reading the official-looking form along with her. "Uh-huh?"

"Daisy Braxton sent you the dog from Los Angeles?"

Yes, her hippie sister Daisy Braxton, a.k.a. Moonbeam, who took a musician lover on her fortieth birthday, quit her job as Assistant Director of Artistic Planning at the Los Angeles Philharmonic, and ran off to join him on the European leg of some dreadlocked rock star's tour. Chaney nodded for the staffer.

"You're right. The dog's a yellow *Labrador* retriever," the staffer announced. "His name's Tony."

Chaney looked down at Tony, lying patiently in the crate. From the recesses of her mind, Chaney recalled why. "Yeah," she mused. "She named him after Tony Soprano."

Just then, the staffer laughed. "Your dog's named Tony?!" she hooted. "*Tony Braxton?!*"

Suddenly, Tony stood at attention in his crate. "Wuh!" he barked.

Chaney sighed. *So the joke's on you, too, huh, fella?*

While the staffer still nursed the vibe she got from the joke, Chaney signed the waybill for Tony and paid the outstanding $280 shipping fee. Again, Daisy making life interesting and expensive for her. But, Chaney guessed, when one looked like her sister—light-skinned, model-tall, with an ass like a cream puff and big, round titties, life was just a bit kinder to you.

What are you thinking? Chaney looked down at Tony in the crate, stared at his little yellow doggie face. God bless him, he sat up, patiently taking in his surroundings as the most understanding skycap on the planet—an older black man in a blue woolen uniform, requisite cap, and the demeanor of a Southern brothah who'd seen it all—

rolled the massive crate on his cart through National's sanitary terminals, into the shiny-bright elevator, and into the always-packed, well-lit parking lot in terminal B.

The minute they got outside, Tony's nose began twitching furiously as he inhaled the currents of crisp March Virginia air. "Not the same as L.A. smog, but you'll be all right," Chaney said to him, then rolled her eyes. *You're talking to the fucking dog!*

"What?" the skycap asked.

Huh? "Oh, nothing," Chaney said, as they rolled up to her prized possession: her champagne-colored Nissan Altima 2.5 S, her vanity purchase to celebrate becoming a business owner, like sixty-hour weeks and no social life actually were worth it.

While Tony proceeded to strain his powerful retriever neck muscles against his inadequate, too-short, blue nylon, Wal-Mart leash and drag Chaney around the lot so that he could pee on the tires of every car, the skycap opened the trunk and shoved the massive crate inside. Chaney could feel the resistance of the thick, nonrecyclable plastic against the metal of the trunk as she shut it.

Chaney tipped the skycap, put Tony in the backseat, and watched helplessly as he stomped his long-nailed paws against the baby-soft leather in his quest to find a comfortable spot. She shook her head. "Daisy, I'm gonna kill you when you get back!"

They got on the road, Chaney looking back at Tony as she navigated the circuitous route of roads and highways that were supposed to get her out of the airport. She blanched as she watched him shift and dig his claws into the leather, then shake and spew tons of yellow hair all over her leather and gray carpet. This was probably why they'd never had pets as children. Anna Lisa, her older sister, was too busy keeping them a family after their parents died to make room for one more mouth to feed. Chaney herself didn't mind so much . . . nothing to get attached to that would suddenly leave. And she couldn't have imagined herself walking a dog late at night in their Brooklyn neighborhood.

Chaney remotely heard the bleating tones of her Blackberry and turned down the soothing Sade track on WHUR—Howard University Radio. She reached into her purse in the passenger seat, took out the Blackberry, and instantly recognized the number with the 718 area code in the digital green window. *Anna Lisa.*

Chaney pressed the TALK button. "Hello, Worrywart," she said.

"Hello, Dr. Hypersensitive," Anna Lisa returned in her proper, affected speech.

Chaney could picture her sitting behind the desk in her twelfth-grade classroom at Sojourner Truth High School, staring from her perch at the desks in a semicircle. Deep in the background, she could hear a voice drone on over the school's P.A. system. Chaney didn't miss that life one bit.

"I was calling to see if you'd gotten the dog," Anna Lisa declared.

"No, you were calling to remind me of how big a sucker I was to ever agree to do this shit."

Anna Lisa laughed such an all-knowing, old-lady laugh for someone who only just turned fifty. "How is the beast?"

Chaney looked back briefly. Tony was now sitting up, leaving sloppy, wet nose marks on her just-cleaned back windows as he stared out at his new home. The leather seats in the Altima comfortably cradled his bony canine butt. "Huge! I think this dog is actually her man."

"Have you ever known your sister to keep one man around for four years?"

True enough. Daisy was like a black Samantha on *Sex and the City.* "Moonbeam swears she was in love with each one of those men she was getting her swerve on with," Chaney laughed.

"Uggh! Chaney Regine Braxton," Anna Lisa sighed, her tone one used with the afflicted. "Must you speak like that? You have a Ph.D., for heaven's sake."

Chaney just laughed again. She enjoyed pushing her sister's buttons sometimes. "So, you're going to kick in some money to help me with Dogzilla?"

"Certainly not," Anna Lisa declared. "That's between you and Daisy. Not like I don't have my own problems."

The hellions. "What's the name of the latest juvenile delinquent?"

"Fahtir," Anna Lisa declared scornfully. She had no respect for anyone who didn't have a European name.

"Oh, no, not you turning up your nose. You with the son with the ghetto name!"

Chaney could hear Anna Lisa scoff over the phone. "His name is not ghetto; why do I always have to explain that his name comes from *The Decameron,* that beautiful novel by the Renaissance author

Boccaccio," she said. "If people'd crack open a book every once in a while, my son wouldn't have to be profiled!"

"That's probably why D's not speaking to you now."

"No, he's not speaking to me because I challenge him to be more than a killer for the rest of his life."

Like she was talking about a hit man, not a decorated Marine and Gulf War veteran. But Chaney knew this was a sore spot with mother and son. She changed the subject. "Anyway, what did this Fahtir do?"

"We were discussing *Giovanni's Room.*"

"Can't go wrong with James Baldwin."

"Oh, no? I asked Fahtir to give me the basic theme of the book. To which my little opportunity for personal growth says, 'Why you gon' ask me about some faggoty-ass book, Mrs. Hall?' "

"To which you said?"

" 'Well, Fahtir, the so-called "faggoty-ass book" in question is on the curriculum, which means that if you don't read it, you won't graduate in three months.' Then this future leader and contributor to my social security says, 'Well, how 'bout I bust your faggoty ass?' "

Chaney gasped. "He threatened you?"

"Oh, it gets better. This kid is, like, six-foot-forever and looks like he could probably bench-press my Benz."

"So . . . ?"

"So, I calmly took my purse out of my desk drawer, counted out the last five twenties I had for groceries, and put them on my desk. Then I said, 'Of course, you could bust my . . . what did he call it, kids?' And the students were riveted; this was the only time this year I had their undivided attention. They all said, 'Faggoty-ass.' 'Yes, faggoty-ass. Of course, Fahtir, you could do that, but the second you're done, I will give this hundred dollars on the desk here to Mike Townsend over there so that he could do the same to you.' "

Chaney remembered Mike. "Jesus, I taught Mike Townsend. That kid was so huge he was shaving in the fifth grade."

"I know!" Anna Lisa laughed. "And Fahtir looks over at Mike and sizes him up. He says, *'Pfft!* Mikey T.'s my niggah. He won't step to me.' And Mikey T. mumbles, 'Yeah, Fah, you's my boy, but for that paper, you best believe I'll wax that ass.' "

"I don't know why you just don't retire," Chaney said. "You're already twenty-plus years in."

Anna Lisa merely laughed. "The boy can't help it, Chaney," she said. "I just had a parent-teacher conference with the child's mother . . . all 200 pounds of her, with her finger waves, and gut baring midriff, and . . . I do believe the Robin Williams quote was 'pants so tight you could tell what religion they are?' "

Chaney grimaced. "Nothing like seeing Mom's camel toe to scar a child for life!"

They laughed. Chaney missed her big sister terribly. Just like how she remembered missing their mother for years after she'd died. Sometimes, Chaney got so lonely being in D.C. all by herself. But she knew that the only way she would grow would be to get out from under her sister's shadow.

"Speaking of alternate-lifestyle males," Anna Lisa cautiously began, "Shane asked me about you today."

Chaney's stomach squeezed painfully. Even after five years, that night at the restaurant was as vivid as if it was happening right then. "And why would I want to know that, Anna Lisa?" she asked.

"You can't avoid him forever, Chaney," Anna Lisa said. "Like Ma used to say, 'That's God's breath, you know?' "

"He's as dead to me as Ma is, Anna Lisa, so drop it, okay?"

The second she said it, she regretted it. She loved her mother, missed her every day she drew breath. She hated that Shane still held sway over her, so deeply that he made her disrespect the memory of her own mother. From the backseat, Chaney heard a plaintive whine, and turned to see Tony, staring at her with understanding brown eyes. *What the fuck's wrong with you?*

Finally, after an awkward silence, Anna Lisa sighed. "Let me go," she said. "I'm not going to enable Daisy by giving up money, but I made an appointment for her dog at Rosslyn Veterinary Hospital. On Wilson Boulevard in Arlington. Norm's cousin is one of the owners of the practice. Devin Rhym. He'll get you and Dogzilla straightened out."

Chaney could practically hear the adulation in Anna Lisa's voice when she mentioned Norm. The love of her life, ex-husband, now present boyfriend. *My family's weird!* "Thanks," she said. "Honestly, I've been circling National for so long that Ashcroft and the crew are probably thinking I'm Osama."

"Let me know how everything turns out, okay?"

"Okay. I'm sorry. I didn't mean to snap at you, much less insult my own mother."

"It's okay, baby sis. I left my husband because he cheated on me with women. I couldn't imagine what I would've done if I found out that Norm was on the down low."

In his misspent youth, before he woke up to the fact that Anna Lisa was the best woman on the planet, Norm had never met a vagina he didn't like. "Norm, on the DL?" Chaney laughed. "Never!"

"I know next to nothing about the men in my life . . . your nephew included," Anna Lisa sighed, hopelessly. "Please check in with him for me. I know he's lonely down there at Quantico, but he's too proud to call his mother."

Chaney couldn't understand D, her nephew, even though they were only five years apart in age. Chaney wished she had a mother to rebel against. "Okay," she promised. "Stop being such a mother hen."

"Can't help it," she said. "Well, I'm going to go before both you and I get matching brain tumors."

Chaney moved into the rightmost lane, under the sign that read: GEORGE WASHINGTON PARKWAY NORTH. She and Anna Lisa said their heartfelt but perfunctory "I love you's," then Chaney hung up.

The erect Washington Monument whizzed by in a blur through the passenger side of the Altima as Chaney drove along on George Washington Parkway. Runners jogged at the Lady Bird Johnson trail, next to the gray, snaking Potomac River. Chaney saw none of it. Her mind wandered to what her sister had said. *Shane asked me about you today* . . . He used to seem two towns and five years away. Now, there he was again, making her feel inadequate as a woman . . . so inadequate that he needed to turn to men to feel fulfilled. After him, her life motto was "No plants, no pets, no men." But there she was, with her gay ex-fiancé still on the brain and her sister's hulking dog in the backseat of her car. She looked at Tony, perched comfortably in her backseat. He stared back at her, and reflexively, his paintbrush tail thumped mightily against the seat. For a second, she thought he looked so sweet, so filled with unconditional love for her, like he'd been in her care for all of his four years. The she came to her senses. "Don't get too attached," she warned him. "As soon as your mistress comes back, you're gone."

Instantly, the tail stopped thumping, like Tony knew his place.

Chaney took the Rosslyn Key Bridge exit off of Route 50, and made the left onto Wilson Boulevard, which was packed, as usual. Between the pedestrian traffic consisting of professionals, and military folks

bearing the uniforms of all branches in stark relief with the tall buildings, and the various and sundry luxury cars, Rosslyn at 5:00 P.M. resembled what Chaney imagined Shanghai at lunchtime looked like.
She eased her way through slow-moving traffic and fast-changing traffic lights. Even Tony now sat up, with a look on his doggie face that
appeared to ask, *Are we there yet?*

Finally, Chaney saw the unassuming red brick building with the
neon sign that read *Rosslyn Veterinary Hospital,* next to the equally red
Arlington Fire Station. Chaney cussed like a sailor as she maneuvered
her way from the leftmost lane to the rightmost lanes of Wilson, which
was now a one-way street. *Please, Jesus, let there be parking.* Despite her
lapsed relationships with both The Man Upstairs and His son, there
was. Chaney turned off Wilson, then parked the car in what was an
embarrassing wealth of spaces. She then looked back at Tony, who
seemed hyperalert now, his enormous yellow head darting every which
way on its thick neck muscles. "Come on," she said. "We're going to
get you checked out. Okay?"

Tony just stared at her. Mentally, she kicked herself. *What are you
waiting for, the dog to answer you?*

The very second she let Tony out of the car, he took off, straining
against the leash in her hand. The nylon plaits burned her flesh as he
dropped his nose to the ground and sniffed the earth and nearby
trees with a vengeance. Then he raised his leg and sprayed a yellow
stream of urine on the bushes with startling accuracy of aim. "Again
with the marking of the territory!" she cried.

She struggled to glance down at her watch. The gold hands
pointed out 5:15. She didn't have time for this shit. Her part of the
proposal for tomorrow's meeting wasn't anywhere near done, and
she was there, wrestling with this creature. She gave the leash a
stern yank, then instantly regretted it. The nylon dug deeper into
the soft flesh of her palm. "Let's go!" she commanded through gritted teeth.

The urine stream ceased as quickly as it had begun, and Chaney
dragged Tony toward the red door with glass squares at its top. She
pulled him through the door and onto the other side of another
world. It looked like a regular doctor's office, especially that of Chaney's
friend Macca, who also doubled as her gyno. There was a wall-length
wooden bookcase filled with files, behind an expansive desk where a
woman in scrubs sat. A pane of glass—with the requisite hole in it for

interacting with patients—shielded her from the waiting room. In said room, a color TV, elevated and seemingly suspended in midair in one corner, broadcast Channel 7's 5:00 news, replete with the D.C. area's share of shootings, stabbings, corruption scandals, and other mayhem. Seated in chairs, two pairs of appropriately concerned white animal parents worried, their charges wearing expensive harnesses and held in check on equally pricey, retractable leashes. Chaney looked down at Tony, with his ghetto leash and bad manners, and felt like the parent of a kid like that Fahtir who had so generously offered to bust her sister's ass.

The two dogs—a god-awfully ugly shar-pei and a mean-looking rottweiler—squared their broad shoulders and gave Tony the evil eye, a look that Tony, completely clueless, appeared not to even notice. He seemed to want to play, whereas the other two dogs seemed united in one sole purpose—tearing Tony a new one. Just as Chaney was wondering how she was going to stop an altercation between the three behemoths, the hole in the glass wall opened. "Hi," called the woman in scrubs, from behind a flat-screen computer monitor.

Chaney dragged Tony to safety. "Hi," she said, strained, amidst her efforts to wrestle the dog into doing her bidding.

Suddenly, she disappeared, only to reappear through an open door at Chaney's right. She was petite, with her black curls drawn up in a ponytail away from her creamy, freckled face. Her green eyes focused on Tony. Her name tag read MARIA FABBRI, VETERINARY NURSE. She reached out and took Tony's face into her small, soft-looking hands. "Look at the big pup!" she cried in a voice that Chaney heard used with babies, animals, and idiots. "Hi, Noonie!"

Tony went nuts, wagging his tail wildly. He rose up on his two hind legs; at that height, he was almost as tall as Maria. "Wuh!" he barked as Maria scratched at the scruff of his stump of a neck.

Chaney wrestled with the leash, wondering if Maria was ever going to get around to acknowledging Chaney's presence. Finally, she did . . . but only peripherally. "Who's your momma?" she asked Tony.

Like he can answer! "Chaney Braxton," she said, her irritation level approaching its zenith.

Maria gently guided Tony down to all fours. "Of course!" she said, her eyes lighting up like polished emeralds. "You're Dr. Rhym's cousin. Your sister called in the appointment."

"Cousin by marriage," Chaney corrected her.

Maria homed in on the paperwork jutting sloppily out of Chaney's unzipped Kate Spade. "Is that for me?" she asked.

Mercifully, Maria took Tony's leash, and Chaney fished from her purse the paperwork that the Delta staffer had given her at National. "Yes."

Tony quietly sat while Maria, still holding his leash, perused the stack of carbon papers. Chaney glared at him. *Oh, so you behave for her, but not for me. Traitor!*

Suddenly, Maria looked up. "Tony Braxton?" she laughed.

Tony snapped to attention. "Wuh!"

Chaney looked behind her at the other doggie owners, whose confused gazes seemed to be asking, *Where?*

"Good boy!" Maria exclaimed to Tony, and from somewhere within those scrubs, she produced a small dog bone treat.

Tony separated his mandible from his skull and almost took Maria's hand off in his single-minded quest for the treat. Chaney looked horrified; Maria, like it was no thing. "I'm sorry," Maria giggled. "I didn't mean to laugh. I'm sure you get that reaction all the time, though."

Chaney glared at her. *Whatever.*

Suddenly, Maria became all business. "We've got a room ready for you and everything," she said, the picture of friendly efficiency. "I'm going to check Tony in and make him a chart. Then the doctor will be with you shortly. Okay?"

"Thanks," said Chaney perfunctorily.

Maria led the way through the side door from which she initially came. Chaney and Tony followed her down a short, sanitary-looking hall lit from overhead with stark fluorescent lights, past closed blue-gray doors with numbers like 1, 2, and 3 on them, until they arrived at an open door, emblazoned with the number 4. Maria deposited them into a windowless room, complete with a computer, metal table, cabinets with glass doors, and Formica shelves with jars with tongue depressors, cotton balls, cotton swabs, and the same bone treats that Maria gave up from the confines of her scrubs. Maria waved her to a small, wooden bench on the far wall. "Have a seat," Maria offered. "I'll tell the doctor you're here."

Tony looked longingly at her, and she laughed. Again, she reached into that magical place in her scrubs and gave him a treat. Again, he almost took her hand off. Again, she found that hilarious. " 'Bye, Tony!" she laughed.

Chaney watched in awe. *This dog-owning shit ain't for me!*

Maria shut the door, leaving Chaney alone in the boxy room with a creature that was so alien to her that he might as well have come from another planet. She stared down at Tony, and he stared up at her with those huge brown eyes with long blond lashes. His ears were pricked up, and he cocked his enormous head to the side. Looking at her like that, he was the epitome of cute. "What's your deal, dog?" she asked.

He actually looked like he was about to answer her, tell her his innermost thoughts. But then, he looked down between his sinewy, yellow-haired legs and, with rapt determination, proceeded to lick his pink nut sack. *Typical male.*

Right then, Chaney heard ringing in her purse and retrieved her Blackberry. She looked at the 202 number. *Nathalie,* it said below the number. She was taking this one. "Hello."

She heard clinking of glasses, loud chatter, and bad seventies music over the digital network even before Nathalie spoke. "Hey, girl," Nathalie greeted her in an accent that still betrayed her Alabama roots, even after she'd spent almost twenty years in D.C.

"Where are you?" Chaney asked.

"Georgetown," Nathalie answered—her favorite place, Chaney knew. "Dani and I are having drinks."

The mention of Dani set Chaney on edge. Dani was Marion Daniels, Nathalie's friend from her days as an attorney on the Hill. Dani, with her brusque, know-it-all ways and her overt lesbian lifestyle left Chaney leery. Chaney was the most liberal soul on the planet, courtesy of having lived the bulk of her life in a blue state. But her tolerance for the gay lifestyle had been severely tested after that night with Shane over her shrimp roti at The Blue Mountain Restaurant.

"How's the dog?" Nathalie asked.

Chaney looked at Tony, still giving his balls a spit shine with his long, pink tongue. "He's alive," she said. "We're at the vet's."

"You're such a good sister."

"No, I'm a sucker. I actually feel my head turning into a giant lollipop."

"Did you make my shea butter hand cream like you promised?"

Chaney sucked her teeth. Nathalie, of all people, should have known that Chaney was a woman of her word. Plus, making her shea butter creations was the only thing that kept her sane nowadays. "You have to ask?" Chaney said, her tone laced with mock hurt.

"Could you be more sensitive?" Nathalie asked.

But Chaney didn't hear her. The door opened, and Tony shot bolt upright to attention. Then Chaney saw him. *Damn!*

The first thing she noticed was that he was tall, way over six feet. And a five-foot-ten woman like Chaney would notice that. Then she saw those almond-shaped eyes that crinkled at the corners as he smiled at her . . . a brilliant, lopsided smile with a top lip that was slightly wider than the bottom. His hair was cut short, cradling his flat head. A tiny lock of hair curled just where his forehead began. He was the color of a piece of caramel that she used to suck on all day as a child. He was wearing scrubs, like Maria, the Patron Saint of Treats, only he wore a white coat with his name—DEVIN S.L. RHYM, DVM—stitched on the left pocket in dark blue embroidered cursive lettering.

Chaney looked him up and down, all the while being remotely aware of Nathalie droning on in her ear. This kid couldn't have been Norm's cousin. He didn't look a day over thirty.

"Chaney!" Nathalie snapped through the phone.

Chaney covered the mouthpiece with her hand. "I gotta go," she whispered.

"But what time should we come over?" Nathalie cried, sounding slighted at being dismissed so abruptly.

"I don't know. An hour. I gotta go," Chaney said, this time forcefully, and then hung up.

"There you are!" he cried ecstatically, like he was happy right down to his toes to see her.

"You're Devin Rhym?" Chaney demanded.

He pinched the white coat away from a well-developed left bicep. "That's what it says on my pocket," he laughed. "Why?"

"I was . . . I just expected someone older," Chaney murmured.

He laughed, shrugging that off. Chaney imagined he was probably the happiest brothah she'd met in a while. "I want you to meet some people," he said.

The door opened wider, and two women were standing next to him. One was a tall, lithe blonde with legs that seemed to go on forever in her slacks that practically cleaved her in two and tight white sweater. Chaney could recognize fake boobs anywhere, but this woman's were the realest-looking of the fake. The other woman, an Afrocentric sistah with a head full of braids, looked miserable and sick under her flawless makeup, like she was about to toss her cookies at any second. The black shroud of a dress she was wearing couldn't camouflage the growing bump at her midsection. Chaney shot a curious glance at Devin. *Which one of these is yours?*

"Chaney Braxton," he began with a flourish, "this is Marlene . . ." he pushed the blonde forward ". . . and Renee." He indicated the green-in-the-gills sistah with a pat on her shoulder. "My sisters."

Just as Chaney was mulling over in her mind how that was possible, Renee said, "Sisters-in-law."

"Chaney's Norm's sister-in-law," Devin told them.

Marlene's blue eyes lit up. "Yes!" she exclaimed. "Dad told me about Norm. The Marine. His son—your nephew—he's a Marine, too, eh?"

Chaney nodded. "Yes. Decameron. D."

It was Renee's turn to register recognition. "You're Anna Lisa's little sister."

Little sister. Like she was still in knee socks and pleated skirts, not a woman now on the dark side of her thirties. Chaney nodded nonetheless.

"That's the sweetest love story," Marlene waxed poetically about a life that wasn't hers. "How Norm and your sister divorced, then got back together after their son went off to Desert Storm." She covered her heart with her hands. "Please tell me they're still together."

"Yup," Chaney confirmed. "Eleven years and counting."

"Marlene's a hopeless romantic," Renee said, almost apologetically.

Chaney marveled at how no one commented on the years when Norm and Anna Lisa were actually married, when he fucked his way through all the women in Quantico, the surrounding towns, bar girls in Viet Nam, all while Anna Lisa held down the fort, raising her son and two sisters in base housing, until life cruelly opened her eyes. Ah, the other side of romance.

The door opened wider, and Chaney's heart squeezed. Three of the most adorable children she'd ever seen trickled in. Even Tony stood up, made his way over to them, and sniffed them curiously. Little brown hands darted out to stroke him, and Tony's tail whipped around like a windmill. There was a taller boy in traditional boy togs, who looked so much like Renee that it was uncanny. His smile consisted of four permanent front teeth in a crowd full of baby ones. Another boy and a little girl who looked close in age grabbed at Tony's tail, which made him try to wag it all the more. The little girl, all in pink, looked up at Chaney with huge brown eyes. "Is this your dog?" she asked.

Briefly, Chaney wondered if she'd ever experience motherhood. By the time her mother was Chaney's age, she'd had two-thirds of her children. Anna Lisa was nineteen when she had D. Chaney was woefully behind schedule. "He's my sister's," Chaney answered.

Renee snaked a protective arm around the little girl. "This is Cousin Chaney, guys," she laughed proudly. "Say hi."

"Hi, Cousin Chaney," they obediently chorused.

So, this is what she was reduced to . . . old spinster Cousin Chaney. She could practically feel herself age under her smart business suit and open brown trench.

Renee pointed to the older boy, "This is Jeffrey," she announced, then pointed to the little boy and the girl. "And my Catholic twins are Corey and Chelsea."

"Hi," Chaney said.

Marlene looked at her watch. "Well, we'd better get a move on," she sighed, then shot Devin a look. "Eric and I are having dinner at Chauncey's. You should come, kiddo."

He shook that head with that adorable curl in the middle of his forehead. "I got plans," he said.

Marlene looked over at Chaney and winked. " 'Plans,' " she said mockingly. "That's code for 'girlfriend I don't want to introduce to my family.' "

He merely laughed, shooting Chaney a convivial look. "What is it with married people? Always recruiting for the team."

"Misery loves company," Renee laughed wearily. "Come on, kids, let's go. Say 'bye to Uncle Devin."

" 'Bye, Uncle Devin," they again chorused.

Chaney watched as the kids, then Marlene, then Renee lavished kisses on Devin's cheeks. For some reason, she felt left out. She looked away, down at Tony, who looked up at her with a *Now what?* expression. " 'Bye!" Devin called after them.

They trickled out of the room in a trail of hushed chatter and spring coats, leaving Chaney, Devin, and Tony alone in the boxy room. Chaney shot him a sideways look. The boy was fine, in a Tiger

Woods sense. But then again, he was just that . . . a boy. Chaney wondered about the many jams from her childhood that he'd never rocked to, how many TV shows whose dialogue she could quote that he'd never seen, how many historical events she'd lived through that had happened when he was still swinging in the safety of his dad's nut sack.

He crossed his arms and leaned against the metal table. "So," he said. "Chaney, huh?"

She nodded, looking away. "Yup."

"What, like Dick?"

Are you offering? Then she realized he wasn't. "Oh, you mean the vice president," she said, half-laughing. "I read somewhere that in Wyoming, they pronounce it like 'Cheeney.' But no, my sister named me after James Chaney. You know, the CORE volunteer who was murdered in Mississippi with Schwerner and Goodman?" *Like you'd know about that . . .*

He looked blank for a nanosecond, before those deliciously limpid brown eyes lit up. "I remember that," he said. *"Mississippi Burning."*

Well, what do you know?

"Plus my dad took me to school," he added. "He's the original black activist."

"And, from what I can remember, an attorney."

He nodded. "Yup. He and my two brothers. As the baby of the family, I was allowed to do my own thing."

"And just how much of a baby are you?" Chaney asked, before common sense could intervene.

He threw his head back and laughed. "I'm twenty-eight," he replied. "Would you like to see my I.D., Cousin Chaney?"

It was Chaney's turn to laugh. Okay, so the boy's bloodline didn't entirely cross with hers, but he was officially chronologically undesirable. She'd have to suspend her fantasies of wondering how many times twenty-eight went into thirty-six. "If Tony doesn't mind your age, then I won't take exception," she said. *Hint, hint. Focus.*

Devin finally looked down at Tony, who was attentively watching them joust and parry. "Ah, yes, Tony," he said.

He reached out and scratched the scruff of Tony's neck, and Tony practically ate it up. "Hey, boy," Devin said, like he was talking to a friend. "How're you doing?"

In response, Tony licked his hand, and Devin smiled his cute, eye-crinkling smile. Devin looked up at Chaney, focusing that smile on her. She felt her heart constrict. "He's great," he laughed, all the while pulling back his jowls and examining his teeth. "Labs are special dogs. Even-tempered. Loving. You're not going to regret doing your sister this favor."

I'm already regretting it. "You're the professional," she commented.

"Oh, so you trust me," he teased, "you know, with me being such a baby and all."

Fuck you! Chaney laughed, shaking her head. "Okay," she said. "You got me."

He got on the phone to Maria, summoning her in, all the while watching Chaney. She returned the favor, watching him watch her. She marveled at this. So, boys in their twenties were gutsier than they were in her day. Like an apparition, Maria appeared, with her calming presence, her implacable smile, and a manila folder with huge numbers on its face. While Devin examined the folder, Maria's hands darted for Tony's neck, stroking him in a way that seemed to calm him. Chaney made a mental note to put that trick in her repertoire.

After a moment of silence, Devin shut the folder and set it on the metal table. "Okay," he stated, all business, "we've got the basics on Tony from the paperwork your sister sent. But there are some gaps in his chronology. So, we're going to examine him and take some blood here. It would help, though, if your sister could fill in some of the blanks with regard to his treatment over the past four years."

Chaney watched attentively as Devin examined Tony with flawless professional acumen. He was no longer a puppy himself, as he, along with Maria's help, listened to Tony's heart with his stethoscope. He expertly took Tony's temperature—rectal—while Tony had a look like, *Hey, what are you doing back there?* Devin stroked that spot between his shoulder blades. "It's okay, dude," he said to Tony, again like they were buds. "It's all good."

When he produced a massive needle and proceeded to take Tony's blood from his left paw, though, Chaney thought she'd faint. The shit looked painful, particularly as Devin had to move the needle in Tony's flesh to find a suitable vein. Devin looked over at her, and he and Maria shared a laugh at her expense. "You okay over there, Cousin Chaney?" he teased.

Chaney turned away as the tube filled up with Tony's red blood. "Doesn't that hurt?" she gasped.

Again, Devin and Maria chuckled. Chaney was pissed that they were making fun . . . of her! *Fuck both of you.* Maria held a squirming Tony while Devin continued to work. "It's probably not pleasant, but dogs have a high pain threshold," Devin said. "He'll be fine once we're done."

Tony let out a yelp as Devin finally withdrew the needle. Chaney's heart lurched. She sensed that Tony had just taken a header over his supposedly high pain threshold. Devin stroked Tony's tensed yellow back. "It's cool, buddy," he said. "All done."

Maria took a blue-soaked cotton ball out of one of the apothecary jars and dabbed it against Tony's paw. Tony squirmed against the pressure she'd applied. "Aww, come on," Maria laughed. "I thought you Labs liked water!"

Tony didn't seem to be amused, and Chaney couldn't blame him. He looked like she imagined she looked after a gyno visit. Tony lay on the cold tile floor, looking spent, like he'd been exhausted by the intrusiveness of the exam. "Cousin" Devin turned to her. "We're going to check his blood . . . you know, his electrolyte levels, and all that," he explained. "Just to get a baseline of how Tony's doing. Okay?"

What else could she do but play along? She looked down at Tony, like the two of them were resigned to his fate. "Okay," she complied aloud.

" 'Scuse me," Maria said, then left the room with the samples of Tony's swabs and bodily fluids.

Devin turned his broad back to her and proceeded to turn on the water in the metal sink. "Just from looking at him, I'd say Tony's in good health," he said over the sound of the running water and squishing, sudsy sounds. "His reflexes are good. His teeth look healthy. Though you're going to have to learn to keep them clean, either by giving him chew toys or treats, or by brushing."

Chaney looked down at poor Tony, who still seemed like he smarted from being so unceremoniously violated. *No fucking way am I brushing your teeth!*

Devin rinsed, shut off the water, and snatched a paper towel from the dispenser on the wall. Drying vigorously, he turned to her. "It'd help, though, if you could get his complete records," he said. "You could even have her fax them here to us, if that'd be more convenient."

Chaney was sure that this entire experience was probably the most inconvenient she'd had in a long time. She plopped down on the bench and sat with her head in her hands. "Here's the problem with that," she sighed. "My sister's run off to be on tour with her latest boyfriend. He's the bassist in a musician's band."

Devin's eyes became rounder in surprise and what looked like admiration. "Who?"

Chaney told him. The eyes became rounder still. "Honestly?" he asked. "That's so cool. I have all of his CDs."

Focus! "Anyway," Chaney said pointedly. "I don't know if she's going to be able to pop into the nearest Kinko's. They're somewhere in Europe."

Devin balled up the wet paper towel and slam-dunked it into the trash receptacle on the counter. Chaney was impressed. But she guessed at his height, he must've spent a good deal of time on the b'ball court. He folded his arms across his chest, and Chaney saw the outline of an impressive six-pack under the green material stretched across his midsection. Reluctantly, she looked away. "She must've told someone where she'll be," he suggested.

Chaney could've smacked her head. How could she have forgotten? The book that came in the mail about a week before Daisy's hasty departure. Chaney dug into her purse, sifting through her Blackberry, checkbook, keys, Listerine power strips, tampons, until she saw it at the very bottom. The book, a thick, laminated affair, half the width of letter paper, bound with a metal spiral coil. She snatched it out of her purse, and then watched, mortified, as two tampons from her purse flew into the air and settled comfortably at Devin's large feet. Her face flamed. *Great. Now he knows I'm on the rag!*

Devin calmly reached down and picked up the tampons, like it was no thing. But then again, he'd just had his gloved finger up a dog's butt not five minutes ago. She sensed that his shock threshold was about as high as Tony's. She reached an outstretched hand to him, and he dropped them in. "Here you go," he said.

Jesus! She couldn't even face him. She looked down at his hands. She saw long, almost dainty, fingers, with painstakingly trimmed nails. She also saw his skin—dry, chapped, like he spent practically all of his time washing them. She recognized the problem immediately. She used to have the exact same problem during the blisteringly cold winters she'd spent in Syracuse. She put the tampons in her purse, then pushed more stuff aside to reveal a sample jar of her shea butter cream. It was the least she could have done for him squeezing her in at the very last moment. "Here," she offered. "For your hands."

Curiously, he took it, opened it, and sniffed it cautiously. "Lavender," he commented. "You make this stuff?"

She nodded. "Keeps me sane." She looked down at Tony, sprawled out on the cold floor. *At least it did before this shit . . .*

Tentatively, Devin dipped one fingertip into the rich, creamy shea butter and scooped out a dollop the size of a dime. Chaney watched as he rubbed it into his hands. "This feels great!" he exclaimed. "You don't know how many lotions I've gone through. Thanks."

Chaney leafed through the book, looking for the March dates of the Rock and Soul Tour. Secretly, though, she felt a swell of pride. "No problem," she said. "Reciprocity."

He laughed, rubbing the butter deeper into his flesh. "It's no big deal," he assured her. "We're family."

Chaney dug her Blackberry out of her purse. *And you're a baby.*

Just then, she saw the name and address of the hotel. "They're in Paris," she said, more to herself than to him.

"Sweet," he commented. "You should've gone."

She could just picture the look on Al McCulligh's face if she were to tell him that, on the eve of their company, Autodidact, acquiring a major government contract, that she was going to run off to gay Paris. But then again, that was never her style. In the drama that was the life of the Braxton sisters, she was the sensible one, the portrait of rectitude. Running off to Paris—or anywhere, for that matter—after some dick was never and would never be her style. "Some of us have work to do," she sighed.

"What do you do for a living?" asked "Cousin" Devin, seeming genuinely intrigued.

The super businesswoman that lived inside Chaney took over. "I'm part owner of an e-learning company," she announced. "We did over two million dollars of government business last year." *Did she sound like an asshole?* "Umm . . . not bragging, mind you."

He shook his head. "Two million's pretty impressive."

She couldn't help herself. "We just acquired six million dollars of a billion-dollar contract with the Navy and Marine Corps. Tomorrow morning, we seal the deal. As a matter of fact, I would've been preparing for that meeting if Tony hadn't popped into my life so dramatically."

"Sounds like you've done well for yourself, Cousin," he said.

It's official. I do sound like an asshole. "And you, 'Cousin,'" she said, intending to deflect from her nervous crowing. "Your own business at twenty-eight? When I was twenty-eight, I was trying to survive and washing all of my clothes together in cold water."

He winked teasingly. "I can use hot water now. I've arrived."

Cute. She shook the phone in her hand. "Well, I'd better make that call."

"Need some privacy?"

"Nah."

As she dialed the country and city codes, then the actual number, she wondered how much this was going to cost her. After three rings, someone answered on the other end. "Hotel Centreville," he near-whispered—sounded like *'Otel Sahn-truh-vee*—but Chaney could still hear the characteristic French snootiness for which they were so famous.

"Daisy Braxton, please," she requested.

"Madam, do you know the hour?" Sounded like *ow-err.*

Her brows knit on instinct. "Pardon."

"The hour. The hour." Sounded pissily like *zee ow-err, zee ow-err.*

Oh! Chaney glanced down at her sensible leather-and-gold Longines. "It's almost seven o'clock."

"Well, here . . ." sounded like *ear* ". . . madam, it is almost one in the morning."

Her Brooklyn ire was about to surface, right in front of cute "Cousin" Devin. "So?" she demanded.

She heard the officious desk attendant huff. "They are sleeping." *Zey are sleeping.* "You call back later." *Lataire.*

Chaney heard a click, then nothing. Shocked, she looked down at the cell phone. *No, this motherfucking frog didn't hang up on me!*

Devin stared curiously at her. "What?"

She silently fumed. "He hung up," she murmured in disbelief. "Something about the lateness of the *ow-err.*"

Devin seemed to understand her frustration. "It's cool," he said, his tone reassuring. "We don't need the information right away. Right now, we're going to do the baseline, which should be normal. If it isn't, then we'll worry. Okay?"

Chaney looked into his face, so young, so open. She wanted to believe him, but she knew her sister and her propensity to bring the drama. Of course, it won't be okay. Of course, they'll need the records. But looking in his face, she was able to forget that . . . at least for a few minutes. "Okay," she lied.

Devin rubbed his now-smooth hands together. "I'm going to see if I can rush Maria on those test results," he said, crossing the expanse of the room in two strides. "Be right back."

In an instant, he was gone, leaving her once again in the room with Tony. She ran it all over in her head . . . the ridiculous expense . . . the cost in time and energy . . . her stress level, which was officially beyond through the roof . . . and the adorable pseudo-cousin who seemed to think this was all something that was going to work out *okay*.

The South Arlington apartment was small, cramped, and redolent of cat piss. From his vantage point on the shit-brown, stressed-out couch, Devin could see the culprit responsible for the stench—a gray tom at the far end of the living room, next to the pressboard entertainment center. The poor cat had its tail caught in the chubby fist of Kimmy's older son. The kid dragged the cat back and forth across a threadbare throw rug that shielded peeling hardwood floors on the losing end of better days. The cat had a look in his green eyes, like he had revenge planned for the second he could free himself.

"Denis, stop that!" Kimmy commanded from her perch next to Devin on the couch.

Denis kept on torturing the cat. Devin was secretly rooting for the cat. He looked around the apartment, with its generic beige plaster walls, third-hand furniture and appliances, television, and boom box from another era. *Salvation Army Chic.*

Kimmy shot a glance at her son, then back to Devin. "Terrible fours!" she laughed uncomfortably.

Devin looked over at Kimmy and mourned her lost potential. He still could hardly believe that this babe next to him in this god-awful place was the love of his life in high school. Back then, at Washington-Lee, Kimmy McKibben had mischievous eyes in a stunningly beautiful face; later, when he actually saw a cornflower, he immediately remembered her eyes being that color blue. Her hair was so blond that when she stood in the sun, its light appeared to permeate her, making her look transcendent. That was the first thing he noticed about her . . . that and a pair of double-Ds in a tight purple V-necked sweater that made his tongue hang from his soaking wet mouth.

This version of her—Kimmy 2002—was a mere shadow of her former self. Her eyes had lost their sparkle, like she'd seen too much of this life that had been so unkind to her after graduation. The blond hair hung in frizzy clumps around her stooped shoulders. She even had black roots. There was no beauty light in this dimly lit apartment. The once-perky double-Ds looked saggy in her gauzy sundress that opened down the front. Attached to the left breast was a newborn dressed in blue, sucking greedily at the pink nipple. Devin looked down at the baby's dark head and struggled to temper his envy. That used to be *his* spot. "So, you're a mommy again," he laughed.

"Yup," she sighed. "Again."

She seemed anything but overjoyed. But, Devin guessed, how thrilled was she supposed to be when the second black baby daddy followed the skid-marked path of the first one and bounced when Kimmy revealed she was pregnant? Devin looked over at Denis. Devin recognized the look of the kid . . . dark curls, light creamy skin. Hell, Devin had The Look, too, the look that said everything . . . impure, racially ambiguous, mulatto, or its polite counterpart, "biracial."

Denis was still messing with the tom, who was now puffed out to twice his size, like he was ready to do some damage. Kimmy looked too overwhelmed to be driven to act. So he did. "Hey, Denis," he called.

Denis was quick to acknowledge a male voice. He didn't speak, though, merely stopped yanking the cat across the floor.

Devin patted the space between him and Kimmy. "Why don't you come over here and introduce me to your little brother?"

Obediently, Denis let go of the cat, got up, and ran across the room to the couch. He plopped awkwardly down between Devin and Kimmy, jarring the baby and knocking the nipple loose from his mouth. The baby's mouth contorted, and he released an irritated squeal from his tiny chest. "Jeez, Denis, be careful!" Kimmy snapped.

Denis looked over at Devin and shrugged. Devin guessed that the poor boy was used to his mother yelling at him. Kimmy lifted her heavy breast and positioned the nipple again into the baby's mouth. That quieted him instantly. "Eww!" Denis said. "He sucking on Mommy."

Devin laughed. Soon, Denis would be thinking that sucking on a tit was one of life's greatest pleasures. "What's your brother's name?" Devin asked.

With gentle little hands with fingernails bitten to the quick, Denis touched the baby's head. "Dante Jaden McKibben," he said proudly.

Devin thought briefly about brothers in general and about his in particular, about how sticky his relationship with them was. He'd actually moved back home to change that. Devin focused on Denis again. "You a good big brother?" Devin asked. "You share with him like a good boy?"

Denis screwed up his little beige face. "He don't like to do anything but cry."

Devin chuckled. Denis was so much like how Devin was when he was four . . . curious, precocious. In moments of imperceptible madness, he could actually see himself as a stepfather to this child, filling in for Denis's absent father like Bill had for Devin. But then there was Dante now. Devin knew he wasn't man enough to care for the seeds of two different men. No matter how much he'd loved Kimmy once.

Devin ran a hand over Denis's head. The boy desperately needed a haircut. And he could make out a dirty ring around the back of the collar of the kid's cotton T-shirt. Tears stung Devin's eyelids. He could hear his voice tremble slightly as he said, "You know, I was like him once."

Denis's eyes widened at the incredulity of it. "Really?"

"Really," Devin said. "I was the baby brother, just like him. Soon, he's gonna be as big as me. But he needs you to watch over him so he can grow up tall and strong."

Denis raised his left arm and made a tiny muscle. "I'm strong, Uncle Devin!" he said, his chest poked out with pride.

Devin felt the tiny upper arm. "Wow!" he exclaimed, his acting damn near Oscar-worthy. "You're a big boy!"

He smiled a smile of tiny white teeth, then he turned to Kimmy. "I gotta pee, Mommy," he announced.

Kimmy smiled, shaking her head. "You know where the potty is, cutie pie," she said.

Denis got up and ran out of the room. "And put the seat down when you're done!" Kimmy called after him.

Alone at last. He wanted to talk to her about adult stuff. "He's grown up so much since I saw him last," Devin observed.

Her proud grin was lopsided. "Yeah."

Devin leaned in and saw—*Jesus!*—lines around her eyes and across her forehead. She was twenty-eight, just like him, and she looked like a prematurely old lady. "How are you *really* doing, Kimmy?" he asked.

She shrugged, avoiding his stare. "You know . . ."

Devin slipped a finger under her chin and made her face him. "How are you?" he asked, this time more emphatically. Though, from looking around at her home and situation, it really wasn't hard to tell.

Kimmy sighed, her eyes moist. "It's a challenge, Devin," she confessed. "You know this wasn't The Plan."

This was so far from The Plan that it needed its own zip code. From the minute he'd met her, Kimmy talked nonstop about blowing Arlington, leaving her drunk mother and chicken-hawk stepfather, and moving to New York City to be a model like her aunt. She'd shown him photos of her aunt in catalogs and magazines. Her aunt had had the healthy, blond, bosomy look that was the shit in the eighties. Kimmy worked two jobs to save up for the headshots she constantly took, because her aunt said she needed a portfolio. He couldn't imagine how The Plan could lead to . . . this.

Nonetheless, he leaned in, looking her straight in her now dull blue eyes. "It's not hopeless, you know," he said.

She scoffed. "Oh, yeah, I'm headed for the runways of Paris!"

"Who says there only has to be one Plan?"

Kimmy dislodged a now-quiet Dante from her breast and rested him against the stained white diaper on her shoulder. She rubbed his tiny back softly. "Devin, everyone's not like you," she said, her tone impatient, like he was bothering her. "You got out. Be thankful."

Deflated, Devin sat back against the back of the couch. *In other words, mind your own business.*

Just then, he felt the corner of the envelope he had for her poking him in the chest. He took it out and looked at it, at her name written in blue ink on its face. He knew what was inside, too—two thousand dollars in cash. He cleared his throat, then offered it to her. "For you," he said quietly.

Tentatively, she took it. With a free hand, she ripped the envelope open and peered inside. She took out the card, read it, and then opened it and saw the money. She sighed tremulously, tears rolling down her flushed cheeks. She looked up at him, and to his surprise, she was smiling. "Devin," she sighed, her tone speaking volumes as to her gratitude. "And you bought a card, too!"

The fact that he could still make her happy swelled him with pride. He blinked away tears. "My mom helped me pick it out."

Kimmy protectively tucked her gift away in a pocket at her expansive waist. "I loved your mom. She fed me all those dinners."

Kim-Chin didn't want Devin to be with her. Kimmy was sexually precocious, not intellectually gifted, and flighty . . . everything a mother didn't want for her baby son. But Kim-Chin fed the girl, because he asked, and because she could see how badly Kimmy needed a mother's love.

Devin groaned. "I just remember her banging on the basement door when we were down there making out!"

"Devin!" Kimmy cried, affecting Kim-Chin's Korean accent. "What you do down there? Playing with you bottom?"

Her imitation of Kim-Chin was dead-on. He laughed so hard, the tears actually came rolling down his cheeks. Only these were tears of joy. "I remember playing with *your* bottom," he teased. "And your top!"

Her laughter slowed to intermittent giggles. "Me, too," she said, a distant look in her eyes. "Me, too."

It was like they were both fifteen again, in young love with each other, listening to CDs together, making out in dark movie theaters near the Arlington Courthouse. Unable to help himself, Devin reached out, touched her cheek. Reflexively, she closed her eyes and reveled in the feel, like she hadn't been touched lovingly in ages. With his thumb, he brushed away the tear lingering on her skin. "It'll be okay," he promised her.

Right then, he heard a resounding burp, and they both realized that it was Dante. They laughed uproariously. Devin pointed at Kimmy's chest. "What you got in there, girl? Beer?"

Kimmy looked at the baby reclined on her shoulder. "My little frat boy," she giggled.

"Well, this is cozy," Devin heard, and turned to see a white man in the doorway.

He was so happy to have been with Kimmy that he didn't even hear a key turn in the front door lock. But he sensed that this was the end of the mirth and frivolity. Kimmy went from happy to downright fearful in seconds flat. She looked like she was trying to play it off, faking a light air. "Don!" she cried. "You're home!"

"Don" was tall, wiry, and very white . . . in that threatening, uniquely Southern way. Devin had encountered many men like him on field trips to "Scary Virginia," which was what he and his boys called the racist hinterlands between the progressive pockets to the north and south of the state . . . anywhere past Manassas and before Norfolk, Hampton, Portsmouth, and Virginia Beach. He wore a navy blue maintenance man's uniform, with an American Red Cross patch on his left pec, and the name tag *Don* sewn over the pocket on his right. In one hand, he held a fistful of keys; in the other, a six-pack of Miller Genuine Draft. Devin's shocked gaze alternated between Kimmy and Don. He wondered when Kimmy started liking white men. And how could she choose this particular white man to raise her two young black sons?

Don stared at Devin, his gaze threatening . . . unwavering. "Hi, dar-lin'," he said, his voice laden with sarcasm. "Who's your friend?"

Kimmy kept emitting that nervous laugh, like a car trying to turn over in the dead of winter. "This is Devin. We went to high school to-gether."

So that was all he was to her . . . someone she went to high school with. Not her ex-boyfriend, whose virginity and heart she'd shame-lessly stolen. Sadness filled him.

Devin stood to his full height as Don came closer. This was, after all, the man's home. "Hello," he said.

Don looked Devin up and down. Don stood at five-feet-ten at the most, and he looked like he weighed about a buck-fifty. But Don flexed in other ways. "So, that's your Navigator in my spot down-stairs," he assumed.

"I'm sorry," Devin said, even though he really wasn't.

Kimmy struggled to her feet, balancing herself to keep the baby still. Devin resisted the urge to reach out and help her. "Don, there's a lot full of spaces," she said, her tone dismissive.

Denis came barreling from the back rooms of the apartment. "Don!" he cried happily.

Don barely checked for the love-starved child; he kept his gaze locked on Devin. "Hey, Denis the Menace," he finally said, ruffling the kid's head with his enormous, gnarly, worn hands.

Devin looked around at Kimmy's strange family. Five—that would be him—was definitely a crowd. "It's cool, Don," Devin said, trying very hard to keep *his* cool. "I was just leaving."

Denis looked up at Devin. "Are you having dinner with us, Uncle Devin?" he asked.

Devin's gaze darted from Denis to Don. He felt horribly conflicted. Devin stooped and gripped Denis by his small waist. "Not tonight, Denis," he said. "Can I do it later, though?"

Denis smiled that adorable, tiny-tooth smile. "Sure," he said, nodding.

Devin stood up and shot a glance at Kimmy. She was looking at him longingly as well, like she was trying to turn back time in her mind to when life wasn't sucking the very marrow from her bones. *Fuck Don.* Devin took her free hand and gave her a kiss on her cheek. "Kimmy," he said, then carefully caressed Dante's head. "Congratulations on this beautiful baby you've got here."

Kimmy squeezed his hand in hers. "Thank you, Devin," she said. She then patted her sundress pocket. *Thank you,* she mouthed.

The tom left his perch in the far corner, skulked over to the couch, raised his leg, and sprayed, all the while glaring at Denis. "Thor!" Kimmy cried, horrified.

Devin laughed. "You know, he'll spray less if you neuter him. Why don't you bring him to my office when you have a moment?"

"Nobody's snippin' Thor," Don decreed. "That's final."

Time to jet. "Well," Devin said. "I'd better be going. Good night, everyone."

As the strange family chorused their good nights, Devin headed for the front door. He exited into the grim hallway with the blood-colored trilobal carpet. The breeze of the door slamming behind him could've actually been the wind of change. As flawed as her process may have seemed, Kimmy had made her own life after he left. It was time for him to do the same.

Chaney pulled the Altima into her spot in the parking lot and killed the engine. All seemed normal in the neat town house ghetto that she called home. Rows and rows of town houses in the planned community, filled with single women—black and white—who had both personally and professionally evolved past men to the extent that they couldn't be bothered with an enormous rambler that would never house children or a husband. And Chaney was one of them. She didn't know how to feel about that. As her mother was so fond of saying, it was what it was.

Moreover, she had more pressing things on her mind, namely one iginormous dog with a touch of heartworm, his exam had revealed. Devin started to tell her that the treatment was two shots in the back over two days, and she resisted the compulsion to fall unconscious at his feet. She still hadn't recovered from the drawing of the blood episode.

Chaney looked back at Tony, who sat alert in the backseat, looking around the parking lot filled with cars, in the middle of the U-shaped ring of two-story town houses with a mix of brick and siding facades. "This is it, dog," she announced. "Home."

Tony looked back at her, ears perked up, like he was ready for the next adventure. Far be it from her to disappoint. She opened the door and got out. Before she could protest, Tony rocketed from the backseat, into the front driver's seat, and out onto the asphalt of the parking lot. In the sparse lighting from the car ceiling, Chaney could see a faint dusting of tiny yellow hairs on the leather. *Say good-bye to dark clothes forever.*

Chaney got the Wal-Mart bag filled with dog food, food and water bowls, and treats from the trunk and headed toward her brick-red front door. Her stoop was even homier with the light from the decorative lamp at her right, light which illuminated the blossoms on the massive tree in the tiny patch of earth that qualified as a front yard. She looked down as Tony fell in step at her left, obediently following her on his leash. Chaney shook her head, remembering what a spectacle he'd made in front of Devin. *Delicious "Cousin" Devin.* "Oh, now you know how to behave," she said, laughing. "You were showing out an hour ago."

Tony looked up at her and began wagging his tail like mad. It amazed Chaney how he responded to her so eagerly, after meeting her only hours ago. He looked at her like he would talk to her if he . . . if he knew how. She rolled her eyes. *Don't tell me I'm bonding with the dog . . .*

"Chaney!" someone called, and she turned to see Nathalie coming out of a black Land Rover.

As always, Nathalie made blue jeans, Keds, and a simple hunter green cardigan bolero look classy. She removed her Atlanta Braves cap to reveal short, straightened dark hair cut close and a smooth face the color of dark chocolate. Her smile was white and even. She looked as friendly as she did the day Chaney met her at Coming Back

Together, known as CBT, Syracuse's homecoming for Black and Latino alumni. She was extolling the wonders of life in D.C. And Chaney, after having spent her first unbelievably hellish winter in central New York, was more than willing to listen.

Chaney felt her mouth break into a smile of her own. Tony squared his shoulders and pricked up his ears; he was in full protection mode. "Wuh!" he barked. "Wuh! Wuh!"

Chaney looked down at him, giving his leash a gentle tug. "It's okay, dog," she said.

Chaney's smile faded, though, when the door to the passenger side to the Land Rover opened, and *she* stepped out. Marion Daniels, a.k.a. Dani. Short, curly hair, green eyes, creamy skin, tall and statuesque, and the way she was dressed—jeans, boots, and a crisp white shirt under a woolen blazer—she didn't look anywhere close to her true age of forty-six. Chaney guessed men must've seen her and her lover, the unfortunately named Sandra Tung, arm in arm on the street in Dupont Circle and thought, "What a waste!"

The back doors of the Rover opened, and Coco Whitman slid out, with her kids Miguel and Juanita in tow. Coco was a study of that old Sesame Street song, "One of These Things Is Not Like the Other," in relation to Dani and Nathalie. She was short and squat, with long, dark curls brushing her sweatered shoulders, and thick glasses obscuring the beauty of her hazel-brown eyes. She clutched a heavy interoffice folder close to her ample chest. Her children, too, were a study in contrasts. Miguel was a tall, dark Latin stunner, like Antonio Banderas must've looked when he was fourteen. Juanita's look this week, on the other hand, was Goth light—all the black clothing and morbid attitude, none of the freakish white face makeup. Coco was a good Puerto Rican woman; no daughter of hers was wearing makeup at twelve.

"What, you got a clown car there?" Chaney laughed as they all came closer.

They all exchanged hugs and kisses all round, with the exception of Dani. She nodded Chaney's way. "Hey," she said.

"Hey," Chaney returned.

Nathalie leaned in toward Tony. "My Lord, you weren't kidding!" she declared, checking Tony out; Tony returned the favor. "He's huge!"

Juanita surprisingly came forward and, without a word, began stroking the dog. Instantly, Tony calmed down. Chaney was admiring how she had the touch . . . then she saw the white bandages on Juanita's wrists. "Umm . . . sweetie," she began, tentative. "What's up with the wrists?"

Miguel rolled his eyes. "*Idiota*," he murmured.

"Tell her," Coco prompted angrily. "Tell Aunt Chaney about your crazy friends and your little suicide gesture."

It was Juanita's turn to roll her huge brown eyes. She sucked her teeth. "Whatever, Mom," she grumbled.

Dani and Nathalie exchanged uncomfortable glances with Chaney. The alarm to change the subject bonged in Chaney's head like Big Ben. "Let's go inside," she suggested.

They headed toward the front door, Nathalie and Chaney hanging back. "I talk to my mother like that, I'm on the end of a *homicidal* gesture," Nathalie whispered in Chaney's ear.

In spite of herself, Chaney chuckled, though the situation was far from funny. Chaney wanted to give Juanita the speech, remind her to appreciate her mother, because one day, she wouldn't be there to shame her in front of her friends, or care that she thought nicking her wrists would be a good way to get some attention. She refrained, though. She was only "Aunt Chaney," and an ersatz one at that.

Chaney unlocked the door and ran to shut off the alarm that instantly began beeping. Tony followed gamely along at her side. She entered the code, then flicked on the lights to reveal the wide open, expansive floor plan of the first floor of her town house. She ushered her guests past the door to the guest half-bath at the right and past the beginning of the staircase, also at the right. They walked down the hall under the vaulted, polished pine ceiling, stopping at the opening to the eat-in kitchen at their left. "Anyone want drinks?" Chaney asked. "Y'all ate already?"

Coco held up a hand. "Not for me," she announced, then tucked the interoffice envelope she was carrying into Chaney's Wal-Mart bag. "I tagged along with these guys, 'cause I didn't think we'd be staying long. I just wanted to give you those . . . the handouts for tomorrow's meeting." Then she scornfully rolled her eyes. "Lissa insisted that I hand-deliver them personally."

Chaney didn't know what the beef was between Coco and Lissa Janus, the other major player at Autodidact. And she didn't want to know. All she did know was that Lissa was the one who provided her with an out. Chaney was about to graduate into joblessness with a fancy degree and no prospects. Lissa had been her teaching assistant at Syracuse. She had everyone in Syracuse's Instructional Design, Development, and Evaluation department chartreuse with envy when she was able to buy into a fledgling e-learning concern at the height of the tech boom. Last year and a half, just as Chaney was packing up her campus apartment at Skytop, dreading the Drive of Shame downstate to sleep on Anna Lisa's couch in the old neighborhood, she got the call from Lissa, offering her a stake in the company. "Okay, then," Chaney said, hoping Coco got the hint that she wasn't going to play along. "Can someone take the dog for a sec? I have to give Nat something in the kitchen."

The unlikely volunteer was Juanita. She happily took the leash from Chaney. Chaney held out a glimmer of hope that Juanita would turn out to be a normal, well-adjusted adult in eight years. "I'll do it!" she offered with as much joy as the estrogen coursing through an unaccustomed preteen body could muster.

Coco led the procession toward the living room, with Dani bringing up the rear. She shot Nathalie a glance that Chaney read to mean, *Make this shit quick.*

Nathalie interpreted it that way, too. "Just a sec," she promised, making an incomplete pinch with her index finger and thumb.

Chaney led the way into the sizable kitchen with pine wood cupboards and ivory-colored Kenmore appliances. Chaney was able to see the goings-on in the living room over the bar in the kitchen that opened to give her a panoramic view of the entire first floor. Coco was supervising Juanita as she stroked Tony, and Juanita resisted mightily. Miguel looked like he was scolding her for mouthing off at their mother. Dani looked bored, thumbing through the *Essence, Jet,* and *O* magazines that Chaney had displayed on the wooden coffee table with the glass top. *No doubt judging me . . .*

Chaney put Dani out of her mind. She could sure use a cup of coffee, but she didn't want shit from her so-called friends. "You sure you don't want some coffee?" she asked conspiratorially.

Nathalie sucked her teeth. "I'm not enabling you in your addiction."

Chaney scoffed, sounding a bit like a cat coughing up a fur ball. "Says the woman who called me from a raging happy hour!"

"Virgin daiquiris," Nathalie insisted. "You know I can't have alcohol and caffeine. Trying to get pregnant, remember?"

Chaney secretly wondered how long it was going to take before Nathalie alluded to Craig, the perfect husband. Corporate attorney (Howard University Law). Greek (Kappa Alpha Psi). Offspring of professional parents (doctor mom, lawyer dad). Provider of mansion-like home on Foxhall Road in Georgetown. Nathalie, Georgetown Law herself and card-carrying member of Delta Sigma Theta Sorority Incorporated, complemented him perfectly. She and Craig Phillips were the Bionic Buppie Couple. "Remember when we in our twenties, and we were trying insanely to *not* get pregnant?" Chaney laughed.

"Now all our friends are on the needle," Nathalie declared; then, seeing the confused look on Chaney's face, clarified. "Fertility treatments."

Chaney shook her head at the irony. In the absence of her very own Craig, she was going to have to settle for being "Aunt Chaney" to her friends' offspring.

Chaney took Nathalie by the hand and led her to a round, French café-style table in the nook in front of the bay windows with the blinds drawn. On its surface was a wicker basket that Chaney had painstakingly painted a creamy white, filled with scented straw and eucalyptus stalks, and packed with a generous assortment of her shea butter creams that she'd blended and packaged in clear jars with black tops—skin creams, lip balms, hair oils. "I could wrap it in cellophane, if you want," she offered.

Nathalie grinned from ear to ear, her dark eyes lit up like tiny Roman candles. She took one of the jars of skin cream, opened it, put it to her nose, and inhaled deeply. She closed her eyes and moaned, hugging herself close. Chaney smiled. That was all the thanks she needed.

Nathalie finally opened her eyes. "This is what you should be doing with your life," she decreed. "Not selling your soul to go into partnership with that shanty Irishman. I could even manage it for you."

Ever since Chaney began sharing the myriad actions that culminated in Al McCulligh being classified as a world-class dick, Nathalie referred to him so often as "that shanty Irishman" that it was like his name. Not that Chaney hadn't thought about it independently . . . without the friendly prodding. There was nothing she'd loved better than spending days in the unfinished half of her basement, making a living out of the hobby that had possessed her since a trip to Ghana.

But she'd already invested practically all of her inheritance and her share of her parents' death benefits in Autodidact. Something sensible with the promise of a respectable return on her investment. The damage, so to speak, had already been done. "I couldn't live long enough to make that many baskets," Chaney sighed, resigned to her compromise. "You just stick to rehabbing houses."

Nathalie leaned in. "I want to ask you," she said. "Why are you so cold toward Dani, anyway?"

Deflect, deflect. "Why are you so warm toward her?"

"She's a great lawyer," Nathalie answered, as if making her own case. "Or she was until she wrote that book about her detail in the Clinton White House. Plus, I know of all the women in this town, she wouldn't try to fuck my husband. You know where you stand with Dani."

"A solid basis for a friendship if there ever was one," Chaney snapped.

"Umm . . . Aunt Chaney!" Miguel called from the living room just then.

Chaney knew when Miguel, the quiet, model Whitman child, raised his voice, it had to be something important. She rushed over to the bar, looked into the living room, and literally felt her blood pressure explode into her head. She must've been having a stroke. Of course, a stroke would produce a mirage, like Tony raising his leg and spraying a lengthy golden shower at the base of her solid pine entertainment center. She watched in abject horror as the pee drained down the polished wood, hit the plushness of the beige carpet, and sank in. Then he moved down a couple of inches . . . and proceeded to spray again.

Finally, the pseudo-stroke passed, leaving the sound of blood roaring in her ears, roaring so loudly that she could barely hear herself but knew she was screaming, "What are you doing?!"

Like the keeper of a magic faucet, Tony shut off the golden stream immediately. Chaney rushed out of the kitchen and over to him. He sat on his haunches, looking annoyingly pleased with himself. Until she grabbed him by the collar. He flinched, squeezing his brown eyes shut. Volcanic fury gave her superhuman strength, enough to haul an eighty-pound dog—at least that was what Devin said he weighed—over to the glass sliding doors. She pushed one open, tossed Tony unceremoniously out onto the deck that led to the small backyard fenced on its remaining three sides with a six-foot-high wooden slat fence. "Stay!" she roared, then slammed the door in his face.

Tony stared back at her, unvarnished remorse on his doggie face, his pink nose pressed against the clean glass, leaving wet smudges. Chaney turned to see ten astonished eyes, staring at her as if she were a crazy woman. And she guessed she was. Daisy's fucking dog was driving her insane by upsetting the balance of her environment. "If I hold that fucking dog . . ." Chaney said, pointing a clenched fist over her shoulder where she assumed Tony was standing.

The Bahamian roots would come springing from her proper-speaking mother when one of her three daughters, more often than not Daisy, would do something so egregious as to make her usually even temper slip. "If I hold this girl . . ." Leah Braxton would say, and her vocal periods of ellipses would imply a fate worse than death if she went as far as she wanted.

Coco broke the silent, staring deadlock. "He's just a dog, Chaney," she reminded her. "He doesn't know any better."

Chaney glared at her. This was the woman whose daughter was a pre-Goth making suicidal gestures.

"Typical male," Dani remarked, shaking her head. "They're all the same. Two legs, four legs . . . doesn't matter."

For once in the year she'd known her, Chaney agreed one hundred percent with Dani. Coco, though, brought Miguel closer to her, as if she thought all the women in the room were about to sacrifice her little prince. Nathalie came out of the kitchen just then, possessively clutching her basket. "Maybe we should go," she said.

"Sounds like a plan," Dani agreed.

Chaney, God help her, thought it was an excellent idea. She watched as they murmured their good-byes and began filing out through the front door. Then she felt guilty. "See you guys later," she sighed. "I'm sorry."

Coco, who was the last one through the door, looked over her shoulder. "Don't worry, *chica*," she laughed.

Chica was the rare betrayal of Coco's Puerto Rican heritage. Growing up in New York, Chaney thought she knew Puerto Ricans. But Coco was from Maryland . . . a kinder, gentler, less attitudinal version of those with whom she grew up. "I'll see you eight o'clock sharp at Union Station," she reminded her.

Shit, the grip-and-grin! Even though it was a done deal, the Auto-didact crew still had to go into D.C., seal the deal, and at least appear appropriately grateful to be the recipients of government money. "Yes, ma'am," Chaney said.

With the closing of the door, they were all a memory. Chaney turned and saw Tony, still staring plaintively at her through the glass door. Then her gaze shifted to the entertainment center, with a trail of urea-yellow pee on its left door. *Fucking dog!*

Unlike Nathalie, becoming pregnant was the last thing on Chaney's mind. So, she went into her kitchen and broke out the Krups coffee-maker. She opened the door to her pantry and found, hidden behind the flour, a baggie with Starbucks French roast that she'd ground just that morning. For someone who protested minutes ago that she didn't have a coffee addiction, she watched, hypnotized, as the coffee dripped slowly into the glass decanter. She reflected on what Dani had said. Was Tony truly the embodiment of every other man in her life who she'd let into her world, only to watch them piss over it?

In her mind, she ran the litany. Her father whom she adored, Reggie Braxton, who decided to take her Bahamian mother on and relocate the family to a pre-Independence Bahamas, only to die with his wife in a plane crash, abandoning her and her sisters. Chaney had just turned five. Then Shane, the straight-gay guy who still haunted her almost half a decade later. *Shane asked me about you today . . .*

After she'd retreated to central New York to seek knowledge, she met Richard, the meathead townie, while lifting weights at the Syracuse Bally's . . . attempting to lose the post-Shane weight that she'd found attached to her ass. There was something so dirty about his clean-and-jerk, about the tight Spandex that molded to his shredded body like a second skin. He'd made all the right noises. *I'm not intimidated by women who have more education than I do,* he'd say, over dinners that included him, her, and Liesl, his scary, jealous rottweiler who Chaney suspected would bump her off if she could master a prehensile grip on a trigger. *I'm impressed by you,* he'd moan after laying the pipe so artfully that Chaney's throat would be raw from screaming.

To prove his ardor, Richard would send her plants and flowers, all of which she'd inadvertently kill with shocking speed and regularity. But she was so horny and cold in her Skytop apartment, so eager to prove that Shane didn't choose to fuck men because of something she'd done, that she actually bought the bullshit, actually fell for his ham-fisted courtship.

That was until they slammed up against the huge deal-breaker in the relationship. In moments of being "dick-mo-tized," as that comic Sommore called it, Chaney had suggested that he move down to Brooklyn with her once she'd graduated. He was adamant. He hated downstate . . . the crime, the drugs, the rude people, the filth, the small, confining nature of the city. He was quite happy at his mechanic's job in Syracuse. *Why don't you broaden your horizons?* she'd finally said to him. *Why don't you narrow yours?* he returned.

Peace out.

Hence Chaney's mantra: No plants, no pets, no men. And Anna Lisa, bless her heart, had ensured that Chaney would need neither. Anna Lisa, being the epitome of anal-retentive, had wisely invested their inheritances and insurance payouts after their parents died. When Lissa Janus told her of an opportunity at the Rockville, Maryland, woman-owned instructional design and e-learning firm that was Autodidact, Inc., Chaney invested her money and became a partner. The only downside to the arrangement was working with Allison McCulligh, the cheap bastard who put the company in his wife Laura's name so that his "woman-owned company" could be eligible for federal affirmative action money. Who better for a new partner than a black woman with a Ph.D. and a nice grip of money? Chaney was like whole-wheat manna from heaven.

The steamy burps from the machine signaled that the coffee was done. Chaney reluctantly returned to the present. She'd taken on Daisy's dog with hyperactive kidneys and tomorrow's 8:30 meeting in the District. She was unprepared for both. From over the bar, she looked at Tony's sweet yellow face, staring through the sliding door. "Wuh!" he barked, the sound muffled by the glass.

Chaney suddenly remembered something Coco once said to her, after anguishing over some idiocy attributed to either Miguel or Juanita. "God made babies and animals cute so you wouldn't run away from the immense responsibility of both," she'd sighed.

No doubt. Feeling like an even bigger sucker, Chaney entered the living room and opened the door to the basement. She descended the carpeted stairs to the unfinished section that housed all of her fragrances, oils, and containers of shea butter. Next to her workbench, she spotted it: the Bissell Pro Heat carpet cleaner. Sighing, she dragged it up the carpeted stairs. After the first few steps, the sweat began to bead on her forehead. She dragged her sleeve across her brow. "This shit better work on dog pee," she mumbled.

Devin parked the Navigator in front of the house on North Garfield Street, the rambling, brick two-story house with white Doric columns in Arlington's Clarendon section. A light next to the hunter green door illuminated the porch and a wood-and-wrought-iron bench. Devin remembered how his mother, in her robe and slippers, would sit on the bench, how she would cry, and chain-smoke her cigarettes, and wait for her husband to get off his latest conquest and drag his ass home. Devin also remembered sitting with Kimmy on that bench, his arm possessively around her shoulders as they talked and laughed.

Kimmy. He sighed deeply. He remembered the exact day he met her. She came to meet her friend at cheerleading practice; of course, Kimmy was too cool for that sort of thing. Devin and ten other newly minted varsity pituitary cases were on the Washington-Lee basketball court, picking and rolling, and shirts-ing and skins-ing, when he looked up and saw her on the bleachers . . . with that tight V-necked sweater and short skirt, with the light from overhead shining right through her. Suddenly, he forgot to move how a point guard was supposed to move and crashed into the small forward. She looked up, concern on her face, as he and the other kid got up. "Sorry!" she mouthed.

Coach proceeded to tear him another asshole, but it was worth it. He'd gotten her attention. Though he couldn't imagine why. Off the court or out of the pool, he was the awkward, tall, smart biracial kid with a massive curly 'fro. If it hadn't been for his boys, who were also in their own stages of teenaged awkwardness and sexual frustration, no one would've spoken to him.

He'd lost his virginity at her house. The stepfather was away on naval exercises in Rhode Island, and her mother was at one of the many jobs she couldn't seem to keep for any length of time. She'd un-dressed in front of him, and she was all woman . . . full breasts with pink, pointy nipples, shapely thighs, pleasing ass. He knew that not all women looked like his mother, who was all straight angles and flat-chested. He started to undress like he was getting ready for a shower after practice. "Slow down," she urged.

Later, he would learn that watching the undressing was an integral part of the act. In that moment, though, he obeyed, slowly stripping off his layers until he was standing naked as the day he was born, in front of her. He used to think of his body as utilitarian. He ate right to have more energy during the games or to do extra laps. He lifted weights to have more strength, to be able to take a charge, to be able to resist the competition hacking him when he had possession of the ball. Only when she looked at him and smirked that satisfied smirk did he realize that his discipline resulted in an aesthetic that was hot! She got her condoms out of her nightstand drawer. "Now bring that big, beautiful black dick over here," she purred.

He looked down at his dick, which was ten minutes ahead of him in the whole experience. It was standing at attention like a divining rod, searching her out like she was water hidden under the earth. Clumsy minutes later, he was a man . . . a man grinning like the village idiot. He was hooked. And like any addict, he wanted more. She was only too happy to oblige, to give him the benefit of her vast experience.

One day, they were at her house, about to head upstairs, but her mom was home. Kimmy wasn't at all pleased. Kimmy's mother was sitting in the tattered kitchen, a Marlboro dangling at the end of her thin bottom lip. She looked like an older, more weathered version of her daughter. "This is Devin," Kimmy announced, without fanfare.

The older cornflower-blue eyes searched him curiously up and down. "What kind of nigger are you, son?" she asked in a voice made deep and husky from years of smoking.

Here we go. The more impolite form of the question. Devin felt the heat sear his face. "The kind that doesn't answer questions like that," he snapped on reflex, before his brain could remind him that this bigot was the mother of his babe, who he should be trying to impress. "Umm . . . ma'am," he added, but he knew the damage was done.

Kimmy's mother looked shocked by his temerity. "Well!" she gasped.

Kimmy snatched his hand. "Let's go!" she commanded, shooting her mother a look of pure scorn as they bolted from the shitty South Arlington house.

They'd sat on the bench on his porch after that. She cried and apologized profusely for her mother, and he'd held her and assured her that it was okay. From then on, they fucked at his house, in the basement. That was, when Kim-Chin wasn't spoiling his rhythm by banging on the door, asking if he was playing with his bottom.

Devin got out of the car, shut the door, and locked it with the remote on his key chain. He always knew that he'd be back here. He never wanted to go to Seattle, but he knew that his mom had to get as far away as possible from his father. One of her men should've protected her. In the wake of the failure of the older one, he, Devin, was it. But when he'd woken up at 6:45 A.M. Pacific time to discover that a plane had hit the Pentagon, and that both his father and his boy, Andre, who were inside at the time, had barely escaped with their lives, he made plans to come back. Bonding with Andre again was a snap. A couple of Georgetown happy hours, and it was like Devin had never left. KL, though, was proving to be a challenge.

Devin opened the screen door, then the front door with his key and found himself standing in the anteroom that had seemed so big when he was a kid. Now, he could jump and touch the bottom crystals of the chandelier that hung from the vaulted ceiling. On reflex, his fingers found the light switch, which he flicked to light up the anteroom and foot of the blue-carpeted staircase. Devin picked up the mail on the floor. "Pop!" he called.

No answer. *Figures.* His father was retired now, no more wars for him to be deployed to, no more unfortunate souls for him to defend in courts-martial. God only knew what sort of mischief KL was getting up to, even at the ripe old age of seventy.

Devin ascended the staircase, stopping at the top to check for prowlers in the bathroom at his left, the guest room, and his father's room . . . all kept neat with military precision. Though he was a slave to his passions in other aspects of his life, KL demanded that his surroundings be orderly. Devin remembered bed check every morning before he went off to school. *Your surroundings are indication of your state of mind, son,* KL stated, just before he did the Bill Cosby-esque white glove dust check, which Devin always passed.

What KL didn't know was that Kim-Chin cleaned up after him, and what KL didn't know didn't come back to hurt Devin.

Devin walked over to the familiar door to his room and pushed it open. Devin thought he'd gotten over it the first time he'd seen it, but it still stung. Any trace of his having spent fifteen years in that room was gone . . . no twin bed, no desk, no Public Enemy or LL Cool J posters. Not even a picture of Devin or his mom. Everything was discarded to make way for KL's office, with a couch, a desk on which rested a computer and printer/fax, and bookcases upon bookcases of military tomes, mysteries, Tom Clancy hardbacks, African-American fiction. It was like KL had erased him from his life. *Son, you disappoint me . . .*

With a shrug, Devin put the mail on KL's desk, then left the room, pulling the door ajar. He bolted down the stairs and into the living room. This room stayed fundamentally as he remembered it . . . a stuffed couch in front of a bay window shielded with venetian blinds, his father's wood carved chair from Ghana in front of a new TV, a full-length mirror over the fireplace, lit from overhead with a fluorescent light, a mantel naked of personal photos. Devin moved toward the dining room, the heels of his loafers clicking on the wooden floor. In the dining room, in front of a wall of windows with the blinds drawn, Devin saw the wood-carved dining table with six chairs, with one placemat at the head of the table. Devin guessed that that was where his father sat; it had an unobstructed view of the TV. That was what his father was reduced to: lonely dinners in front of the TV.

Devin reached out for the stereo case next to the table, opened it, and turned on the radio. His dad was listening to jazz on WHUR. *Typical.* Devin turned the knob to 95.5, WPGC, just in time to catch Rane taking shout-outs from listeners over DJ Flexx's bombastic hip-hop beats. Devin smiled. *More like it . . .*

Devin made his way from the dining room into the small yellow kitchen. He remembered helping his mother paint it when he was four, though he'd gotten more paint on his hands than on the wall. "New mistress of house, new color," she insisted to KL, and in one day, had gotten rid of the pukey green that Daphne, Second Wife, had chosen before she was told to hit the skids. That was the one thing that KL had kept that spoke of their presence in the house.

Devin checked the cupboards of the house, which were full. At least KL was eating nutritious foods. He then went to the fridge, opened it, and began looking inside. Suddenly, though, he felt an arm around his throat, the antecubital part pressed against his windpipe, cutting off his air. His heart pounded in his ears, black spots swam before his eyes. Where rational thought escaped him, his sense of smell kicking in, filling the breach. The ultrafamiliar aftershave played in his nostrils. His heartbeats slowly returned to manageable levels. He tugged at the arm around his throat. "Dad!" he croaked. "It's me! Devin!"

The arm relaxed, and Devin turned around to see his father, a devious smile at the corners of his mouth. "I thought you were a prowler," he said simply.

"A prowler in the fridge?!" Devin demanded, pissed because he knew full well that KL was fucking with him.

Plus everyone in this neighborhood knew who lived on North Garfield. Everyone knew not to fuck with the crazy Marine, much less break into his house.

Devin looked down at KL's constant companion, Sadat, the aging springer spaniel that KL had acquired years after Devin and Kim-Chin left. Sadat, on a retractable leash, sat calmly at KL's boot-shod feet, watching the interplay between father and son.

"Making yourself at home, I see," KL observed.

Devin looked at his father in disbelief. "This used to be my home," Devin reminded him, shutting the door to the fridge.

"Yes, but you have the fancy pad in Georgetown now, right?"

Here we go again . . . KL hated everything about his son's chosen profession, but especially the fact that Bill had helped him buy into the lucrative veterinary practice. What KL didn't know is that Bill had done it so that Devin could come east in his quest to bond with his selfish father who'd almost died a fiery death. "This is your inheritance; take it now," Bill had said. "Go be with your father."

"I ran into a cousin today," Devin said—anything to change the subject.

KL went from seemingly bored with his son to intrigued with the information he had. "Really?"

Devin shrugged. "Well, she's not really a cousin so much as . . ."

"Get to the point, son."

"Our cousin, Norm Hall? She's his ex-sister-in-law."

Now KL was really intrigued. His bushy, graying eyebrows perked up. "Anna Lisa's sister? Which one?"

Devin smiled as he remembered her, in her smart business suit, and her overly harried professional exterior. She was even kind of cute. No, he guessed, you'd call older women classy, not cute. But he did like the look of her . . . her curly hair let loose to hang about her broad shoulders. Her 'fro looked like his when he didn't bother to cut it. And those eyes . . . deep . . . like swimming pools he used to dive into. And he liked that she was tall, that she could look him in the eye when they talked. He tended to have to sit or bend deep in the knees when talking to women, because he was so tall. Mostly, he loved the way she filled out her gleaming white blouse under her sensible blue suit. "Chaney," he announced, his smile growing broader.

KL let Sadat off the leash, and the dog wandered off to his water bowl in the corner. "Damn!" KL exclaimed over Sadat's loud lapping. "The last time I saw her, she was about five. She was a good kid . . . sweet, and so friendly, considering . . ."

Now it was Devin's turn for intrigue. "Considering what?"

KL shook his head. "Tragic story. Their mother was from the Bahamas. When the country was about to become independent, they were going to move down there to nation build. Except Anna Lisa, of course. She and Norm had just gotten married. She was pregnant.

"Well, anyway, the family—minus Anna Lisa—gets down there all right." KL stroked his long chin, shaking his head. "The next day, the parents charter a Cessna to fly to this island called Andros. Bang. Plane goes down. No bodies were ever found."

Devin shuddered. "That's horrible," he murmured.

"Anna Lisa kept that family together," KL said. "She brought the two younger sisters back to the U.S. and raised them, along with her son. At nineteen. While her husband was off in the jungles of the 'Nam. She's one strong sister."

"Seems like it trickled down to this sister. Though she's got her hands full; she's dog-sitting. That's how I met her. Anna Lisa made an appointment for her to see me."

"Tell her I said hi," KL said, and this was one of the few times he'd seen his father excited about another person. "I'd like to have her over for dinner one night."

Devin's mind entertained the possibility. "Okay, I'll tell her; I see her next week."

KL began puttering around the kitchen, and Devin stared at his father. He wondered if he was going to be just like him forty-two years from now. "Why don't I make you dinner?" he offered.

KL, now washing his hands at the kitchen sink, looked at his son in surprise. For one second, Devin thought he'd seen pride. But then, just as quickly, the wall came back down. He turned away. "I already ate," he announced.

Devin stared at his father. *I don't have to be a fucking mind reader; I get the hint!* "Okay," he said, nodding. "Well, I'm gonna go home, then."

KL dried his hands on the dish towel hanging on a hook from the wall. "I'll walk you out."

To make sure I'm really gone so I don't bring any more chaos to your order? Out loud, though, Devin said, "Okay."

Devin headed out the kitchen and along the short hallway to the anteroom, where he'd entered the house. KL followed. They both left the house and stood in the light that the porch lamp provided. "Big car, son," KL commented, staring at the Navigator parked at the sidewalk. "You wouldn't be overcompensating now, would you?"

Jesus, now my dick's too small, too? Masking the hurt, Devin laughed, shaking his head. "Haven't had any complaints, Pops," he said. "And women like the ride, too."

Even KL had to laugh at that one, a laugh that said, *okay, you got me.* "Well, son," he said, with an air of finality, "I'm gonna pull chocks."

In KL's military speak, that meant he was going to leave. "'Night, Dad," Devin said. "I'll call you tomorrow."

"Okay. Just not too late."

There was an awkward moment when Devin waited for a hug, or a handshake even. When he saw that neither was forthcoming, he turned and descended the concrete steps and made his way to the much-maligned Navigator. He settled in and started the engine, then looked up at the porch for one last glimpse of his father. The porch was empty. KL had already gone inside.

Devin popped in JaRule's latest CD and pressed the FORWARD button until he got to the track he wanted. The bouncy cut blasted through the speakers, followed by Ja's gravelly voice and the pumping bass. The booming system in the Navigator did the kick of "Livin' It Up" justice. JaRule could bring the party and make you forget the heavy shit you were going through.

Devin only then realized that his offer to make his father dinner was no joke. He was actually starving. He turned onto Wilson Boulevard, picked up some takeout from Faccia Luna, even though he wasn't really in the mood for Italian.

He was still thumping JaRule as he made his way over the Key Bridge that separated Virginia from D.C. At the light that signaled that he was in his beloved Georgetown, he hung a left, following the other end of M. Street, the main drag. As the dark road wound, he saw the university and all the million-dollar homes that he remembered from his childhood. All his life, he'd wanted to be here, in Georgetown. This was the fun side of D.C., where the power brokers lived and the intelligentsia played, where achievement was tangibly rewarded and greatly respected. As he pulled up to his town house in the 4500 block of Macarthur Boulevard and pressed a button on the garage door remote, he sure did feel like he'd arrived.

Moments later, he was in his very own kitchen, spooning his spaghetti Bolognese into a Peruvian earthenware plate. The first round of March Madness was about to begin on the plasma screen TV in his living room. He took his food and his Coke and took a seat on the couch seconds before tip-off. He looked out the bay windows at the Potomac River rolling majestically about a mile away. Solo takeout on a Wednesday night wasn't his idea of The Plan, just how Kimmy's situation hadn't been her Plan, either. He'd come home to live his dream . . . a successful practice, a good woman by his side, and a repaired relationship with his father.

Devin looked around the sparsely furnished, expansive living room, the gleaming wooden floors making it look even more empty. "Dev," he said to himself, "it may be time for a new plan."

Two

The train lurched, and Chaney woke up, disoriented. Then she panicked. *Shit! My stop!* She rocketed out of her seat, squeezed through the packed-to-capacity train of suited-down commuters, and made it through the double doors just as they were closing, almost catching her leather briefcase. She found herself standing on the platform of the Yellow Line at Gallery Place/Chinatown, getting jostled by the impatient commuters on their way to their government jobs. Just like her.

Chaney joined the throng, walking briskly to the escalator. No one stayed to the right and hung on, waiting patiently for the escalator to take them down. Everybody walked down, carried along by the power of the escalator, and she joined the momentum of the crowd. She got to the platform just in time to slither onto the Red Line train, rubbing between the other drones on the packed train.

She hung on to one of the poles, sharing it with another woman in a black suit and a well-tailored trench coat. She sighed, kicking herself inside. If this were Brooklyn, she never would've fallen asleep on the train. The New York subway could be very unforgiving to those who weren't vigilant. How could she allow a kinder, gentler D.C. to lull her into a false sense of security?

Like she didn't know the answer. *Tony.* His adjustment was not going well. Sometime during the night, after she'd drifted off into a labored sleep, Tony seemed to figure out that if he barked loud enough in that deep, resonant voice, she'd get up and let him out to use the potty. This she did: twice, each time disarming the burglar alarm, then resetting it.

Then, after she'd finally gotten back to sleep, Tony decided that running into the vertical blinds at the sliding door would be a fun way to pass the time. Unfortunately, the blinds slammed into the alarm sensor at the foot of the sliding doors. The alarm siren seared through the quiet of the night, sending Chaney's pressure spiking dangerously close to the stroke zone. She shot up in bed. *Someone's in the house!*

She ran downstairs, brandishing a Jimmy Choo pump, only to realize that the only someone in the house, other than her, was her sister's attention-seeking dog.

That morning didn't hold out any promise of getting better, either. Daisy, in her sales pitch to Chaney, explained that Tony was primarily an inside dog. So, against her better judgment, Chaney left Tony in the house and, just to be on the safe side, closed all the doors to the bedrooms where he might be tempted to do some damage. Chaney remembered the rapt attention on his doggie face when she explained to him that she had to go to work. In response, he proceeded to jump on her as she was going, his long paw nails leaving an intricate network of runs in her panty hose. Cursing in a seething rage, she changed into slacks that didn't match her blazer, shrugged into her tan trench coat, and rushed in the Altima to the Huntington metro stop. Of course, changing set her back fifteen minutes. All the good spaces in the parking structure were gone, forcing her to park in the hinterlands, and then run to catch her train.

Which led her to the street outside one of Union Station's many entrances, to where Coco was standing, looking appropriately cold and peeved. Coco saw her just then and gave her the face she usually reserved for Juanita. "You're fifteen minutes late," she announced, mother guilt on overkill. "I want to be spared from taking shit from your friend Lissa."

They began walking briskly, dodging fellow commuters. "I'm the boss," Chaney said simply in an attempt to neutralize her. "Blame me."

"Bag the delusions of grandeur, sweetie. You're *a* boss; you're not *the* boss. How many pieces you got of the woman-owned pie?"

Coco was right. Chaney owned twenty percent of the fifty-one percent of estrogen in Autodidact—twenty percent compared to Lissa's twenty-one and the other ten owned by Laura, Al McCulligh's wife. Al owned the remaining forty-nine percent. That didn't exactly translate into much juice on Chaney's part. She guessed she'd better increase her speed.

But then she was distracted by a dreadlocked brothah with a table laden with incense, along with the scented oils she used for her shea butter skin preparations. She looked down at her watch. *Do I have a minute?* Coco followed her gaze and read her mind. "No!" she commanded, like she was speaking to Tony.

Once they'd finally made it to the CNN Building, they encountered the usual gauntlet of security. "Here's where they crawl up your ass with a microscope," Chaney whispered as she handed over her identification and put her briefcase and laptop on the nearby conveyor belt to be scanned.

"Osama, the instructional designer," Coco whispered back with a laugh as she, too, handed over her identification and bags.

Just then, one of the security guards turned, and both Chaney and Coco got a glimpse of a frighteningly real holstered pistol. In an instant, Chaney remembered seeing the plume of black smoke in her rearview mirror; recalled the fear as she continuously speed-dialed Anna Lisa on her cell phone, only to have the call drop; remembered hearing on the radio that the plume of smoke was actually the result of one jumbo jet crashing into the side of the Pentagon. It was then Coco's turn to read Chaney's mind. They exchanged glances. Joke Time was officially over.

The security guard gave them their visitors' tags and called upstairs for their escort. Chaney stared longingly at the coffee shop across the atrium. The craving hit her at the very cellular level of her body. "Let me at least get a cup of coffee while we wait," she pleaded with Coco.

Coco stared at her with mock disdain. "Nathalie's right. You do have an addiction."

From behind them, Chaney heard, "Good morning, ladies."

They both turned to see Doug Thornton coming toward them from the elevator banks. Chaney had met him once before and imagined that if Mr. Potato Head had come to life and had become a civilian contractor for the Navy, he would look like Doug. He was squat and balding with gray eyes squinting behind wire-framed lenses. He wore a white shirt with sleeves that were too long, a navy blue tie that was too short, trousers belted at a rotund waist, and black lace-up shoes with thick soles.

Chaney slipped seamlessly into her professional façade. "Good morning, Doug," she said with a controlled smile.

He shook the hand she extended. "Chaney," he said with a pinched twitch that, Chaney guessed, was meant to be a reciprocated smile. "Good to see you again."

Chaney brought Coco forward. "This is Socorro Whitman," she announced. "She's going to be our senior instructional designer on the project, once we work out all the details."

"Well, that's where the Devil is, I'm told," he laughed.

She laughed along, too, a polite laugh that reminded her that even though he was full of shit, he, as senior project manager, had the power to green-light the six million dollars to Autodidact. Mentally, she calculated what her twenty percent of six million was. Her laugh got even louder.

"Good to meet you, Socorro," Doug said.

"Please, call me Coco," she said. "Easier on the tongue."

Doug looked relieved at not having to pronounce something as positively un-American as *Socorro*. "Coco it is," he declared, rubbing his hands together. "Well, then, shall we join the rest of the crew upstairs?"

Chaney and Coco followed Doug onto one of the four elevators, and with practically no time for more useless small talk, they arrived at the client offices. Doug ushered them through the double glass doors and a labyrinth of gray cubicles, then another set of smaller double glass doors that led to a conference room. "We've got two more," Doug announced.

The usual suspects murmured their greetings and salutations. Al McCulligh, resembling a rumpled bed in his steel-blue suit reserved for grip-and-grins, looked up from the conversation he was having with Laura, his Plain Jane, bespectacled wife in her usual Laura Ashley, Little-House-on-the-Prairie look, and a perky blonde in a black suit dress. He had a Polaroid picture in his hand, and Chaney caught the tail end of the conversation. "Yeah, it's got nine bathrooms," he was saying.

Chaney instinctively knew to what he was referring in that Polaroid: the Bethesda mansion that he and Laura were remodeling. Al had sent that very same picture, along with others, over the Autodidact e-mail system to her and to the rank-and-file staff to show how mighty he was . . . the very same staff that joked that a man as full of shit as Al was would probably need nine bathrooms. After all, here was a man whom his mother, with her own pretensions to grandeur, named *Allison,* thinking that it made him sound further removed from his ancestors who came through Ellis Island with only the lint in the pockets of the threadbare clothes on their backs. The unfortunate moniker, though, only served to get him beat up in school and to give him license to be an asshole. This was the man who, when Coco had had a brain aneurism almost burst as she sat toiling away at work last year, made sure that she got in her weekly forty hours on her projects. The only reason anyone tolerated him was because his particular talents, extrapolated into a business context, translated into his knack for detecting how much a client could spend and for engineering the fall of all those dollars into Autodidact's coffers.

Laura, his idiotic better half, stood proudly next to her husband, who looked like he'd lost the fight with their iron. She was an owner of the business on paper only. Her true talents lay in frequenting Bethesda society luncheons and shuttling their three children to soccer practice and violin lessons. At Autodidact, she did the payroll—badly—and calculated paid annual leave, or PAL—erroneously, more often than not—to the company's advantage.

"The gang's all here!" laughed Al, with a wide, sweeping gesture and an even wider smile.

Fake motherfucker. In the office, he barely spoke to Chaney, and that was just how she liked it.

"Hello, Al . . . Laura," Chaney said.

The blonde came barreling forward. Chaney had seen her type before on contracts: the Overeager Beaver archetype, dying to prove her worth to the project. Until you crossed her. "And I'm Callie. Callie Bruce," she announced, snatching both Chaney's and Coco's hands, respectively, in a cold, clammy, bloodless handshake. "I'm an instructional designer, but I'm consulting with Doug as a project manager. I guess I'm his wingman."

"Wing *person,*" Doug corrected her.

They all laughed uproariously at Doug's attempt at P.C. Chaney resisted the urge to roll her eyes. *Twenty percent of six million dollars . . .* She joined in the laughter.

"We're waiting for one more person," Doug announced, then waved in the direction of the bank of windows that afforded a view of the Washington D.C. skyline. "Ladies, there's coffee, tea, and bagels and donuts at that table over there. Please help yourselves."

Chaney's gaze followed the waving hand over to the gray table on which goodies were spread out. *Coffee.* "You said the magic words, Doug," Chaney said.

Over at the table, too, was the only person who made her partnership in Autodidact bearable. *Lissa.* Chaney recognized her from the back of her curly head and her petite frame. Chaney, even with her confusion concerning homosexuals, readily admitted that she had a harmless girl crush on Lissa from when they were at Syracuse together. Lissa was different from anyone she'd ever met: a biracial sistah with spiral curls and nondescript eyes that were either light or green, depending on her mood; a sistah who was also an observant Jew, who had even been bat mitvahed, courtesy of her mother. In short, Lissa was light and airy Los Angeles; Chaney was dark and gritty New York. They complemented each other perfectly.

More importantly, Lissa showed Chaney strategies to tolerate Al and Laura while getting her work done, maximizing her share of the bottom line. She helped her with her project management skills, like creating a budget that was in line with the Office of Personnel Management, or OPM, the agency through which they went to secure contracts with government agencies. Lissa was her godmother, her wing *person.* Despite how Coco felt about Lissa, Chaney loved her, her loyalty to her boundless.

Chaney sidled up next to her and looked over at her flawlessly luminescent face. "Just leave me hanging with those folks, why don't you?" she whispered.

With plastic sticks, Lissa stirred her coffee in an environmentally unfriendly Styrofoam cup. "I can't deal with all that manly glad-handing," she whispered back. "I was about to grow a dick just listening to them go on."

Chaney choked back a laugh, glancing guiltily over her shoulder to see if anyone heard them. They hadn't. She grabbed one of the dark chocolate crullers. "Girl, I'm starvin' like Marvin," she whispered.

Lissa, the dedicated gym rat, glared scornfully at the cruller. "You might as well spread it on your thighs, 'cause that's where it's going."

From behind her, Chaney heard hands clapping. "Okay, we're all here," she heard Doug say. "Let's start, shall we?"

Chaney and Lissa turned simultaneously, and Chaney's hormones stood at attention.

The brothah walked into the office like he was the master of the universe, and Chaney's breath caught in her throat. She dug how his matter occupied the confined conference room space. He was basketball-player tall, one of her requirements, and as dark and delicious-looking as that cruller in her hand. He wasn't handsome in the classic sense, but his face wore the lines of time beautifully, giving him character. His bald dome reflected the fluorescent lights from overhead. He radiated cool, from the expression on his square-jawed face to the way he wore his gunmetal gray suit, with a blood red tie. "Sorry I'm late," he said in a voice as smooth as honey. "Carrying water uphill, as usual."

Chaney leaned in toward Lissa, who was also mesmerized. "Can I spread *him* on my thighs?" she whispered with a naughty giggle behind her hand.

Then Chaney became aware that the brothah was having the same effect on all of the women in the conference room, from blend-into-the-woodwork Laura, to uber-perky Callie Bruce, to even ultra-Catholic, ultra-married Coco! "Take a number," Lissa whispered back.

Everyone took their seats at the conference room table, and Doug, like the meeting's cruise director, elicited introductions. Everyone went around the table, introducing themselves, stopping at the brothah, who was seated at Doug's right hand. "And this is Randy Tyree," Doug announced. "Our ex-Navy lieutenant and SME."

"The unfortunately late Randy Tyree," he interjected.

That resulted in fake laughs from everyone, including Chaney. *Twenty percent of six million . . .*

"Now, Chaney's going to explain to us how we're going to get people at our call centers trained," Doug announced.

On cue, Chaney moved to the laptop and projector that Doug had already set up. While Chaney put the CD holding her PowerPoint presentation in the disk drive, Coco distributed the handouts to all present, then killed the overhead lights. The opening slide—*Navy Help Desk Customer Service Computer-Based Training Course (CBT)*, along with Autodidact's information and logo—appeared through the magic of projection technology on the silver screen at the front of the room. "Now that we've all had our coffee," Chaney said, shooting Coco a pointed barb in the semidarkness, "let's begin. You all should have received electronic copies of Autodidact's management plan via e-mail yesterday."

"We all did," Doug confirmed.

So far, so good. "Excellent," Chaney said. "For the first part of this presentation, I'm going to tease out the highlights."

Change slide. "From the information you provided for us, we devised this instructional goal." Chaney read off the slide. "The instructional goal of the *Navy Help Desk Customer Service* intervention is for participants to demonstrate knowledge of the process for managing help desk calls, from beginning to end, as it applied to current relevant U.S. Navy guidelines."

Chaney saw Callie's ghostly white arm shoot up, reflecting the ambient light from the projector. *Here we go.* "Which current U.S. Navy guidelines are you talking about?" she asked.

"That's a good question, Callie," Chaney lied, a device she learned to use during her dissertation defense: stroke the ego of purveyors of the dumb question before blowing them off. "But, as you probably know, being that you're an instructional designer, the instructional goal isn't meant to be specific. We get into specifics once we discuss the actual objectives of the course."

The response had far from the desired effect. Callie began to perform. "Are there any COTS products that we could use, in addition to this proposed course?" she asked.

Another acronym-rod. Government contracting was filled with them. For some reason, some genius thought that the use of acronyms made one seem smarter than one really was. "I'm sure you can find a *commercial off-the-shelf* product for anything these days, Callie," Chaney said. "But that's outside the purview of what Autodidact's being contracted to do here. Of course, we're always open to follow-on work!"

Everyone in the room laughed. "Of course we are," Al said.

Probably thinking of adding a tenth bathroom.

Chaney changed the slide. "Back on track, then," she said. "So here are the terminal objectives for the course."

Callie was on fire. "You know," she said, with a laugh that seemed meant to be conspiratorial, "I know it's the terminology of the field,

but I always found the words *terminal objective* so negative! I mean . . .
terminal. Sounds like a fate worse than death!"

In her mind, Chaney could picture all of the instructional design
pioneers turning over in their collective graves. Her life's work was
being treated to the vagaries of this babe before her, for no other
reason than that a critical aspect of it sounded like "a fate worse
than death." Just as Chaney was wondering how she could take one
for the team and still seal the deal, the late Randy Tyree spoke, his
voice resonating out of the semidarkness. "I hear you, Callie," he
said, apparently using the same device as Chaney had minutes ago,
"but I'm not an instructional designer. I'm the subject matter expert. I'm interested in the content and how it's going to be presented. I'd like to hear Chancy get to that, then open the floor to
questions."

Callie giggled and if it weren't for the darkness, Chaney was sure
she would've seen Callie blush. Callie put a hand over her flat chest.
"Of course, Randy!" she whinnied. "Please. Chaney. Go on."

Chaney stared at him, marveling at the power of a big black man to
calm the waters. He met her gaze and smiled. "Yes, Chaney," he echoed.
"Please go on."

So, with his blessing, she did.

Chaney looked at the embarrassment of oils on her office desk:
bottles of multicolored jasmine, patchouli, sandalwood, and others of
various earthy, fruity, and flowery scents. Coco, on the other hand,
wasn't so impressed. From her place in the guest chair in front of
Chaney's desk, she stared at the bounty, shaking her head disapprovingly. "You actually bought that Rastafarian guy out," she said.

"My food pellet for sitting through that meeting," Chaney declared. "And I didn't get any complaints from you about the last batch
of butter I made for those iron feet of yours."

Coco giggled coquettishly, like a new bride. "Mike does like it," she
confessed. "My feet don't scrape him under the covers at night anymore."

"Another satisfied customer," Chaney stated.

"Speaking of that meeting, what was the deal with that Callie?"
Coco asked. "Talk about over-the-top."

"I know!" Chaney laughed, a bitter tinge to it. "*Terminal objective* sounds so negative! I'd like to hear what Gagne or even Dick and Carey have to say about that shit."

Everyone working in the field of instructional design cut their teeth on the seminal works of Robert Gagne, Walter Dick, and Lou Carey. "She's going to be a problem," Coco predicted.

The memory of Callie jockeying like Willie Shoemaker for power in the group was fresh in Chaney's mind. Sometimes she truly wished that she could retreat to the basement with her oils, like Nathalie had suggested, and make a living at her hobby. But Autodidact and the bills it paid were her reality.

Right then, Carly stuck her unkempt, graying head in the office. Chaney could see dandruff flakes lingering at the part down the middle of her hair and cringed. "It smells nice in here!" she said.

"Speaking of problems," Coco murmured under her breath.

Carly Fincher-Barnes was messy, nosy, and harried from her unique project management style. She was forever putting out fires of her own making. It was small wonder that the rank-and-file staff, filled with dread at the prospect of working on any of her projects, nicknamed her *Cluster Fuck* Barnes.

Nonetheless, Chaney was polite. After all, in a year, the woman had managed to steer clear of her. "Hey, Carly," she said.

"Just talked to Al," Carly announced. "You're the woman of the hour, it seems."

Chaney was mildly surprised. She didn't think Al had anything positive to say about her; God knew she had very little to say to him and about him. "Al said that?"

"He sure did," she said. "I'd like to work with you sometime. Just let me know if you need my help on this project."

Chaney shot a glance at Coco. *No!* she mouthed, the look on her face resolute.

Chaney suppressed a chuckle. "Thanks for the offer, Carly," she said.

"Anytime," Carly said, then disappeared down the hall.

"Don't you let that woman near this project," Coco commanded.

"Okay, okay," Chaney laughed.

Just then, the phone rang. "Uh, duty calls," Chaney said.

Coco made her exit, and Chaney picked up the receiver. "Hello?"

" 'Cawfee,' huh? You must be from New York," he said from the other end.

Chaney smiled a million-watt smile. "And the way you say *water* like *wooder,* you must be from Philly," she laughed.

"West Philly, thank you."

She sat back comfortably in her chair, gazing through the picture windows at bustling, late-afternoon traffic on Rockville Pike. "Randy Tyree. We last talked, what, like two hours ago?"

He laughed that honey laugh. "It seemed longer than that since we 'tawked.' Where in New York?"

"Brooklyn."

"Bucktown."

She was impressed. "Home of the original gun clappers," she laughed, biting the line from that old Smif-N-Wessun rap, *Bucktown.*

Like she knew anything about guns. She was a straight-up nerd at Midwood High. In the Arista society, to put an even finer point on the matter. But what he didn't know wouldn't hurt.

"I just wanted to touch base with you after the meeting to let you know that I'm eager to start working with you," Randy said.

Chaney beamed, unable to fight the good feelings he was bringing. Somewhere deep in the recesses of her mind, she remembered the mantra: No plants, no pets, no men. Plus, everyone knew you didn't dip your pen in company ink. Still, she couldn't stop herself from flirting. "So folks from Illadelph have manners," she teased.

"Unlike people from New York," he shot back.

She laughed. "It's cool. I understand where the inferiority complex is coming from."

He laughed, too. "Well, back to business. I can't wait to start."

"Me, too." And she meant it.

"And don't worry about Callie. She's manageable."

Chaney had several managerial strategies in mind for her, none of them legal, unfortunately. "Well, I manage stuff for a living, so that should be no work for me," she declared.

"All right, Phenomenal Woman," he teased. "We'll talk soon."

He actually reads . . . and quotes Maya Angelou, no less! "Count on it," she returned, secretly wondering who the cocky bitch who'd suddenly inhabited her body was, and why said cocky bitch was doing all the talking.

The dial tone sounded in her ear, and she hung up the phone. *Randy Tyree.* That was a nice surprise.

A knock on the heavy wooden door snatched her to the present, and Chaney turned away from the picture window and saw Lissa, grinning from ear to ear. "I just talked to Doug," she announced. "They want Autodidact to develop the training. They want a design document, and a CBT package with instructor and learner guides, and they want us to stay on for an additional six months to train their trainers, and maybe even line staff!"

Chaney's enormous grin matched Lissa's. *Twenty percent of six million . . .* "Yeah, baby!" she laughed.

Lissa came in, and they hugged. Chaney practically dwarfed her, having to double over to complete the embrace. "Al is so happy, he could shit!" Lissa laughed. "He's planning another wing on that house in Bethesda."

Leave it to the mention of Al to dampen the euphoria. "Of course," she commented. "Why actually invest that profit in the business?"

Chaney sat back down in her chair, and Lissa eased down on the corner of the desk, careful not to disturb the oils. "Plus, with everything you've done for the company . . . with the investment, then using your contacts to secure us this deal, then writing that section on instructional design for our new OPM proposal," Lissa said, calling the roll, "Al can't touch you. You're bulletproof!"

Chaney wondered if the tide could actually be turning for her. She certainly knew that she was overdue for some goodness in her life. Professionally, things were looking up. Randy Tyree invaded her brain just then. Maybe it was time to rethink the mantra . . .

Lissa got up and smoothed out the front of her pants suit. "Well, we've been at it all day, and I'm going home," she declared. "I suggest you pack up your shit and do the same."

Chaney looked down at her watch. "Oh, at a quarter of five," she laughed. "How big of you!"

"Of course, you'll pay tomorrow by incorporating their revisions to the management plan," Lissa said, with a faux diabolical chuckle. "But for tonight, go home. Savor our victory!"

She barely remembered packing up her oils, riding down to the ground floor of the huge office building. Nor did she remember all of the details of crossing nearby Chapman Avenue to the Twinbrook metro and getting on the train for the evening rush hour crush. *Randy Tyree.* For the first time since Shane, a man had made Chaney feel warm and mushy inside. She practically giggled to herself for the better part of the hour-long train ride from Twinbrook to her car at the Huntington metro parking lot.

In the car, she eschewed the usual soft tunes of WHUR for Hot 99.5, just in time to hear JaRule wax poetically about how J.Lo's ass had him sprung, followed by her shallow-throated beginnings of "Ain't It Funny." Though she was more into Public Enemy and A Tribe Called Quest, she was beginning to have a healthy appreciation of how the new school brothahs broke it down. There was no ambiguity with them. They were adept at articulating their needs, sexual or otherwise. Chaney could hardly remember inspiring such primal reactions in a man. She wondered if she still had "it," if any man— Randy Tyree included—would ever be moved to recite poems about her ass.

Deliberating the proposition made her fifteen-minute drive home from the metro seem like half of that. She parked in her usual spot and came back to reality at breakneck speed. *Tony.* She could see him through the gossamer curtain obscuring the glass panels in the front door. His ears were perked up, and he stared at her like she was the beginning and end of his world. She could hear a muffled, repeated "Wuh!" from behind the door. She readily admitted to herself that that was sweet. Usually, she came home to an empty, dark, silent house.

She was so focused on Tony that she only barely saw her neighbor coming out of the door to Chaney's left. The frumpily dressed older woman held a chocolate Lab on a retractable leash. "Hi, Mrs. De'Ath," Chaney said, then prepared herself for the unpleasantries.

She nodded. "Chaney," she said in her broad Yorkshire accent. "You have a dog?"

Chaney noticed that she was "Chaney," but the old lady was "Mrs. De'Ath." Forever pulling rank. "I got him yesterday," she said.

"He has been barking all day, scaring my Hershey," Mrs. De'Ath declared. "It's very unsettling for us both."

What do you want me to do? Chaney looked down at Hershey. She was wagging her tail happily and panting, her pink tongue hanging out of her doggie face, which was pretty much how Hershey looked every time Chaney had seen her. Aloud, though, she said, "Thanks for letting me know."

Mrs. De'Ath took to the sidewalk with Hershey in tow. Chaney shook her head. *Dog people.*

Chaney turned the key in her lock. The second she opened the door, Tony bum-rushed her. To the tune of the bleating alarm, he barked, and jumped, and danced around her legs in apparent unadulterated joy. He left a healthy swath of yellow hairs all over her black pants, her trench coat. She watched the spectacle, her mouth literally hanging open. *What the hell?!* "Wuh!" he barked, slurping at her hands.

"Oh my God!" she laughed.

He leapt up and slurped at her chin. "Okay, okay, okay!" she laughed. "I've got to turn off the alarm!"

She shut the front door, locked it, and walked down the short length of the hall to the alarm panel. She quickly punched in the code, which silenced the beeping. Then she turned on the light in the hall and heard herself scream, felt her belongings slip from her hands and to the floor.

She ran into her living room and looked at her surroundings in utter disbelief. In the middle of the floor was a sea of stuffing from ripped throw pillows. Magazines that were once intact on the coffee table were torn to shreds. Strewn across the carpet was an indiscriminate trail of chewed-up CDs and videos, the laundry basket he'd apparently dragged from upstairs.

She ran into the kitchen and saw the plastic trash can, shredded at its handles by teeth marks. She saw trash ripped from the plastic bag and scattered all over the linoleum floor. Papers from her presentation that she'd left on the kitchen table had joined the trash in a heap of ripped detritus. Her blood pressure spiked, though, when she saw the buttery leather satchel that Anna Lisa had given her for graduation from Syracuse. It, too, was on the heap, its pockets and zipper mangled almost beyond recognition.

Through her near-homicidal fury, Chaney looked down at her feet, at the force of nature responsible for such wanton destruction. He looked up at her, panting happily. "Wuh!" he said.

If I hold this dog . . .

Somehow, Chaney found her purse on the floor and rummaged through until she found the card for the Rosslyn Veterinary Hospital and the book for the tour. She calmly got the phone and sat on the couch among foam beads of pillow stuffing. She found the number to the Hotel Centreville and dialed. After two rings, she heard, "Hotel Centreville."

It was the same whispering French snot from the previous night.

"Daisy Braxton, please," she requested, again feeling like she was in a hellish time warp.

Apparently, he recognized her voice, too. "Madam, *zey* are sleeping," he snapped.

Chaney clutched the phone in a death grip to keep from flinging it across the room. "Yes, I know!" she spat. *"Zee ow-err, zee ow-err.* I need to leave her a message."

Silence. He seemed to be able to do that. "What is the message, madam?" Sounded like *zee messahge.*

Success. "Please tell Miss Braxton to have her vet in Los Angeles call this number and arrange to have her dog's records faxed," she said, then gave him the number.

"My pleasure, madam," he lied after an appropriate silence, in which Chaney was to assume that he was writing down the number to Devin's office.

Refraining from a good-bye, Chaney hung up and looked up at Tony. He was now quiet, like he sensed he was guilty of something very bad.

She looked down at Devin's card in her hand again. *What the hell?* She counted to ten, took a deep breath, and dialed. On the third ring, someone picked up on the other end. "Rosslyn Veterinary Hospital," the man said.

Only he sounded just like the man she just hung up with from across the Atlantic. *What is this . . . Attack of the Annoying Frenchmen?* "Hello?" she asked.

"Yes, to 'oom would you like to speak?" he asked.

"Dr. Rhym," she said.

"Er . . . ee has left for the day. I'm Dr. Didier. May I 'elp?"

"I really need *him*!"

"Trust me, madam. I am also a veterinarian. I can 'elp."

Time to play her only ace in the hole. "This is his cousin, Chaney Braxton. I really would prefer to speak with him, if you don't mind."

" 'Ello dere!" he laughed, perking up. " 'E and Maria told us about you. 'Ow's de dog? 'Ow's de treatment for eez 'artwom?"

Huh? "Umm . . . " she began, trailing off. What was the protocol when one couldn't understand a word the vet is saying?

Fortunately, he saved her from having to find out. "I will locate eem, and 'ave eem to call you back," he promised.

It took a minute as Chaney ran it through the translator. "Okay," she said finally. "Thank you."

Chaney pressed the TALK button again, hanging up. She breathed in and out in an attempt to calm herself. She looked down at Tony. She clapped her hands. "Let's go!" she commanded.

Immediately, Tony snapped to attention, following her as she stormed toward the sliding doors. Seconds later, he was on the deck, peering at her from the other end of the glass. She wondered how she ended up there, right in that spot . . . particularly after the wonderful beginning to the day.

And the characters at the Rosslyn Veterinary Hospital didn't seem to be any help whatsoever. There was the insanely perky nurse, the unintelligible Frenchman, and, lastly, the child who dispensed medical advice and reassurances like Pez.

She went up the stairs, suppressing a shudder at the chewed-up trash cans that Tony had somehow extracted from the laundry closet. She opened the door to her office, one of the spare bedrooms she had furnished with office furniture and her numerous books. She sat in the black swivel chair, behind the solid wood desk, on which her flat-screen monitor and Dell Pentium 4 rested. She turned on the CPU and watched as it booted up. *What am I dealing with here?*

In less than a minute, desktop icons, superimposed over a picture of the three Braxton women as wallpaper, displayed on the screen. She clicked on the Internet icon, watched as the Autodidact home page appeared. Immediately, she typed in the URL for Google. At the search field, she typed in DEVIN RHYM, then clicked GO.

Seconds later, her page filled with blue writing, URLs, and descriptions with Devin's name highlighted in bold. On the top status bar, she saw the words 1 of 2,400 hits. *Two thousand, four hundred hits!* For the first ten pages, until she got tired of clicking, she found his impressive curriculum vitae . . . papers he'd written while at the University of Washington and at Washington State University . . . presentations and symposia on veterinary medicine . . . even photos of him scoring as a point guard for the Washington Huskies . . . photos of him in a Speedo, swim cap, and goggles as he launched out of the starting blocks into a shimmering blue pool.

Holy shit! How could she have doubted him? Worse, how could she have gone on at length about her tiny presence in her tiny company, when, in the veterinary world, he was The Shit? There was nothing to do but shut up and wait . . . for the call.

Devin stacked the bottles of Heineken in a tiny pyramid on the last shelf of the fridge. Behind him, he could hear the sound of the pre-game pundits pompously waxing on the plasma TV about what college team was going to win tonight's basketball game. "That's bullshit!" Andre shouted at the TV, apparently not feeling the pronouncements. "Gonzaga? Whoever heard of fucking Gonzaga?"

"Anyone who knows anything about Washington State," Devin countered defensively.

Andre gazed across the expanse of the town house living room to see Devin in the open kitchen. "Oh, 'scuse up on me," he commented. "I forgot that you pledge allegiance to that *other* Washington. Go put on a Pearl Jam CD. Or some Soundgarden. Or that Alice in Chains shit."

Even in the faint light, Devin marveled at Andre's uncanny resemblance to eighties' singer Al B. Sure, an attribute that he used to its advantage to score with the ladies. " 'Scuse up on *me*, Mr. Ho-ell, for not having such a narrow mind."

" 'Ho-ell,' " Andre laughed sarcastically at the bastardization of his real last name—Joell. "That was clever the first hundred times I heard it from y'all, especially from you, Soul Brothah Number Two."

"Oh, Biracial Humor!" Devin laughed. "Too clever for me!"

He laughed, but the comment stung. It always had. It meant that even his closest friends saw him as inauthentic, the fake McCoy, a Halfrican.

Jamal, who'd been listening to the exchange from his seat on the couch, got up and headed toward the kitchen. "The *other* Washington," he commented. "They're letting ugly Americans into the Air Force these days."

"Same way they're letting ugly Jamaicans into Howard University Hospital," Andre countered, calling after him.

"Give me one hour in an exam room with him," Jamal whispered to Devin. "That's a dick just begging for a Foley catheter."

Devin resisted the urge to cup his package. "Ouch!"

These were his boys, fellas he'd known since they'd ended up sharing crayons in kindergarten at Patrick Henry Elementary School.

They'd kept his place for him while he was in exile in Seattle and welcomed him back as if he'd never left. Devin had been toying with the idea of moving back to Virginia, but it was Andre's near brush with death at the Pentagon that helped him make up his mind. Then there was Jamal Bain—nicknamed Mali in moments of male affection—still wearing his scrubs from work. Mali's mother came to the U.S. from Jamaica when her extraordinarily bright son was barely school age and worked as a domestic to give him opportunities that led to him being a third-year resident at Howard University Hospital.

Jamal looked down at his watch. "Hey, where's your brother with the pizza!" he called out to Andre, and Devin could hear traces of his Jamaican accent. "I'm coming off a double shift, and I'm starving!"

"Have some cheese with that whine, motherfucker," Andre said.

Devin, the peacemaker, opened one of the white cupboards and handed him a box of Cheez-Its. "After all these years, you don't know Ryan's late for everything?" he scolded.

Jamal eagerly took the Cheez-Its and cracked open the box. "Boy must be an honorary West Indian," he said, shoveling crackers in his mouth.

The doorbell rang right then. "Guess who?" Devin laughed.

"It's about fucking time," Jamal murmured, the mouthful of crackers muffling the sound.

Devin went to get the door. A glimpse through the peephole revealed that it was, indeed, Ryan Joell, Andre's older brother. Devin opened the door, and Ryan, carrying a mountain of pizza boxes, stepped into the room. "Am I late?" he asked with wide-eyed innocence.

"Is water wet, Negro?" Andre called from the couch.

Devin relieved Ryan of the pizzas, then proceeded to head over to the wooden coffee table and spread the boxes out. "How much do we owe?"

He shrugged his thick, broad shoulders. "My treat," he said.

That was typical. After all, it was Ryan who, because he was seven years older than the rest of them, would take them into R-rated movies, would drive them to D.C. and Maryland to buy them beer, as well as get them into clubs on U Street. "Thanks, man," Devin said.

Ryan shrugged off his jacket and, as he went to hang it up in the coat closet, Devin saw his gun in the small of his back. He loathed guns. He vividly remembered fearing the one his father carried. "You're off duty, for crying out loud!" he cried. "Couldn't you leave that thing at the office?"

Ryan protectively patted the small of his back. "You wouldn't be saying that if some shit jumped off here, would you? I'd have to hear 'Where's a cop in D.C. when you need one?' "

"Your brother leaves *his* gun home."

"My brother works with computers. The worst thing that'd happen to him is that Windows would crash and wipe out all his little reports."

"Bring it over here!" Andre called with a full mouth of pizza. "We can shoot the TV if Gonzaga wins."

"No one's shooting Devin's TV," Devin declared, then said to Ryan, "Please put your gun in the closet with your jacket."

Begrudgingly, Ryan obliged, and they all sat in front of the TV. Devin fondly remembered his days playing b'ball in college . . . the camaraderie, the travel, the girls, the roar of the crowd when he stepped with his teammates onto the court. Even though he played to afford his tuition, he still loved it. That was why he still played. Each of his friends indulged him. He lifted weights with Ryan, played b'ball with Jamal, did D.C. Happy Hour with Andre, the ladies' man. "Washington's got this," Devin decreed.

Andre made a hissing sound through pursed lips. "Washington ain't got nothin' on Maryland!"

"They're named after an angry snapping turtle," Jamal reasoned.

"If the Terps win this, I'll eat a bug," Ryan declared.

"You're on, bruh!" Andre declared.

He and his brother pinky-swore, and Devin and Jamal looked on in surprise. "What are you two, like, ten?" Jamal asked.

"Eat your fucking pizza," Andre commanded.

Obediently, Devin reached for a pepperoni slice, folded it, and took a bite. He exhaled to cool the cheese and oil that seared the top of his mouth. "Shit is hot!" he cried.

Clearly, no one else was feeling his pain. They were chowing down and pounding their Heinies . . . especially Jamal. Only Andre came up for air as the game went to commercial. "Hey, Dev, 'member that honey we met at the Rhodeside last week?" he asked.

Devin searched his mind, but for the life of him couldn't remember. "Naw, he was sulking because we dragged him to a bar in Arlington, instead of his precious M Street," Ryan commented.

He was right, of course. The *Washington Post* was calling the

Clarendon section of Arlington County "the New Georgetown," but Devin wasn't feeling it. Anywhere you had to go to an ABC Store to buy liquor was hardly down with the times.

Andre leaned in, a devious smile on his face. "Any-hu," he continued, "the honey wasn't feeling me."

"Shocking!" Jamal commented, with a sarcastic laugh. "Could it be because you called her a 'honey'?"

"Another country heard from—literally," Andre commented, then again turned to Devin with the sales pitch. "She's a student at Georgetown. I got the digits and hit her up, but she said that she was more interested in my friend that looks like Tiger Woods. In case you haven't passed a mirror lately, that would be you, bruh."

Devin laughed, shaking his head. After Tiger had won the Masters in 1996, Devin officially went from nondescript, wooly-haired freak to fuckable in literally eighteen holes. He was thankful that Tiger Woods had made him acceptable in the eyes of greater America, but this was ridiculous. "I'd like to score my own women, thanks," he said. "'Huggy Joell.'"

"Just looking out for you, Dev," Andre said. "This monastic shit you're working with is hazardous to your health. Mali can tell you about the perils of blue balls firsthand, can't you, Mali?"

Jamal looked up from his slice long enough to flip Andre off.

"Did I tell you guys I saw Kimmy yesterday?" Devin said.

The rest of the posse groaned. "Oh, man, Dev, that's majorly old history," Andre declared. "Why you wanna hook up with an anchor with a kid?"

Devin tossed the rest of his slice in an empty corner of the box. Suddenly, he wasn't hungry anymore. "Two kids," he corrected.

"Making the point even stronger," Jamal interjected.

"How is she, Devin?" asked Ryan, the sole mature voice in the bunch.

Devin took a liberal swallow of his Heineken. "Living in a shithole on South Glebe and shacked up with this redneck," he summarized.

"So, what's the attraction, Devin?" Ryan asked, his gaze deep and probing, like he was really interested.

Devin laughed, shaking his head. "Maybe I can save her," he said. *Is that really true?*

"*Jesus* saves," Andre said. "You ain't Jesus."

Just as he was thinking of a comeback, the cell phone in the front pocket of his cargo pants beeped. *Saved by the bell*. He snatched it out and began pressing buttons. "I'm on call tonight," he announced to his guests.

He took the phone and wandered over to the kitchen. On the green screen of his cell phone, he saw that he had one text message. He pressed all the necessary buttons, then read on the screen: 911. CALL COUSIN CHANEY. 703-555-9697. DIDIER.

His curiosity sufficiently piqued, Devin picked up the cordless phone on the kitchen wall nearest the fridge. While he dialed her number, he also stored it in his cell . . . for potential future use. After three rings, he heard the phone being loudly snatched up. "Hello," he heard.

She sounded harried, stressed-out beyond belief. Instinctively, he became the antithesis. "Good night, Chaney, it's Devin," he said, keeping his voice calm and even. "My partner, Dr. Didon, said you called to speak to me."

She said. "I don't hate animals," she declared. "I mean, as a concept, they have their place. But I'm not feeling this dog! I mean, if he was a person who totally destroyed my home, I could just ask him to leave. But he's a dog!"

Her fury made her New York accent even thicker, especially when she said the word *dog*, like "dawg." "What happened?" he asked.

She continued her alternating monologue. "If I were my mother—or my sister, even—this dog would have a shoe in his ass."

"Well, as a rule, I don't recommend corporal punishment," he said, maintaining his tone. "You really only have about a half-hour window to consequence pets. After that, Tony doesn't know what you're mad at, just that you're mad. So, he wouldn't form any correlation between the crime and the punishment."

"I admit it; I don't know what to do," she confessed.

The basketball game he'd been waiting for all day was practically blazing on the TV in the background, and he could've cared less. What was it about his soft spot for women with problems? His mother. Kimmy. Now Chaney. "I could come over if you need me to," he said, keeping his tone professional. "Would you like that?"

Suddenly, the heat left her voice, replaced by uncertainty. "Umm . . . I don't know," she murmured. "It's not like I'm really going to hurt the dog."

"I don't think you'd hurt Tony," he said, though he wasn't entirely sure. "You're overwhelmed; I understand that. I'm just offering to help."

Silence. He waited and waited, and his anticipation grew exponentially with each moment he listened to her breathing, wondering—he assumed—what she was getting herself into. Finally, she said, "Let me give you the address."

Minutes later, the fellas were staring at Devin as he laced up his Tims and shrugged into his pea coat. "I've gotta go," he said.

"Must be important for you to blow off the game and all," Andre said simply. "We'll tape it for you."

He knew they'd understand. "Save me a slice."

Devin raced down to the garage, fired up the Navigator, and, following her directions, he made it to Alexandria in less than twenty-five minutes. With the help of the dashboard light, he drove around the neighborhood of town houses until he entered a cul-de-sac and saw one with a red door. The numbers 3702 glowed atop the door, illuminated by a bright porch light.

Devin parked, rushed in the brisk night up to the door, and rang the bell. Instantly, he saw Tony's yellow head appear through the gauzy curtain in front of the glass panels in the front door. "Wuh!" he barked, his ears perked up.

"Tony, come down from there!" Devin heard Chaney scold him from behind the door.

The door flew open, and Devin saw Chaney, scowling, clutching Tony by this thick black leather collar. She looked damned near homicidal until she saw him. Then relief replaced the anger on her face. *That pretty face.* He smiled. "Good night," he said, still using the friendly but firm professional tone.

She sighed. "Hey. Thanks for coming."

"We're cousins, right?"

That made her laugh. She moved aside. "Come on in. But be prepared."

Devin entered the anteroom, looking around as he did. Her crib smelled deliciously fragrant and was homey in an Afrocentric kind of way. She had some of the same types of collages and tribal masks that his dad liked and used to decorate the house on North Garfield. Then he saw it: the remnants of a gigantic mess in the middle of her living room floor. Even with the broom, dustpan, and vacuum strategically placed nearby, the flurry of chewed objects and torn papers still seemed massive. He looked over at her, and she at him, looking like, *see, told you so.* "I guess I'd be tempted to strangle him myself," Devin conceded. "But you didn't."

"It wasn't easy," she said, moving over to the cleaning implements in the middle of the living room floor.

He watched her walk, a strong, confident walk that said she didn't take shit from anyone. Girls his age had that come-over sidle, like they needed horny bastards like him to validate their womanhood. Not "Cousin" Chaney. Everything about her, even with this dog she didn't understand, screamed confidence, security in her skin. Not that she wasn't sexy. She bent over for the dustpan just then, and he saw right down her blouse, got a nice eyeful of cleavage furrow.

Peeling off his coat, he joined her amidst the mess. "Let me help," he said.

She pushed the vacuum cleaner his way. "Be my guest."

They put Tony onto the deck, and with two hands, made quick work of the mess, filling two kitchen trash bags. Reluctantly, she let Tony in, and he came straight to Devin. He rubbed Tony's big head. "It's okay, boy," he said. "You're gonna get adjusted in no time."

She looked up at Devin, with a *yeah, right* expression on her face. She began tying a bag, and tossed what was formerly a stuffed clown before Tony had gotten to it. In a shot, Tony ran after it, grabbed it in his mouth, and brought it back to her. She took the clown out of his mouth and stared incredulously at him. "That's different," she commented.

Devin laughed. Poor woman, so out of her depth! "He's a retriever," he said simply. "It's what they've been bred to do."

She looked like she was trying to absorb it all. She sat down at the foot of her carpeted stairs and sighed wearily. He joined her. "They're smart dogs," he said, continuing the sales pitch. "My friend Ryan's a D.C. cop. He hangs out with these Customs officers. They love labs."

"Well, if I decide to make a career change to drug interdiction, I'll be prepared."

He laughed. "You got jokes."

Devin studied her profile. He could see some gray streaks in her 'fro. He wondered if it was as soft as it looked. In this light, being so close to her, he realized how physically attractive he found her . . . her 'fro with those cute spirally curls, her full mouth, which looked even fuller with the shade of red lipstick she was wearing. Blowjob Red,

Andre would've called it. Sitting down, he got an even better look down her blouse, the only thing stopping him being the line of a black bra. She moved just then, and he felt her thigh brush against his. Common sense told him to shift a little, to break the contact between them, before he was tempted to bone his fake-cousin right there on the stairs.

"I'm like, the worst hostess," she said, with a sheepish grin. "Can I get you a drink or something?"

Devin shook his head. "I'm gonna leave in a few minutes."

Chaney looked down. He saw it, too, at her foot . . . a chewed-up .45 record. She sighed, looking up at Tony, who was now lying where the mess was in the living room. She looked like she wanted to cry. "Look at this," she said, picking it up. "I loved this record."

From the unchewed part of the label, Devin could make out the title and artist: *What You Won't Do for Love*. Bobby Caldwell. He knew the cut. "Hey, I thought that group, Intro, recorded that song first."

She looked at him like he was a pitiful young 'un. "Naw, man, Bobby Caldwell," she said, shaking her head like she had to take him to school. "This was the jam—1978."

"I know who Bobby Caldwell is," he stated in his defense. "Common sampled him on 'The Light.' "

She looked up at him, seemingly impressed. Then she looked away, dark eyes darting back and forth. "What was I doing in 1978? I was about to start seventh grade. Wow! What were you doing back then?"

Right then, he felt like a pitiful young 'un. "Umm . . . eating paste?" he guessed. "I was only four."

Chaney chuckled. "Cousin, you are a tenderoni!"

"Hey, the eighties called—they want that word back!"

She burst out laughing, bumping him so hard he nearly fell off the step. He made her laugh like that. That made him feel good.

Soon, though, the laughter died, and she got all serious. "That's a good question, don't you think?" she said. "What wouldn't you do for love?" She scoffed, looking over at Tony, who looked back at her. "You'll allow yourself to get guilted into watching a dog that you can't manage."

Devin thought about KL. *You move back to try to bond with an emotionally bankrupt father before he dies.*

He thought of Kimmy. *You hold on to Kimmy in some sick way, even though she's obviously moved on.*

"You gotta factor self-love into the mix," Devin suggested. "Whitney Houston said that learning to love yourself is the greatest love of all."

"Ah, but George Benson said it first," Chaney informed him.

Devin chuckled, shaking his head. "You're too old school for me, big cuz."

"I've literally got teeth that are older than you, little cuz."

"Okay, you opened the door. Just how old are you anyway?"

"I'm thirty-six," she announced.

Devin's mouth dropped open. "No way!"

"Yes way!"

Kimmy looked older than her. "I would've thought thirty, thirty-one, tops."

Chaney looked at him and smiled. He felt his mouth returning the favor. "Guess that stress-and-coffee diet is working well," she laughed.

He loved how she said coffee, like *cawfee*. "That means you were . . ." he quickly did the math " . . . eight when I was born. What was going on in your life then that was so interesting?"

The laughter really took a vacation then. "My parents died when I was five," she announced. "I was three years into figuring out how a God that was supposedly so benevolent could take them away from me."

What do I say here? "I'm sorry," he said quietly. "My dad told me about your parents."

She snapped her fingers. "I remember who your dad is now!" she exclaimed. "KL. The last time I saw him, you weren't even a glimmer in his eyes yet. He was married to this white lady."

His family's checkered past coming out to haunt him. "Daphne," he confirmed. "My sister-in-law, Marlene, is her daughter-in-law. Moms is wife number three."

"Your dad's a stud!"

He knew he wouldn't be able to keep track and juggle all the women his dad had gone through over the years. "That he is."

"You too, Cousin?" she teased.

He felt himself blush. "This apple fell far from the stud tree," he declared.

"Well, tell your dad I said hey."

"I will. He wants to have you over for dinner."

She got up, and he did the same. He sensed their interlude was wrapping up. "Just say when," she said.

Chaney tossed the demolished record into the living room. On instinct, Tony caught it and brought it, covered in spit, back to her. "You'd better take that from him," Devin said, back to the helpful, kindly veterinarian. "Sharp edges."

Chaney did so, tossing the record on the pile of trash ready to be taken out. "So much for that," she sighed.

Devin looked down at his watch. He doubted he'd still see the fellas *or* the game when he got back to the house. "Well, I better go," he said, then reached into his pocket for his cell phone. "Listen, why don't you give me your e-mail address? I'll send you some articles on combating anxiety in dogs and managing destructive behavior."

The expression on her face said she was down for that. "It's S-Y-R-A-Q-Q," she announced.

He stopped punching in the letters for a sec, looking up at her. "Oh," he said. "Syra-cuse! I get it!"

She gave him the letters of her ISP, and he punched it into the phone, too. "I went to school there," she explained. "I know; it seemed like a cool idea at the time."

"I'm not hatin'," he laughed. "My personal e-mail is D-Riddim. That sounded cool at the time, too."

"You can also send it to my work e-mail addresses—Cbraxton@ autodidact.tv."

Laughter punctuated an uncomfortable conversational lull. Until Chaney finally spoke. "Thanks for coming to help me," she said. "I know you missed the game. I heard it over the phone when we were talking."

Tawking. He shrugged, like it was no thing. "I really only start paying attention when they get down to the Sweet Sixteen, anyway."

From the kitchen counter, she produced a large, clear jar, like the mommy of the little one she'd given him the day before in the exam room. "Here," she said. "More."

He took it from her, tentatively opened the jar, and smelled the creamy contents. The scent was spicy and inviting. "I'm going to have the most kissable hands in D.C. if you keep this up," he chuckled.

To his utmost astonishment, this woman who was so together and professional giggled. "You're funny," she said. "You need to travel with your own rim shot machine."

He got his coat off the handle of the stair banister, shrugged it on, and tucked his jar of hand cream inside one of the pockets. "Well . . ." he said.

They spent a second or so staring at each other. Devin knew she was thinking the same thing he was. *Shake hands? Hug?*

Finally, Chaney opened her arms and pulled him close. It was an innocent enough hug, but damn, if he couldn't smell her perfume, sense every curve of her underneath that suit, feel the hair of her head softly brush his cheek. Even though she wasn't really a blood relative, he felt a little strange about the feelings he was having toward her.

He ended the embrace, looking down to see her smiling up at him. He liked it when she smiled. "Listen, call me or e-mail me if you're feeling overwhelmed," he urged. "I don't care what time it is. Okay?"

She nodded. "Okay."

They headed for the door. Devin sensed Tony behind them. At the door, he bent and stroked Tony's soft, thick coat. " 'Bye, buddy," he said, sending Tony's tail whipping about in concentric circles. Devin looked up at Chaney and winked. "You be good, okay?"

"Wuh!" Tony barked, and Devin truly believed that Tony understood him. Even after years in the business, animals still amazed him with the things they did.

Minutes later, Devin was on the outside, staring at both Chaney and Tony through the gauzy window treatment.

The traffic was lighter still on Route 1 as he made his way from Alexandria to Arlington and over the Key Bridge to Georgetown. And with Jigga bringing the knowledge over a thumping beat about "Girls, Girls, Girls," it seemed like it was no time before he was in his garage once more. He killed the music and the engine, and thought again about the question: *What you won't do for love.*

Devin looked in his wallet, sifting through the photos in his billfold, until he came across a black-and-white photo strip of him and Kimmy. They'd taken it at a photo booth at Ballston Common, the mall in Arlington, before he'd left for Seattle. The first two shots, they were typically mugging for the camera. The last two photos on the strip, they were locked in a passionate kiss that had made his teen-aged body shake. *If you loved yourself, you'd move on . . .*

Maybe if he wasn't so horny, he'd be able to think straight. He did the math in his head and came to the realization that he hadn't had a date since moving home almost six months ago. Hugging "Cousin" Chaney made him acutely aware of the itch in his pelvis that needed to be scratched.

He entered the town house to find empty pizza boxes and dead soldiers of the Heineken variety strewn about the coffee table. Andre was making a half-assed attempt at cleaning up. He looked over his shoulder at Devin. "You solve the world's problems, Superman?" he teased.

Andre didn't need to know about his inner conflict just yet. "Where's everyone?" Devin asked, looking around.

"Ryan took his gun and left after Maryland won," Andre said. "Mali went home to pick out a bug for Ryan to eat. So that just leaves me, and I'm gonna make tracks like homeless in a minute."

Again, Devin looked over at the empty pizza boxes. *These greedy motherfuckers!* "You guys didn't save me any pizza?"

Andre headed to the kitchen, and Devin followed. With a dramatic flourish, Andre opened the oven. There, on a large piece of foil, were four slices of each variety that Ryan had brought. "We saved you some beer, too," he announced. "In the freezer. Ice cold. Just how you like it."

Devin smiled, shaking his head. "And I doubted you."

Andre sucked his teeth. "You know you's my boy."

Devin took two Heinies out of the freezer and popped the tops with the bottle opener on the counter. He passed one over to Andre. "Listen," he began. "That girl you were talking about earlier?"

Andre's eyes lit up. "The honey from the Rhodeside."

Devin began to wonder if this was such a good idea. "Yes, the honey from the Rhodeside," he snapped.

"I ain't a doctor like Mali, but I know the symptoms," Andre teased. "Someone's got a raging case of blue balls."

So like Andre, to draw this shit out. "Oh, just give me the fucking number!" he laughed.

Looking too pleased with himself, Andre pulled out his cell, and Devin pulled out his. He read the number off his cell, and Devin punched it into his. "Her name is Zoe," Andre said, and Devin input that, too.

There he was again . . . on the verge of the indiscriminate use of his dick. With someone's sweet daughter named Zoe. He couldn't stop;

after all, he was KL Rhym's son. With Andre enabling him, he was a hopeless case.

Andre patted Devin on the back, then took a healthy sip of his Heinie. "You're doing the right thing," he insisted. "You're young, and there's a world full of women out there. Leave that blonde alone. Time to let go."

Devin looked down at Zoe's number glowing on his green cell phone screen. He swigged his beer, then raised his bottle Andre's way. "Here's to letting go," he said.

Andre's smile brightened, his smile flattening out his unibrow. He clinked Devin's raised bottle. "To letting go," he said, all the naughty implications of that carried along on his voice.

Three

Careful of getting yellow hairs on her black suit, Chaney sat down on the small wooden bench on the far wall of one of the Rosslyn Veterinary Hospital's windowless examination rooms. Tony, on a brand-spanking-new retractable leash, lay on his belly under the metal table. He looked up at Chaney with the ears-perked, head cocked look for which he seemed to know she was a sucker. Chaney pressed her Blackberry to her ear, listening to the silence over the phone. She was holding. "Don't you give me that look," she said to Tony, and he began swishing his tail from side to side. "I'm still mad at you."

From over the phone, from across the Atlantic, Chaney heard, "One minute, please, madam. I will connect you to that room."

Chaney looked down at her watch; the hands pointed out 8:30. What a difference the cold light of day made on the disposition of the Hotel Centreville's employees. Where the nighttime desk attendant was the height of snitty, this daytime desk attendant embodied politeness. There was another hollow-sounding pause before Chaney heard her sister giggle, "*Allo?*"

When did you get so French? "Daisy, it's me," Chaney announced.

Daisy gasped. "Chanes!" she squealed. "Girl, I wish you were here! I'm looking out from my room at the Eiffel Tower. The fucking Eiffel Tower!"

Chanes. She was only *Chanes* when Daisy wanted something. Chaney pictured her sister, staring out at the Paris skyline, languishing her tall body in a lace teddy, stretching herself over miles and miles of million-thread-count cotton sheets. Chaney tempered her envy. "Well, I'm looking at the inside of the fucking vet's office," she mock-squealed. "Oh my God, you should see it. It's got a computer, and jars with treats and stuff, and it's got a yellow dog in it!"

"Oh, Chaney, you're so funny!" Daisy giggled again. "Talk to Ricky."

Chaney heard a muffling sound as the receiver was passed, and before she could protest, Ricky was on the phone. "Hi, Chaney," he said, his voice deep and resonant, like that of a singer. "Your sister's told me so much about you and Anna Lisa, I feel like I know you two already."

So Cock-Diesel the Bass Player was named Ricky. "I wish I could say the same about you, Ricky," Chaney said before she could stop herself.

"We're gonna meet sooner than you think," he promised. "Well, here's your sister again."

More muffling sounds as Ricky passed the phone back. Chaney heard the lip-smacking goodness of long, leisurely French kissing. Irritation suffused Chaney. She looked down at her watch, at the time ticking by. Then finally, Daisy reappeared on the phone. "I'd tell you two to get a room, but you did that already," Chaney said.

Daisy laughed, more like purred . . . sounding quite like a well-laid woman. Chaney barely remembered the last time she'd made that sound. "Listen, Chanes, how's my baby dog?" Daisy asked.

Chaney looked down at Tony. *Again, with the licking of the balls!* "He's got heartworm, and he's wrecking my house. Other than that, we're getting along great."

"How'd my baby get heartworm?"

"I don't know, Daisy. I just know he has it. I'm at the vet here, getting it treated. Some barbaric practice involving shots in the back."

"Oh, my poor baby dog!" she cried. "Does that hurt?"

Chaney could actually feel Daisy's love for Tony in that moment. She obviously had to, to sign up for the challenge that owning him provided. Sometimes her sister actually surprised her. Perhaps she wasn't as frivolous as Chaney thought. "I don't know, Daisy," she confessed. "It can't be fun. He's gonna be okay. Norm's cousin is his vet, and he's very good." *And very cute, for a juvenile . . .*

That seemed to reassure her a bit. "You're the best, Chaney. I love you, girl!"

Chaney softened some, but not too much. "I love you, too, Daisy. So when are you coming home?"

"It's our last day here," Daisy announced. "Tomorrow, we're heading off to *Barthelona!*"

Chaney couldn't help but laugh. Yes, Daisy was making her life miserable, but that was funny. "I also had the vet fax Tony's records to the number you gave the desk attendant yesterday," Daisy said. "If you're there, he should have them."

"I'll check once he comes in."

More lip-smacking emanated from over the phone. "Hello?" Chaney snapped.

Daisy laughed seductively. "Girl, I have to go," she said. "It's our first free day here, and we want to make the most of it."

I bet you do! Far be it from her to begrudge her sister some dick. "Go," Chaney prompted. "Call me later at the house."

"Kiss my baby for me," she implored.

Chaney glanced at Tony. He was sitting upright, staring at her, as if he knew his mommy was on the phone. His expression seemed to read, *did she ask about me?* Chaney puckered and blew Tony a kiss. His yellow tail thumped the hard concrete floor. "I just did," she said.

But Daisy was no longer there. Chaney heard a click, then looked in the screen of her Blackberry. *Call ended,* she read. *Another sistah "dick-mo-tized."*

The door opened just then, and Devin appeared in the doorway. Tony was up like a shot, tail whipping around like the blades of a windmill. Chaney broke into a shy smile. "Big cuz!" he laughed.

There were no scrubs, Tims, or cargo pants today. Under his personalized white coat, he wore a white shirt with a gray tie, Hunter green corduroys with medium wales, and black loafers. He looked quite the young urban professional. "You've got to perk down a notch, little cuz," she pleaded. "I haven't had my morning coffee yet."

He leaned against the metal table. In an instant, Tony leapt up on his hind legs, pressing his front paws against Devin's chest. "Tony!" Chaney cried, mortified.

Devin guided Tony gently to all fours, all the while surreptitiously inspecting the insides of Tony's ears. "Sit, Tony," Devin commanded, then pressed an index finger softly at the base of his back, where the tail met his body.

Instantly, Tony dropped to a sitting position, and Chaney stared in awe and admiration. She mentally stored that trick away for future reference. "Good boy!" Devin said, then, from that magical place in his coat, extracted a treat.

Tony nipped it out of Devin's fingers, then chewed impolitely, soggy crumbs falling to the floor from the insides of his doggie mouth.

Devin turned his attentions on her. "Let's talk about you," he said, in that same soothing tone he'd used to talk her off the ledge last night. "How are you doing?"

Given her license to bitch and moan, Chaney went full tilt. "I'm at my wit's end with Tony, and the destructive behavior. I have a million-dollar project that I should be working on, but I have to be here, dealing with this problem, while my sister is off having the best sex of her life with some bassist named Ricky." *And it's Day Three of my period, and my cramps are killing me!*

Devin's brows flew up. "All-rightee then!" he laughed.

She sensed she might have gone too far.

"While the sex thing is way outside of my scope," he chuckled, "I can probably help you manage Tony. Let's start with the good news first. This morning, your sister's vet in L.A. faxed the records over, and I'm reviewing them. But right about now, nothing jumps out as a problem. We've found the heartworm, and we're going to treat him for it today and tomorrow, okay?"

Chaney took it all in. "Okay."

"Now, about the destructive behavior," he began. Chaney was all ears. "The poor guy's most likely having separation anxiety. He just made a move three thousand miles across the country. I've made the trip several times, and it grates on me! So, I can only imagine how it must affect a dog who doesn't understand what's going on. He's probably nervous, and the chewing and the destruction are the way he gets it out of his system. He can't talk and say, 'Hey, I don't know you, and I'm scared, and I miss my mommy.' "

Chaney looked down at Tony's sweet face, and he returned the favor, with his cute, head-cocked-to-one-side look. A wave of guilt washed over her. *Poor dog!* "I didn't realize," she murmured.

Devin playfully touched Tony's pink nose, and Tony licked his hand. "What happened last night just isn't this breed's M.O.," he assured her. "Labs tend not to destroy and chew wantonly, because they're retrievers. You saw that last night. Their job is to retrieve game in their mouths and bring it back without damaging it."

"Okay," she said. "So, he's not supposed to do what he's doing. But he's still doing it. What happens if he doesn't stop?"

"I e-mailed you the articles we talked about last night," he said. "They have some recommendations, some things you could try. I'd say just watch it. If the destruction continues, then we might want to discuss using medication to control the behavior."

She laughed incredulously. "What, like doggie Prozac?"

He laughed, too. "Yes, there's been some use of Prozac with dogs, but we're jumping the gun here. I don't like using medication for behavior modification unless it's absolutely necessary. Let's just wait and see for now. Okay?"

Chaney stared at him, amazed. So this was how this child could garner two thousand, four hundred Google hits. He knew what he was talking about. "Okay, I agree to wait and see for now," she said.

Devin peeled back the hairy flap of one of Tony's ears. "Just one quick thing before you go," he said. "See that?"

Chaney peered inside. All she could see was reddened flesh, leading down to a dark hole. She recoiled. "What's that about?"

"He's scratching," Devin said. "It could be nervous behavior, or just dirt. You're going to have to learn to clean his ears."

She looked on, compassion for Tony being replaced with scorn. "How am I supposed to do that?"

"I'll send you home with some ear cleaning solution," he said. "You wet a Q-Tip or a cotton ball with it, and then put it in his ear."

Chaney looked down at her attire. *Not in my good suit!* Devin shook his head teasingly, like she was hopeless. "I'll show you," he offered.

Chaney watched as Devin prepared six long, generic cotton swabs on the metal table, wet them with cleaning solution from a bottle with a pointed tip. "Now hold his ear," Devin instructed.

Chaney reluctantly obeyed, and Tony jumped. Devin came around and slipped the swab effortlessly into Tony's ear. "They tell us not to put Q-Tips in our ears; why is it okay for him?" Chaney asked.

Devin swirled the swab around in Tony's ear, and Tony moaned, his eyes rolling back in his head as he enjoyed his own little eargasm. "Because a dog's ear is shaped like an L," he said absentmindedly, deep into the task at hand. "There's no way this swab's gonna turn the corner and perforate his eardrum."

He pulled out the swab, and Chaney cringed at the chunks of brown ear wax on the once-white cottony tip. "Jeez!" she exclaimed.

Devin held out the remaining five swabs. "Your turn," he prompted.

Apprehensively, Chaney took the proffered swab between her thumb and forefinger. Awkward minutes later, Tony had the cleanest ears he'd probably ever had, and Chaney's good suit was covered in dog hair. Devin patted her on the shoulder. "You got skillz, cousin!" he laughed.

Chaney spotted a tiny run in her black pantyhose, starting at the calf of her right leg. Courtesy of Tony's long nails, no doubt. "Now who's got jokes?" she snapped.

Devin took her hand and helped her to her feet. "Oh, Chaney, you're gonna be all right," he assured her. "By the time your sister gets back, you'll have this down."

"Gee, something to look forward to."

Devin went around the metal table and reached into one of the drawers. He pulled out a lint roller and handed it to her. "Here," he said. "A must-have if you've got a pet."

Pleasantly surprised, Chaney took it, then looked up at him. *Smart and considerate.* "Thank you," she said.

"No problem," he returned, then all of a sudden, became the picture of professionalism again. "So, you'll leave Tony here with us. We're going to give him the first shot for the heartworm, and then watch him for any reactions. After work, you can come and pick him up. We're here until seven. If it's all good, we'll do it again tomorrow."

Oh, joy! She held up a hand. "Just not the ear cleaning," she mock-pleaded. "I can't take any more of that."

Devin laughed. "Have a good day, Chaney. We'll see you back here at seven."

Chaney nodded. She stared at him, marveling at how wise and calm he was at his age. Twentysomething boys: Who knew? Chaney doubted she was ever as self-possessed as he was. "Seven," she repeated.

She patted Tony's head as a good-bye and headed out the exam-room door. Halfway toward the clearly marked exit, she turned to see him staring after her, with Tony on the leash doing the same.

Devin crushed up his sandwich wrapped in the Red Hot and Blue barbeque bag and tossed it into the trash. He was about to grab the keys to reopen the office for the post-lunch shift when Didier entered. "Devin, we need to talk," he announced.

He looked so serious. Reflexively, Devin sought to lighten the mood. "You wanna break up?" he teased.

In response, Didier tossed a vertically folded copy of a newspaper onto Devin's desk, knocking over his ceramic replica of Harry, the Washington husky. "What's this?" he asked, more of himself than of Didier.

"The *Alexandria Gazette*," Didier answered. "Look at the article at the top of the page."

Devin did as he was told. He read the headline out loud. " 'Potomac Yards Pet-Thenon Opening Set for June.' "

"You know who they are, don't you?"

"Of course I know who they are," Devin said absentmindedly as he scanned the staff reporter's story and photos for facts and clues. "That chain of pet stores out of Oregon. With that tacky building façade that looks like the Parthenon."

"That shopping center, Potomac Yards, is less than ten miles away from here," Didier stated. "These chains have a history of coming into neighborhoods and stealing away business."

Devin handed Didier back his paper. "I'm not going to sweat this right now, Didier," he said. "There are enough sick animals in the D.C. area for the work to go around. Plus the procedures we do are more specialized than your average practice."

Didier didn't seem convinced. "I think we should review the business plan and see what changes we need to make," he declared.

Devin was seeing a whole other side to Didier. When he'd met with Bill and Devin to explore the prospect of buying into the practice, Didier, though unintelligible at some points in the negotiation, was aloof, the picture of Gallic cool, as if a partnership would've been nice, but he could take Devin and Bill or leave them. But Didier was older and had more experience. That counted for something. "I can't even begin to tell you how much I value your opinion, Didier," Devin said. "And I agree; we should take a look at the business plan. But it's Friday. I also have an FHO in about a half-hour, and, with checking in on my cousin's dog, I'm backed up. So it won't be today."

That seemed to satisfy Didier . . . if only for the moment. "Okay. You do your femoral head osteotomy. But early next week, we handle this. Okay?"

Devin righted the husky on his desk. "Okay," he promised.

Didier walked out, his coat flapping on the breeze he made. Devin held his head in his hands. *Neurotic, French-Canadian partners. Fraidy-cat, pet-sitting fake-cousins. Matchmaking boys. Nit-picking fathers. Ex-girlfriends making dumb choices.* Devin felt his pulse crash through his head like a tidal wave, destroying all rational thought in its wake. He needed some kind of release.

Then he remembered. The phone number. *Zoe.* He looked down at his Ironman watch. He had about twenty minutes in which to knock this out. He took out his cell phone, searched for the number, then looked down at the ten digits on the green screen. *Should I?* What was she going to want from him? What did he want from her? Was it still in him to hit it and split it? Would he get attached and end up getting played?

Fuck it. He pressed the TALK button, and heard the digital tones sound as he put the phone to his ear. She answered after only two rings. "Hello?"

She sounded like a kid, with that high-pitched voice that younger women of all colors seemed to have. And Devin, for the life of him, couldn't even remember if she was black or white. *Play it cool . . .* "Hi, is this Zoe?" he asked.

"Yes," she said, sounding tentative, like, *who are you and what do you want?*

"My friend Andre gave me your number," he said, to answer her unasked questions. "You met him when we were at the Rhodeside last week."

She laughed seductively, and in his state, it felt to his ears like silk being shimmied over his skin. "I remember you," she said. "Tiger Woods."

He laughed. *God bless Tiger.* "Actually, my name's Devin," he said.

"So, what's up, Devin?" she asked.

He hated the hoops you had to jump through to secure a woman. Just once, he wished he had his dad's charm. Women came to KL, not the other way around. "I wanted to call, introduce myself, see what's up with you."

"It's all good. I'm headed to class."

"Andre mentioned you went to Georgetown."

She giggled. "What else did Andre say?"

"That's it. I figured I could get to know you better myself."

"So, what did you have in mind?"

This was easier than he'd thought it'd be. She seemed available, as available as he was horny. *What do I have in mind?* "What are you doing tomorrow?" he asked. "I thought I could take you to dinner."

Immediately, he kicked himself. How he could have forgotten advice from his boys, his brothers, from Rob Reiner in *Sleepless in Seattle:* drinks first, then, if everything goes smoothly, progress to dinner.

"Dinner sounds great, but unfortunately, I've got plans for tomorrow," she announced.

"Would another day be better?" he asked.

"Let me see," she said; then there was dead air for a second.

Just as he was planning another cold shower, Zoe came back on the line. "How's Wednesday?" she suggested. "You know . . . Hump Day?"

All rightee then! His brows flew up in his utter astonishment. He cleared his throat. "Wednesday's good for me, too," he announced. "Seven o'clock?"

"Seven's good," she said in agreement. "I'm on campus. At Copley Hall. They give you tons of shit letting guests up, so I'll wait for you downstairs. What kind of car do you drive?"

"Look for a black Lincoln Navigator," he said.

She made a noise that sounded like the aural equivalent of curiosity and excitement. He suspected that his ride drove his stock up a notch. "Excellent, Devin," she decreed. "I have you down for Wednesday night at seven. I'm gonna save your number in my phone so I can call you . . . just in case I have to cancel."

From the tone of her voice, Devin realized he was being dismissed. "Well, Zoe," he said. "See you on Wednesday."

They hung up, and Devin looked down at the phone. *Mission accomplished.*

Fuming, Chaney stared out the picture window at the Pike. Maybe Nathalie was right. Could she actually make shea butter products, in her house, by herself, and not have to deal with idiots? In her mind, she relived that awful moment in which she wanted to leap across the conference table and strangle the life out of Callie Bruce.

An hour ago, Chaney was sitting behind her laptop in Autodidact's darkened conference room. This time, the clients were their guests at the Rockville office. Projected on the wall was Callie's attempt at a performance objective. "Students will be able to—abbreviated SWBAT— answer phone calls coming to the help desk," Callie read.

Doug sighed . . . a deep, frustrated sigh. "Looks fine to me, Chaney," he said. "I don't see the foundation for your objection."

Because you're not a fucking instructional designer . . . and neither is your wing person, by the way. Aloud, though, Chaney said, "An instructionally sound performance objective has three components: the behavior, the conditions under which the student will perform the behavior, and the degree to which you judge that performance as satisfactory. The objective we're deliberating over is only one-third effective."

"It was effective when I taught fifth grade," Callie declared.

"According to our learner analysis, the average Navy's customer-service desk worker hasn't been a fifth-grader for some time, Callie."

Lissa shot Chaney a look in the semidarkness, a look that said that maybe she should throttle back on the sarcasm. Chaney looked away. *I hate clients.*

"Maybe the objectives aren't clear because your task analysis in this draft design document is not well defined," Callie stated sulkily.

"I don't understand it either, Chaney," added Doug. "Frankly, I think it's a little convoluted."

Callie sat smirking, with the confidence of someone who'd turned popular opinion her way. Just when Chaney had thought all was lost, salvation came in the form of Randy. He'd been sitting quietly, absorbing the group dynamic, and, Chaney saw more than once, checking her out. She tried to focus on the two vipers at her table, but even in a heightened defensive state, she sure could appreciate how handsome he looked, with the sleeves of his white shirt rolled up to reveal strong forearms. "I don't think it's convoluted at all," he announced.

Callie began her equine-sounding laugh, in the face of Randy's objection. "I disagree, Randy, but of course, I could be persuaded with some evidence to the contrary."

Randy rose to his full, impressive height. "Okay, Callie," he said. "We can flow the whole customer service process. Chaney, you have Visio on your laptop?"

Chaney smiled. She wasn't big on men coming to her rescue, but just this once, she was willing to make an exception. In response to his question, Chaney accessed the software on her laptop. In an instant, a blank grid, with a vast array of flow-charting boxes, projected onto the silver screen in the conference room. Randy grabbed a marker and moved effortlessly over to the easel, equipped with newsprint, in the far corner of the room. "Ready?" he asked Chaney.

Was that a loaded question? Was she indeed ready to handle him? "Ready," she said, nodding.

Chaney watched the cars zip along the Pike . . . watching them stop at the light . . . watching the light turn green . . . watching them pick up speed . . . driving toward and away from her. With every second she watched, she felt her nerves become less raw, less frazzled. *I want to run away, too.*

There was a knock at her door, and Chaney turned away from her automotive therapy to see Randy at the door. "Hey," he said simply, slipping into his trench coat.

The smile that appeared when she saw him morphed into a wide grin. "Hey," she returned.

"So, where can two coworkers go to get a drink in your 'hood?" he asked.

Chaney got her purse from her secret desk drawer. "I know just the place," she laughed.

A short walk later, they were seated at the bar in the Ruby Tuesday's in Federal Plaza. The crowd was as thin as a supermodel, and they were enjoying that pleasant lull between lunch and dinner, when you could actually hear the conversation of your companion, actually listen to the sports on one of the four TVs surrounding the bar.

Chaney was getting a subtle, warm buzz from her merlot. She stared at him as he watched the March Madness coverage on ESPN above their heads. She watched him intently as he smiled, like he liked the results he'd heard, as he sipped liberally from his glass of beer. He wasn't cute, by any means. "Cousin" Devin was cute as a button and happy like he was *tabula rasa*. No, this Randy Tyree was attractive in the way he carried himself, like experience made him exude an aura of powerful confidence, which she gravitated toward despite the calcified notions about men she willingly harbored, despite No plants, no pets, no men.

The body, though . . . damn, that was just right. He was tall; there'd be no setting her drink on this brothah's head. And his lean strength was made even more evident in his choice and cut of suits. He looked like a b'ball coach on the sidelines, instead of an ex-Navy lieutenant. She could imagine him, though, in those crisp dress whites that made Debra Winger lose her mind in *An Officer and a Gentleman,* the same dress whites that made women all over D.C. slip off their chairs when a naval officer entered a room.

He shifted his gaze from the TV to her suddenly. She felt her stomach tighten. He pointed up to the TV. "Sorry," he said. "Reliving my glory days."

"You played ball?" Like she had to ask.

He nodded. "Temple. Class of '78."

That put "Cousin" Devin's age deficit further in perspective. When Devin was four, Randy Tyree was walking down the aisle to "Pomp and Circumstance." She tried to lighten the mood a little. "You folks from Philly," she commented. "Only you guys could pronounce S-C-H-U-Y-L-K-I-L-L like 'Skoo-kull.' "

Chuckling, Randy turned on his stool to face her head-on. "So, who is Chaney Braxton, this phenomenal woman from Brooklyn, New York?" he asked.

Deflect, deflect. "What've you heard?"

"I heard the sistah got a Ph.D. from Syracuse. Great school, horrible b'ball team."

She held up a hand directly in his face. "Talk to the hand, bruh! NCAA Final, 1996. We only lost, 'cause Kentucky got lucky."

He sucked his teeth in mock disdain. "Whatever. Obviously, I didn't hear she's got insane school spirit."

"Hey, I paid enough for the damned degree. I should big up the school!"

He laughed, letting the conversational lull punctuate the moment. Then he looked at her over the rim of his glass. "Married?"

She looked at him over the rim of her glass. Maybe Shane being hetero-flexible was meant to lead her right there. In that moment. On that stool. "No. You?"

He grimaced. "Divorced. Kids?"

"No. You?"

A smile of unvarnished pride replaced the grimace. "Yup. Two teenagers. A boy and a girl. My ex-wife and I share custody."

Randy drained his glass, then signaled the bartender for another. "You?" he asked.

She covered her glass with her hand. "I'm good."

The bartender popped open a bottle of Heineken, gave Randy a fresh chilled glass, then blended back into the mirrored wall of booze, ice, and soda fountains. "How long were you married?" Chaney asked.

"Ten years," he announced. "Until she got accepted to law school at Georgetown. That's how we ended up down here, from Philly. She stayed in the Navy. I retired from active duty. And our marriage exploded in our faces."

She saw pain in his eyes, and she wanted so badly to make it stop. *What's up with you and these wounded brothahs?* Instead, though, she managed a safe, "That's unfortunate."

Much to her surprise, he smiled brilliantly. "I have my children," he said. "They gave my life meaning, no matter what happened with their mother. Wanna see pictures?"

So, the flirtatious mood had evolved into the Family Hour. "Sure," she said.

Randy took out his wallet and pulled a 3x5 photo from the billfold. Chaney stared at Randy, in between two tall, rather attractive children, who had creamy brown skin and spirally curly hair. Obviously biracial. Her guard rose up some, the classic involuntary reaction every sistah experienced in the face of a brothah-white girl coupling. She wanted to ask, *Help me out here; just what is the lure of white pussy?* Especially to this guy who was so obviously black. But she let it slide. "They're adorable."

"R.J. and Taina," he announced. "They're my heart."

Chaney took a fistful of the Goldfish in the dish before them. "I'm sure you're a great father," she offered.

He shrugged. "You do your best, you know?" he said. "I wish they didn't have to come from a broken home. My parents are still married. I couldn't imagine what it'd be like to have to spend one weekend here, one weekend there."

She gave his forearm a tender squeeze, and felt muscles bounce back against her fingertips. "Hey, I went to school with kids whose parents stayed together for the sake of the children," she declared. "They're just as jacked up as the kids who came from the so-called broken home. Shoot, Eric Harris and Dylan Klebold came from so-called nuclear families. Look where they ended up . . . in the Trench Coat Mafia."

Randy set his elbow on the bar, set his chin in his palm, and stared at her. His smile was one of appreciation . . . admiration. "Yeah," he said in quiet agreement. "But I'm surprised you don't have kids."

Chaney chewed her Goldfish. "I taught fifth grade for three years.

That cured me of any desire to procreate. Plus, my patience is already being tried by my sister's dog. I'm babysitting him while she . . ."

Oh shit! Tony! She looked down at her watch . . . almost 5:30. Devin said they'd be there until 7:00. She pitched up, draining her wineglass. "I gotta go!" she cried.

He got up, too. "Go where?!"

It was going to take her at least an hour and a half to get the train, pick up her car, then drive to fetch Tony. She reached into her purse and began throwing bills onto the surface of the bar. "I'll explain later," she said breathlessly. Right now, if I don't get to Twinbrook metro, my dog will have to spend the night in jail."

He looked puzzled. "Huh?"

She slinked into her coat. "I promise, I'll explain tomorrow."

With that, she headed out the double glass doors and into the beginnings of dusk.

Chaney got the hint that she was ridiculously late when she saw Maria standing patiently on the sidewalk outside the veterinary hospital. Tony, surprisingly well-behaved, sat on his haunches, his leash connected like an umbilical cord to Maria's hand. He shot up on all fours when he saw her get out of the Altima. "Wuh! Wuh! Wuh!" he barked, doing his little dance of joy.

Chaney marveled at that. *What the hell is this?* "I'm sorry I'm late," she said to Maria.

Chaney guessed Maria didn't have an angry bone in her body. "It's perfectly all right," she assured Chaney. "Some of our pet parents get tied up at work. Totally unavoidable."

Chaney didn't have the heart to tell her that the only thing she had been caught up in was some naughty, alcohol-fueled flirting with a fine coworker. Guiltily, she relieved Maria of the leash and looked down at Tony. *Cock blocker!* "Hey, boy," she laughed, nonetheless.

Tony leaned heavily against her as she stroked his coat. "Wuh!"

The glass double doors opened, and Devin appeared. He, too, looked like he was happy from head to toe to see her. He flashed her a broad, sweet smile. "You're here," he said.

This was the Devin she'd seen last night, not the ultraprofessional doctor from this morning. She preferred this model. "Yes," she said. "Finally."

Tony transferred his fickle affections from Chaney to Devin. He leaned against Devin's long legs, and Devin reached down to stroke his head. "You did good today, didn't you, boy?" Devin asked, and Tony looked up into Devin's face like he could understand him.

"While you two males bond," Maria laughed, "I'm gonna go. My man needs his dinner."

Chaney couldn't picture Maria as the little woman, slaving over a hot stove. She kept that to herself as she and Devin watched Maria unlock the nearby black Honda CR-V, get in, and head toward Wilson Boulevard.

After she left, Devin scratched the blond furrow between Tony's perked-up ears. "Tony took the treatment very well," he announced. "He might be a bit quiet tonight and again tomorrow, but if he acts strangely in any way, I want you to call me here. I'm covering the office tonight. Okay?"

"I never owned a dog," she reminded him. "Everything he does is strange."

"If he whines, or vomits, or starts having seizures . . . like that," he clarified.

Chaney stored that away in her head. "Oh," she said. "Okay."

"Can you do me a favor?"

After all he'd done for her, she couldn't imagine refusing him anything. "Sure," she said. "What?"

He laughed sheepishly, his upturned almond eyes making him look like a two-legged Tony. "Can you make me some more of your hand cream?" he pleaded. "Maria and Didier have been using mine all up."

Chaney laughed. *Was that all?* "I'll make you a basket," she promised. "On the house. I imagine by the time Tony goes home, our favor bank will be empty."

"Don't be silly, cousin," he said. "Whatever you need, you know . . ."

"I know."

What's going on here? Was "Cousin" Devin also mounting an assault on No plants, no pets, no men, too? She pointed at her car. "Well, I'd better . . ."

"Yeah," he said, then suddenly exclaimed, "Wait!"

More than mildly surprised, Chaney's eyes followed his hands down to the right pocket and watched as he took out a CD in a clear jewel case. "What's that?" she asked.

He handed it to her. She looked down at the writing on the gray face of the CD. " 'What You Won't Do for Love,' " she read.

He looked pleased with himself, and happy, too, that he could do her a favor. "I burned you a copy of the single," he said.

She looked down at the CD again, then up at him. "Thanks, Devin," she said, genuinely touched.

He dismissively waved a hand. "It's no thing," he declared. "Didn't want you to go without your old school jam." He then pointed over his broad shoulder. "Well, I gotta go."

She stared him up and down. So, men had the power to surprise her, after all. "See you tomorrow, then."

"Tomorrow," he said, then in five long strides, he was gone inside.

Four

Macca stared down at the chart in her hands. "You gained weight, Chaney," she observed.

Chaney tried in vain to wrap the paper gown around her bare midsection, then glared at Macca from a supine position. "Gee, what gave it away?"

Macca just laughed. She patted Chaney's right knee. "You can get up now," she said.

Chaney huffed and puffed as she tried to dislodge her stockinged feet from the stirrups. After what seemed like a lifetime, she was successful. She sat bare-assed on the white paper that covered the leather examination table. And tried again to smooth the paper gown into her lap. "Chaney, I've been your doctor for over a year now, and I still find it hysterical that you insist on keeping your socks on," Macca said, shaking her head. "What's that about?"

"Because in the most invasive moment of my life, I would like to at least keep my dignity."

Oh, Macca silently mouthed, noted something in the chart in her hands. Chaney wondered if she wrote, *Keeps socks on during examination.*

"Well, Chaney," Macca began, "structurally, everything seems normal . . ."

"So, it's normal to bleed for ten days?" Chaney snapped. "That's twice as long as my periods used to be. And they never used to be this clotted. My periods are practically solid."

Chaney knew she could only get away with being such a problem child because she and Heather McDaniel grew up together in Brooklyn, both daughters of West Indian immigrants.

"If you'd let me finish," Macca said pointedly, "I was going to say that, when I palpated your belly, though, I thought I felt a fourth mass. I'm speculating it's another fibroid. Of course, I'd like to schedule another sonogram to confirm that."

Chaney tugged at the robe again for coverage. "Just great," she mumbled. "Those are such fun . . . the full bladder about to explode, the ice cold gel on my stomach, the big stick up my vagina. I can't wait."

Macca flipped through the pages in the chart. "Yes, the one you had last year spotted three," she said, her eyes scanning the ultrasound photos and the corresponding report. "All on pedicles outside of the uterine wall. The largest of the three was four-by-three by two-point-seven centimeters."

At the thought of things growing unchecked inside her, Chaney felt her skin produce a fine film of goose bumps. "Can I have them removed now?"

Macca sat in front of her on a small, rolling stool and scratched her head. "The thing with fibroids, Chaney, is that more often than not, they tend to recur after surgery. And it doesn't make sense having the surgery if you don't plan to get pregnant in the immediate future. You plan on having kids any time soon?"

Chaney sighed. "I don't know. I mean, when I was with Shane, I thought about it. After him, though, any sex I had was insanely protected. The past year and a half has been ridiculously slow."

"What, lack of desire?"

Chaney laughed, woefully shaking her head. Lack of desire for sex was truly a concept only a married person like Macca could grasp. Until fairly recently, Chaney was close to shorting out the motor in her blue Rabbit sex toy. "Lack of opportunity," she stated.

Macca looked down at the chart again. "How old are you now, Chaney?" she asked absentmindedly while scanning her papers.

First "Cousin" Devin, now her? "Thirty-six," Chaney said.

Macca, shaking her head, sucked air into her chest through pursed lips. "Hmmm . . ." she said, intensely perusing the chart.

Chaney's eyes widened. She clutched the inadequate robe close to her chest. "What's . . ." she mimicked the pursed-lip-air-sucking sound " . . . 'Hmmm . . . '? What does that mean?"

"You're in a good spot now at your age," Macca said. "But after forty, the chances of getting spontaneously pregnant drop precipitously, Chaney. The older you get, the worse it gets."

Spontaneously pregnant. Chaney laughed bitterly. "Is that, like, spontaneous combustion?"

"No, that's like everything we were fighting against in our twenties with the pill and condoms," Macca said. "Isn't it ironic?"

It was like Macca was in her kitchen last week. "I was just saying the same thing to Nathalie," Chaney said.

Macca nodded. "She's a prime example. She's, what, thirty-nine? And look at how much trouble she's having getting pregnant."

Chaney threw up her hands. "Well, I'm not seeing anyone right about now. I don't even know if I want kids, Heather. What do you suggest I do?"

"Have you ever thought of freezing your eggs?"

Chaney looked her up and down; Macca was dead serious. "You're kidding, right?" Chaney asked in disbelief.

"You'd be surprised at how many sistahs are doing it," Macca said. "Sistahs delay having children for their career; this is D.C., for crying out loud. They want to have children, but don't want to use old eggs to do it. Those cryogenic places are popping up all over the place."

"Like Walt Disney," Chaney remarked.

"Like Walt Disney," Macca repeated, nodding. "Only they don't freeze a head. They preserve your eggs in a tank of liquid nitrogen until you've decided whether or not you want to be a mother. But I have to tell you. A thirty-six-year-old egg is certainly more viable than a forty-year-old one. Something to think about, Chaney."

With her sitting there, bare-assed in a paper gown, it suddenly hit Chaney. *This is what the biological clock looks like.* "I'm running out of time," she murmured. "This is so depressing."

Macca got up off the stool and went over to the sink in the counter. She washed and dried her hands, then balled up the paper towel and dropped in into a hole in the counter. She then turned back to Chaney, concern etched on her face. "How are you doing really, Chaney?" she asked. "I hardly see you anymore, and when I do, you're certainly not the easygoing sistah that I remember from home."

She wondered if that was really true. "I was never all that easy-going."

"Yeah, yeah, you were a tight-ass and obsessed with getting things done; you're from New York. That's a given. But you were fun!" Macca laughed. "Nowadays, you're on edge. You're irritable. I'm sorry, my sistah, but one could actually think of dropping the B bomb when it comes to you."

Chaney gasped. "You're saying I'm a bitch?!"

Macca held up a hand. "All right, all right, slow your roll, Chaney. I'm just concerned that your recent behavior may be a symptom of something more serious. Talk to me."

The room sounded so quiet all of a sudden. The silence, though, facilitated Chaney's introspection. She thought of the minutes of staring at the traffic on Rockville Pike . . . minutes that sometimes turned into hours. She thought of her anger at Callie and her nit-picking. She wondered whether the sudden weight gain was due to ordering out massive portions of fatty foods—the sport of Autodidact Champions—or whether she was actually overeating as a comfort mechanism. And then she thought about all the trouble with Tony . . . *Is there something really wrong with me?*

Finally, she faced Macca's curious expression. "I have had a lot going on lately," she confessed. "What with the business and my idiot clients. And now I'm watching Daisy's dog for her while she's following her boyfriend on tour."

Macca rolled her eyes. "Girl, when are you going to stop letting Daisy sucker you into these things?"

"What things?" Chaney asked—unconvincingly, as it turned out.

" 'What things?' " Macca echoed. "Didn't she get you to 'watch' her piano while you were in Syracuse, and you had to end up transporting it home to Brooklyn . . . at great personal expense, I might add. And didn't she come to your graduation in Syracuse with a one-way ticket, and you had to lend her money to get home? And now you're watching her dog?"

From Macca's mouth, she did sound like a sucker. Chaney held up a hand. "Okay, okay," she conceded, her mind flashing on her parents in their watery grave. "Daisy's got issues. But she's my sister. She, Anna Lisa, and D are practically all the family I have."

"Duly noted. But that doesn't mean you have to be her doormat."

Chaney sighed. "Yes, Macca—sometimes, I can't concentrate. Sometimes, I overeat. Sometimes, I feel so overwhelmed that I can scream. All of the time, I'm worn out and dog-tired, which is probably why I drink too much coffee. I have a lot on my plate. But don't all black women? Isn't this just that 'harried woman's syndrome' I've been hearing about?"

Macca stared at Chaney, her gaze unwavering. "Have you ever thought that you might be depressed, Chaney?" she asked.

Chaney stared back, stunned. Then she followed her first impulse: denial. She sucked her teeth. "I'm not depressed, Macca. You know your Jamaican mummy would say that's for those delicate little white girls who can't handle pressure, and I would agree."

"Ever since I've known you, Chaney, you've been grace under pressure. You thrive on it. But everything you just said to me makes me think you may be clinically depressed," Macca declared. "Lack of concentration. Change in eating habits. Chronic fatigue. Those symptoms sound like they could be right out of the DSM-IV." She saw the puzzled look on Chaney's face. "The fourth edition of the *Diagnostic and Statistical Manual of Mental Disorders,*" Macca explained. "It provides criteria and guidelines for diagnosing the most common mental disorders."

"Oh," Chaney commented. "It makes me feel so much better that you think I'm psycho, Heather."

"And," Macca pointedly continued, as if she hadn't even spoken, "it's not just white folks who get depressed. If more sistahs and brothahs, given all the mess we have to go through in this life, were open to accepting this diagnosis instead of thinking that we can just 'walk it off,' or 'seek Jesus,' then we'd have less misery in our community."

For a second, Chaney actually entertained the thought that something might be wrong with her. She sure didn't feel like herself. But something inside her resisted the possibility that Macca could be right. "I'm just tired," she sighed.

"Okay," Macca said. "Maybe you're right. You're just tired. I'm going to give you a referral for this psychiatrist. I did my residency with his son at Hopkins. He's Sean Tolochko. As luck would have it, his office is practically right up the street from you on Huntington Avenue in Alexandria. You know psychiatrists are also MDs. If you're just tired, he can prescribe you some heavy-duty iron pills. But if you're really depressed, he could diagnose that, too."

Resist, resist. "Oh, come on, Macca. You know if you're a hammer, every problem is a nail! He's a shrink; of course he's going to see mental illness."

Macca shook her head. "Not necessarily. Just go, Chaney. You won't know if you don't go. You know I'd never steer you wrong, right?"

From Brooklyn days on Flatbush Avenue and Maple Street, Macca had always been a straight shooter. There was no reason to think she'd change now. Chaney felt her resolve steadily weakening as she sat there, emotionally vulnerable and physically half-naked. She tucked what was left of that useless paper strip around her. "Okay," she finally sighed. "Okay. I'll go, but I know it's going to be nothing."

Macca smiled triumphantly. "I'll write you a referral."

Devin pulled up in front of the majestic spires of Copley Hall on the Georgetown University campus. He did a mental check of all the date systems. First of all, he was dressed to impress in his thick black turtleneck, khaki cargo pants, Tims, and a leather jacket, with just the right amount of Dolce and Gabbana scenting his skin. The fragrance mixed in nicely with "Cousin" Chaney's spicy sandalwood body cream. He had both plastic and the right amount of cash in his wallet, tucked safely away in his back pocket. In that wallet, too, he had a strip of Durex condoms. Just in case. On the sound system, Aaliyah's "We Need a Resolution" was bumping. He suspected that it said about him that he was into good music and was also sensitive; Aaliyah's tragic death almost seven months ago was still on everyone's minds. *We're good to go.*

Then he saw a girl huddling under an overhead light in the cool night. She was petite, with bangs across her forehead and long hair spilling down the back of a black coat. Some Asian girls he knew wore the same 'do. She wore black jeans and black boots with high heels. From the distance between Copley Hall and his vantage point in the Navigator, she looked attractive enough. *Is that her?*

Devin turned Aaliyah down, then rolled down the automatic passenger-side window. "Zoe?" he asked.

In the overhead light, she turned his way and smiled in recognition. Then she came closer to the car, and the fantasy was over. He could see weave tracks in the crown of her head, that all that hair on her head was probably manmade. And her eyes were too green to be anything but contact lenses. "Devin?" she asked.

For a second, he wondered if he should hit the gas. He wished he'd pressed Andre for more details. Then he thought, *Am I that shallow? Maybe we can have interesting conversation.* "Yup," he finally said.

Her full red mouth slowly spread into a smile. She was rocking the Blowjob Red lipstick, too, like "Cousin" Chaney the other night. He wondered if the color would live up to its hype.

She eagerly hopped up into the passenger seat and shut the door with a loud thud. Devin stared at her. *Easy on my doors!*

She extended her left hand, and he caught a glimpse of her acrylic nails that matched the lipstick. "Nice to finally meet you, Devin," she said, lowering her head to give him a coquettish, fake-green stare.

What about this babe is real? Aloud, though, he said, taking her hand, "Same here."

She fondled his hand for a second before releasing it, trailing those nails along the black-hand side. "So, what do you have planned for tonight?"

"Dinner. At Ruth's Chris. You been there before?"

The green eyes were like emerald fire. "On Connecticut?" she gasped, unable to contain herself. "Not on *my* work-study salary."

Despite the initial first impression, Devin admitted to himself that he was getting a charge out of impressing her. He laughed. "Let's go, then."

Devin drove confidently through the streets of Georgetown, navigating the busy Wednesday night streets on D.C.'s semi-logical grid. Over Aaliyah's sweet voice, they made small talk. He got her last name—it was *Blocker*—figuring it was only right that he should know a little more about someone he was entertaining putting his dick in. She was from Atlanta and had no plans to go back. "That flag is a big downer, *Showty*," she said, her comfort level with him allowing something of an accent to peek through her practiced speech, in the way she called him *Shorty*. She was studying law at Georgetown. He grimaced when she told him that. *Can't escape.*

Every disclosure he made to her seemed to make those fake green eyes practically luminescent, from the fact that he was a vet (a doctor!), to the fact that he lived in Georgetown (assumed wealth!). When he mentioned that one of his brothers—Eric Rhym—went to Georgetown Law, she nearly lost her mind. " 'Big Tort' is your brother?" she laughed.

Confusion set in. "Pardon?"

"We study your brother's exploits in class. He's Mr. Civil Action. They call him 'Big Torturer.' 'Big Tort,' for short. A tort is like a civil suit."

He knew that. KL made sure that Devin knew practically everything about the law without having set foot in a law school. But Eric? His tight-ass brother. Called "Big Tort," a play on the name of "Big Pun," a rapper who he'd probably never even heard of. *Who would've thought?*

The expression on her face was one of awe as the valet took the car, as they were whisked right past the waiting line of poor souls who hadn't thought to make a reservation, into one of the intimate, secluded corners of the restaurant. When she took off her coat to reveal a black sweater midriff that showed off a flat brown stomach with a pierced innie navel, as well as her apple bottom, it was Devin's turn to stand at attention . . . almost literally. At least the body appeared to be the very real thing. She looked down at him and smiled, satisfied that he'd seen the goodies and that she'd made her point. He looked away, forcing himself to think about sports, spreading a crisp white linen napkin across his lap . . . just in case.

When the black-suited waiter came over and made the requisite fuss, she ate it up. He did the usual hello-would-you-like-to-see-our-menus, then looked over at Zoe. "And what would the lady like to drink?"

"Apple martini," she announced. Devin had heard somewhere that that had surpassed Cosmopolitans as the drink-*du-minuit* for twenty-something ladies.

Not missing a beat, the waiter said, "And may I see the lady's ID, please?"

Devin watched as she begrudgingly produced her Georgia license, and the waiter decreed that she was of legal drinking age. Obviously, she was embarrassed at being carded, and Devin was equally embarrassed that for a second, his date may have been thought of as jailbait. The happy feelings in his boxer briefs caused by her dramatic unveiling disappeared just then.

Throughout dinner, it seemed that all the conversation from the car had suddenly taken a vacation. He tried to draw her out by having her talk more about herself, but she just wouldn't bite. Then he was forced to become that asshole that Marlene and Renee told him women hated . . . the one who talked about himself constantly on dates. But she just focused on her steak smothered in butter and onions, and the potatoes au gratin, and the broccoli with cheese, and the New York cheesecake with strawberries. He wondered how she kept that delicious body . . . the one genuine article about her, it seemed. He stared at her quizzically. "You okay?" he asked.

She nodded, polishing off her third apple martini. "Uh-huh," she said. "Why?"

So much for the sparkling conversation. "Nothing," he lied, then signaled the waiter for the check.

In the valet line for the car, Devin glanced over at her. Her eyes were glazing, like she was working on a nice buzz from the drinks. She stared out at the traffic on Connecticut, her hands shoved deep inside the pockets of her coat. Belatedly, he realized that it was rather cold for mid-March. The cold wind played against them, making their eyes water. Tentatively, protectively, he slipped an arm around her slight shoulders and rubbed his hand down the length of her arm. She looked at him, and she looked irritated, like he was taking all kinds of liberties in touching her. Despite the fact that she'd flashed him what she was working with less than two hours ago.

He took his arm away, mentally weighing the evidence . . . the near bankroll-busting dinner, the lack of chemistry between them, the quasi-golddigger persona dress-up in acrylic, fake contacts, and man-made hair, and the fact that she didn't want him touching her, so she probably wasn't going to want to be with him. It was official: the date was a bust. Back to the monastic lifestyle that Andre ridiculed him about.

Mercifully, the valet brought the car around, and they got in. He belted himself in, and she did the same. He ejected the CD and was pressing the dials in search of ESPN radio when she touched his hand, right there on the console. He stopped what he was doing and looked up at her. *Okay, I'm confused.*

The seductress was back. "I want to see where you live," she announced.

He glanced at the clock on the console. The numbers that were about as green as her eyes glowed out ten o'clock. "Really?" he asked, surprised.

"Uh-huh," she said. "Really."

Don't overthink this, Devin. He pushed the CD back into the player, and Aaliyah began singing "More Than a Woman."

She sat on her side, facing him, all throughout the drive back to

Georgetown. Devin glanced over at her every once in a while and smiled. Her eyes never wavered, and it was evident to him what she had in mind. And who was he to question her motives? He just knew that he was working on more wood than he'd ever had in his life, resting against the cotton of his confining shorts, and he could've cared less about yielding to pedestrians in the crosswalk, or about D.C.'s restrictive traffic laws. His objective was his town house; with everything else, he was channelling his inner Ludacris, screaming at bitches to get out the way.

He damned near collapsed with relief as he drove into the garage, pressed the button on his visor, and allowed the mechanical door to close. They entered the house through the garage door, and Zoe looked around at the vast expanse of room, dimly lit by strategically placed lamps and the light over the stove in the kitchen. "This is it," Devin announced.

She unbuttoned her coat, and he came up behind her just in time to slip it off her shoulders. That sweater gave him a quick glimpse of the small of her back . . . and her T-bar, where her thong rested comfortably. He got harder still.

"Want something to drink?" he called to her from the foyer as he hung up both their coats in the closet.

"A beer, if you got it!" she called back.

He appeared as she was looking at his DVD collection on the console that held the plasma-screen TV. "You're not big on furniture, are you?" she asked.

Devin shrugged. "I haven't decided what look I'm going for yet," he said. "Single-guy bare will have to be it for now."

She headed toward the kitchen, and he followed, his eyes glued to that round ass. It was literally a chore to force himself to be witty, to not jump her right there on the hard wood floor. He reached into the fridge, got two Heinekens that were left over from boys' night in, and popped the tops. "Martini chaser," he said as he handed her hers.

She took a sip, her red mouth lingering on the top of the bottle. He found himself envying the bottle. "Thanks."

"What's that saying, though? Is it liquor, beer, in the clear; or beer and liquor, never sicker?" he asked. "I can't remember."

She laughed. "How about gimme a beer, 'cause I don't care?"

He laughed, too. So, this was the uninhibited Zoe, certainly not the one on the sidewalk who looked at him like he was a leper. "Whatever works for you, baby," he said.

She moved toward him, and air stood still in his throat. Then he realized that this babe-in-the-woods—barely twenty-one, according to her ID—was trying to work him. *Time to flip the script.*

He took her hand, lacing his fingers within hers, and pulled her close, pressed every inch of himself against her. This close, though, the eyes seemed more fake, as did the hair. He closed his eyes and molded her against him. He ran his fingers across the small of her back, letting them rest against the satiny softness of that T-bar. He slipped those same hands under the back of her sweater, relishing the feel of her skin against his. He'd practiced this move many times . . . reach up to the small of the back, unclasp the bra. The metal hooks gave way, and against his chest, he could feel her breasts spring free.

She tiptoed and turned her face up toward him. He opened his eyes, focused on that delicious red mouth. He kissed her softly at first. He opened his mouth wider, teased her tongue with his, tasted the soft wetness of her. She moaned breathlessly, as did he, like they were singing the same lyrics to the same song. The kiss deepened, and he felt like he was going to lose it. He pulled away, still clasping onto her hand. They stared into each other's eyes, breathing heavily in and out, like they'd been running the same naughty race. "What kind of CDs you got?" she panted.

"The usual," he gasped.

"Play something for me," she said.

He looked down at the huge bulge in his pants. *Now?* But somewhere in his gauzy, feverish mind, logic struggled to be heard, told him that if this was what it took to get what he wanted, then play on.

Devin let her hand go, then moved from the kitchen over to the far wall, where he kept his state-of-the-art system and hundred of CDs. He looked at her as she stalked on over to him, wondering what music would get her out of those clothes. He put in all of the neo-soul that he could get his fidgety fingers on . . . Glenn Lewis, Craig David, Musiq Soulchild, the Roots . . . then hit Shuffle, then Play. As if prophetically, the smooth acoustic guitar of "Fill Me In" filled the room, then Craig David's voice slid into the moment like honey.

Just then, she was behind him, her hands working the top button of his pants. He looked down, watching as she worked the zipper. He gasped as his pants hit the floor. *Oh shit!*

Eagerly, he pulled his turtleneck over his head and tossed it away. He turned to face her, and to his extreme delight, she'd already opened her sweater, exposing small but perky breasts with little black dots as nipples. He reached out for them, and his large hands practically gobbled them up. She tossed her jeans and boots, standing before him in only her thong and trouser socks. "Oh, that is so hot!" he whispered.

She giggled, a little-girl giggle that was so dirty it gave him goose bumps. She kept giggling as she reached for the waistband of his boxer briefs. Those acrylic nails grazed the outside of his thighs as she pulled them down. There he was, exposed, vulnerable, itching for her. And what she did next shocked the hell out of him. Just as he thought that this would be the moment to grasp for the condoms, Zoe dropped to her knees and took him into her soft, wet mouth. *Blowjob Red for sure!*

He clasped his hands to his head, a moan from deep inside his chest resounding out, competing with Craig David. She sucked and released with just the right pressure . . . out and in . . . out and in . . . He locked his fingers into that tangle of fake hair. She ran her tongue along the head, and he screamed like a little girl. In and out . . . in and out . . . His knees went weak, his muscles tensed. He stood there with fistfuls of her hair, his grip tightening as the contracting waves rolled through his groin, and rolled, and rolled until he couldn't contain himself. "Shit!" he yelled.

His muscles contracted, and six months of abstinence bottled up inside him released. She pulled away just in time, just as his pelvis thrust wildly, and he came, hard and heavy. Thrusting . . . thrusting . . . thrusting until he was empty and shattered, his leg muscles all wobbly.

He looked down to find her looking up at him, her red lipstick smeared over her cheeks. "Thank you," he breathed.

Then he saw it . . . a long, stringy clump of white genetic material clinging to her bangs. His genetic material. *Oh, shit!*

She ran her nails up and down his thighs, making him tingle all over. "Good?" she whispered.

He took her hands and helped her up. "Phenomenal," he said, smiling. He pointed her in the direction of the half-bath next to the coat closet. "Go clean up. When you come back, I'll take care of you."

Obediently and mercifully oblivious to the wad of cum in her hair, she tiptoed away on those stockinged feet. He watched that ass and smiled. He shook his head. *Damn!*

Once she came back, they graduated to the vastness of the master bedroom. In the king-sized bed with the ultrafirm mattress, they repeatedly became a mass of tangled limbs and flesh, separated only by a thin sheath of rubber. Like a wild man, he pulled her up and wrapped her sinewy legs around his waist, invading her with just the right frequency and hardness until it was her turn to scream out in the darkness like a little girl. After the shortest refractory period in his entire sexual existence, he bent her over the stuffed chair in the bedroom, alternately clutching her ass and the back of the chair until he came again, holding her close, both of them slippery with the other's hot sweat.

Later, they lay in the bed together, staring at each other, deliciously exhausted. Then came the awkward part. That Clash song came immediately to mind: *Should she stay or should she go?* He searched his mind in vain for anything they had in common, except for the mutual, earth-shattering release they'd just experienced. Did he want a girlfriend? Was that what she wanted to be to him?

His eyelids were getting heavy. Whatever she wanted to do, she would have to decide right then, or nature was going to make the decision for them both. "Hey," he whispered. "Should I be taking you back to Copley?"

"Do you want to?" she asked.

Lobbing the ball effectively back in his court. *Damn!* He looked over her head at the digital alarm clock—the numbers glowed out 2:10 P.M. "I got an early day tomorrow," he said. "And you probably have classes, right?"

Please take the hint. She sighed. "I guess you're right. Don't wanna jeopardize my scholarship."

He suppressed a sigh of relief. "Let's get dressed," he suggested.

They retrieved their twisted and mussed clothes from the living room and dressed in silence, which was the rehearsal for the ride home. No Aaliyah this time, just subdued, romantic slow jams from WHUR's Quiet Storm. Devin focused all of his energies on staying awake and on the road . . . and also on how to execute the proper good-bye under these circumstances. He tried to remember what had worked for him in the past, but for the life of him, he couldn't recall any effective exit strategies. Then the tension and the nagging pain that had suddenly begun in his neck kept him awake.

Copley was still lit up like a Christmas tree at 2:30 in the morning when Devin pulled up in front of the dorm. "Here we are," he announced, then realized how stupid that must've sounded.

They turned to face each other. She looked like a used Kleenex, all her date façade worn off now. "I had a nice time," she said.

A wave of memories of all the things they'd done hours ago flooded through his mind. His smile was twisted. "Me, too," he said, which was true.

She turned up her mouth for a kiss. He looked down at her mouth. *Nope, had my dick there.* The forehead was the other alternative, but then he remembered that stream of cum that had hung there for a brief moment. So, he dropped a quick kiss on the only area that was safe: her cheek. She looked hurt, and immediately, he began to hate himself. "Can we do it again?" she asked.

He searched her face with his gaze. What was the answer to that question? What would be the best way to get out of this and not hurt her feelings? Then he asked himself the ultimate question, which was immediately followed by a flood of self-hatred: *What would Dad do . . . ?*

Chaney sat cross-legged in one of two brown paisley stuffed chairs in the office. She studied her surroundings: tons of books, diplomas, and certifications from Harvard, Yale, and Hopkins, a thick wooden desk, and another swivel chair in front of her. *No couch,* she observed.

The man Macca had spoken so highly of sat in front of her, looking quite like she imagined a psychiatrist would look like: white shirt, black tie, black pants, sensible lace-up shoes. Gray eyes under a shock of salt-and-pepper hair stared out at her. He tapped his notepad with a Montblanc pen. "So," Chaney said to break the ice, "Sean Tolochko. The Irish Russian. That's a unique combination."

"Got me beat up a lot growing up in Fells Point," he commented, then stopped tapping. "So, why are you here?" he asked.

Why am I here? She looked down at her watch. Nine o'clock on a Thursday morning. Wasn't like she didn't have somewhere else to be. Namely, working on her project, talking herself out of strangling Callie Bruce, and ogling Randy Tyree. "Heather McDaniel, the doctor who gave me the referral, seems to think I'm clinically depressed," she finally explained.

"And what do *you* think?" he asked.

"Obviously, I disagree," she declared.

"That brings us back to my first question: Why are you here?"

Chaney pointed a finger at him. "Oh, you're good," she laughed.

His face was expressionless, somehow telling Chaney that it was time to focus. "Well," she sighed, "I'll tell you what I told her. I have a lot to do, and I'm stressed out, and I guess my reaction to it is becoming counterproductive."

"How is it becoming counterproductive?" he asked.

So she told him about the moments of distraction that led to lost hours of watching the traffic outside of her office. She told him about how her clothes didn't fit anymore. She told him about her irregular, difficult, and unusual menstrual cycle. "In between waiting for my period to come, then actually having it," she sighed, shaking her head, "I probably have only twenty-six good weeks a year."

She took the appropriate pause, waiting for him to say something. When he didn't, she went on, telling him about her company and its demands on her life, from the pressure of a multimillion dollar contract, to dealing with the idiots who managed the coffers. Again, she waited; again, he sat there listening. *This is interesting* . . . Usually, people listened with a view to inserting their own bullshit opinion at the perfect pauses.

But then she realized: this wasn't a conversation. This was therapy. Therapy she was paying for at $120 an hour. So, she went on to discuss her problems with Tony, and how her sister held sway over her, to her benefit. All the while, Tolochko's gray eyes were stable, focused on her, except when he jotted down notes with the pen in his hand.

When she finished, she sighed deeply. Begrudgingly, she admitted to herself that talking about it was a tad cathartic.

"Hmmm," he said, then started writing in his notepad again.

Hmmm? She poured out her soul, and the best informed opinion he could give her was *Hmmm?* She peeked over at the notepad and saw successive lines of black, manly scrawl. He flipped the page and continued writing, then flipped the page again. *What the hell?*

"Have you had a physical recently, Chaney?" he asked. *Writing . . . writing . . . writing . . .*

Chaney looked up, trying to actually remember. "Yes," she announced. "Six months ago. Heather gave me a clean bill of health."

Writing . . . writing . . . writing . . . "Hmmm," he said.

Chaney glared at him. *Again with the Hmmm . . .*

Finally, he looked up from the notepad. "Tell me, Chaney, have you ever taken an antidepressant before?" he asked.

Chaney threw up her hands at that one. "Wait a minute here!" she exclaimed. "Aren't we rushing things just a little? We haven't even decided if I'm actually depressed."

Tolochko again focused that deadly serious gray gaze on her. "There's no question in my mind, Chaney, that you're clinically depressed," he declared. "All of the symptoms you described to me are classic. And as you passed your last physical, then there are no physiological reasons for the symptoms you're having."

"But, from what I know about depression . . . I mean, I don't want to hurt myself or anything like that." Briefly, she thought about Callie Bruce; if anything, she wanted to hurt other people.

"There are different types and degrees of depression, Chaney," he said. "Depression can range from serious forms like manic depression or bipolar disease, to something milder, like the type you have. It's called dysthymia. It's number 300.4 in the DSM."

Again with the fucking DSM! "Well, if the DSM says I'm depressed, then I must be, right?" she declared sarcastically.

"Chaney, when I look at someone like you, who's intelligent and has so much to offer the world, and when you tell me you have . . ." he flipped back a couple of pages in the notepad " . . . twenty-six good weeks a year, I find that a tragic waste of potential. Think about what you could do if you could have all that time back."

She tried to imagine it . . . clear, focused thought instead of trying to stop her mind from bouncing around in her brain . . . more productive ways of managing her temper . . . strategies to accept that, even though she loved her hobby, her chosen profession was what she was good at, what paid the bills. But were pills the remedy? Or was he yet another medical professional shilling for the all-too-powerful drug industry? "I think I want a second opinion," Chaney announced. "I am leery of such a drastic solution. Plus, I think there are more culturally appropriate solutions to this . . ." *Problem? Matter?* " . . . issue."

He finally averted his eyes, staring off briefly. He seemed to be processing what she'd just said. Chaney was satisfied that she'd made her point.

Then again, he focused on her, his eyes an intense slate gray. Chaney gulped, her hard-as-nails exterior softening, against her will.

"Of course, a second opinion is your prerogative," he said. "I highly recommend them. But I can assure you that there is no plot here to turn you into a medicated and docile instrument to serve 'The Man.' As a matter of fact, the culturally appropriate doctor sent you to me. I'm only here to help."

Chaney ran it all over in her brain . . . the brain she deeply valued. Her power to think and to strategize had gotten her out of many scrapes, and had helped her to achieve goals she'd set forth. The last thing she wanted to do was mess with its chemistry. She wondered, though, if chemicals could help her better manage her life, enhance the quality of her relationships. Still, she held out. "Can't we just talk?" she asked.

He nodded. "We will talk. The drug is meant to facilitate and increase the effectiveness of talk therapy. One of my patients is a swimmer. I use an analogy he made. He said dealing with life was like swimming against the tide. He said the drug helped him work on the issues he wanted to without having to battle resistance. Simply put, it made the tide go away."

She digested that one for a minute. Her life was one never-ending high tide. Like Alice in Wonderland, all she had to do was take a pill, and that would make it all better. The very notion took her in. Plus she trusted Macca implicitly. If she, her friend and doctor, suggested this as a solution, then how could Chaney not consider it? "So what's this pill called?" she asked.

Dani and Nathalie sat, listening to her with rapt attention as she relayed the story. She sipped her merlot and looked around at the patrons in the Georgetown bar. "It's called Fluexa," she announced. "The chemical name is fluoxetam bromide."

Dani made a sour face. "And how long are you supposed to be taking this poison?" she asked.

Chaney stared at her, like *who gave you a hand in this poker game?* "Obviously, you disapprove," she commented.

Nathalie slapped Dani's forearm. "Dani!" she cautioned, then turned to Chaney. "Seriously, though, how long are you supposed to be taking this antidepressant?"

Chaney liberally sipped her wine, savoring the taste. "He gave me some samples, and a prescription to fill," she said. "He suggests treatment for six months, going from ten milligrams to twenty and up while we meet every other week to talk. After that, we'll see if I need to keep taking them."

"Girl, you need Jesus, not a pill," Dani declared.

Chaney stared incredulously at her. *Fuck holding my tongue!* "This, coming from the lesbian," she said with an ironic laugh. "You know Dubya calls your lifestyle amoral."

Dani's face clouded over, and Chaney knew she'd hit the right button. As far as Dani was concerned, there was only one president: William Jefferson Clinton, who was the subject of her book about her detail in the White House during his presidency. Chaney and Nathalie joked that Bill was probably the only man alive who could excite Dani.

Dani sucked her teeth. "Fuck George W. Bush," she declared. "Election thief. Now he's trying to get us to invade Iraq."

"Okay, okay," said Nathalie, the prevailing cooler head at the table. "Chaney, personally, I don't think it's for me, but who am I to talk about the evils of drugs? I'm shot up with hormones and fertility drugs on any given day. If it works for you, girl, do it. If it'll calm your ass down and stop you from drinking all that coffee, then it'd be a success."

Chaney laughed. "Well, he didn't say anything about coffee, but he sure said no alcohol while taking the pills," she sighed, holding up her glass of merlot. "This is my last dance here for six months. I'm dead woman walking!"

Nathalie rolled her eyes and wrapped her lips around the straw in her 7-Up. "You'll live," she declared. "Wait until you try to get pregnant. No alcohol indefinitely."

Chaney looked away. She decided not to divulge the contents of her upsetting conversation with Macca about her own fertility. But still, it resonated in her head. *After forty, the chances of getting spontaneously pregnant drop precipitously, Chaney.*

She put her glass down on the table and looked around. "Where's the bathroom?" she asked. "I've gotta pee."

Dani got up. "I'll show you," she offered.

Andre drained his glass of draft beer, then looked down, checking the blue tie of his airman's uniform for any spillage. He focused his gaze on Devin, raising and lowering his unibrow. "So, Dev, you're still gonna hold out?" he asked. "You're still not gonna tell us about your date with the honey?"

Devin resisted the urge to cringe. Instead, he sipped his lager, looking around at the inquiring eyes of Andre, Ryan, and Jamal. "Her name's Zoe," he reminded him. "And gentlemen don't kiss and tell."

"Do gentlemen fuck and tell?" Andre asked.

Devin laughed, saying nothing. He just looked through the bar's picture window at rush hour on M Street. And he prayed to God that he didn't see her and her law school friends on this, the main drag of Georgetown. "Why're you so interested?" he asked. "I thought you were getting enough for all three of us at this table."

"Just curious if you whipped that Cablanasian love on her," Andre declared. "That's all."

How could he even begin to articulate how much that hurt . . . calling into question his blackness? He thought over the years, his skin would've been thicker. That was the one thing he missed about Seattle. There seemed to be more people who looked like him there than so-called monoracial blacks. And as much as he loved being back home, it was times like this moment when he wished he could blend in, be less conspicuous, not have his boys point out how different they thought he was.

Surprisingly, Jamal came to his rescue. Devin guessed Mali must have sensed Devin's discomfort. "All right, leave the brothah alone," Jamal said. "If the cops pulled him over, he wouldn't be above having a plunger shoved up his ass, too, like Abner Louima."

Ryan rushed in to defend the cop brotherhood. "Hey, that was a rogue element of the NYPD," he declared. "We're not all about putting plungers in brothahs' asses."

"Can we get off the topic of asses in general and mine in particular?" Devin asked of no one in particular.

"They'd have to find his ass first," Andre continued, as if Devin hadn't even spoken.

Jamal nodded in agreement. "No offense, bruh, but you look like you been taking your Noassatall pills religiously," he laughed.

"All of you can kiss my Cablanasian no-ass," Devin declared, then turned his gaze to Andre. "Especially you, Unibrow."

As if on cue, Jamal, Ryan, and Devin started singing, to the tune of Al B. Sure's "All Alone You Get Off on Your Own (Girl)" *"I've only got one eyebrow/I've only got one eyebrow/I've only got one eyebrow/brow/brow/ brow!"*

Sweet revenge! Devin laughed as Andre sulked and glared at the fellas at the table. When they finished in riotous laughter, Andre sucked his teeth. "Fuck y'all niggahs!" he cried, then turned to Ryan in mock hurt. "And you! My own brother. Why don't you hang out with people your own age?"

Secretly, Devin wondered the same thing but never openly questioned it. He enjoyed Ryan's company, thought he brought the civilizing effect of maturity into the mix. "And miss all this?" Ryan laughed. "Sorry, bruh, but that shit was funny!"

Andre got up. "I'm gonna bounce!"

Jamal got up, too, pointing to the bar thick with the suit-and-tie Happy Hour crowd. "No, you're not. The next round's yours. Go get it."

"I should piss in y'alls' beers," Andre declared.

"Speaking of which," Jamal said. "Gotta make a pit stop."

Andre headed for the bar, and Jamal made a beeline in the direction of the men's rooms, leaving Ryan and Devin alone. "Seriously, Dev, how'd the date go?" Ryan asked.

Devin shook his head, wondering if Ryan would think any less of him in the face of the unvarnished truth. "You really want to know?"

Ryan shrugged. "Only if you wanna tell me. No pressure."

So Devin did . . . about the first impressions, Zoe's exceedingly user-friendly nature, getting back to the apartment, the initial sexual encounter. And Ryan made a face. "Damn!" he laughed. "In the sistah's weave? Bruh, you need to work on your aim."

Devin laughed. "You know . . . heat of the moment."

"So, how did you leave it?"

Devin couldn't even look at him. "I can't explain it. I just didn't want her to stay. In my space. I'd had my fun, and I wanted her gone."

"So, you took her home . . ."

"And as she's leaving, she asks if we could do it again."

"And?"

"It was like I became my father," Devin sighed, recognizing the inevitability of it. "I used to hear him on the phone, blowing off women he fucked around with . . . women who had the balls to call the house. I flat-out told her that I was busy. To which she said, 'You weren't too busy when you had your dick in my mouth.' So, I actually put it on her. I told her if she was going to act like that, then I probably should leave her alone to do some soul-searching into her needy behavior. And I left her there. Right at the front door of Copley."

Ryan looked like it was no puzzle. "Dev, she had to know that she wasn't wifey. Especially after the way she used my brother to get to you. And when she decided to fuck you on the first date, all bets were off. I would've thought it was a one-night thing myself."

Devin sighed. Is he just telling me what I want to hear? "This shit was so much fun ten years ago . . . you hook up, hit it, and leave. What happened?"

"You're actually a grown-up now," Ryan offered. "Look at how much your life's changed since you were eighteen. How does 'someone to do' fit into that?"

"I don't want 'someone to do,'" Devin declared.

"So you're looking for a girlfriend?"

Devin thought, his head cocked to one side. "I'd like to have something exclusive now," he confessed. "But see, girlfriends inevitably want marriage. And wives want kids. Look at my fucked-up family history. The best way to not become KL Rhym is to avoid going down that path. Like he did. Three friggin' times!"

"Becoming the anti-KL is still him having influence over you, you know," Ryan laughed. "Just do Devin, man." Sounded like *main*.

As he was trying to figure out just what that was, Andre and Jamal returned to the table, each of them holding two beers each. Ryan looked up at his brother. "You've stopped sulking like a little bee-otch, I see," he observed.

Andre was actually smiling. "I'm so past feeling y'all clowns," he declared, staring over at the bar.

From the crowd of yuppies, a blonde rocking business-casual gear looked over at them and waved. Jamal shook his head in disbelief. "I don't get it," he said. "I'm the doctor. I'm wearing fucking scrubs, and he gets the hookup. It's so unfair."

"Women love men in uniform," Andre theorized. "What can I say?"

"Looks like you're working on a couple of potential little halfricans yourself." Devin laughed at the irony. Andre, who rode him the hardest about his ethnicity, was about to go the interracial route himself.

It was Andre's turn to be all smug and full of himself. "Yeah, you suckahs have fun with Palmela and Fistina," he laughed.

But Devin wasn't listening. Something had drawn his gaze away from the blonde at the bar to the doorway that had led to the restrooms. He stared at two women, both tall and striking, one of whom, as she came closer, he realized he knew. *D.C. can't be this small!*

She was about to pass the table when he stood up in front of her. "Chaney!"

She went from ready to cuss the obstructionist to, once she recognized him, giddily happy in seconds flat. "Cousin Dev!" she exclaimed. "What's up?"

"Boys' night out," he explained. "Let me introduce you."

Then he called the roll, announcing each of his boys. Their expressions ran the gamut from a cool Andre to an engaged Jamal, and then a puppy-dog look from Ryan, who was more interested in the woman with Chaney than in Chaney herself.

Chaney brought her friend forward. "This is Dani," she announced.

"Hey, fellas," Dani said, seeming friendly but sexually disinterested at the same time. Devin studied her clothes—jeans, sweatshirt, cowboy boots—and got a vibe of the non-heterosexual kind off her.

Chaney scanned the table of eager, horny brothahs before her . . . Devin included. "So, who are you guys, the Junior Mafia?" she teased.

Cute. He laughed, then proceeded to translate for his boys. "See, my brothahs, my old-school, fake cousin thinks I'm a—what was that ridiculous eighties word?—*tenderoni*, and reminds me of this every chance she gets. Like now."

Jamal winked deviously. "You know what they're saying; young brothahs are the new black," he said. "Or 'half-black,' in the case of my man here."

Devin rolled his eyes, changing the subject. "So, what are you guys doing in Georgetown?"

Chaney pointed over his shoulder, and he turned to see a pretty black woman at a table for three, waving back. "Our friend Nathalie," she said. "She's the ultimate Hoya—even though she went to Syracuse."

"Despite the fact that you need seven dollars and a well-placed blow job to park around here," Dani added sarcastically.

The look of admiration on Ryan's face deepened. "Can anyone lend me seven dollars?" he laughed, looking straight at Dani.

Dani and Chaney exchanged a private glance. Devin's gaydar began to blip in earnest right then.

"Well, we're gonna head back," Chaney sighed. "We're about to call it a night."

Dani said the perfunctory nice-to-meet-you's. Chaney tapped her on the shoulder. "Catch up with you in a sec," she said.

Dani advanced ahead a few steps, and the fellas began their own separate conversations. Devin took Chaney's hand. Damn, if it wasn't soft, probably from that delicious hand cream she made. "Good to see you," he said, and he really meant it.

"Same here, little cuz," she said.

"How's Tony?"

"Good. Still laying waste to the crib and my purse, but what you won't do for love, right?"

He nodded. "Right."

Chaney leaned in toward him, and he was treated to a delicious whiff of floral perfume. "And tell your friend that he's not Dani's type. She's more into Ellen DeGeneres and the Indigo Girls, if you catch my meaning."

Bingo! He looked down at Ryan, watched as he stared at Dani at Chaney's table. "I'll break it down," he laughed.

After Chaney left, Devin took his seat again, just as the fellas ended their side conversations. " 'Cousin Devin,' huh?" Jamal teased. "Cousins make dozens!"

Even Andre joined the fray. "Yes, she seems nice, Dev," he offered. "She ain't no Rhodeside honey, but she got skillz. Class. Like what these honeys'd be working with ten years from now."

Devin turned and looked over at the table. She looked a little sad, but she seemed like she was enjoying her friends. Every time he saw her, she got cuter, the icy cool melting by tiny degrees the more she let him in. Just then, she looked up at him and smiled. He returned the favor with a tiny wave. Then he wondered if it made sense for him to spend the next ten years in hip waders, slogging through the current talent, when what today's women his age would be like in ten years was sitting there. In the present. About five tables away . . .

Five

Chaney again found herself sitting cross-legged in her usual of the two brown paisley stuffed chairs in Dr. Tolochko's office, amidst his books, diplomas, and certifications. She stared out at the drops of rain plopping onto the picture window, then streaking down the transparent surface. Focusing on the rain was her futile attempt to take her mind off the headache that felt like both Maurice and Gregory Hines were stomping on the top of her skull. *Why the fuck isn't this ibuprofen working?*

Tolochko sat in his usual chair in front of her, this day wearing a gray tie that competed in intensity with his eyes. He didn't seem to mind that she wanted to spend the first ten minutes of the session staring out the window. Finally, though, after fifteen minutes, he said, "So, you've been taking the Fluexa for a week now. Are you tolerating it well?"

"I'm depressed about these side effects," she declared, looking at him with eyes bleary with fatigue. "I have a headache all the time. The heartburn is awful! And I get less sleep now than when I did when I was stressed out."

Writing . . . writing . . . writing . . . "Watch the side effects," he said, over the sound of the pen scratching over the notepad paper. "Treat it with over-the-counter meds. If it gets worse, though, let me know. We'll play with the dosage until we get the right amount for you."

Chaney nodded, then instantly regretted it. The tapping on the top of her skull became heavier . . . harder.

Tolochko stopped writing. "How are you doing otherwise?" he asked.

Chaney shrugged. She wasn't feeling this therapy shit and resented having to play along. But still . . . only twenty-six good weeks a year . . . what kept her hooked was the remotest possibility that Tolochko and his Fluexa could fix it all. "Like you say, it's only been a week."

"What's going on in your life?"

She thought for a minute, wondering if she really should complain. But then again, he asked, so she let it rip. She told him about Callie, the client from Hell, and Doug, her spineless cohort. "This Callie woman is hell-bent on sabotaging the project, or on playing a role bigger than the one she'd been designated. This babe has a certificate in instructional design and she insists on challenging me . . . the one with the PhD in the subject. And I'm also sensing some strain in my relationship with my partner, Lissa," she announced.

He seemed to tease out just what he needed from that declaration. "Do you like being an instructional designer?"

Chaney smiled past her headache, the smile one would smile when an old, faithful lover was mentioned. "I like the logic of it," she said. "You actually look and see if there's a performance gap, and how you could close it. You look at your learners. You look at your tasks. If the performance requires training, you develop assessable objectives for your learners. You use the right testing instrument. Instructional design takes the guesswork out of instructional strategies. It demystifies concepts like the 'master teacher.' "

Chaney was grateful to see that Tolochko was still alert, that his eyes weren't glazed over by Chaney's detailed explanation of what she did. "It sounds logical," he said.

"It has logic and order," she announced.

Writing . . . writing . . . writing . . . "Is logic and order all that important to you in other aspects of your life?"

Huh? "What do you mean?" she asked.

He referred back to those infernal notes. "You talked about Tony, how he's upset the balance of your perfect home. You talk about this woman, Callie, who is trying to change the dynamics of your project. I wonder if this need for logic and order is a common thread that runs through all of your life's activities."

"You make me sound tight . . . inflexible."

"I'll ask the question differently," he said. "What do you do for fun when you're not working with the logic and order of instructional design?"

What do I do for fun? She had to think about that one for a second. She shrugged. "The odd drink with friends, I guess," she finally said. "I'm trying to build a business. I don't have time for fun."

"Ah," he said, then began writing again.

Ah? Chaney could literally feel her patience waning.

He stopped writing after a while. "Are you seeing anyone, Chaney?" he asked casually.

Immediately, Chaney's hackles rose up. *What the fuck does that have to do with anything?* "No," she confessed.

Writing . . . writing . . . writing . . . Her eyes widened at the sheer volume of ink being expended to document the fact that she wasn't getting any. "Is that relevant?" she asked.

Tolochko looked up. "It may be," he said. "Later on."

For some reason, she felt compelled to let him know that she wasn't seeing anyone because she was discerning, not desperate. "I do have a crush on someone," she said, though, to her ears, she was sounding a tad desperate. "His name is Randy."

He seemed about as interested in her revelation as he was in her explanation of instructional design. "Tell me about him."

She smiled privately, remembering the afternoon they'd spent together, confessing their hopes, dreams, and shortcomings over drinks at Ruby Tuesday's. Some days, he was the only impetus for her to get dressed and go into the office. Him and twenty percent of six million. "He's sweet. He's attractive. He's articulate. And he doesn't seem to want anything from me but to spend time talking."

Tolochko held up his hands. "Are you pursuing this any further?"

She sighed. "He's a coworker. You know what that's like."

Tolochko finally rested his pen down. He looked Chaney straight in the eye. "Can you tell me, Chaney, when was the last time that you experienced any joy in your life?" he asked, point-blank.

Chaney blinked. Stunned, she let the question sink in to her painful brain. *When was the last time you experienced any joy in your life?* The fear of having to admit to herself that she might not have an answer to the question made her deflect it back to him. "Isn't that the same question that Bob Greene asked Oprah in that *Making the Connection* book?" she demanded.

He shrugged. "It's possible," he said.

"This is why I question the cultural appropriateness of this type of therapy," Chaney declared.

His brows creased. Finally, an actual reaction—albeit a tiny one—from him. "I don't understand."

" 'When last have I experienced joy,' " she reiterated. "Please don't take this the wrong way, but that's such a white question. With the exception of my hippie sister, black people don't talk about joy like that . . . in a secular kind of way. Besides the odd Blackstreet or Anita Baker song. We talk about racism . . . conquering obstacles . . . getting the job done . . . going for ours."

"And this is what you do at . . ." he flipped way back in his notepad " . . . Autodidact. Get the job done? Go for yours?"

"Precisely," she declared. "I can't sit around, navel gazing, talking about joy. I have twenty percent of a business to grow. That's Chaney Braxton's mission and vision for her life. Not some ridiculous quest for something as abstract as joy."

Tolochko looked away, like he was deep in thought. Again, Chaney was pleased. She was so sure that she'd articulated her position, had made herself clear.

Then Tolochko spoke. "Last week, when you came in here, you told me that your cycle was irregular, that you drank too much coffee, that you basically have only twenty-six good weeks a year." His gaze seared her like a laser beam, exacerbating her throbbing headache. "Have you ever thought, as much as you may like instructional design, that your mission and vision might be hazardous to your physical and mental health? That they may be killing you?"

Oh snap! Chaney looked away. As much as she was conditioned to fight what he was saying, it nagged at her that somewhere deep within her, she thought he made sense. "Well," she said, finally. "That was . . . blunt."

Tolochko throttled back a bit on the intensity of his stare, sat back in his chair, and picked up his pen. "I wanted to bring it up so that we could talk about it in the remaining time we have. But I want to suggest that you actually think about my 'white' question," he said. "Let me reframe it. I heard an interview with Toni Morrison. She was at a career crossroads, wanted to know what she was supposed to do with her life. Finally, she said to herself, 'If I don't do—blank—I will die.

Her answer to—blank—was to mother her children and to write. What would yours be, Chaney?"

Chaney looked away, back to the picture window streaked with spring rain. Her head thumped mercilessly, like her brains were about to explode all over his nice diplomas, certificates, and books. But her sadness was just as palpable as the pain in her brain. Sadness, because Chaney Braxton, as smart and tough as she was, who was always quick on the draw, had absolutely no answer for the question.

Devin sat on a stool and looked around at Marlene's fabulously appointed kitchen. It resembled a layout he'd seen in *Better Homes and Gardens*, when he was trying to find a look for the Georgetown crib: Italian ceramic tile floors, creamy white tiled counters, immaculately white cabinets with pewter drawer pulls, white porcelain sinks with delicate fixtures, a butcher block island, over which hung a wrought-iron lattice. Pots that Devin doubted Marlene ever used hung from the lattice.

Marlene was standing in front of the white microwave oven that was suspended over the white gas stove with six burners instead of the usual four. "I want you to taste this," she said, looking over her shoulder at him. "The caterer gave me samples for our ladies' luncheon next week, and I've tasted so much of this stuff, I need a second opinion."

Devin glanced at his watch. The NCAA Final game between Maryland and Indiana was about to start in one hour. "Only if we can do each other's hair next," he teased.

Marlene made a face. "Hah hah, Smarty Pants!" she said.

"Can we at least turn on the TV? If I'm gonna be doing this chick shit with you, I should at least be allowed to watch my game," he reasoned. "Keep my testosterone levels in check."

With a laugh, Marlene went over to the nearest counter and turned on the little thirteen-inch color TV she kept in the kitchen. It sure was no match for his massive plasma screen joint at home, but it would have to do. The pre-game prattle with the color commentators was going on and would be for another fifty or so minutes. "I love you," he said, and he truly did.

Marlene ate it up. She held up her left hand, and that Gibraltar-sized engagement ring and complementary platinum wedding band glinted in the light from the fixtures overhead. "I'm taken," she declared. "Find your own babe."

Here we go . . . He mentally prepared himself for the usual grilling over his lack of companionship. "If I frosted a babe like that and she left me, I'd be highly upset," he laughed. "But then again, my brother's got better taste in both women and bling. Did you know that the students at Georgetown Law call him 'Big Tort' . . . like 'Big Torturer'?"

Marlene thought for a minute. "No," she said. "Who told you that?"

Oh Lord, he opened the box. He made a piss-poor attempt at a casual shrug. "Some babe I met," he said, being intentionally cryptic.

Marlene, alas, was too savvy to let that slip pass. " 'Some babe,' huh?" she commented. "You know, you need to find yourself 'some babe.' You're not going to be young and cute forever, you know. Before you know it, you'll be looking for a doctor to give you Botox and a ball lift."

Devin looked down at his package. He couldn't imagine letting someone take a scalpel to his basket. "I'll never be that old!" he laughed.

"Never say never," she said with a giggle. "Your brother's thought about it."

Devin shook his head, not even wanting to entertain a vision of his brother's balls. If there was surgery to remove the stick out of his ass, though, Devin would have recommended it to Eric immediately. "Where is my brother, anyway?" he asked.

"In the den," Marlene said. "Working with the baby birds."

"Baby birds" was her code for Eric's clerks. It still amazed Devin that people looked up to his brother, revered him, the guy who used to share his room when he'd come from California to visit KL. The room that KL turned into an office and thus removed any memory of their existence.

Devin was curious about one baby bird in particular. "Is Liz still with him?" he asked with a naughty smile.

Marlene's smile was equally naughty, with a little bit of devious sprinkled in for good measure. "Yes, Liz is still clerking with him," she replied. "I heard she just recently broke up with her boyfriend, too. Some bench-warming jerk on the Wizards."

The Washington Wizards. So, she liked tall men in general and basketball players in particular. Devin was 2 and 0 right there.

Marlene went back to watching the microwave. "She's here tonight," Marlene offered.

Devin could taste the adrenaline in his mouth. "She is?"

"Yes, along with another girl. Ayanna. She's new."

Old cow and *new cow.* "Umm . . . maybe I could see them before I go," Devin said.

"I don't see why not," said Marlene, trying to play it cool, but Devin could practically hear the wheels turning under all that blond hair. "They should be taking a break any minute."

The microwave beeped, and Marlene took out a clear Pyrex dish with a pair of padded oven mitts. She whirled around to face him, and she looked like June Cleaver on the reruns of *Leave It to Beaver* that he'd seen on TVLand. "Here it is," she announced, whipping the lid off the dish with a flourish. "Pasta and pine nuts."

"I didn't know pines had nuts," Devin teased.

But Marlene looked past him. "Ladies!" she exclaimed. "We were just talking about you."

She'd said the magic word: *ladies.* Devin turned and got an eyeful. He gave Liz the once-over. Twice. He'd been trying to get to at least first base with her for the six months he'd known her. She was classy, always dressed like a Wall Street lawyer in tailored suits. That night, she rocked a navy blue pantsuit. She was petite but statuesque, with flawless cocoa-brown skin, her black hair combed in place. Devin guessed that she was what Maxwell might have been talking about when he said his girl had "that cocoa cure" for whatever ailed him. She was born in Chicago, but she'd spent the first ten years of her life in London, so when she spoke, her American accent sounded so high-tone that she could make him hard just by reading the phone book. Even as she rebuffed him, she did so with a great conversational touch, and, being half-Nigerian and half-African-American, they shared a mixed heritage. Devin stood up straight, making himself look more impressive. "Miss Ijeoma," he said. "Looking good."

Her smile turned her pink mouth up like a bow at the corners. "Dr. Rhym," she returned. "Day off from your practice today?"

Devin looked down at his gear: a gray Nike skull cap, gray hoodie sweatshirt over a waffle-knit Henley, baggy jeans, and a pair of Nike high-tops that had seen better days. Certainly not dressed to impress. "If I'd known there'd be ladies present, I would've spent more time in the closet," he said with a laugh, shooting a pointed glance at Marlene.

But then the Liz cloud lifted, and he became aware of the babe next to Liz. She looked bored with the verbal foreplay unfolding in front of him. But damn, if she wasn't all woman. In her suit that hugged her in all the right places, she looked like the Tits-and-Ass Channel on two shapely legs with three-inch stacked heels. She had one of those highly textured 'fros that brothahs were wearing lately, the spicy brown color complementing her hazel eyes. For a nano-second, she reminded him of a shorter, younger version of Chaney. But he made no mistake. This sistah was a hard rock; Chaney was a polished gem.

Marlene closed the cover on her pine nut dish. "I'm going to go check on my husband," she declared, her smile conniving.

Devin, Liz, and the girl watched Marlene go. Then Devin broke the ice. "Who's your friend?" Devin said to Liz, all the while checking the old girl out.

"Devin Rhym, this is Ayanna Lewis," Liz announced, with the ap-propriate directional hand gestures.

Ayanna looked him up and down, then turned her attentions to the game behind him on the TV set. "Maryland's got this," she de-clared.

No hello? The testosterone coursing through him made him spread his metaphorical plumage for her. "Naw, man," he said. "Indiana's on fire this year."

Now it was Liz's turn to look bored. Devin stood there, mulling over his dilemma: Liz, permed and classy, or Ayanna, Afrocentric and extremely confident, spilling out of her blouse, built, as KL would say, like a brick shit house.

Fortunately for him, Ayanna helped him along in the decision-making process. "Hey, I know some folks who're gonna tear the roof off if Maryland wins," she announced. "Around eight tomorrow night in College Park. Wanna come with me?"

He was amazed . . . no effort required on his part at all. Devin's gaze darted to Liz, who looked away, smiling knowingly. He wondered what, exactly, did Liz know. But then Ayanna made a *pfft* sound with her full, pursed lips. "Oh, that's cold, bruh," she laughed, a laugh meant to mask her being wounded. "You gonna leave a sistah hanging like that?"

What the fuck? Liz didn't seem interested in him . . . as usual. And there was a serious shortage of other fish in the sea. "Okay," he said.

Devin looked over at Liz, who was still smiling that all-knowing smile. He winked. "You wanna come with us, Liz?"

"Liz is married," Ayanna teased. "To the law."

Marlene reappeared, with Eric in tow. In his khakis and powder blue V-neck pullover sweater, Eric looked like the perfect picture of legal tight-assedness. He entered the kitchen, took one look at Devin's gear, and raked Devin with a gaze of disapproval. "Devin," he said.

His brother was like KL, minus all the height and melanin. "Big Tort!" Devin laughed. "How's it going?"

Eric gave him a look, like *not in front of the help.* "Sorry we're antisocial," Eric said. "Lots of work to do."

Ayanna didn't hear her boss. She was practically glued to the TV, watching as the players from Maryland and Indiana finished the national anthem, with massive hands pressed against jersey-covered chests. Devin checked her out again. She was built, and she loved sports. Two pluses right there. "But they're about to tip off!" Ayanna protested.

"And we're about to get back to work," Eric said, no shortage of authority in his voice.

Ayanna looked like a petulant child, pissed off at a parent. Devin instinctively knew that her days in his brother's office were numbered. Eric didn't abide slacking of any kind.

Just as Maryland and Indiana were about to tip off, the cell phone in Devin's hand rang, to the tune of Diddy's "Bad Boy for Life." He held up a finger. " 'Scuse me, Ayanna, I gotta take this," he said, then looked her over again. "But don't you go anywhere."

The second Devin put the phone to his ear, he heard a little boy's wrenching cries, over the loud shouting of a man and a woman in the background. Belatedly, Devin thought he recognized Kimmy's voice as that of the woman. "Hello!" Devin said.

"Uncle Devin!" Denis sobbed hysterically from the other end of the phone. "Please come!"

The blood drained from Devin's face. He was at the coat closet near the door in five running strides. "Denis," he said, trying his hardest to remain calm in the face of the child's obvious distress. "Tell me what's going on."

"Please, Uncle Devin!" Denis screamed from the other end. "Please come help my mommy!"

Devin's heart constricted so violently that he nearly doubled over in agony. He shrugged into his jacket. "Devin, what's the matter?" Marlene called after him.

He turned and saw four pairs of eyes staring at him like he was crazy. He pressed the phone over his left breast. "I gotta go," he whispered. "I'll call y'all later."

With his keys in his hand, Devin ran to the Navigator. All the while, though, he listened to Denis's hiccupping sobs over the phone. One thing drove his movements: getting to him and Kimmy, and the baby. "You okay, little man?" Devin asked. "What's going on over there?"

"Don's screaming at Mommy," Denis cried, his voice now hoarse from the exertions. "Please come here." Sounded like *hee-or*.

With his free hand, Devin started the car and gunned it toward Route 7. "Okay, dude, I'm coming, okay?" he promised. "Just stay on the phone with me, okay?"

But then a loud crash resounded through the phone and straight into Devin's ear. "Ow!" he screamed, almost dropping the phone on the floor of the car.

He put the phone to his ear again and heard nothing but dead silence. *Denis!*

All through the ten-minute drive to Arlington, Devin frantically dialed, then redialed Kimmy's number. Each time, he got the voice mail, with Kimmy sounding as happy as he'd ever heard her sound, definitely not like, on the other side of that voice mail message, some redneck was beating her in front of her terrified, helpless children.

Finally, he arrived at the parking lot of that shitty apartment complex and drove to the usual spot in front of the building. Don's shiny blue Ford pickup was gone from the spot, so Devin pulled into it, tires screeching. He stormed out of the Navigator, locking the car with a chirp from his key chain remote. Once inside the foyer with the threadbare carpet, he took the stairs two at a time and ran the extra couple of feet to her door. He knocked with authority on the metal fire door. From behind the door, a tiny voice asked, "Who is it?"

"Uncle Devin, Denis. It's cool; open the door!"

The door opened slowly, and Denis, wearing a pair of faded, droopy Spiderman pajamas, stood in the doorway that dwarfed him. His face was red and streaked with tears, his little brown eyes bloodshot and puffy. His little chest heaved, and Devin could see the bony outlines of his clavicles through his shirt. "Uncle Devin," he wept.

Devin picked him up and held him close. Devin rubbed Denis's tiny back in an attempt to soothe, but he doubted it was working. Devin could feel Denis's heart thumping at the speed of a hummingbird's wings. "It's okay, Denis," he assured him. "It's gonna be all right."

Denis wrapped his legs around Devin's waist as much as he could. Devin came inside the apartment and shook his head in awe. The place was trashed. The cheap entertainment center was tipped over, and all the secondhand appliances littered the floor, all of them shattered to bits. Books and pictures were tossed across the room. Ripped papers were strewn all over the floor and the depressing furniture. In the pile of mess sat Thor, swishing his gray tail vindictively from side to side. Devin stared at him, and he stared right back. *I've got a nice syringe of Ketamine back at the office for you.*

Just then, Thor decided that he had to be in another room right away and rushed madly away. At the same time, Kimmy came tearing from the back of the apartment. She saw Devin, with her son in his arms. She narrowed her eyes, and cornflower blue became pissed-off blue. "What are you doing here?" she demanded.

Denis looked guiltily at his mother. Devin ran a hand over the boy's head. "Denis called me," he answered. "What happened here?"

Kimmy came closer. "Denis, how many times do I have to tell you about using the phone without my permission!" she yelled.

Devin felt every muscle in Denis's body tense. Devin rubbed his back again, and slowly, the boy unclenched. "He was just trying to protect his mommy," he said.

Kimmy pointed an index finger with a chipped nail in his face. "Don't you contradict me in front of my child!" she commanded.

Devin took a deep, cleansing breath. He knew she was stressed. He'd seen the same erratic behavior from his own mother. He was probably Denis's age when his father went from charming to philandering asshole with a quickness. "I didn't mean to," he said calmly. "I'm sorry."

Kimmy raked chipped nails through her black roots, and he could see that her hair was stringy, like she hadn't washed it in at least a week. Neglecting her personal hygiene was so unlike Kimmy, the former aspiring model. She looked at the mess around her and sighed deeply.

Now to deal with that fucker. "Where is he?" Devin asked; he wasn't even worthy of a mention by name.

"He went out."

"Dante?"

"I just put him down. He finally went to sleep."

Maybe I can save her . . . "You eat yet?" he asked.

Through her astronomical stress, she smiled. On instinct, Devin touched her face. She shook her head no. "Dinner's on the floor in the kitchen," she sighed.

Where Don threw it, Devin guessed. He shook Denis in his arms. "How 'bout some pizza, little man?"

Denis's reddened eyes widened. "Pizza!" he cried happily.

"Well, your mom's going to take a hot bath, and you're going to be a big boy and help me clean up this mess, okay?"

"Okay," Denis agreed.

Pizza took an hour to come. Of course, it was the night of the NCAA Final Four Basketball Championships, and Maryland, the local favorite, was playing. Still, in that time, Denis, true to his word, helped Devin with the items a four-year-old could lift. His mother allowed him to stay up an extra hour to have pizza, which made his day. Devin guessed she was overcompensating to make up for exposing her child to her man's violence.

They set the broken appliances by the door, and Devin laid the slats from the wrecked entertainment center against the wall. They were done by the time the pizza came . . . an appropriate reward. Kimmy, now scrubbed and practically glowing, ate a whole pie by herself. Devin stared at her. *You must be starving!*

"All right, baby," Kimmy said to Denis as she wiped tomato sauce from his mouth. "Time for bed."

"Aw, Mommy," he whined. "I wanna stay up with Uncle Devin."

"It's a school night for both you and Uncle Devin," Kimmy declared. She pointed Denis in Devin's direction. "Now kiss Uncle Devin good night."

Obediently, Denis leaned in and gave Devin the stickiest, sweetest kiss on the cheek. Then he pressed his tiny hands against Devin's face. Devin laughed out loud. Then he found himself kissing the child back on the forehead. He doubted that he wanted to be a father. He'd seen firsthand how parents wounded their children, whether intentionally or inadvertently. But this kid was fast making him rethink his position. " 'Night, Uncle Devin," he whispered in Devin's ear.

" 'Night, Denis," Devin said. "You were a good boy tonight. Thanks for your help."

Devin watched as Denis then wrapped his arms around Kimmy's neck and kissed her good night on the cheek. Devin silently prayed that people were right about kids, that they were resilient. Something told Devin that this kid had seen more than his share of grown-up shit in his four years on the planet.

"Don't forget to brush your teeth!" Kimmy called after him.

"Yes, Mommy!" he called back, then disappeared in the back of the apartment.

Devin wondered how he would bring it up to her without embarrassing her, or hurting her feelings. Then he just thought, *Fuck it!* He produced the Payless shoe box from under the table. "Is this what set him off?" he asked. Don was still not worthy of mentioning by name.

Kimmy went ashen. With shaking fingers, she opened the box filled with hundreds of Polaroids. Devin looked her straight in the face. He didn't need to see those pictures again. The images were indelibly etched in his gray matter from when he'd scooped them up off the floor: Kimmy in various states of undress . . . a brothah with a black redwood of a penis, thrusting it into any and every hole in her body that would fit it. There were shots of doggie style, shot from awkward positions, pictures of the top of Kimmy's head, with the dick thrust mightily in her mouth, shots of the dick between her creamy breasts with pink nipples. Just to name a few shots that stood out. Devin found himself boiling with anger and envy, and Kimmy hadn't been his woman in over ten years.

She nodded. "That's TC," she whispered. "Dante's father." All of a sudden, her eyes grew wide. "Please tell me Denis didn't see any of these!"

Devin shook his head. "I got to them before he did."

Kimmy sighed. "Don had a hard day," she explained. "He has this new boss, and she's riding him pretty hard."

Yeah, yeah, whatever! Even the look on her face said she knew she was making lame excuses. "When I moved in here with him, I put practically all of my stuff in the cage in the basement downstairs. I didn't even realize I still had them until he found them down there tonight."

"Kimmy . . ." Devin interrupted.

"Devin," she continued over him. "He's very sensitive about this thing, with me and the children's fathers. With them being black."

She sounded like the cliché of the abused woman. "Kimmy, he knew who you were coming into the relationship," he reminded her. "He's tripping over some pictures now?"

Kimmy turned away, and Devin could see fresh welts made by the contact of an open hand with her cheek. She looked bone-weary and defeated. "I don't want to talk about this with you," she said. "Obviously, you've made your mind up about him."

Devin wanted to grab her and shake some sense into her. "Does he hit the children?" he asked, then hated himself for the judgmental tone he took with her.

She looked him point-blank in the eye. "No!" she cried.

Devin looked at her slumped in the chair. "Obviously, he hits you," he said quietly.

She looked away.

"What's in it for you, Kimmy?" he asked.

She kept avoiding his gaze. He wondered why . . . shame? "I'm twenty-eight years old," she sighed. "I've got two kids for two different black men. In the South. In spite of that, he gives me love and a roof over my head."

When did your love become so easy to buy? "And the occasional open-handed smack," he murmured.

She stood up and pointed at the front door. "Thank you for the pizza," she said, dismissive. "I'm sorry you came all this way. Denis just overreacted."

He stood up, too, towering over her. "He's four, and his mommy was being smacked around like the stepchild with ring-around-the-collar," he insisted. "He acted appropriately. If he were older, he probably would've done like Warren Moon's son and called the cops."

Kimmy stormed over to the door. "I can handle this, Devin," she said, her hand on the knob.

She threw open the door and pointed to the hallway. He didn't have to be a genius to see that she wanted him out. And it was her right to want him gone. After all, she was the mistress of this fractured home that smelled like cat piss. Devin moved slowly to the door. "You're twenty-eight," he said. "Denis is four. You think he can handle it, too?"

Kimmy glared at him. "Get out!" she commanded through gritted teeth.

That he did, stepping into the hallway. She slammed the door so hard that she nearly hit him in his ass with it. He looked over his shoulder at it, wondering if he could let what happened behind that door rest. But what could he do?

He wondered this as he made his way out of the depressed building and out to his car. Don was still nowhere to be found. He was probably out getting Kimmy a Whitman's Sampler and a gas station bouquet of flowers. His father brought home many such apologies after he'd demoralized his mother in front of Devin.

Devin started the Navigator, then drove from the darkened parking lot . . . at the speed limit this time. It was too quiet in the car, though. So he turned on the radio, just in time to hear the announcer say, over the roar of a passionate crowd, "It is pandemonium here in College Park at the University of Maryland campus. It's official. The Terrapins are the 2002 NCAA Final Champions!"

The crowd roared like spectators at the ancient Roman Coliseum. The Terps were the gladiators who ate Bobby Knight-less Indiana alive. Suddenly, out of nowhere, he remembered. His shitty mood took a hiatus, and he laughed out loud. Maryland won, which meant one Detective Ryan Joell was going to have to eat a bug.

Chaney stirred sugar and her own half-and-half into her coffee, in a huge black Mad Hatter tea mug. Another sleepless night, courtesy of the Fluexa. She looked around at the coffee room that also tripled as a lunchroom and a station for copiers. As if on cue, Callie came in, wearing a yellow boucle jacket and matching skirt, like she was getting a jump on spring. Unfortunately, with her coloring and the fluorescent overhead lights, she looked like a walking urine sample. Immediately, Chaney put her guard up.

"Hi, Chaney," she said in a high-pitched voice that Chaney imagined made all the dogs in a ten-mile radius howl.

Fake bitch. "Good morning, Callie," Chaney returned, managing a wan smile. "You're in early."

She eschewed the whole sea of vendor mugs next to the microwave and helped herself to an eight-ounce Styrofoam cup.

Fake, environment-killing bitch.

"I meant to thank you and Lissa for giving me, Doug, and Randy that extra office space," Callie said. "I live in Friendship Heights. This is much closer than the other office at Union Station. Which is great, because you're on fire! We just got your latest revisions to the design document. Fast turnaround, girl!"

The upside of Fluexa-induced sleep deprivation was that Chaney was getting tons of work done. Often, she went straight from the chair in her office at home to the chair in her office at work. "Whatever it takes to make the client happy," Chaney said, the usual reflexive bullshit that clients took for meaningful conversation, for genuine caring about satisfying their personal, rather than their business, needs.

"I still think the objectives could use a little tweaking," Callie declared. "It's not really apparent what the end user will know after going through the training."

Chaney bristled inside. On the outside, though, she continued to calmly stir her coffee. "Well, Callie, since we've moved on from the analysis phase of the project to the design phase, your point is probably moot. However, about the objectives, we've phrased them so that they can genuinely assess whether learning has occurred. At Syracuse, I was taught that any objectives that use the words *know, learn,* and *understand* outright were taboo. You can't crack the learners' skull to see if they've learned something, but if they completed the task, then they've demonstrated the knowledge of that task. We can assume that learning took place."

"Syracuse, huh," she said, with a little clipped nod. "You must've read that 2000 *Training* magazine article that said that instructional design went downhill once universities started offering programs in the subject."

The old Chaney would've laughed. Right in her face. This time, though, she merely kept stirring, sizing Callie up. Maybe, after weeks of sleeplessness, gas, and blinding headaches, the Fluexa was beginning to work. "I sure did read it," she said. "Though I found the rebuttals to that article from established instructional design professionals even more interesting than the article itself. Did you read any of them in your certification program from . . . where did you get certified again?" *Point made.*

Callie turned away, pouring coffee into her cup. "Online," she mumbled.

"Ah," Chaney said. "Online. Well, a lot of universities are developing online components of their programs. Which online university?"

Callie smiled a fake, pinched smile. "I could give you the URL if you'd like."

Pitiful. This babe with her dime-store online certificate that she probably printed out on a dot-matrix printer was a joke. "Okay," Chaney said. "Maybe we can compare and discuss instructional design theory sometime. Away from the project."

The smile grew more fake, more pinched. "Sure," she said.

The Fluexa had reached the limit in Chaney's system. One more minute in that room with Callie, and Chaney was going to let the leash on her Brooklyn 'tude loose. She set her mug down on the counter. "Please excuse me, Callie," she said.

"Okay," Callie said eagerly.

Chaney left the coffee room and walked through the labyrinth of blue-carpeted halls. As she walked, Tolochko's words resonated in her ears . . . *Have you ever thought that your mission and vision might be killing you?*

Days like this, she just wanted to run, like her Southern dad used to say, "like a nigger who stole something." But not her. Escaping from responsibility was the *modus operandi* of one Braxton sister: Daisy. Anna Lisa didn't run at the darkest hour in the history of their little family. Chaney was reliable to a fault. But sometimes . . .

Chaney left Autodidact's double glass doors and headed down the hall to the ladies' room. She knew she had to do something. Just what, though, escaped her.

She arrived at the white door to the ladies' room, pushed it in . . . and got a whiff of the most pungent odor that cut her breath and made her eyes water. "Gat-DAMN!" she cried on the foul air she'd mistakenly breathed into her lungs.

She turned to run when she heard the familiar voice echoing off the tiles of the bathroom. "Chaney, that you?"

Chaney held her breath. "Coco?!" she called on the little air she had left in her lungs.

"Hold on a minute!" Coco called.

Chaney heard a spraying sound, then she became aware of a chemical smell. Now it smelled like Lysol and shit in the bathroom. Chaney stuck her head out for a much-needed whiff of air. "Girl, I'm gonna be outside!" she called.

"Be right out!"

Chaney stepped into the hallway and gulped in fresh air. She crossed her arms over her chest and waited until Coco, on a current of shit and Lysol, left the bathroom. Coco pulled her aside, into the stairwell, and waited for the red metal door to slam shut. They were there huddled close in the stark, concrete area between two flights of stairs. "What's with the Oliver Stone shit?" Chaney asked.

"I just thought you should know," she said.

The old Chaney would've been irritated. The Chaney in the grip of Fluexa counted to ten. "Know what, Coco?" she calmly asked.

"Lissa," Coco answered. "I heard her talking to Al. She and that Callie are out to fuck you over. Apparently, it was Callie who asked for the extra office space for her, Doug, and Randy. She actually said to Lissa, 'I don't think Chaney knows anything about instructional design.' That bitch Lissa didn't even defend you."

Chaney looked away, letting it sink in. "Did you actually hear the exchange between Callie and Lissa?" she finally asked.

Coco's eyes darted back and forth behind her glasses. "Not exactly," she admitted. "I heard her say it to Al."

Chaney thought for a minute. This sounded like Callie, but certainly not Lissa. Granted, they weren't having the best moments in their relationship, but why would Lissa want to sabotage a six-million-dollar project? Plus, Lissa herself had said that Chaney was "bulletproof," to use her word. It didn't track, but Leah Braxton didn't raise no fool. "Thanks for telling me, Coco," Chaney said, then headed for the door.

She opened the door and looked back at Coco. "Coming?" she asked.

Coco looked puzzled. "Who are you?" she asked. "You're not the Chaney I know."

Chaney shrugged. "What do you want me to do? Scream my head off? Lose it, because a client may or may not have called my credentials into question? Nah."

"What are you going to do?" Coco asked.

"Nothing," Chaney said. "For now."

For now, she was going to watch it and wait . . .

Devin ran across his office to get his cell phone, repeatedly ringing out Puffy's "Bad Boy for Life." He set the business plan in his hand onto the desk, snatched up the phone, and opened it before it went to voice mail. He was not in the mood for any calls. He and Didier had gone over the business plan in detail, in an attempt to head the Pet-Thenon off at the pass. "Hello," he snapped.

"Devin Rhym," came the naughty, suggestive purring voice from the other end.

Who the fuck is this? "This is Devin Rhym," he said tersely.

"How quickly men forget," she said in his ear.

He thought . . . and thought . . . and thought some more. Then it hit him. "Ayanna!" he exclaimed, snapping his fingers. "Ayanna Lewis."

"Yeah, buddy," she laughed.

He could picture her in that suit, the embodiment of ripe womanhood, coffee-colored titties and a round ass that he wanted to clutch in his hands. "I'm sorry I didn't recognize your voice," he apologized. "It's been a week."

"And I didn't hear from you after you bounced from your brother's house."

Yes, he remembered that Denis's heart-wrenching phone call made him make tracks just as he was on the verge of sealing the deal with her. "Wait, you were gonna call me about that Terps victory party in College Park," he reminded her.

"Yeah, well, it turned into a little victory riot, as you probably saw on the news," she said. "Figured we should stay away. Nobody's going to want to hire a lawyer who's been in jail. Plus it took me a week to get your number from your sister-in-law."

Devin smiled, shaking his head. *God bless Marlene!*

"Umm . . ." she began, surprisingly awkward for someone so forward. "I'd still like to kick it with you, though."

He wondered what "kicking it" with her actually entailed. "What did you have in mind?" he asked.

"I figured we could play it by ear," she said. "You come get me, and we'll see what happens."

Devin laughed louder. *He* was actually being courted, not the other way around. This was an interesting switch . . . naked sexual aggression aimed at him. *Run with it, Devin.* "What day did you want to 'kick it?'"

"How about tonight?" she suggested.

What the hell? He was curious to know what it was like not to have to do all the heavy lifting. She relieved him of having to go through his bag of tricks to see which ones would be effective to get him to the ultimate goal: a home run. His Zoe fix was wearing off fast. And Pamela and Fistina were getting old. "Okay," he conceded. "Let's do it."

Chaney's fingers flew across the keyboard as she put the finishing touches on the latest revisions to the design document. Begrudgingly, she had to admit that Tolochko was right. Physiological side effects of the drug aside, she noticed that her preoccupation with life's usual bullshit had lessened. Her focus had sharpened. She could envision all mental barriers parting like the Red Sea, allowing for laser beam concentration on her task. Fluexa had actually allowed her to tune out the clients so she could focus on the creative aspects of her job that she liked.

She took a break and optically scanned her flat-screen monitor, reading the stimulus material that she'd written on the fly. Callie and Doug were still fucking with the design document. The stimulus material for the actual training was months away, but that didn't stop her from wanting to get a jump on it. Make the client happy. Although, with that miserable bunch—excluding Randy, of course—she doubted that they'd ever be happy.

Chaney took a brief moment to indulge in what was becoming an occasional occurrence now—staring out the picture window at the traffic moving on Rockville Pike. It was dark now, and all she could see of the cars were their sleek lines and beaming headlights. She smiled. Randy . . .

He'd been gone a week, something about taking his daughter Taina to Florida on a basketball retreat. She found herself missing him, which surprised even her. She mostly missed him in meetings with Doug and Callie, when everybody, except Coco, sat back and watched as Callie drew first blood and Doug lapped it up. Where Randy was missing, the drug more than made up for his lack of presence. Chaney had handled herself masterfully—not with sarcasm, but armed with the facts and with solutions to even their most ridiculous requests. *Terminal Objective* sound too negative? *Boom!* Chaney called it the *End Goal* instead. Task analysis unclear? *Boom!* Chaney wrote an addendum to the document, clarifying Callie's unfounded, uninformed speculations. *Twenty percent of six million . . .*

Randy... She missed his smile, their exchanges that had just enough detachment to make them professional but with the right amount of heat to make it interesting. A meaningful glance in meetings, a surreptitious brush against those rock-hard biceps, thighs touching as they sat next to each other while reviewing documents on the lobby bench downstairs. Just thinking about him made her chemically treated brain remember the scent of his crisp, clean cologne, mixed in with this own unique scent. Just sitting next to him gave rise to all the familiar physical reactions: the cold sweat above her top lip, the hardening of the nipples inside the confines of her bra, the whooshy wetness in her panties. Far from shunning the feelings, she welcomed them. They meant that at least one side effect of the antidepressant didn't apply to her: sexual dysfunction.

A knock on her door startled Chaney, and she looked away from the window. Lissa was standing in the doorway. Chaney regarded her warily. Their relationship officially took a hit when Lissa sat in the client meetings and allowed her shitty client discipline to tacitly co-sign Callie's behavior. And if what Coco said in the stairwell that day was true, then Chaney knew she needed to watch her ass in earnest. Nonetheless, she smiled. "Lissa," she said. "What's up?"

Lissa took her key card out of her purse. "Just wanted to say good night," she said. "See how you're doing. We haven't had a chance to talk since we got the contract."

Chaney laughed, sizing her up. Could she really have gone from being her godmother at Syracuse to a caramel-colored cottonmouth in a cream-colored pantsuit? "Doing good," she declared, then stared at her, narrowing her eyes. *Let me fuck with your head* . . . "How are you, Lissa?"

Lissa looked puzzled. She laughed nervously, looking away. She pressed her hands to her flat chest, her plucked brows raised. "Me?" she gasped. "I'm fine! Why do you ask?"

Chaney's Fluexa-induced clarity helped her focus on the moment. Instinct met the signs she'd been missing, and right then, she knew that Coco was telling the truth. Chaney stared at her and felt a tinge of sadness. "Nothing," she said. "I'm starting on the actual training, if and when our client decides to move on to the next level."

Lissa leaned forward conspiratorially. "She's a frigging dim bulb, that Callie," she whispered. "But, you know . . . clients."

"Yeah," Chaney said. "Clients." *And friends . . .*

Lissa buttoned up her jacket over her suit. "Well, I'm gone," she said. "Lock up our little candy store when you leave."

" 'Bye."

Chaney watched her go. She wondered what she was going to do now . . . all leveraged into a company, where she hated the clients and, now, where she couldn't even trust the partners.

Devin saw the Navy Yard go by in the pitch blackness through the driver's-side window. "I didn't know you lived in Southeast," he commented in passing.

Though he wouldn't have figured a law student to be setting up shop in the most hardened corner of the triangle that was D.C.

"Why not?" Ayanna asked, looking at the same view from the passenger-side window. "How am I gonna protect my brothahs and sistahs from injustice when I live in someplace like Great Falls or some fucking place like that?"

Point taken.

She sucked her teeth. "And ain't like your brother's giving up some major cheese," she added. "That gig is just a means to an end."

Okay, shitting on his brother was not exactly the best way to make a good impression, but she was right. Eric was as cheap as they came. If it hadn't been for Marlene's style and influence, Eric still would've been living in the same crappy apartment he'd had before he'd gotten married, sleeping on a money-filled mattress.

Devin glanced over at her. She looked cute—baggy jeans that rode low on that deliciously round ass and a V-necked, long-sleeved cotton blouse. Her coffee cleavage was pushed up and accentuated, the light inside the car shimmying off her bosom. He forced himself to think about sports before he created his own stick shift. "You look great," he commented.

She turned her hazel eyes on him, too, raking them appreciatively over his denim shirt, jeans, and Lugz . . . all under a black sport jacket. She did one of those quick LL Cool J lip licks that didn't need any translation. "You're looking fine yourself," she declared. "Smell good, too. What are you wearing . . . Dolce and Gabbana?"

He laughed, pleasantly surprised. "Yeah, it is. How'd you know?"

She laughed cryptically. "It's nice on you. Calvin Klein would probably smell good on you, too. CK1 or something like that."

What a strange case of role reversal! She wanted *him* to wear something nice for *her*. He was starting to feel a little like her bitch.

"So, what you got planned for me?" she asked.

He shrugged. "I figured we could go for drinks in Georgetown," he said.

She scoffed. "White Boy Land? No thank you!"

That stung more than a little. "Hey, I live in Georgetown."

Other people would've tap-danced to cover their ass. Not her. "Figures," she commented.

"What does that mean?"

She shook her head. "Just, you being a single doctor and all that. I bet a Georgetown address'd get many honeys out of their drawers with a quickness."

He stared over at her. *Strike One.*

"Let's go to a club. On U Street," she suggested. "Got some nervous energy I wanna work off, and Wednesday's Ladies' Night."

Devin hadn't been clubbing on U Street since high school. With his boys and with Kimmy. Immediately, he banished memories of his first love to the back of his brain, wanting to enjoy a night alone with a lower-maintenance woman. As he thought back, he realized he hadn't really been to the club since he used to deejay for extra money at U-Dub. He nodded. "Sounds like a plan," he said.

"But I want to eat first," she said.

He moved into impress mode. "There's this great Korean place in Chinatown."

She screwed up her face. "Can't we get some real food?"

Okay, shitting on his mom's heritage. That was officially *Strike Two.*

"Let's go to Adams Morgan," she suggested, blissfully unaware. "There's a great Nigerian restaurant there that Liz recommended. I wanna check it out. You down?"

Liz. Now that's who he really wanted to be on a date with. But this was reality, and he was here with Ayanna, who was clearly running the show. Devin took the next exit off of Route 295. "Sure, I'm down," he said.

She cranked NPR on the stereo, listening to the commentators discuss a possible invasion of Iraq, as they made their way toward Adams Morgan, one of the more youth-oriented, trendy enclaves of D.C., filled with a multiracial, multicultural mix of students, yuppies, pages who worked on Capitol Hill, and other people who were young and hip. Adams Morgan was usually on the list of places to go when he and his boys were in middle school, and Ryan had just gotten his license. She just laughed as he circled like a great white in the seemingly futile quest for parking . . . until someone reversed and he shot into one of the curious sideways parking spaces.

Moments later, they were upstairs at a table in the crowded Pride of Benin restaurant. He looked around, wondering if there was truly credence to the myth that, whenever a government fell, three new restaurants opened up in Adams Morgan. They were surrounded by other couples who looked like they were on awkward first dates as well.

Devin admitted to himself that this was different. He was with the most aggressive woman he'd ever known. At a restaurant where there were no utensils. "Did Liz happen to recommend what to order?" he asked.

Ayanna smiled, relishing her role as the one in charge. "I'll order for us," she said, then snapped her fingers. "Waiter!" she called.

Over dinner—a hardened farina and codfish soup combination called fufu and egusi that you ate with your fingers—Ayanna began to perform. "Your brother says you're from Seattle," she said.

Devin mimicked what she'd previously done, fashioned the fufu into a ball, and dipped it into his bowl of egusi soup. He popped it into his mouth. It was like eating spicy, fishy Cream of Wheat. *Interesting.* But, he thought, far be it from him to dog out other people's cuisine. His boys still didn't know how he could crave *kimchi* with just about everything he ate. "You and that smelly cabbage," Andre would chide him. Jamal was right; Andre was the ultimate Ugly American.

"Actually, I'm from Virginia," he clarified. "But I moved to Seattle when I was fifteen."

"Seattle," she said, letting it roll off her tongue. "No black people. Two hundred and twenty-nine overcast days a year. Suicide capital of the nation. I see why you left."

He hardened. Obviously, she hadn't heard about Jimi Hendrix or Sir Mix-a-Lot, to name a token famous few. "There are black people in Seattle," he declared. "And it was great there. I only left because I wanted to come back home."

"To Virginia," she said, again with that judgmental tone. "Folks in D.C. give Virginia a wide berth."

It took some work, but he summoned his easygoing side. "Where are you from that's so wonderful?"

She looked at him, like *can't you tell?* "Harlem," she replied.

She had him there. Neither Seattle nor Arlington could compare to what the Cradle of African-American civilization had to offer. "Oh," he murmured, sufficiently shut up.

Ayanna dipped her fufu into her egusi, then took a swig of Nigerian beer. "How could someone from a tree-hugging town like Seattle drive that big, gas-guzzling ride?"

Again with the attacks on his beloved Navigator. First from his demanding dad, then from Don the redneck, and now her. He shrugged casually, but inside, he was beginning to take it personally. "I like having a big ride," he explained. "That car's got everything I need inside it. Plus, I'm tall; there's no way in hell I'm getting into something like a Geo Metro."

She looked naughtily at him over her beer. "I don't know, bruh," she said, shaking her head. "You know what they say about men with big rides . . ."

She and KL were singing from the same hymnal. His ardor toward her was definitely cooling at this point, but he briefly thought about whipping it on her, just to be spiteful while, at the same time, proving a point. He feigned ignorance. "What do they say about men with big rides, Ayanna?" he asked. "Big gas bills?"

She laughed. "Not quite," she said, then held up her pinky, then bent it, as if driving home her assumption.

It was his turn to laugh, his turn to gaze naughtily at her over the top of his beer. "Well, maybe later, you'll be able to tell me what you think," he declared.

She did the LL lip lick again, checking him out with those probing hazel eyes. "Sounds interesting," she said. "Why don't we just see what happens?"

Devin was tempted. But just as he even entertained the possibility, he looked up, and his blood chilled cold. In a serious case of when worlds collide, he saw his past coming up the stairs, on the arm of a bald, buffed, suited-down Mandingo of a brothah. *Zoe!*

She still wore those ridiculously fake green contacts, but the weave, longer and streaked with blond, was different. He shuddered inside as he remembered her mouth wrapped around his dick, her screams as he fucked her over the stuffed chair in his bedroom. Tonight, she wore a fuck-me black dress and fuck-me-harder black pumps. Her eyes scanned the room before her, and Devin's heart practically thumped out of his chest. *Please don't look over here! Please don't look! Please don't look . . .*

Wishful thinking. She looked. Their eyes met, and he at first saw recognition, then hurt on her whole face. She shot him a lopsided smile, and he returned the favor. He waved at her. The same feelings he'd had when he'd unceremoniously deposited her on her dorm steps returned with a vengeance. He looked on as, in an instant, she and her date disappeared into the nether regions of the restaurant.

Before he could process what had just happened, he looked back at his table . . . and realized that Ayanna had just witnessed the brief exchange. "Who's she?" she asked, more like demanded.

Guiltily, he looked away. "Just a friend," he said.

Ayanna sat back in her chair and folded her arms across her chest, making those round melon titties poke further through the V in her blouse. "You fucked her, didn't you?" she concluded.

He felt his traitorous face go red. He stared at her in shock. Then he found his voice, laughing nervously. He picked up his water and took a healthy sip, concentrating to regulate any tremors in his hand. He looked away, his eyes scanning the restaurant. "Ayanna, you really should learn to say what's on your mind."

Strike Three.

Chaney saved her document, then looked up from the monitor. She worked her head around in a circle on her aching neck. She took a quick look out her window. The rain that the weatherman had been predicting all day came down in torrents, slashing water across the glass. April showers had begun. The tires on the cars on the Pike were hydroplaning on the asphalt.

She was glad she'd left Tony inside. This time, though, she read all of Devin's articles, including some he'd written on separation anxiety. She'd left the TV on, so Tony wouldn't feel so alone. She'd put up a perimeter of baby fences to protect the entertainment center and other open areas. She'd left his toys in the middle of the floor. In short, she'd created an environment that she hoped he'd find cozy, make him feel less compelled to destruction. But even for the most patient dog, this was a long day. The numbers on the digital clock she'd hung on the office wall glowed out 7:30. It was time to call it a night.

Chaney picked up her coffee cup and was about to head to the pantry. Suddenly, she sensed she was being watched and looked up in the doorway. Her heart leapt up into her chest, and she screamed. Then she saw who it was. *Randy!*

Goose bumps dotted her skin. He stood in the doorway, looking so smooth-brothah fine in his suit pants and shirtsleeves, with a black backpack over one broad shoulder. He looked tanned and well-rested, flashing her that brilliant white smile that nearly made her slide off her chair. "Chaney Braxton," he said, his voice indicating the joy he felt at seeing her.

Chaney giggled, shaking her head. "Randy Tyree," she said. "You're back!"

He looked down at his watch. "What are you still doing here?"

Chaney shrugged. "You know me," she said. "President of the Women Without Lives Club. More importantly, why are you here?"

"Moving stuff into the office space," he said.

Chaney looked away and nodded. The office space that Callie asked for so that she could fuck with Chaney from closer proximity. "Ah, yes, the office space," she commented, then abruptly changed the subject. "Enough about that. How's your daughter? How was Florida?"

His smiled widened, that of a proud father. He held a hand over his heart. "She was great," he said. "She handled herself so well; it made her old man feel so good. She's two years from even thinking about college, and scouts were all over her."

"That's great, Randy."

He laughed. "Yeah," he said. "And she penciled me in for some sightseeing. I actually took my daughter to the club!"

Chaney's brows raised. "You were in the club?" she laughed. "I would've paid to see that."

He reached into the backpack. "You won't have to pay," he said, waving a CD jewel case in her direction. "You got some time to see some photos?"

She was sure even Tony wouldn't begrudge her a few minutes of affection. "Sure!" she squealed. *Settle down, Chaney.*

Randy grabbed one of the guest chairs and dragged it over next to her behind the desk. He reached across her and pressed the release on the computer's CD drive. "Let me just put this in your thing here . . ." he murmured.

Chaney's mind formed all kinds of filthy visions, just from those few words. She studied his profile, taking in the side view of the dome, the nose, the silhouette of his full mouth. Before temptation got the better of her, she turned her head away. Suddenly, she felt the muscles going down the side of her neck painfully twinge. "Ow!" she cried.

He looked over at her. "What's wrong?" he asked, concerned.

Chaney held her head down and massaged the base of her neck. "My neck," she moaned, her voice muffled by her bosom. "I don't know what I did."

"How about sitting at the computer until 7:30?" he suggested, getting up. "Let me help you."

Just as Chaney was wondering just what he had in mind, he came up behind her in her swivel chair, then put his hands against her neck. She jumped at the feel of his touch. *Oh, shit!*

He laughed. "Ease up, girl! What's wrong with you?"

"Sorry!" she squeaked.

He ran his thumbs up and down the length of her neck . . . the sides . . . the base, just where her collar met her skin. Characteristically, she felt the perspiration film creep across the top of her lip, felt the little droplets of sweat dot her forehead. She moaned softly, moving into his touch. She rolled her head in the direction that he massaged and kneaded her flesh, until the kinks slowly began to lessen. "That feels good," she sighed, on reflex. "You got the touch."

He pulled her back, so that the top of her head rested in his tight midsection. He held the top of her head and tilted it to one side, all the while kneading the muscles on the exposed side of her neck. "Haven't heard that in a while," he said.

So, he was probably just as horny as she was. And this probably wasn't helping either of them to keep their head. But she'd be damned if she was going to tell him to stop.

He tilted her head in the other direction, then massaged the flesh on the other side of her neck. Under the gentle pressure of his fingers, tensed muscles relaxed and flattened, releasing the pain. "You smell good," he said, a huskiness to his voice that was rather new to her. "What's that . . . lavender?"

"Umm-hmm," she groaned. "My own stuff. I make it at home."

The massage became a caress, moving from the sides of her neck to her throat. "Suits you," he said.

Chaney's eyes flew open. Her logical mind finally woke up, came out of the shadow of her horny flesh. She rolled her chair toward her desk, away from him. She whimpered as those delicious hands disappeared from her skin. "Umm," she said, then cleared her throat. "Maybe we should look at those pictures, huh?"

The figurative professional curtain descended between them. He took his seat again in the chair at her right and grabbed the mouse. He looked at her like nothing had just happened between them. He was the same polite Randy he'd always been. "Okay," he said.

Chaney glanced down at her watch. Poor Tony. She envisioned him with all four legs crossed, his bladder ready to explode. "Just a few, though," she said. "I've got to get home and let my dog out."

"I'll be quick," he promised.

Randy took the mouse, and instantly, thumbnails of photos appeared in succession across the screen, above numbers in the right corner of the photographs. Chaney could make out the tiny images in each photo. Randy's eyes scanned the screen. "Let's see . . ." he said.

He clicked on one photo, which became larger to reveal a young woman in a Nike T-shirt and long red Spandex shorts. She looked deadly serious as she handled a Spaulding rock. Her green eyes focused somewhere off in the distance, her curly ponytail mid-swish. Chaney remembered her from the pictures Randy had shown her weeks ago at the bar. "She's a beautiful kid," Chaney said, committing her face to memory.

Randy's smile was practically incandescent. "That's my Tai," he laughed.

"I want to see one of those of you clubbin'," Chaney laughed.

Randy moved the mouse across the photo array, squinting his eyes as he looked at the thumbnails. Suddenly, he gasped, then clicked. "Here's one."

The thumbnail exploded, and the image of Randy and Tai, in their party finery, appeared onscreen. Chaney's eyes darted from Tai—

whose sporty façade was now gone, replaced with full-faced makeup, a skimpy black lace-up halter top, and skin-tight chocolate leather pants—to Randy, who was decked out in all black . . . short-sleeved black dress tee that revealed the outline of his abs, to sleek black slacks. Perfect for April in Miami. Chaney nudged him. " 'Scuse me, *papi chulo,*" she teased. "Not bad, Temple, Class of '78."

He laughed shyly. "I thought I was going to be laughed out of that club in South Beach," he said. "Girl, you would've been surprised at how many other forty-six-year-old men were trying to hit on women my daughter's age."

Chaney studied his image again. "I bet none of them looked as good as you," she murmured, realizing just then that she'd said it out loud.

He ran an index finger along the length of her jawbone. At first, she jumped, startled. Then she closed her eyes and got into it, enjoying the feel of his skin against her skin. "I love you for saying that," he said. "Especially since you're a little tenderoni yourself."

Instantly, Devin came to mind . . . them on her steps in her house, and then with his boys in Georgetown, when she accused him of being the very same thing. She laughed loudly, more like squawked. Like lightning, the finger went away, and she could tell that he thought she was laughing at him. "I'm sorry," she blurted out.

He shrugged, darting right back into his professional shell again. "No biggie," he said.

She looked down at her watch: 7:45. "I have time for one more," she said, even though she really didn't.

He smiled again, and Chaney assumed all was right between them again. "Okay," he said. "One more."

He clicked on the last thumbnail in the bunch. All of a sudden, a photo of him popped open. He was standing in the foamy surf. Water caught rays of the sun and glistened on his bare brown skin. The only thing between him and nature was a pair of skimpy, shimmering black swim trunks. She got an eyeful of well-developed pecs, rippling abs, bulging biceps and triceps, and strong thighs. Mostly, though, she got an inviting full frontal view of the massive bulge lying to the left. In her head, she imagined all the damage he could do, the hours of untold fucking he could do . . . they could do . . .

She cleared her throat and turned to look at him, to see him looking at her with the crystallized clarity of his intent. "That's a hell of an advertisement," she confessed.

His gaze never wavered. "What are you doing tonight?" he asked.

"Umm . . ." she pointed over her shoulder " . . . I've got to go . . . you know . . ." *You stuttering asshole!*

He nodded. "The dog," he said.

She nodded. "Uh-huh."

"What about after that?"

She blinked. "After that?"

"Yeah, after that."

She thought. "I don't know."

"I want you to come over to my house."

Oh shit! "To do what? Work?"

He laughed, his voice deep and throaty. "If that's what you wanna call it."

Chaney looked around her all of a sudden, just then remembering where they were, and what his place was in the grand scheme of things that was Autodidact. After all, she was having enough problems on this project without adding fucking the key subject matter expert to the list. But she looked at that picture again. Had she been that focused on building her career that she hadn't realized that the last time she'd gotten any was Richard's angry, passionate breakup sex last year, before she and her broadened horizons left him and Syracuse for D.C.?

"Do you think this is wise?" she asked quietly.

His smile was lazy, seductive, and she could feel herself getting sucked in toward that dick that lay to the left. "No, it probably isn't," he said. "But I'm overdue for doing something that may be stupid but feels so good."

She shook her head. He was truly appealing to that side of her that said she should chuck responsibility and live a little. "Me, too," she sighed.

He leaned in until he was inches from her face. Her heart beat so loud it threatened to choke her. She offered up no resistance when he brushed his lips against hers. As if triggered by a switch, she felt the familiar thumping between her thighs. "Randy," she whispered.

He held her face in his hands and kissed her again, and she thought she'd die from sheer pleasure. "You gonna come over?" he asked.

She heard her answer in her head. *Yes, yes—fuck, yes!* Outside her head, though, all she heard was the annoying ringing of her desk phone. Guilt set in. It was the voice of God, or Lissa, or Al, intruding on the moment, punishing her for even thinking of fucking her client. She broke away from Randy, who was sitting opposite her, mid-pucker. "I better get this!" she breathed.

Randy took her hand and laced his fingers between hers. "They'll leave a message."

Chaney glanced at the green screen on the phone. *Nathalie Phillips,* along with her number, showed up. She wondered why Nathalie would be calling her at her office, and not on her cell phone. "I've got to get it!" she cried.

She snatched up the receiver. "Nathalie!" she gasped.

"Chaney, thank God!" Nathalie cried.

Lusty heart pounding became fear-filled heart pounding. "What?" Chaney demanded. "What happened?"

"Why aren't you answering your cell phone?" Nathalie asked.

Because I was about to hook up with a coworker. Chaney opened the bottom drawer of her desk, took out her purse, and dug for her Blackberry. Lo and behold, the little envelope, signaling that she had messages, appeared on the screen. "I didn't hear it ringing," she said. "What's going on? Are you okay?"

"The Fairfax County police called," Nathalie announced. "And your alarm company tried to reach you, then they called me as the alternate contact. The alarm is going off at your house!"

Chaney shot to her feet. "Oh my God!" she cried. "What did they say? Is someone trying to break in?"

"I don't know, Chaney," Nathalie said. "You better get home as fast as you can. I'd go, but I'm up in Baltimore with Craig. It'll take me just as much time as you to get there."

Then Chaney's heart lurched. "Oh, shit! Tony's in the house!"

"You better go!" Nathalie commanded.

Chaney hung up and took deep breaths, trying to collect herself. All types of horrible scenarios ran through her mind . . . her house was being burgled . . . her house was on fire . . . something happened to Tony, and now he was dead. Daisy'd be beside herself with grief.

Randy stood up, concerned. He held on to her hand. "What's the matter?" he asked.

"I gotta go," she insisted.

"You're always leaving me," he said, his smile lopsided. "If I were sensitive, I could take this personally."

Chaney took one last look at that shot of him in a swimsuit before she ejected his CD and shut the computer down. *Damn!* "It isn't you," she assured him. "The alarm is going off at my house. I gotta go check it out."

"You need me to come with you?" he asked.

She looked at him and smiled. *I love you for that.* She reached behind the door and grabbed her jacket. "You're so sweet," she said. "But the cops are on their way, so I'm good."

He stood there, looking so bereft, watching her as she walked out on him for the second time. Impulsively, she ran up to him, held his face in her hands, and kissed him squarely on that adorable mouth. "Rain check?"

He laughed. "Most definitely. You have my home number. Call me. Tell me how it all turns out."

She rushed toward the double glass doors. "I will!" she promised.

All through the metro ride to Alexandria, Chaney's mind went from worrying about her home and Tony, to reliving that kiss and that deliciously naughty invitation from Randy. She remembered learning about the concept of harmonic convergence in college . . . when a good thing happens in life, it is balanced out by an opposing bad thing, so as to keep the karmic balance of the universe intact. So, she thought, if the house were being robbed or worse, with Tony helpless inside, at least she would've had, for one moment, known something purely good with Randy Tyree. Not a fair trade-off, but close enough.

In exactly one hour, she was at the Huntington metro station, with her prime spot in the parking garage, safe from the torrential elements. She floored the accelerator in the Altima, skillfully maneuvering the slick, wet roads. She shaved five minutes off the drive that usually took her fifteen, pulling into the parking lot just as two male uniformed Fairfax County cops, wearing rain gear and oppressive crew cuts, were moving away from her intact town house. She sighed with relief.

Chaney parked in her spot, then got out into the rain that had now become an annoying drizzle, and approached them. One cop went around to the passenger side of the dark blue-and-white cruiser, the other approached her. "Ma'am, do you live here at 3702 Suffolk Court?" he asked.

This is where they ma'am me to death. She held her tongue. As progressive as Northern Virginia was, it was still the South. Black folk who mouthed off at cops had a nasty habit of disappearing down here. "Yes, that's my house," she admitted. "What happened?"

The cop came closer. Even with all his grown-up policeman's gear, he still looked like a child playing cops and robbers. The flesh on his unlined face was smooth and full. "Your alarm company called us after they couldn't reach you," he explained. "They said that something had tripped the sensor on your sliding glass door."

Chaney's eyes widened. "Someone's in the house?"

To her ultimate surprise, the cop smiled at her. So much for her paranoid fantasy of getting into the squad car and being driven into Black history. "No, ma'am," he said. "My partner and I scoured the perimeter of the house. We even jumped your fence in the back and inspected the sliding glass door. The only casualty was my partner's pants leg that got ripped on your fence. The home's intact. Whatever set it off must have done it from the inside."

"From the inside?" she asked, puzzled. "What on earth could've set it off from the . . ."

Then it hit her: *Tony!* Chaney went from worried about him to phenomenally pissed off with him in mere seconds.

"Do you have a pet inside, ma'am?" the baby cop asked. "A dog or a cat?"

Chaney looked toward the house, shaking her head. Tony! He caused her a heart attack for nothing . . . again. Much less deprived her of a night of potentially earth-shattering but possibly career-destroying sex. "Do I ever," she commented.

The baby cop laughed. "Sometimes, they touch the sensor and upset the connections," he said, his tone reassuring. "It happens more often than you think."

Just then, the partner with the ripped pants leg joined them. He looked sufficiently pissed and rather happy to be handing the baby cop a yellow copy of something. "I'm sorry, ma'am, but we're going to have to give you this summons for the false alarm," baby cop said, handing her what looked like a yellow carbon paper Post-It with the sticky back. "It could've been worse."

Chaney sighed. He was right. The house was standing. The dog was all right. She didn't fuck the client. She took the summons.

The officers headed toward the cruiser. Once at the car, baby cop tipped the brim of his hat. "Good night, ma'am," he said. "Don't forget to pay that summons."

"Thanks, officers!" she called after them.

They drove off, their tires splashing through the standing water on the asphalt.

Chaney fished her keys out of her purse and headed toward her front door. As she was working the front door, Tony's big yellow head popped up behind the gauzy window treatment. "Wuh!" he barked, scaring her half to death.

She screamed, dropping her keys on the concrete stoop. *If I hold this dog . . .*

As she bent, she became aware of Mrs. De'Ath staring at her through her gauzy window treatments, giving Chaney that puckered, tight-ass British look of disapproval that was her trademark. Chaney guessed Mrs. De'Ath was probably not surprised that the cops would be at the door of a black person. Chaney politely waved. Mrs. De'Ath turned away from the window. Chaney guessed that thicker window treatments made good neighbors.

Chaney worked the lock and entered the darkened hallway, which was illuminated only with the ghostly light from the TV's images. Instantly, the alarm bleated, and Tony jumped on her. "Wuh!" he barked happily. "Wuh! Wuh!"

"Okay, okay, okay!" Chaney cried, reaching for the light switch.

She lit up the hallway, shut the door, and locked it. Then she ran over to the alarm control panel and punched in the code. Immediately, the alarm went silent.

Tony ran the length of the hall, then ran back and jumped on her. He poked his nose into her crotch. He ran rings around her. God help her, she went from wanting to strangle him to laughing her head off, in spite of herself.

Chaney rubbed the scruff of his neck. He leaned into her hand and moaned low in his throat. He sounded kind of like she did when Randy was expertly massaging her neck and throat. She headed for the caged-off living room, and he followed, lingering near the scene of the crime: the glass sliding doors. Then she remembered: he'd been in the house for over twelve hours. Of course, he probably had to pee like a racehorse.

Chaney opened the blinds, then opened the doors, and let Tony out onto the deck. Quickly, he ran down the stairs to his spot across the yard, near the tool shed. He raised his left leg, and a stream of piss arced from his dangling pink penis. He had a look on his face like Tom Hanks in the classic scene at the urinal in *A League of Their Own* . . . orgasmic relief.

She found a ratty towel under the kitchen sink and met him on the deck. She bent and toweled his wet paws dry, so that he wouldn't track rain and mud into the house. His tail whipped around furiously. "Tony," she laughed, shaking her head.

As if in response, he slurped her chin. She giggled. "You probably just got a mouthful of Clinique," she said.

She finished with one paw, and obediently, he lifted the other and stood patiently on the remaining three legs as she toweled the last paw dry. So, something was sinking in. Somewhere in his skull, either from Daisy, or from instinct, or from his own doggie mother, he'd gotten some inkling of how to behave. "Tony, we're gonna have to come to an understanding," she said, and he stared at her, like he had command of the English language. "If you're gonna stay here with me while your mommy's away, we're gonna have to peacefully coexist."

The look on his face was curious, but vacant. Chaney shook her head at the hopelessness of her inability to communicate what she needed and wanted. To yet another man. This one, with four legs. So, she did the only thing she could do. She opened the door and let Tony inside.

The deejay was on fire! He would play cuts from Jay-Z's *Blueprint*, then just as Jigga'd turn the crowd into a frenzied mass of bodies gyrating on the floor, the deejay would seamlessly mix in Mary J., then her voice and beats would give way to that of Andre 3000 and Outkast . . . cuts off *Stankonia*. Devin was in heaven.

He'd never been the best dancer. Being tall and biracial were a twin curse, making him look goofy if he did the popular dances of the day. He'd mastered the shifting from foot to foot, rolling back the shoulders, and bouncing in place, what Snoop had made cool. Every once in a while, he'd throw his hands in the air, moving his hands through the air, then cross them across his chest in a nanosecond pose. To that day, no one looked at him like he was a nondancing freak.

Ayanna watched him move and eyed him appreciatively. Then she turned, with her back toward him, and he got a full view of her shaking that ass. That more than made up for the horrible start to the night. She backed into his midsection, and that ass was inches away from his crotch. In response to the engraved invitation, Devin rolled up on her, rubbing against that delicious ass, his arms outstretched as they moved to the thunderous rap. Here he was, after she tried to take the reins all night, he was the man after all . . . the man with a granite-hard dick pressed up against her ass.

She turned around to face him, and he laughed, taking her hands in his. They were soft, warm, and a little sweaty, but he didn't care. Just the anticipation of human contact with her of the sexual kind made him care about little else but being with her. So what if her personality was the equivalent of a klieg light in the face? The little head wasn't thinking about that.

Ayanna stood on her tippy, tippy toes and wrapped her arms around his neck. "You wanna leave?" she said, softly enough to be seductive but loudly enough to be heard over the music.

He caught his bottom lip under his top teeth. In his mind, he pictured all the different ways he could have his way with her. He nodded.

"Let's have a drink first," she said.

Again, he nodded. He was down for whatever it took to get her where he wanted her.

Under the riot of swirling lights and thunderous music, they held hands and made their way over to the island of tables in a dark alcove. A waitress came over in time, and they ordered drinks. He watched, getting all kinds of hot and bothered as she sipped her drink through a red straw. Clearly she was enjoying the fact that he could drill holes through the table with his dick.

Finally, she finished her drink and sat back in her chair. "Want another?" she asked, with a wink.

He smiled, shaking his head. What he wanted from her wasn't going to fit in a glass. She laughed. "Okay, okay. I'll put us both out of our misery." She stood up, smoothing the fabric of her slacks over that divine ass. "I'm going to the ladies' room. I'll be right back."

Devin watched her go, and he wondered what he was doing, being led around by his dick, about to fuck this girl that he would have to spend the next few weeks blowing off, because they had absolutely nothing in common other than the fact that she had a vagina, and he wanted to fill it. But that old urge . . .

As he nursed his Heinie, he noticed through the corner of his eye that another girl had approached Ayanna's seat. "Is anybody sitting here?" she yelled over the music.

"Yeah, but we're leaving!" he yelled back.

She slid into the chair and bobbed her head to the music. She flashed him a smile, and he returned it.

Devin was finishing his beer when Ayanna appeared, her face looking like a made-up thundercloud. He stood up. Secretly, though, he wondered why she was so pissed off. "Hey," he called. "Ready?"

But Ayanna didn't even acknowledge his existence. She tapped the girl on the shoulder. "Excuse me," she said. "This is my chair."

The girl looked Ayanna up and down, then tilted her head in Devin's direction. "Your man said y'all was leaving," the girl said.

"We haven't left yet," Ayanna declared. "Obviously."

The girl rolled her eyes. "Your man said it was cool," she insisted.

"It's definitely not cool," Ayanna declared, doing the cobra thing with her neck. "Can you please move?"

Devin stared in disbelief at the scene unfolding before him. This was new.

The girl turned in her purloined chair to face Ayanna. "You want me to move?" she asked. "Then move me, bitch!"

To which Ayanna grabbed the girl by her shoulders, lifted her from the chair, and pushed her against the padded wall. The girl had a look of unvarnished astonishment on her face. "Okay, you got your wish," Ayanna declared.

"Ayanna!" Devin shouted. "What are you doing?"

"She called me a bitch," Ayanna explained.

Neither of them saw the next thing coming. The girl had balled her hand up into a fist and clocked Ayanna right in the face. Ayanna didn't even flinch, staring at the girl with rapt attention. "That's all you're packing, sistah?" she yelled.

The girl had a shocked look on her face, which was probably

matched only by Devin's. She also seemed to sense that Ayanna was about to beat that weave out of her head. Some arcane message flooded Devin's brain, telling him that he should intervene. He bounded over the table and grabbed Ayanna's hand, just as she was about to crunch it into the girl's face. "Ayanna!" he cried.

"Let me go!" she screamed at Devin.

Just then, two gorillas in suits equipped with body mikes descended into the fracas. They didn't say anything. They didn't need to. It wasn't like they didn't know what was going on. Next thing Devin knew, they were being pushed out of the club and onto the sidewalk. "Fuck you!" Ayanna screamed after the bouncers.

Devin stared at the people who were standing on the sidewalk, waiting to go in. As if they were all on the same page, the crowd of rejects waiting in line broke into thunderous applause, cheers, and whistles. He could feel the heat travel up to his face. He only prayed that it was dark enough on U Street so that nobody else could see how ashamed he was.

Then Ayanna turned on him. "Thanks for all the help," she spat.

Devin exploded. "'Scuse me for not helping you beat the shit out of someone, because she took a seat you didn't need 'cause you were leaving!" he shot back.

"It was the principle," she insisted. "She called me a bitch!"

"After you menaced her for taking a chair," he reminded her. "A chair!"

"She disrespected me, and you deprived me of getting mine!"

So, I'm the problem. Devin stared at her, shaking his head. She was nuts. He looked down. Fear and loathing had turned his wood into a limp sapling. "I'm outta here," he declared. "Come if you want to."

He turned on his heel and began walking the block and a half to the car. He heard her heels clicking on the concrete behind him. Once in the car, they rode in silence. He mashed his foot on the gas, eating up D.C. real estate in his quest to get her home and gone. At last, he saw the front façade of her fucked-up, of-the-people tenement and parked the ride in front. He didn't even look at her. "I'll walk you to the door," he said.

She sucked her teeth, opened her own door, and jumped down onto the wet sidewalk. As promised, he got out, came around, and walked her the short distance to the door. She regarded him with downcast hazel eyes. "So, you're not coming up," she concluded.

Not even if you had Halle Berry chained up inside, holding the Oscar. Aloud, though, he said, "Naw, I think I'm gonna call it a night."

"So, you're just gonna pussy out," she said.

He couldn't believe her mouth. *While we're being honest . . .* "Yeah, Ayanna, I guess I'm gonna," he said. "I'm afraid your dick may be bigger than mine."

She looked at him, like *oh no, you didn't.* "Well, this was a huge waste of time," she declared.

"At least we agree on something," he said.

She raked him with her gaze, sucking her teeth. He got a parting view of that ass that he'd found so fascinating as she went inside, then worked the lock of the inside door, then entered the lobby. She stared at him briefly through the glass reinforced with metal.

Devin headed toward the car, got inside, and hit the gas. He never looked back. Not even once.

After the rain let up, Chaney dressed Tony up in his harness and took him for a walk on his retractable leash. She was amazed at how he went crazy when it was time to take a walk, how he associated the sliding door with going potty and the front door with going for a walk.

They strolled down the wet sidewalks, Tony with his nose to the ground, sniffing all of the new scents of Virginia up his monstrous nose. Strangely, he knew to walk to the left of her, until she let the leash extend, and he'd walk ahead of her, sniffing and stopping to spray a stream of piss on a stray bush or two. Marking his territory.

About a half-hour later, they'd walked the main street that split the development down the middle and were headed back when Chaney saw Hershey. She was gamboling on a retractable leash held by a tall teenager in black, with his black hoodie pulled up to hide his face, à la Kenny from *South Park*. Chaney shuddered, then later realized it was Jon, the De'Ath's grandson. *Death Walks a Dog.*

Hershey looked at Tony, and he looked at her, the ears on their massive Labrador heads perked up. Her hazel eyes met his brown, and she made a whimpering sound. He squared his shoulders and said, "Wuh!" Chaney watched in awe. Tony was, in his unique doggie way, stepping to Hershey, and she appeared more than receptive.

Tony dragged Chaney over to Hershey and Jon. Jon turned his

head, so that Chaney could now see his unshaven face. There was a surprised look in his vacant eyes. "Oh, hey," he said, tone flat.

His blank face, his interaction without affect. Chaney put two and two together: *weed smoker.* "Hi," she said. "How are you?"

"Rock on," he said.

Chaney stared at him. *Okay . . .*

She turned her attentions to Tony and Hershey. The two dogs nuzzled each other, licking at each other's faces, pink tongues searching out and dueling. Chaney laughed, amazed. Tony was getting more action than she was. "Oh, shit, they're frenchin', man!" Jon laughed.

"Hershey, you ho!" Chaney giggled.

Tony moved on to her hindquarters and proceeded to sniff Hershey's behind. She looked back, and Chaney could've sworn she saw a smile on her brown face. Chaney shook her head. If only courtship of the human variety could be so honest and devoid of all the head games.

She decided, though, that it was time to break up the canine love fest unfolding before them. Jon looked like this was as close as he got to having sex. "Well, good night," she said.

Tony's claws practically dragged on the asphalt as Chaney led him away from Hershey. Hershey herself looked like Maria saying goodbye to her own Tony, like from *West Side Story.* "Come on, boy," she said quietly, outside of Jon's earshot. "She ain't nothing but trouble."

Back at the house, Chaney opened her mail while eating a bowl of soup. She paused briefly, spoon halfway to her mouth, to reflect on her situation. *Soup for one.* "Girl, you're such a spinster cliché," she sighed.

She checked her messages. There was one . . . from Daisy. "Chaney, *theeth eeth* your *theethster, Daithee,*" she said from the digital mailbox, affecting a bastardized Castilian Spanish accent. "We *juthst* left *Barthelona* and are headed for *Authstria,* or as they *thay,* Oesterreich."

Chaney howled with laughter, nearly spitting her soup across the room. Boy, a change of scenery and some amazing dick could sure improve a disposition. Not that she would know . . .

On the message, Daisy became herself again. "Okay, I'll stop," she giggled. "I just sent you and Tony a postcard. I sent our evil, judgmental sister one, too. I love you both. Kiss my baby dog for me."

Chaney looked down at Tony, who sat on his haunches, staring up at her. He sure did look kissable. He would have to settle, though, for a tiny pat on the bony knot at the top of his head.

She took a shower, letting the water beat down on her painful neck. Alas, the showerhead was no substitute for Randy's hands. She had to settle for running her soapy hands over her skin, her throat . . . her breasts . . . between her thighs . . . waiting for the explosive feeling to happen. Alas, it didn't, and she began to prune in the water.

Minutes later, shea buttered and berobed in flannel, Chaney sat at her computer, checking her e-mail. She opened one titled: Sorry, Auntie! It was from D, e-mail address: DoubleD. "Sorry I didn't return your message," Chaney read aloud. "I was busy 'pushing up on a cutie.' This one's serious. I want you to meet her."

Chaney laughed. "My nephew, the pimp," she said.

D was his father's son, insanely responsible on the job, but spending his free time in the quest to get as much punany as possible in one lifetime. Despite what D said, Chaney doubted that the shelf life of this new babe was going to rival that of a Twinkie. Chaney hit the Delete key.

She heard jingling of metal and looked over her shoulder to see Tony skulking into the room. Chaney wondered if it was her imagination, or if he was looking repentant for having scared her to death earlier that night. "You booty hound," she laughed. "You got Hershey all twisted up."

Tony came closer, set his head in her lap, and looked up at her with such innocence that it immediately sucked her in. *This is new and different* . . . Chaney scratched the top of his head. Could it be that he was finally warming to her? She channeled her inner Sally Field. "You like me," she laughed. "You really, really like me."

Tony's tail thumped the carpet so hard it echoed throughout the room. "Guess that's yes," Chaney said.

Just then, she heard a digital tone coming from the computer and looked up. A tiny screen had appeared on her monitor, and someone named D-Riddim sent her an instant message that read: "Hey. You're still up!"

It took a second for it to register. Then she remembered who it was: Devin!

She began to type:

SYRAQQ: Hey, little cuz. Isn't it past your bedtime? ☺
D-Riddim: You got jokes.

SYRAQQ: u ok?
D-Riddim: Just had the worst date.
SYRAQQ: That bad?
D-Riddim: Well, I can cross getting in a bar fight off the list of things to do b4 I die.

Damn! She wondered who these chicks were that he was dating. But then again, with everything he was working with—a cute, smart, single doctor—he must've been chickenhead catnip.

SYRAQQ: Yeah, cuz, that's bad.
D-Riddim: What do women want, cousin?

Chaney chuckled. *God, that date must've really fucked with his head.* For Devin's sake, she pondered the question.

SYRAQQ: Can't speak for all women, Devin. I know what I like.
D-Riddim: What?
SYRAQQ: I won't lie. Physical attraction. Especially height. Tall sister like me's got a height requirement. But I like someone I can talk to, someone who's kind and considerate.

With a big dick, she thought, but didn't think it prudent to share that little tidbit.

D-Riddim: So u r one of those rare women who doesn't want a thug.
SYRAQQ: Don't believe the hype. That shit's for MC Lyte raps. Sure u r not part of the problem, cousin?
D-Riddim: I admit. I'm a little spoiled. Moms is Korean. Men are special in her culture. She used to tell me stories about how she and her sisters would give up their beds for her brothers to sleep in. The men would eat meals first too before the women. She treated me like a prince.

Chaney knew right off that there was no way she could ever live in Korea. But in retrospect, though, she did like the combination that Korean and Black produced. He had a different look from your aver-age brothah, but at the same time, he carried himself with the confidence that she thought made black men so attractive. The best description of it that she could think of was "sensitive flava." He made the combination work.

SYRAQQ: What about your dad?
D-Riddim: Dad was aggressively the reverse of her. The Marine couldn't have his boy going soft. He still hasn't gotten over me being a vet. Not manly enough.
SYRAQQ: r u happy?
D-Riddim: When Moms and Dad separated, she moved me away, all the way to Seattle. I was your typical angry teenager. My stepdad and his animals saved me from screwing up my life, from becoming a cliché.
SYRAQQ: A cliché of what?
D-Riddim: You know, the confused, messed up biracial kid.
SYRAQQ: So, that's a yes. That you're happy.
D-Riddim: LOL. Yes, that's a yes.
SYRAQQ: So, u r a balanced guy who's happy in his career. Doesn't sound like there's anything wrong w/u. ☺
D-Riddim: LOL. u r good 4 my ego.
SYRAQQ: Don't worry about the dating thing. It'll get better. When I was your age, men were offering me sex all the time.
D-Riddim: u say that like u r, like, Jurassic. u r hot.

Chaney laughed, actually feeling herself blush. She'd never been the hot one, always the smart one. It was her turn for a much-needed ego stroke. Now, if only he wasn't a child and a distant relative, then the compliment would've meant more.

SYRAQQ: & u r sweet, lil cuz.
D-Riddim: Well, just wanted to say hey. Not gonna keep u. Thanks 4 the advice. U made me feel so much better.
SYRAQQ: wat r cousins 4? Have a good night.
D-Riddim: u 2. Pet Tony 4 me.
SYRAQQ: Will do.

The digital tone sounded again, then the line "D-Riddim has signed off," with the time, appeared in the tiny screen.

Chaney logged off and shut down the computer. She looked down at Tony, whose head remained comfortably resting on her thigh. "Cousin Devin's having women trouble," she said, then laughed. "You had a better night with Hershey."

Tony's tail loudly thumped the floor.

"Come on," she said. "Let's go to sleep."

That night, the first since he'd arrived, Tony slept on the floor, at the foot of her bed. She glanced down at him as he moaned and whined in his sleep. At least she could say that she had one man in her bedroom. *The most satisfying relationship I've ever had with a man.*

Chaney laughed, turned over, and tried to defy the Fluexa by willing sleep to come . . .

Six

"I should spank you," he said over the phone.

Shocked, Chaney looked up from her monitor. " 'Scuse me?"

"You heard me," Randy said. "You were supposed to call me to let me know how things turned out at your house. When you didn't come in to the office today, I was worried."

Chaney tried to come up with something witty to say, but she heard plaintive whining and looked down at Tony. He lay next to her feet, with his paws covering both his ears. All day, he'd been fitful, pacing back and forth, but the whining and rubbing of his paws against his ears was a new development. "Everything's okay," she assured him. "The dog set the alarm off somehow. I'm working at home today, because he's acting really strange. I wanted to be here to watch him."

"You and that dog," he said, sounding like someone who was unequivocally not a dog person. "You must love him."

Chaney watched as Tony uncomfortably shifted positions. *Do I?* "I love my sister more," she declared. "If something happened to him, she would be so hurt. I wouldn't be able to forgive myself."

"You know Doug and Callie are circling the wagons," he announced.

"My stock is plummeting with those two," Chaney sighed. "I may have to end up having to blow Doug to bring him around to my way of thinking!"

The tone of the conversation shifted so suddenly that Chaney imagined she felt the air pressure in the room drop. For a second, she wondered if she'd gone too far with her little attempt at humor. "Umm . . . are you still there?" she asked tentatively.

"Yeah," he said in a voice she didn't even recognize. It sounded thick . . . dripping with sexual tension. "Just a second."

She heard him put the receiver down, then seconds later, heard the door close in the background. "Hey," he said when he returned, in that same seductive voice. "Can I ask you a question?"

"Sure," she said.

"Tell me what you're wearing."

Huh? Chaney looked down at her favorite pink J. Lo velour sweats that rode low on her hips that were less fleshy, courtesy of one positive side effect of Fluexa: weight loss. "Why are you asking?"

"I'm trying to form a mental picture of you on your knees, blowing Doug," he laughed softly. "Only it's not Doug in the picture. It's me."

Oh my God, what have I done? "I was just kidding!" she insisted.

"That doesn't make my dick any softer right now," he declared.

Oh shit! Chaney could just picture him, touching his fly in his closed-up office, all the while gazing at the commuters gathering on the Twinbrook metro platform. "I didn't mean . . ."

"Too late. Why don't you tell me what you like."

"What, sexually?"

"Uh-huh."

"You first."

"I'll ask, and you can tell me yes or no. Okay?"

No, this is not okay! She tried to imagine what Leah Braxton would think, looking down from heaven on her baby talking dirty on the phone with a man she only remotely knew. But there was that side of her, talking her into mischief, urging her to play along, assuring her that if it got hairy, that she could stop. She hesitated. "Okay."

"If I was to eat your pussy, would you like that? Like, suck your clit and fuck you with my tongue, would you like that?"

Her insides shuddered. "I think I'd like that," she croaked.

"What else would you like me to do to you?" he asked.

She said the first thing that came to mind, the one thing she actually missed about making love. "I love to have my titties sucked," she said, shocking even herself.

He laughed, a soft laugh that rumbled over the phone. "My dick is so hard right now," he whispered. "Would you like it if I put it in your mouth? Would you suck it until I came all over your face?"

Okay! That was it. The line had officially been crossed. "You know, Randy, stop. I'm not really comfortable with this," she declared.

"Why?" he asked. "It's just phone sex. Not the real thing."

It sure felt like the real thing. She was hot, and sweating, and aroused like it was the real thing. "Despite what you and Bill Clinton might think, sex is sex," she explained, but at the same time, she did feel like the world's biggest prude. "Call me old-fashioned, but we should probably go on a real date first before I start acting like *Girl 6*, don't you think?"

Randy just laughed. "Where do you want me to take you?"

Something inside her told her she was out of her very square element. But love-starved as she was, she let her common sense get the better of her. "Take me to a club," she said. "And wear that suit you wore in Miami."

"I think I know just the place."

But Chaney didn't hear him. She looked away from the monitor and down at Tony. He was scratching his left ear furiously, howling so painfully that Chaney's heart squeezed. "Oh, boy!" she cried. "What's the matter?"

Tony shot up and started rubbing his ear against her hand, whimpering as he pressed his head in her hand with the full strength of his powerful neck muscles. "What's wrong, baby?"

She peeled back his floppy yellow ear and shuddered. The flesh was reddened and swollen almost shut. Streaks of blood oozed from scratch marks that ran along the floppy part of his ear. "Tony," she gasped.

He whined and pressed his ear into her hand. Whining became howling at her touch. In the face of his extreme agony, all else was secondary. "I gotta go," she said to Randy on the other end of the phone.

Randy sighed impatiently. "I know," he declared. "The dog."

"Make the arrangements for the club," she said. "I'll come; I promise."

"You will, if I have my way," he said.

Chaney hung up the phone, too worried about Tony to be impressed by Randy's promissory play on words. This was fast becoming a ritual. "Come, Tony," she called, heading for the stairs. "We're going to Cousin Devin's."

Tony eagerly followed behind her, his heavy steps echoing on the stairs as he ran down them and toward the front door.

Tony lay in the front passenger seat well, close to Chaney's feet, as she sped through the Route 1 afternoon traffic toward Rosslyn. Her heart pounded in her chest. She looked down at him periodically. Forever the trouper, he seemed to swallow his pain, pressing his paw over his left ear. "Hang on, Tony," she pleaded. "We're almost there!"

Once they got to the hospital, all Chaney had to do was show Maria that ear, and immediately, Maria ushered them into the usual examining room, number four. Chaney sat on the bench and immediately began rubbing Tony's ear. He pressed his head further into her palm with such power that her biceps and triceps began to ache. She bent her head, leaning in close to his good ear. "It's okay, pup," she quietly assured him. "You're gonna be okay now."

The door opened just then, and Devin entered. Chaney sighed, relieved. "Oh, thank God!"

He smiled, a smile meant to soothe, as he gave her a quick once-over. "Look at you, all J. Lo'ed out," he said. "This is you outside of work?"

Tony leapt up and trotted over to him. He pressed his ear into Devin's thigh and whimpered. The message was clear. "Hey, Tone," Devin said, then slipped him a doggie treat.

Chaney tried to contain her innate cynicism as she looked at the spectacle. Even supposedly in pain, Tony still had enough of an appetite to nearly crunch off one of Devin's fingers in the quest for the treat. While Tony munched, crumbs spilling out the sides of his mouth, Devin lifted the flap of the ear. Where Chaney had recoiled, he dispassionately assessed the situation. "Hmm," he said, then looked up at her. "I'm sure he let you know this doesn't feel good."

Understatement! "He's been whining all day, practically," Chaney confirmed.

Devin continued his examination, tilting Tony's head to get better perspective on the damage. "How'd you notice it?"

"He hasn't been himself all day," Chaney explained. "That's why I worked from home. About an hour ago, he started holding his paw to his ear and whining. That's when I brought him here."

He continued to study the problem; surprisingly, Tony let him. "What were you doing at the time?"

Chaney winced. *See, this is God punishing you for your filthy mouth, telling that man to suck your titties and put his dick in your mouth!* She squirmed in her seat, as she wondered if he would judge her, or if he would find this whole situation as funny as she would've found it, if she hadn't been totally mortified. "Umm . . ." she began, " . . . I think I was having phone sex."

He immediately looked up at her. No disapproval in his smooth cocoa face, just extreme surprise. "Okay," he said, drawing out each syllable in the word; then he smiled. "Well, if you're not sure that's what you were doing, then it must not have been that good, huh?"

Whew! She laughed. "Hey, at least I didn't get in a bar fight," she fired back.

It was his turn to grimace. He rolled those perfect, almond-shaped eyes. "Point taken," he said.

Chaney watched intently as Devin gloved up, then examined Tony's ear with the otoscope. Tony squirmed, and whined, and twisted in his grasp. Chaney watched, on edge. "Is he gonna be okay?"

He continued the task with laser beam focus. "Sure," he said. "Animals know when you're trying to help. Plus, dogs with this type of ear tend to get infections and mites. At his age, he's probably had more than his share."

Just then, Tony let out a piercing yelp, and Chaney's heart leapt. Tears welled up in her eyes at the thought of him in pain. She clutched a fistful of her hoodie in the hand over her chest, just to have something to do. "Now that probably *did* hurt," Devin said, then gently stroked Tony's head. "I'm sorry, boy. I didn't mean it."

Finally, Devin finished, tossing his gloves and tip of the otoscope in the trash. Tony scurried away, hiding in the relative safety that the space under the examining table provided. "So?" Chaney asked.

"He's definitely got a virulent ear infection," Devin decreed. "It's most likely from a combination of wax buildup, from him scratching at his ear, and, I'm swagging this, a food allergy."

Confusion made her brows knit at the bridge of her nose. "Swagging?"

He hit his head, like he could've had a V-8. "SWAG," he said. "Scientific Wise Ass Guess."

Could I feel like a bigger idiot? "Oh," she said. "But what makes you think he may have a food allergy?"

He shrugged. "Well, he's scratching his ears. I've noticed him licking his paws and his butt every time I've seen him, either here or at your house."

Chaney looked down at Tony cowering under the table. *Poor dog!* "What are we gonna do?" she asked.

Devin took up residence behind the computer on the counter and began typing furiously. "I'm gonna give you some antibiotics," he said. *Type . . . type . . . type . . .* "Give them to Tony twice a day until they're gone. I'm also gonna give you some Rimadyl for his pain. It's an NSAID for animals."

She looked down at Tony, still cowering under the table. He looked like he'd been traumatized enough. "Please tell me I'm not gonna have to shove these horse-sized pills down his throat."

He shook his head. "Nah, they're liver-flavored tablets. He'll think they're snacks."

"And about this food allergy?"

Type . . . type . . . type . . . "I'm gonna change his food to a different formulation. He needs something with either fish or lamb. We sell the Waltham food here. They're really good for managing pets' dietary issues. Later on, we can do a blood test to see what exactly Tony's allergic to."

Probably more expensive than the high-end supermarket food she'd been giving him, but one look in Tony's scared brown eyes, and she could practically feel her wallet opening up on its own. "Whatever he needs," she sighed.

He rubbed his large hands together. "Okay," he said with finality, looking up from the computer. "Maria'll have that waiting for you at the front desk when you're ready to go."

Chaney looked up at him. His generosity and open heart made him even more adorable. "Thank you, Devin," she said. "Yet again. Tony must be the patient from hell, huh?"

He laughed as he crossed the room with his leggy stride and plopped down next to her on the bench. He stretched those long legs out and crossed them at the ankles. "Not even close," he assured her.

Suddenly, he looked cuter to her. He must've been due for a haircut, because she could see some texture to the hair that crowned his head. She actually noticed a dimple in his right cheek when he flashed that brilliant, near-perfect smile at her. At the V of his scrubs, she could make out a triangle of curly hair. Suddenly self-conscious, she looked away. *Are you nutting over this man-child? Minutes after your slutty phone performance?*

It was like he'd read her mind. "So who's this man you were talking dirty to on the phone, cousin?" he teasingly demanded.

She cringed, holding her red face in her hands. It was time to come clean. "This guy, Randy," she moaned.

The teasing tone ratcheted up a notch. "And how do we know Randy?"

"*We* work with Randy."

"Is that smart?"

He couldn't imagine how many times she'd asked herself that very same question. *Deflect, deflect.* "I can't believe I'm being interrogated by Doogie Howser, D.V.M.!" she laughed.

"I'm old enough to know, like my dad used to say, you shouldn't dip your nib in company ink," he declared.

"Hey, there is no nib dipping, thank you," she said. "Just an intense flirtation. He feeds my affection monkey. You're old enough to know what that's like, aren't you?"

"Yeah, I think we covered that yesterday in kindergarten," he laughed.

Just then, Tony tentatively eased out from underneath the table, inched closer to her, then finally rested his head in her lap. She gently stroked his head, and his tail loudly thumped the cold, hard floor. She chuckled. "Plus, any nib dipping is always thwarted by our little blocker here."

"I'd trust Tony," he said. "Dogs have good instincts."

"So, when did you start dating Laila Ali?"

Devin playfully nudged her. "Hurt yourself changing the subject?"

"About as much as you hurt yourself avoiding mine."

Devin threw his head back and laughed. Chaney loved the sound of his laughter; he sounded like a happy, joy-filled kid. "'Laila's' one of my brother's law clerks," he declared.

"Now who's dipping their nib?"

"Anyhu," he said pointedly, "I actually wanted to date the other clerk, but this one—Ayanna—she asked me out, and I wasn't doing anything. Cliff Notes, we're in the club, and this girl takes her seat. Ayanna asks her to move, the girl drops the B-bomb, and next thing I know, the girl cold-cocks Ayanna in the face! I was like, this is what women are into now—throwing down like the fellas?"

"Not all sistahs," she assured him. "So what's the other clerk like?"

The almond eyes lit up as he looked off into space. "Liz," he sighed, shaking his head, like *damn!* "She's classy, and fine, and sweet, and smart. She could be the Future Ex-Mrs. Devin Rhym, if she plays her cards right."

Chaney laughed at the wit. "How could she not leap at that?"

"You know, like father, like son."

"So what's the puzzle? Ask the clerk out."

"I did," he insisted. "But she had a boyfriend. Then they broke up and now she's . . ." air quotes ". . . 'healing.'"

"'Healing,'" she scoffed. "That's code for 'It's gonna be a little harder for you to get in there, but if you make the extra effort, it'll be worth it.' You can't be deterred by 'healing.' "

Devin slipped an arm around Chaney's shoulders and squeezed her close. She felt strong, well-developed pecs and traps pressing against her body. She looked up at him in surprise. *What's this about?* "Oh, cousin," he laughed. "I need to come to you when I'm having woman trouble."

"Yeah, I'm giving love advice," she murmured. "I just had phone sex with a guy I work with. Without dinner and a movie, even!"

"Well, I don't know about a movie, but I want you to have dinner with me and Pops," he said. "Next Tuesday. I'm gonna cook and everything."

She felt warm inside. "That's so sweet," she said. "Do you need me to bring anything? You know, Bahamians say that you don't go to a dinner invitation . . ." she affected her own bastardized version of a Bahamian accent ". . . 'swingin' ya hands.' Shall I bring some Pepto Bismol?"

He unfolded himself and got up; she followed suit, as did Tony. "Cute," he laughed. "Just bring yourself." He ran a hand over Tony's head. "And bring my man here, too. He can keep my dad's dog busy. His name's Sadat."

Chaney looked down at Tony. "You want to have dinner at Cousin Devin's?" she cooed, and Tony's tail whipped around, slicing the air and dropping fine yellow hairs on the ground.

"I think that's yes," Devin laughed.

She clipped on Tony's leash. "We better go," she said. "I got tons of work left to do at home."

"You should make your creams for a living," he suggested. "Didier and Maria raided the basket you made me. And my friend, Jamal. Mali. You met him the other day, remember?"

"Was that the poor brothah who was so besotted with Dani?" she laughed. "I hope you set him straight. No pun intended."

"No, that was Ryan, and yes, I had to break the poor boy's heart. Mali's the doctor, the one in the scrubs."

She headed for the door. "I'm taking orders, so let me know what they need, and I'll make it for them."

"I'll do that," he promised.

She patted his arm. That was as much affection as she trusted herself to give him. "Thanks again, Devin," she said. "I can't tell you how much I really appreciate this."

In response, he encircled her with his arms, pulling her close. Every muscle in her body tensed. "You're my girl, Chaney," he laughed, and she felt his voice vibrate from his chest to hers.

She laughed softly, enjoying the feel of him molded against her. Innocently enough, his hands brushed the small of her back, where her sweats hung low. She didn't know what he was feeling, but this hug, which she assumed was meant to be fraternal, was wreaking havoc with every cell in her body. He felt so hard and warm against her. Her face fit in the hollow of his throat, and she inhaled the subtle scent of his spicy cologne.

Inevitably, she did the comparative study. Randy's embrace the other day was raw, overtly sexual, pure heat. Devin's, on the other hand, was familiar, and warm, like home. That mental experience, coupled with having his obviously hard body complementing her soft curves, though, had the same effect . . . the perspiration pooling above her upper lip, the goose bumps running down her spine, the subtle stirring in her sweats. *What the hell is wrong with you, girl?*

Chaney pried herself away, and, aggressively avoiding his eyes, worked the doorknob to the exam room door. After what seemed like forever, she threw open the door. "See you, cousin," she said, heading straight down the hall toward the front desk.

"Hey, Tuesday at 6:00," he called cheerily after her. "Don't forget—Maria's got the address, Tony's food, and Rimadyl!"

She waved, not looking back. "Okay!" she returned.

As she turned the corner, she snuck a peek back down the hall. He was staring after her, his smile wide and white. Just then, she admitted to herself that yes, she was truly conflicted.

Devin stood in the middle of KL's kitchen and ran through his mental checklist. Salad was in the fridge. Dessert—Kim-Chin's famous Devil's food cake—was under glass on the far counter. Rice in the electric rice cooker had been done for about an hour. Old and new *kimchi* were in respective airtight containers in the fridge. The *burkoki*, the Korean beef dish that Kim-Chin had taught him to make, sat covered in a skillet on the stove.

He moved over to the kitchen door and stared through the glass panes at the red-tinted deck. His father had set the table with the good dishes, yellow linen napkins, and bamboo chopsticks. He'd also strategically placed lit tiki torches to complement the light that the naked bulb against the house brought forth. Devin hadn't seen KL this excited in a very long time. He was actually making an effort for a woman he wasn't trying to get with.

Speaking of KL, he entered the kitchen with a bottle of wine in his hand. He was wearing his good woolen argyle vest, ivory oxford shirt, and khaki chinos. He'd brushed back his salt-and-pepper hair, making it look less than Don King's. He'd suspended his reading glasses on a gold chain. Devin looked his father up and down. *This is new.* Now that he was retired, KL hardly broke out the trendy threads.

The ever-faithful Sadat trailed behind him. Sadat looked some days like he was feeling every minute of his ten years on the earth. His spaniel face was actually graying around his brown dapples. But he came up to Devin and pressed in against his legs. "Hey, boy," Devin said, distracted as he ran his mental checklist again.

He focused on the bottle in KL's hands. He snapped his fingers. "Wine!" he exclaimed, scaring Sadat, who jumped.

"I found this downstairs," KL said.

"It needs to chill," Devin insisted.

It was KL's turn to look *him* up and down. "No, son, *you* need to chill," he declared, mocking the slang word with a rolling of his eyes. "Is it just us, or are your brothers gonna grace us with their presence?"

He'd called Chauncey and Eric, but they didn't seem too eager to spend time with their father. "Just us," he said. "Jeffrey's got a play at school that Chauncey and Renee are going to, and Eric said he was busy."

KL made a face, then positioned his reading glasses on his hawkish nose and studied the wine label. "Polishing the stick in his ass, no doubt," he declared.

Briefly, Devin marveled at how they could be brothers and all be so radically different. "I don't know about that boy," KL said, shaking his head. "His mother Daphne, is such a beautiful, free naked spirit."

Ewww! Devin held up a hand. "Yo, Pops, T.M.I.," he cried. "Don't want to hear about your second wife's naked spirit, okay?"

KL put the wine in the freezer. "Now who's a tight-ass, son?" he asked.

Silly me, only wanting to imagine you with my mother.

KL got food from the cupboard and proceeded to feed Sadat. "So, what's Chaney like?" he asked.

What's Chaney like? She was like comfort, and friendship, and loyalty, and intelligence, big-hearted kindness, and sometimes, introspective self-doubt. He doubted, though, that a warrior like his father would understand a woman in the abstract. So, he went for the concrete. "She's hot," he confessed. "She's tall, working the T&A. She's very New York."

"I'm not surprised," KL said. "Those Braxton women are easy on the eye. That Anna Lisa was a stunner. I think that's why Norm lost his mind. He was so young, he didn't know what to do with this beautiful, smart girl who loved him with all his fatal flaws. Male inadequacy is a dangerous thing, Devin."

Again, Devin looked his father up and down. *Speaking from experience?* Devin remembered all the times KL had made his mother feel so small, her punishment for her only crime—loving him and wanting to make his life easier.

"So I'm told, Dad," Devin commented.

"Well, this calls for some wine," KL said. "I'll go see if we have any downstairs."

Devin stared at his father. *Are you kidding?* "Dad, you just brought some wine up," he said. "You just put it in the freezer. Remember?"

KL had a blank look on his face. Then it filled up like an angry thundercloud. The quickness of it stunned Devin. "Of course I remember, Devin," KL finally snapped. "Don't be obtuse."

Devin recoiled. This was his father at his most unpleasant. The signs were all too familiar.

Mercifully, the doorbell rang right then, sparing him from experiencing the full brunt of KL's fury. Sadat raised his head from his aluminum bowl and barked low in his hairy throat. The anticipation of seeing Chaney counterbalanced the feelings his father produced in him just then. "That's her," he said.

He headed through the kitchen to the front door. Sadat followed closely behind. Devin cocked one eye and looked through the peephole. Through the fish-eye view, he saw them: Chaney in a gray pantsuit and black pumps—no J. Lo sweats this time. She was holding Tony on his red retractable leash. God help him, his heart began to palpitate furiously. *What's that about?*

Devin opened the front door and smiled at her from behind the glass of the outside door. She smiled, lowering her head to look at him from behind the dark lenses of her sunglasses. He threw open the outside door. "Hey!" he greeted her. "You made it."

She crossed the threshold and stepped past him and inside. "Yeah," she said.

Devin closed the door behind her and watched her out of the corner of his eye as she looked around the anteroom. He wondered what she thought but dropped that. This was KL's castle, not his. Instead, he ran a hand over Sadat's flat head. "This is Sadat," he announced.

Chaney bent and touched the dog's head, too. "Hi, Sadat," she said, her tone a few decibels higher than normal. "Sadat, this is Tony."

Sadat and Tony sized each other up and appeared to judge each other mutually benign. Sadat was so underwhelmed that he turned on all fours and headed back to the kitchen. Devin laughed, shaking his head. "He's ten," he explained. "Been there, done that, seen it all. Kind of like what you want me to believe about you, cousin."

The smile on her face said, *got me.* "Comparing me to your dog," she said. "This evening's getting off to a great start."

He chuckled, taking her hand into his. It felt soft and warm. "Come on," he prompted. "Let me introduce you to my dad."

They found KL outside, checking the tiki torches on the deck. Sadat darted—well, as much as a 70-year-old dog can dart—out onto the deck, descended the stairs, and headed out into the backyard. "Go on," Devin said. "Let Tony play."

Chaney unclipped the leash. They both watched as Tony instinctively followed after Sadat.

"Dad, look who's here!" Devin called.

KL looked up from the torch. Instantly, his face lit up. He traversed the deck in his long, authoritative Marine stride to approach her. Devin couldn't remember the last time he'd seen such pure joy from his pops. Ever. "Come here, girl!" he commanded.

Devin heard Chaney gasp as KL locked her up in a strong bear hug. "Hello," she said, "sir."

KL let her go. "Girl, call me KL," he said. "I haven't been 'sir' since I retired."

She tried it on for size. "KL."

KL took her hands and looked her over. For once, his father gave a woman a look that didn't signify anything sexual. If anything, it was more father to daughter. "Look at you," KL said, shaking his head in disbelief. "Last time I saw you, you were knee-high to a blade of grass."

Devin laughed. Every once in a while, his father would become that Southern gentleman from Crewe, Virginia—right down to his speech.

"That was a long time ago," she said. "God, who was president then?"

"It's good to see you again," KL said, and Devin really believed he meant it. "Think of this as your home."

"Thank you," she said.

There was a lull in the conversation, and Devin exploited it. "Well," he said, rubbing his hands together. "Shall we eat?"

"Sounds like a plan, son," KL declared.

"Let me help," Chaney offered.

He nodded. "Okay."

Devin held the door open and watched as she headed inside ahead of him. He even shocked himself by sneaking a long, uninterrupted glance at her ass as she stepped up into the kitchen. He liked what he saw, curves which allowed her trousers to rest on her backside, then flare out to create a look that made her already long legs look even longer. *Nice.*

She put the leash down in the corner and began washing her hands in the kitchen sink. Meanwhile, Devin put the stove on warm under the *burkoki*. Drying her hands on a piece of hand towel, she came up behind him. "That smells delicious," she said. "What're you cooking?"

He uncovered it to give her a full view of the riot of beef, onions, and carrots in a brown sauce. "*Burkoki*," he answered. "It's Korean."

He took one of the pieces of beef up in the cooking spoon. "Wanna try?"

"Okay," she said eagerly.

He plucked it up between his fingers and extended it her way. He watched intently as she encircled his thumb and forefinger with her mouth, suppressing a shiver as she sucked the beef out of his grasp. He waited as she chewed, her eyes darting every which way. "I taste onion," she announced, eyes still darting. "And garlic. Oh, and soy sauce."

He nodded with approval. "Yes," he said. "I'd tell you the rest, but I'd have to kill you."

She laughed and elbowed him. "Just show me where your serving dishes are."

Devin watched her at work, and he completely understood the value of a woman's touch. He was used to helping his food from the pot, eating in front of the TV, and scratching his balls when through. She brought a touch of class to the operation. She helped the rice, the *burkoki,* and both old and new *kimchi* into glass serving dishes he didn't even know KL had—all ready for him to take to the table. She filled a glass pitcher with water and ice, wrapped the chilled wine in a dish towel, found glasses, and gave them to him to take out as well. The result, a perfectly laid table on the deck. He was genuinely impressed. Apparently, so was KL. "This is beautiful," he decreed.

Devin filled his plate, enjoying his own cooking. She and KL had two helpings each as they talked about her sister, Anna Lisa, and the good and not-so-good old days. He loved it that they enjoyed and appreciated his efforts. For once, KL appeared to be pleased with him.

Devin began filling glasses with merlot. She covered her glass with her hand. "None for me, thanks," she said. "Just water."

He was curious, but he heeded her wish, filling her glass with ice water. He stored that moment away for future analysis.

Later, after they'd had their chocolate cake, they lingered over coffee and wine on the deck. Sadat and Tony lay curled up at their respective masters' feet. "When I saw Anna Lisa that day she left Quantico, I knew she was hurt," KL said.

"Because her husband had screwed a swath across Northern

Virginia and Southeast Asia," Chaney declared. "I mean, I love my brother-in-law, but enough was enough."

"Norm couldn't help himself," KL said. "Norm loved Anna Lisa, but he couldn't help being a pussy hound."

Devin nearly did a spit take with his merlot. His father was being full-on Marine tonight, salty language and all.

Chaney wasn't buying KL's explanation. "Yeah, he could've," she said.

"The Rhym men are hard-wired that way," KL said.

"Suppose the shoe was on the other foot, Dad?" Devin asked. "Norm probably would've gone postal."

KL looked at Devin and shook his head, like Devin was beyond hope. KL leaned in toward Chaney. "My son, civilization's last sensitive man," he commented. "The last girl I'd seen him with was that Kimmy from high school."

Devin laughed to cover his overwhelming sense of impending doom. "Oh, God, make it stop!" Devin moaned.

Chaney winked, like she was going to help put him out of his misery. "I'm sure li'l cuz needs no help when it comes to the ladies," she said.

" 'Cause he's a Rhym man," KL stated. "My baby son one day comes home from kindergarten. His cute little face is screwed up, like he's so confused. I'm wondering, 'What the hell could make a five-year-old so upset?' "

Devin cringed. He knew what was coming. "Dad, stop!" Devin pleaded.

KL didn't even look in his direction to acknowledge his protest. "So I say, 'What's the matter, son?' And he says, 'Daddy, I have the biggest penis in the whole kindergarten. Is that supposed to be like that?' "

KL and Chaney laughed wildly, and Devin looked away, a rueful smile on his face. "I was the proudest father on the block!" KL laughed.

Chaney rubbed his arm, meaning to soothe. "You know, Devin, that's not such a bad thing with the ladies."

Devin winked at her, dragging his top teeth over his bottom lip. "I know," Devin said.

"Oh!" KL exclaimed, then he and Chaney looked at each other and laughed.

Devin drained his wineglass. "Yuck it up, you two, at old Dev's expense. I'm gonna start cleaning up."

"I'll help you," Chaney offered.

"Don't hurt yourself," he said.

Chaney stood up, began grabbing now-empty serving dishes. "Oh, un-pucker your cheeks, Devin. We're just kidding."

"Watch my puckered cheeks leave," he said with mock hurt.

He took glasses and dishes into the kitchen, and she followed.

Despite the expressions of his wounded male pride, she stayed and helped him clean up, stack the dishwasher. While they cleaned, they talked and laughed about everything and nothing in particular until, before he knew it, the mountain of dishes was gone, and the food was tucked away in the fridge.

Devin stared at the clean stove, sinks, and countertops. "This used to take forever when I was a kid!" he laughed.

She hung the dish towel on the hook on the wall. "The dishwasher's the key," she said. "When my sister, Daisy, and I were growing up, we begged our sister to get a dishwasher. She looked us up and down and said, 'I have two.' "

Devin chuckled. "Your sister sounds like a piece of work."

"She takes no shorts, that's for sure."

"I'd like to meet her one day. My dad seems to love her. When I talk about you, his mind immediately goes to her."

Chaney leaned against the counter. "Seeing him brought it all back. Your dad was the one who came to our apartment in Fredericksburg to sort Norm out," she said. "Norm wasn't having that. He was the man; he was gonna do what he wanted to do. Your dad helped us pack our stuff, drove us all the way to Union Station, and made sure we got on a train to Brooklyn. Not to put a fine a point on it, your dad saved our lives."

Devin stood there, taking it all in. His dad actually saving three women; did that counteract the pain he'd brought to his own three? Did that equalize his father's karmic balance sheet? "I didn't know," he said.

"I'm sure there's a lot you don't know about him," she said. "He's good people, your dad."

Chaney looked down at her watch. "Well, I'd better go," she announced. "No rest for the weary."

"Gotta go see Randy tomorrow, huh?" he teased, before he could stop himself.

She shook her head. "You just get your own love life together, Doogie," she said.

"I'm on it," he promised.

"Good," she said. "One of us should be getting some real sex."

He followed her out onto the deck, where KL was tossing balls to eager doggie mouths down in the yard to fetch. She clapped her hands together. "Come on, Tony!" she called. "Let's go!"

Tony stared right at her, his head cocked to the side, with a red ball crushed between his powerful jaws. He then ran across the yard, his ears flapping. Sadat followed behind. The two dogs leapt up the deck stairs and spat their saliva-coated balls into KL's waiting hands. Tony came over to Chaney, and she clipped the leash onto his harness. "Good boy!" she laughed, and his bushy yellow tail swung furiously in a concentric circle.

"You're leaving?" KL asked, disappointed. "Don't go! Let's all sit and talk some more."

"Spoken like someone who's retired," Devin commented.

"I'm sorry, KL," she sighed. "Gotta work tomorrow."

"Okay," KL relented.

Devin looked on as KL kissed her cheek, then hugged her, careful to keep the spitty balls away from her clothing. He closed his eyes tightly and smiled. "It was so good to see you again," he said. "Thanks for coming."

"Thanks for having me."

"You come back anytime."

"Okay."

Chaney said a quick 'bye to Sadat, then Devin led her and Tony inside. Again, he caught a surreptitious look at her ass, and again wondered what was going on with him. "You wanna take some food with you?" he asked.

She patted her flat stomach. "Devin, if I eat one more bite, I'm gonna explode," she laughed. "You save it for me for when I come back."

So she liked everything. He felt an enormous swell of manly pride. "I'll walk you to your car," he said.

They strolled leisurely from the house down to the Altima, parallel parked between two SUVs at the curb in front of the house. She unlocked the car with a key chain remote, then opened the back door and ushered Tony inside. "Go on, boy!" she commanded.

Obediently, he leapt in, and made himself comfortable on the leather seat. He realized that was probably why he didn't have a dog.

As much as he loved animals, he loved the leather seats in his ride more.

She shut the door. "I'll have you over to my house next," she said. "Cook you some Bahamian food."

"That sounds nice," he said. "Just say when."

She leaned against the driver's side door. "Well . . ." she said.

He shoved his hands into his pockets. "Well," he said.

In seconds, his mind replayed the night, and he felt a warm, comfortable vibe. He realized he'd enjoyed her company, he'd enjoyed the kinder, gentler version of his father that she'd brought out. Mostly, he just enjoyed the ease of being with her. There was no pressure, no pretense. That was hotter than Zoe's come-fuck-me clothes, or Ayanna's titties poking out of her blouse.

It was almost natural how he opened his arms, and she moved into his embrace. He buried his chin into the crown of her head and wriggled it. "That tickles!" she giggled.

"Not you, the Iron Maiden, all giggly," he laughed.

"I had fun tonight," she said.

He relished the feel of her breasts pressing into his chest. "Me, too," he said.

He probably could've stayed out on the street all night, holding her like that. But she backed away, like she'd reached her affection quota for the evening. "I'll call you," she promised, then opened the car door and slunk into the driver's seat.

He shut her door for her, then stepped away and watched as she started up the smooth engine and slowly drove away down the block to the red traffic light where Garfield met Wilson. The light turned green, she hung a right, and was gone into the night with all the other cars. He sighed. *Chaney* . . .

Devin went back into the house and found his dad sitting on the deck with Sadat. Devin sat down next to him. Together, the Rhym men silently enjoyed the stillness of the cool May night. "Chaney's a good woman," KL finally said.

Devin nodded in complete agreement. "Yeah, she is."

"You two were brewing up some chemistry like the Curies, man," KL observed.

Can't get anything past you, Pops. Devin laughed self-consciously. "Isn't she family, Dad?"

KL looked over at him. "This is Virginia, son," he reminded him.

"You're allowed to fuck your second cousin's ex-wife's sister. No one would even blink."

"Good to know, Pops," Devin said sarcastically. "What's with the no drinking? Did you notice that?"

"Maybe she wasn't drinking 'cause she was driving," KL suggested. "Doesn't mean she's in a twelve-step program. Stop trying to find fault where none exists."

Am I doing that? "Would it be finding fault to point out the fact that she's older?" Devin asks. "She reminds me of it all the time."

KL chuckled low in the throat, sounding devious. "Cocky young brothah like you could use an older woman to turn you out. You're my son, so I know you're well-endowed, but she could show you what to do with the equipment. An older woman is a rite of passage, son. Mine was the choir mistress in my mother's church, back in Crewe. I was seventeen and so wet behind the ears, I could've sailed away." The chuckle became deviously confident. "Let's just say she was proficient on two organs, okay?"

Devin got that sick feeling every child experienced at the thought of a parent getting busy. And the nausea mingled with confusion. There they were, talking about a hypothetical hookup with Chaney, when he was still trying to sort out his feelings for Liz. "Thanks for sharing, Dad," he said. "No disrespect, but you were married three times. Shouldn't you be the last person giving advice about women?"

"I'm the perfect person," KL declared. "Gain knowledge from my experiences so you don't make the same mistakes I did."

Devin mulled that one over, took it in and rolled it over in his mind as he sat next to his father in silence.

The arena at the MCI Center was packed with a robust crowd of Washington Mystics fans. Between the noise of the crowd, along with the music, and the applause for the group of dancing teens and tweens that was the Mystic Mayhem, Chaney began to feel more than a little overstimulated.

This outing was Dani's treat. Like many lesbian couples, she and Sandy, her lover, were season ticket holders. They shared their fistful of tickets with their straight basketball friends, like Chaney. This was how Chaney became sandwiched in the upper tier, between the happy same-sex couple—Dani and Sandy—and the happy hetero couple—

Nathalie and Craig. *This is some kind of Fellini-esque Hell.* Only in 2002 D.C., it was halftime at a Washington Mystics preseason game.

Charm, the blue bunny rabbit that was the Mystics' mascot, tried to pump up the crowd by doing backflips and somersaults, and by taking out a pneumatic gun and shooting T-shirts into the stands. Then the unseen deejay started bumping RuPaul's "Supermodel."

"Oh, baby, this was our jam!" Craig laughed.

"I know!" Nathalie laughed.

Chaney eyed them, her with the Halle Berry coif and Craig looking like the legal profession's answer to Tyson Beckford. "I hate you two," she declared. "You two actually have your own 'jam.' "

"Listen to the sixth toe," Sandy teased.

Chaney stared at her, too. *How bad does your love life have to be that you have a Chinese lesbian making fun of you?*

"Don't hate on us," Nathalie laughed. "We've been hearing about this fictional 'Randy' for weeks now, but have we met him? No!"

Chaney couldn't have planned it better. Just as RuPaul was having his one thing to say—You betta work!—the Jumbotron began its Fan of the Game series. People in the stadium would jump and dance and hope like hell to get the camera focused on them. After the first succession of hefty women who appeared to be Presidents of the Clean Plate Club, the Jumbotron broadcast the image of a young girl wearing Mystic forward Chamique Holdsclaw's #23 jersey. Chaney recognized her immediately. After all, she'd seen two pictures of her in her father's wallet and on CD-ROM. Speaking of her father, he was seated beside her, sporting basketball 'nalia and chewing gum. Suddenly, they were aware that they were on camera. The girl, Taina Tyree, jumped out of her seat and started doing the Harlem Shake to the beat. Randy looked up at his image on the Jumbotron and was the epitome of the cool brothah. He just waved and laughed.

Unbelievable! "That's him!" Chaney squealed.

"Who?" Dani yelled over the music.

Chaney pointed at the Jumbotron. "Him!" she cried happily "That's Randy!"

Her companions didn't look convinced. "Sure, it's him," Sandy said, rolling her eyes, which didn't take much.

"I'm telling you—it's him!" Chaney cried.

Four pairs of eyes looked at her like she was pathetic, like she had to insist that some Jumbotron stranger was her man so that she could save face. She was facing the flesh-and-blood embodiment of the Smug Marrieds that Helen Fielding wrote about in *Bridget Jones' Diary*. Even lesbians were getting laid when she wasn't. *To hell with all of you!*

Chaney's eyes scanned the crowd until they came to rest on what she recognized as the back of Taina Tyree; her front still appeared on the Jumbotron. She and Randy were seated a few rows down, near the floor. Chaney got up. "See y'all later," she said.

Four smug pairs of eyes turned into four puzzled pairs of eyes. "Where are you going?" Nathalie demanded.

Chaney left her seat and picked her way across Dani, then Sandy, then Nathalie, and lastly, Craig. "How are you getting home?" Dani asked.

"After the game, you guys wait for me at the Gallery Place-Chinatown Metro where we came in," Chaney said. " 'Bye!"

With that, Chaney descended the stairs, tier by tier, until she came upon where Randy and his daughter were sitting. Which wasn't easy to do in her work pumps. She finally reached their seats, where Taina sat down, and Randy, wearing jeans, sneakers, and a Mystics throwback, slipped an arm around his daughter's shoulders.

Taina looked up first, giving her that jaded teenaged look that said *who are you?* "Hi," Chaney said.

Randy looked up. Far from the effusive greeting she'd expected, his smile was cool, distant. "Hey," he said, smiling nonetheless. "What are you doing here?"

Chaney pointed tiers up at Dani and her crew. "I'm here with my friends," she said. "I saw you stylin' on the Jumbotron and had to come over. Is D.C. small or what?"

Randy got up, reached over his daughter, and hugged Chaney. It was like a hug one would give a friend, not someone who he wanted to have suck his dick mere days ago. *What's going on here?*

Randy turned to his daughter. "Tai, this is my friend, Chaney," he announced.

Taina looked Chaney up and down. Chaney found herself eagerly awaiting this girl's approval. "Hello," Taina said.

Chaney sensed she meant *fuck off.* She looked away, focusing on the line of ridiculously tall women coming onto the court. Randy moved over one chair, leaving a seat vacant between himself and Taina for her. He shot Taina a look, then shrugged. Chaney understood it immediately. Here Chaney was, inserting herself into a girl's precious night out with a father she probably only saw on the weekends. Randy leaned in. "She'll be okay," he assured her.

Chaney knew she probably wouldn't be . . . not for a long time. That was the downside of getting involved with a man with children. However, there was an upside. She wouldn't have to be some guy's broodmare, spitting out babies so that he could prove that his dick worked. Especially not with her fibrous husk of a uterus. The pressure would be off, and God knew she needed less pressure.

The game whistle sounded, and the point guard, Helen Luz, all five-foot-eight of her, took possession of the ball and viciously man-handled her counterpart from the Charlotte Sting. The crowd erupted in a noise that sounded like, "Boooo!"

Chaney leaned in to Taina. "Why are they booing her?" she asked. which, to Chaney's ears, sounded like they were booing.

Taina rolled her luminous light eyes. "They're not booing," she explained. "They're saying 'Luuuuuzzzzz!' Like her name?"

Indeed. Chaney could practically feel her cool points decreasing as Luz passed the ball to star forward Chamique Holdsclaw for the two.

Far from overjoyed that her team was spanking the Sting like a toddler, Taina looked past Chaney at her father. "Dad, I'm going to grab a Coke," she announced. "You want anything?"

"No, baby," Randy said. "Thank you."

Taina left the row and took the steps up the tier two at a time. Chaney watched her leave. She would've loved a Coke, too, but she didn't want to press her luck with Tai. She was going to take the gentle touch.

No sooner was Tai out of his line of vision than he became the Randy who'd offered so generously to suck her clit days ago. She laughed as he took her face into his hands. He pressed his mouth against hers, and she practically melted in her borrowed seat. *Feed me,* her affection monkey screamed. And he did. He kissed her face, her mouth, her forehead. She was gasping for breath by the time he'd stopped. "I'm glad you're here," he whispered.

He slipped his arm around her shoulders. She leaned against his chest, her smile clocking a hundred watts. "Me, too," she said.

After the game, after the Mystics had practically demolished the Sting, Randy, Chaney, and Taina made their way through the crush of the crowd to the curb of F Street outside. Chaney held one of his hands, and Taina held the other. Chaney knew she didn't have to be Freud to see the symbolism . . . the potential lover and the adoring daughter sharing the same man, with varying degrees of success. *This is going to be complicated.*

"Where are your friends?" Randy asked.

They headed toward the Gallery Place-Chinatown Metro. Through the crowd of folks breaking out, Chaney saw the happy couples, milling around, holding hands. Chaney became ever so conscious of Randy's hand in hers, and, deep down inside, she finally felt worthy to be in their presence. With her free hand, she pointed. "There they are!" she cried.

They headed toward her friends. Suddenly, four pairs of eyes looked up, watched them coming. They seemed to try to suppress their astonishment but failed egregiously. Pride swelled Chaney's chest. They thought she was deluding herself, but she was going to show them.

Nathalie ran her eyes over Randy and Tai. "Chaney!" she laughed breathlessly. "Who's your friend?"

Chaney pointed to each one as she began the introductions. "Dani, Sandy, Nathalie, and Craig," she said, "this is Randy Tyree and his daughter Taina."

Inside, though, she was laughing. *Joke's on you!*

Later, as she waited on the underground Metro platform with the couples, she smiled, reliving the time spent with him on her mind. "Where'd Randy and his daughter go?"

"They drove here," Chaney announced. "He's taking her for ice cream."

"You were holding out on us, Chaney Braxton," Craig teased. "Where'd you meet him?"

Here we go again . . . "At work," she announced.

Nathalie and Craig looked away, shaking their heads, as did Sandy. The only one with an opinion—typical!—was Dani. "That's the stupidest thing you could do, Chaney," she declared. "The partner who fucks clients is the partner who loses her partnership."

Chaney looked at her and laughed bitterly. She was seriously wrecking her high. " 'Scuse me, NostraDaniels," she said. "Didn't you meet Sandy on your detail at the White House?"

Sandy smiled, all warm, fuzzy, and nostalgic. She slipped an arm around Dani's waist. "Yes, she did."

"But neither of us works together anymore," Dani reminded Chaney. "Men want to fuck who's available. Men like easy access."

"Not necessarily," Craig inserted.

Chaney would've laughed in her face, if she hadn't been exhausted from hearing what a bad idea hooking up with Randy was. "Wait, you're giving me man advice?" Chaney asked her. "Vegetarians don't give meat advice."

Nathalie and Craig looked away, snickering behind their hands.

"I had my share of meat before I became a . . . vegetarian," Dani declared. "I'm telling you. Getting involved with him is a bad idea. But you're not going to listen. You're going to do your own thing, Chaney. As usual."

Chaney drew breath to counteract Dani's argument, but she felt the pressure drop in the tunnel, saw the lights in the platform begin to blink. The train was coming. Was the light at the end of her single tunnel hope? Or was that also another train?

Once home, Chaney opened the door and flicked on the light switch. Light filled the anteroom. Immediately, the alarm bleated, and she rushed over to punch in the code to shut it off. Seconds later, silence filled the vacuum the sound of the alarm once occupied. "Tony!" she called.

Nothing. That was peculiar. It wasn't like he could pick the lock and leave the house. With the infection still roiling in his ear, the last thing she thought prudent would've been to leave him outside, getting dirt in that very same ear.

She locked up and went over to the entrance to the kitchen, the entrance separated by a white baby gate to keep him confined in a smaller space. "Tony!" she called again.

This time, she heard a low howl, then an intermittent, high-pitched whine. Her heartbeats sped up. *What now?*

She moved the gate aside, entered the kitchen, and switched on the kitchen light. Then she gasped. There was Tony, lying curled up on the tiled kitchen floor in a yellow ball. There were pieces of a chewed-to-be-damned brown bottle, with chunks of its familiar white cap, all over the floor. Belatedly, Chaney recognized it as remnants of the plastic Rimadyl bottle that she'd left on the top of the counter, supposedly out of his reach.

Chaney dropped to her knees and snatched up the bottle. She saw what was left of the label from Rosslyn Veterinary Hospital. Chaney did a quick count on her fingers. Devin had prescribed fifteen tablets last week. Eight had been left since then. Tony had overdosed on eight tablets.

Oh, shit! Chaney approached Tony, who was still in a ball on the floor. He didn't even do his I'm-so-glad-you're-home dance that he usually did when she came home. He looked up at her with eyes filled with pain. Her heart lurched. She ran a hand over his head. "Tony," she singsonged. "You okay, boy?"

He nudged her with his pink nose and let out a whimper.

"Tony, why'd you do this?" she asked.

She looked at him, waiting for him to answer. Then came that realization again, the realization that he was a dog and he thought he'd scored some great beef-flavored treats, not that he was taking medicine that could practically fry his little liver. *Where's the phone? Gotta find the phone . . .*

Chaney struggled up to her feet, ran out into the living room, and found the cordless phone. She willed herself to calm down, searched her mind for the number. *Can't remember the fucking number!*

She ran over to her purse on the anteroom's credenza, emptied it out on the floor, and clawed through the contents, looking for Devin's card. She found it next to some Listerine Pocket Strips and a red lipstick. She turned it over for his personal cell number, then dialed haltingly, looking away at the card simultaneously, until she'd entered all ten numbers.

He picked up after three rings. "Hello," he moaned sleepily into the phone.

"Umm . . . Devin," she sputtered. "It's Chaney."

There was a seven-second delay over the digital air space. "Chaney," he breathed. "Hey, girl."

What was he going to think? That there she was again, with her negligent self. Only this time, it wasn't ear infections and heartworm shots. Because of her carelessness, Tony could die. Just the thought of having to tell Daisy . . . "Sorry to wake you," she began.

"What time is it?" he asked, seeming a bit clearer now.

What time is it? She looked down at her watch and winced. She was going to owe him a shitload of hand cream after this one: "11:30," she said.

"Fell asleep watching TV," he explained, half-coherent. "You okay?"

"It's Tony," she said, then vomited out the rest. "He got into the Rimadyl. I think he ate about eight of them. He's whining and curled up in a ball. What should I do?"

"Emesis," he murmured.

Her brows crinkled. "What?"

"Did you stick your finger down his throat? Make him throw up?"

Chaney's gut roiled, feeling the waves start to push all the hot dogs and popcorn and Coke she'd had at the Mystics game toward her throat. She swallowed hard. "No," she groaned. "I just got home and saw the bottle. I don't know when he did it. It could've been hours ago."

"Okay, I'm up," Devin said. "Don't do anything. Just meet me at the office. If we leave at the same time, we should get there in a half-hour."

Chaney began scooping up her stuff into her purse. She breathed a grateful sigh. "Okay," she said.

She clicked off the cordless, put it onto the counter, and went back into the kitchen. "Tony?" she said to the yellow ball.

He looked up at her; his eyes seemed to implore her for help. Chaney would've been crying if that infernal Fluexa in her blood-stream would've allowed the release. She helped Tony to stand on all fours, took him by the collar, and led him gingerly toward the door. "Come, sweet boy," she said. "We're going to Cousin Devin's."

Again, Tony lay in the front passenger seat well, close to Chaney's feet. Again, she sped through the night along Route 1 toward Rosslyn. Again, she looked down at him as he whined intermittently. "Tony," she whispered. "Please be all right."

She screeched into one of the front parking spaces at the veteri-nary hospital. She found Devin, bleary-eyed, standing against his big black ride. Chaney got out of the car, went around to the passenger side, and gently helped Tony down. Devin came forward, and Chaney wanted to hug him for getting out of his bed to help them. She clutched a hand to her chest. "Devin," she sighed.

Sleepily, he scratched his head. "Hey, Chaney," he said.

He looked down at Tony. Even in pain, Tony wagged his tail, slug-gishly, but nonetheless, he let Devin know he was glad to see him. "Let's go inside," Devin suggested.

He pulled out a fistful of keys and unlocked the double glass doors. Just like at Chaney's house, an alarm sounded—this one like a long, high-pitched ping. Devin rushed through the door that led to the examining rooms. Seconds later, he appeared behind the glass panel that separated reception from the glass wall, behind which Maria sat. The alarm suddenly stopped. He pointed to the door that led to the examining room. "Come on through!" he called, his voice muffled by the glass and the distance between them.

Chaney obeyed, going through the door. He met her in the hallway, and together, they walked to the usual examining room. He went through his usual task in silence, listening to Tony's heart with his stethoscope, examining his eyes, his ears, nose, and throat. Chaney sat on the bench, the suspense closing around her throat.

Devin squinted his eyes closed and scratched his head with his hands. "Okay," he started. "Here's the thing, Chaney. Tony's suffering from Rimadyl toxicity. This is very serious. If he ate eight of those pills, he could be looking at total organ failure."

Oh, shit! Chaney's hands flew to her mouth. "What?" she cried. "Is there something we can do?"

Devin stroked Tony's face, all the while looking deeply into his eyes, Chaney assumed, for anything out of the ordinary. "I'm going to put him on an IV drip for twenty-four hours," Devin announced. "Gotta flush all of that drug out of his system. After that, we'll do some blood tests to check the health of his organs."

The enormity of it hit Chaney squarely in the face. "This is all my fault," she murmured, going over the events in her mind that led them to that very moment. "I kept him in the kitchen, because I *thought* I was protecting him from getting dirt in his ear. I put the drugs on the counter, out of reach. At least I thought so."

Devin shook his head. "Chaney, you can't blame yourself. He's a dog. He's gonna do shit like this."

"That's not comforting," she said.

Devin sat next to her on the bench, and by the expression on his face, Chaney could immediately tell that he wasn't finished, and that part two was probably going to be even worse. "Chaney," he said.

"What?" she said.

"As I said before, this is very, very serious," he said. "I'm going to treat Tony the best way I can, but things can happen with something this serious."

She gulped. "Like what?"

"He could arrest on the table. There are three options you'll have to consider. First, there's the full code. If Tony arrests, I'll use every option available to me to bring him back. Then there's the partial code. I'll do what's available . . . drugs, defibrillation, but nothing invasive. Last, there's no code. That's where I'll keep him comfortable, but just let nature take its course. You understand?"

This was going from bad to worse. She stared incredulously at him. "It's that bad?" she asked.

He nodded.

Chaney weighed the options in her mind, then looked down at Tony's huge brown eyes, with his blond eyelashes and his pink nose. The answer was obvious. "Full code, of course," she stated.

Again, Devin nodded. He patted her knee, like she'd made the best choice. "Let's get ma man here on the drip," he said. "Are you going to wait? Through the night, at least?"

Chaney glanced down at her watch. Shit, it was already midnight, and she doubted she was going to get any sleep worrying at home about him. She couldn't bring herself to leave him. Just in case . . . "Where can I wait?" she asked.

"I'll show you."

They left the room and turned left, rounding the bend of corridors away from the examination rooms. Soon, they came to a white door with Devin's name—DEVIN S.L. RHYM, DVM—on a brass nameplate. He pushed it open, letting her and Tony in. Chaney cursorily studied the crowded desk, the books, the comfy leather couch against the white wall with ivory wainscoting. He shrugged. "It's not much, but it'll work for tonight," he said, pointing to a pile of folded scrubs and a blanket. "You can put those on, if you want."

Chaney nodded. So, she was camping out at the hospital.

Tony whined again, and Devin ran a comforting hand over his head. "You want to come with me?" he asked Chaney.

Chaney blanched, and Devin laughed. "I take it that's a no," he said. "You stay here and get ready for bed. I'll fix him up and be back."

Devin led Tony out of the office. "Come on, boy," he prompted.

Chaney watched them go. *Oh, please let him be okay . . .*

Devin closed the door behind him and Tony. Chaney sighed, looking around the office. "Okay," she sighed.

She undressed, looking all around her, just in case there were peepholes she couldn't see, peepholes where prying eyes may try to get a glimpse of her in her black lacy bra and matching boy shorts. *My tig old bitties and my lumpy ass.* She folded her clothes neatly and set them in a pile on the couch. Then she unclasped her bra. Her skin breathed, and she moaned with relief as her soft breast tissue expanded to its natural fullness. She stretched a hand across her chest, with the other hand flapped open the top of the scrubs. Hurriedly, she yanked it over her head. It ballooned around her like a big green tent. Then she pulled the scrub pants on, one leg at a time, then cinched the drawstring at the waist. Even they bagged around her. *So, I'm not as huge as I thought . . .*

She put her clothes on top of her pumps on the floor, plopped down onto the couch, and unfolded the blanket. She lay on her side, with her head propped up on her hands. Only then, in the relative quiet of the office, did she realize how dog-tired she was. Her breathing became even, less labored, as she settled in to her surroundings. The blanket cradled her in warmth. The leather felt like a second skin against hers. Finally, it felt like her body had begun to cooperate with the Fluexa, like the drug was finally going to allow sleep to come.

She felt gentle shaking and started into consciousness. Then she saw his face, practically in front of hers. He was stooped down. "Devin!" she gasped, then sat up, propping herself up on an elbow. "How's Tony?"

Devin produced something that looked like a baby monitor. "Fine. He's sedated, on an IV drip. I brought this back so we could hear him. We just have to wait."

Chaney lay back down on the couch, feeling so helpless. He was a few rooms away, and she couldn't do anything to help him. "Just wait," she repeated.

"Well," he said, pointing at the swivel chair behind his desk. "Good night."

Chaney lay back against the leather pillows. He was sacrificing his space for her. That was hardly fair. "You're gonna sleep there?" she asked.

"Yeah," he said, nodding.

"That's not comfortable."

"It's gonna have to do."

Chaney thought for a second. What could it hurt? Plus, she doubted that she had to be wary of him trying to cop a feel. She scooted back, and then patted the couch. "Come on," she said. "I already got you out of bed. I don't want to be responsible for your chiropractor bill, too."

For a second, he seemed amenable. Then he waved his arms, shaking his head. "No. It's okay."

"Okay," she said, her tone cautionary. "Just think of those long legs all cramped up, seizing up like a big, painful pretzel . . ."

He looked like he was envisioning it, too. He screwed up that adorable sleepy face. He turned off the light and came over like a lion stalking comfort. Chaney's heart skipped a beat. He kicked off his sneakers and shrugged off his hoodie. Chaney imagined what he must look like, disrobing before he made love to some nubile twenty-something honey. Which she wasn't.

There was an awkward moment, when he slid in under the covers next to her. They laughed as his long legs found hers and intertwined until they found a compromise where they fit together, facing each other like two complementary puzzle pieces. He felt like cotton and socks, smelled of toothpaste, waning aftershave, and spicy deodorant. And like Devin. She didn't realize how much she missed snuggling and cuddling with a man until right at that moment. "This is nice," he laughed.

She grinned. It sure did feel nice indeed, lying there with him in the semidarkness, with a sliver of light coming through the crack in the ajar door. "Just don't try anything," she mock-cautioned.

He rolled his sleepy eyes. "Chaney, I'm too tired to even raise a question."

It was her turn to laugh. "I thought you young boys pitched a tent whenever the wind blew."

"And I thought you older sistahs took forever to warm up—is that true?"

"Depends on who's in the kitchen, boy."

He looked away, like he was thinking about what she said. "I'll keep that in mind," he said.

Chaney sighed. "My sister's going to kill me," she moaned.

"Let's just wait and see. This'll probably be something you could tell her long after she takes Tony back home."

Chaney secretly hoped so. "I can't even begin to thank you," she said.

"Keep the cream coming," he said. "That's some good stuff. How'd you get into that, anyway?"

Chaney swallowed hard and looked away. This was going to be hard. "I was engaged once, you know," she announced, still avoiding his eyes.

He seemed intrigued. "Really?"

Time made it easier to be flippant now. Five years ago, Anna Lisa was close to scraping her up off the floor. "Yeah, but I'm lying here with you, so obviously it didn't work out."

She could feel him staring curiously at her. "I'm sorry."

"When it ended, I knew I was going to Syracuse, but there was a long summer before I was gonna change my scenery. And Anna Lisa was going to Ghana with one of her teacher friends. Then one day, she comes to me and says, 'Deidre's pregnant. You want to come to Africa with me?' I was, like, 'Is a duck's ass waterproof? Of course I wanna go to Africa!' "

" 'Is a duck's ass waterproof?' " he repeated, laughing.

She laughed, too, laughter that slowly subsided as she found herself back in the moment. "I cried clear across Ghana, from Kumasi, to Accra, to the Cape Coast," she sighed. *Mooning over the homosexual love of my life.*

He reached up from under the covers and ran a hand over her cheek. "He's an idiot," he said.

Bless your heart! "I bought the shea butter in a market in Accra," she announced. "It was in this unassuming bag, like the ones you put produce in at the supermarket. I brought bags and bags of it back with me. Then when I went to Syracuse, with its ten months of winter. I would've been a raisin if it hadn't been for that stuff. Then I used to go home to Brooklyn, or go to Harlem in the summer, and buy oils from brothahs off the street, and I'd experiment. I know this may be hard to believe, but I can be something of a tight-ass."

"*Pfft!* Naw!" Devin teased.

She pushed him in the chest, and he clutched onto her to stop from falling off the couch. "What I meant to say," she laughed, "was that I can be a little . . . tightly wound, and when I start making my creams, it chills me out. Relaxes me."

"I know you're a little neurotic, Chaney," he grinned. "That's what I like about you."

You like me. She blushed. But her knee-jerk reflex kicked in. "I thought men your age liked lobotomized, uncomplicated women."

He looked her straight in the eye. "Maybe I'm not your typical man my age," he declared. "Ever think about that?"

She turned away from him, not wanting him to see the vulnerability on her traitorous face. "Every day," she said.

It seemed so natural when he moved up behind her, wrapped his right arm around her waist. He molded against her, his knees bent in the hollow her bent knees made. Her head fit just under his chin. She could hear his even breathing, felt her own chest rising and falling in synch with his. She could get used to this if she allowed herself to.

"This reminds me of those dumb camping trips my brothers and I used to take with my dad," he said, mid-yawn. "When I was five. Chauncey'd make up these corny jokes, wordplay on pop culture icons."

She tried to imagine it. "Like what?"

He laughed low in the throat. "Like . . . what do you call a flatulent boxer?"

"What?"

"Gaseous Clay."

She grimaced. "Yeah, that's bad!"

"Or what you call a thieving man of the cloth?" He waited the appropriate time for the punch line. "Felonious Monk."

"Now I see where you get your jokes," she laughed. "Oh, I got one. What do you call a sponge that sings R&B?"

She felt him shake his head. "What *do* you call a sponge that sings R&B?" he repeated.

She made him wait for it. "Loofah Vandross!" she giggled.

He exploded with laughter. "Loofah Vandross!"

She giggled, feeling good inside that she made him happy. She relaxed into him as he pulled her closer and hugged her. "Loofah Vandross," he murmured.

Minutes later, they were both asleep.

The hot May sun, combined with the heat percolating up from the grill and reflecting off the aluminum foil on the grate, made Devin sweat like a pig. Devin pressed a spatula against each of the searing hamburgers, all while wiping his brow with a white towel. So, bonding with his family meant standing on Chauncey's deck on Memorial Day, grilling under the magnified rays of the sun, while practically everyone else either splashed around in the pool or stayed in the air-conditioned comfort of Chauncey's Capitol Hill house.

Except for his father, the grill master. He stood at Devin's left, clutching a cold Heinie in his hand. "What are you doing?" he demanded. "You're burning 'em, son!"

Devin struggled to remain calm. "I'm not burning 'em, Pops," he insisted. "Renee said to make 'em well done, kill any E. coli. She's pregnant, and we don't wanna harm the children."

Chauncey and Eric came over to critique, open Heinies firmly in their hands. "Little bruh's on the grill," Chauncey laughed. "He's a man now."

Devin rolled his eyes and blinked as sweat from his forehead dripped into them. He dabbed his brow again. He didn't have the heart to tell them that his mother had taught him how to do what he was doing. The manly Rhym men probably would've passed out if they had an inkling that someone with a vagina knew the secrets of the grill. "Can someone get me a beer, please?" he asked.

Eric handed him his. "I don't like beer that much, anyway," he said.

Chauncey and KL looked at each other over Eric's head, a look that said, *pussy*. Devin took it and practically poured the whole thing down his throat. It felt cold and satisfying going down. His chardonnay-sucking brother didn't know what he was missing. He opened up his throat, and an earthquaking burp came out. "Whoo!" he cried.

Chauncey and KL looked at him in admiration; Eric, disgust. "You're a pig," Eric said. "How on earth did Ayanna find you attractive? You know, she quit because of your disastrous date."

A part of him wanted to tell his brother the real truth, but at the same time, he didn't want or need the bad karma. He pressed the spatula against the hamburgers for the last time. "Keep your mind on your own love life, please, brother," he said.

Renee, wearing a black one-piece and tentlike pareo over her expanded belly, waddled forward with a tray covered in a hand towel. Chauncey patted his wife on her ass, and she beamed. "Hey, baby," he said. "When are we gon' eat?"

"Right now, sweetest," she promised. "As soon as my brother puts those wonderful burgers on this platter."

Devin complied, helping the burgers off the grill and onto the tray. He shot KL an I-told-you-so glance. "All well done, just like you asked," he declared.

He closed his eyes and smiled as she kissed his sweaty cheek. That was love. She winked at him. "Liz is here," she said. "Marlene invited her."

"Devin's not using my pool of clerks for his dates," Eric protested. "Liz is like my right arm. I'm not going to lose her, too."

Devin closed the lid on the grill. "Married people," he remarked. "Don't hate me 'cause I'm single."

He left them there on the deck, pulled open the sliding door, and went inside to the kitchen. What he didn't want to tell them was that he'd already spent the most enjoyable night of his life ever with some-one—Chaney. He'd asked her to come here with them, but she said she'd already made plans. She was going to Rehoboth Beach in Delaware with her friends, to take in some sun and watch the beauti-ful gay men.

They hadn't even held hands, or kissed, even. The closest he got to a home run with her was spooning on the couch. Yet, he still couldn't get her out of his mind. Talking and laughing with her that night, see-ing the look on her face in the morning, after he'd saved Tony's life, seemed to fill up every empty, lonely space inside him.

But she made it clear that he was still in shorts and knee socks, as far as she was concerned. Their age difference colored every conver-sation they'd had, every interaction between them. And even after they'd spent the night together, that didn't seem like it was going to change anytime soon.

Devin headed toward the half bath off to the side of the open kitchen. Just as he was about to knock on the closed door, though, it flew open, and Liz, a vision in an orange string bikini, appeared in the doorway. His mouth dropped open as he took in all of the bare brown skin, the swell of her small cleavage, the pierced navel in the middle of a flat, ripped belly.

She reached up and clasped her shoulder-length black hair in an orange Scrunchi. "Devin!" she exclaimed. "Hey."

"Hey," he said, then to try and cover his ass for staring practically through her, he pointed behind him. "Umm . . . Renee says it's time to eat."

"Okay, thanks," she said. "Bathroom's all yours."

Liz brushed past him. He ran the entire starting Redskins lineup in his head to keep his dick from saluting as he watched her swish her way across the kitchen and through the sliding doors. That same dick that made him think, *Chaney who?*

Devin sat by the pool and looked around at the activity that surrounded him. This was why he'd come home. If he was still in Seattle, he would've missed how they'd all joined hands around the shimmering pool while Renee said the mega-mix of grace over the food. He would've missed the pangs of envy he'd felt seeing his dad, hopped up on his share of Heinekens, playing on the backyard swings with Jeffrey, Corey, and Chelsea, while Sadat barked loudly at them. He would've missed talking shit with and being ridden by his big brothers. He would've missed running the litany of available, fuckable women with Marlene and Renee.

Speaking of fuckable, he would've certainly missed a soaking wet Liz, coming up the stairs of the swimming pool like an *S.I.* swimsuit model. The drenched bikini clung to her like a second skin, nipples hardened to points by the cold water evident in her top. He didn't feel so lust-crazed when he caught Chauncey and Eric also staring at the vision in orange. Marlene, herself looking hot in a more sensible black bikini, passed in front of the men. "Tongues back in your heads, fellas," she laughed.

As the sun set, Chauncey and KL lit citronella candles and torches, and Renee put in CDs of old school music. KL, Eric, and Marlene sat at one of the beach tables, nursing their drinks and winding down. On the lit patio, Renee and Chauncey slow-dragged by the pool, their respective arms around each other's dueling girth. Jeffrey, Corey, and Chelsea sat around them in a circle, staring lovingly up at their parents. As much as Devin rebelled against his brothers' and sisters-in-law's efforts to couple him off, right then, he himself wondered if he was missing something flying solo. He imagined having someone to come home to, someone to help him fill his cavernous Georgetown crib, someone to give him physical and emotional love, love that he could return. Didn't that trump coming and going as he pleased, happy hour with the fellas, indiscriminate fucking around?

The fair Liz, now dressed in a T-shirt, white linen capris, and blue Keds, sat on a white Adirondack chair and watched the happy family by the pool. Occasionally, she smiled, snapping her fingers to Earth, Wind, and Fire's "Fantasy."

He broke out two Cokes from the cooler on the deck and headed toward her. "Hey," he said.

She looked up at him and smiled warily. "Hey, Devin," she said.

He sat down on the chair next to her and handed her one of the Cokes. "Having a good time?" he asked.

She took the can and nodded. "Your family's great."

He popped the top on his can and took a nervous swig. *What do I say?* He decided to cut to the chase. "So, are you done healing?"

Liz stared at him, her mouth open in mock shock. Then she laughed, shaking her head. "Gee, Devin, don't hold back!"

He smiled, quite proud of himself. "I figured I'd better hurry up before you gave me the gas face," he laughed.

She smiled at him. "When have I done that?" she asked.

He looked at her, shocked. "All right, Miss Short-Term Memory," he said. "All those times you shot me down."

"I thought Ayanna was more your type," she teased.

He held his head in his free hand. *Ayanna.* That was five hours of his life he desperately wanted back. "I don't want to talk about that," he declared.

"So, if I got with you on this hypothetical date," she said, "where would you take me?"

That Nigerian restaurant in Adams Morgan was definitely out. Too much former date foot traffic. "Anywhere you want to go," he promised.

Her dark eyes widened. "Anywhere, huh?" she asked. "Give me a taste."

He searched his mind for hot spots that were all the rage in D.C. "Dinner at Jordan's," he said. "We might even see Mike there."

"Oh, you know Michael Jordan?"

He forged ahead, not allowing the fact that Michael Jordan probably had his hands too full with trying to save the sorry-ass Washington Wizards to care about lowly Devin Rhym to get in the way. "After dinner, we could go dancing at Dream."

Liz laughed. "Okay, okay, you can ease up on the hard-court press, Devin," she said.

"Well?" he asked, filled with hope.

The CD shuffled just then, and the first five hard-charging beats of "Never Too Much" exploded from the speakers. He was almost in there with Liz, and all he could think about just then was that night with Chaney. *Loofah Vandross.* He laughed, holding his hand to his mouth.

Liz stared curiously at him. "What's up?" she asked.

He shook his head. "Nothing," he insisted. "So, are we sealing the deal?"

Liz's mouth was open, her lips looking ready to form the word *yes* when they both heard a goose bump-raising scream. They turned to see Marlene rushing and Renee waddling over to KL, who lay on his back on the grass, in front of the last step on the deck. Sadat was bent over KL, licking his face. Devin's heart lurched. *Dad!*

Devin threw his Coke down and rushed over to where the family was congregated. They all looked down at KL. Obviously, he'd fallen, his legs turned strangely in relation to his waist and chest. His eyes were closed, his face slack and blank. Reflexively, Devin dropped to his knees. "Dad," he said calmly, tapping his cheeks.

Nothing. Devin took his father's pulse, which was a little slower than normal. "Pops, come on," he said, his tone calm, but his insides running riot.

Nothing. He turned on the mini Maglite he kept on his key chain, then opened KL's eyes one at a time and checked his pupils. They reacted to the light. *Normal.* "Grampa, wake up!" Corey shouted from above.

That seemed to do the trick. KL moaned, opened his eyes, and stared at Devin hovering over him. He squinted. "Who are you?" he barked, irritated.

"Dad, it's me," he explained, and when it still didn't appear to register to KL, he said, "Devin, Pops."

He seemed to think for a second. "Of course you're Devin," he snapped. "What, you think I'm stupid?"

Same old Pops. Devin looked up at the others. "He's fine," he assured them.

Chauncey and Eric helped KL up, after which KL snatched his hands away. "I'm fine," he bellowed. "Stop treating me like a pussy."

Renee clutched the children to her. "Dad!" she cried.

Chauncey held his father by the waist. "Pops, we're taking you to a hospital," he said.

"Stop infantilizing me, Chauncey," KL commanded. "I used to change your diapers, boy."

Marlene came forward. "Dad, Chauncey's right," she said. "I saw you take a header off that deck. Go to the hospital. Humor us, eh? We just want to know you're okay."

That seemed to do the trick. But then again, KL always seemed to have a soft spot for Marlene. "I'm not driving in Devin's penis mobile," he declared.

Devin looked around at everyone, and everyone returned the favor, especially Liz. He knew his face was pink under the brown. "Is it okay if I follow behind in my penis mobile?" he asked.

Eric took out his keys. "Marlene and I will drive you, Dad," he said. "Let's go."

Renee stayed at the house with the kids and Sadat. Eric, Marlene, and Chauncey drove KL in Eric's sleek black Beemer, and Devin followed behind in the black penis mobile. He was pleasantly surprised that Liz came along with him. And brought them all coffee as they waited in the near-empty waiting room at George Washington University Hospital. Devin detected a vibe passing between Liz and Eric as she passed him a paper cup of coffee. *What the fuck is that?*

He glanced over at Marlene, who seemed happily clueless. In fact, she was talking to a nurse, trying to get some word on KL's condition. Devin shook his head. *I'm worried about Dad, and I'm seeing things.*

Liz eased down next to him and handed him the final cup of coffee. "For you," she said.

Devin took it and looked down at the milky brown liquid. Then he looked up at her. Grace under pressure. "Thanks for being here with me," he said. "You didn't have to come."

"It's never dull with you and your family," she laughed.

She was so pretty, all flawless cocoa skin and huge, dark eyes. Looking at her was the perfect distraction from fretting about KL and what that tumble from the deck did to him. "If you knew what was good for you, you'd run," he said.

"Not without my dinner at Jordan's and dancing at Dream," she said.

"Oh, now you say yes," he said. "That's what it took? My dad taking a header off the deck?"

"You should thank him. I couldn't kick you when you're down."

Just then, a young white doctor in scrubs not unlike those Devin wore at work came into the room. "Rhym?" he said, and he pronounced it right, much to Devin's surprise.

They all shot up in unison. "That's us," Eric announced.

The doctor looked them all up and down, and Devin recognized that look. He'd seen it all his life, a look that questioned how this group of people of races, creeds, and colors could be a family. None-theless, he came forward with his chart. "Mr. Rhym's fine, physically," he announced.

Everyone in the room sighed, relieved.

The ER doctor continued. "He sprained his ankle and bruised a couple of ribs. There was some disorientation, but he'll be fine. For a seventy-year-old, he's in great shape. Must be his military training. You can come back with me and be with him, if you want."

They all murmured the affirmative, following the doctor to the back where the gurneys were. KL was giving a male nurse a hard time, slapping the nurse's helpful hands away. "Mr. Rhym, you have to get into the wheelchair," the nurse pleaded. "It's hospital policy."

"That's a negative," KL declared.

Eric sighed. His brows were furrowed into lines so deep that his forehead looked like an accordion. "Dad, just get in the wheelchair," he ordered. "Please!"

Marlene elbowed Eric and gave him a stern look. "Dad, would you get in the chair if this guy was a cute nurse with a short skirt?"

KL smiled for the first time that evening. "Maybe," he said.

Devin laughed. His father, even painful and sore, had punany on the brain. KL was going to be just fine.

Marlene took the reins of the wheelchair. "Come on, Dad," she prompted. "Let's get you home and to bed, okay?"

KL hobbled on his bandaged ankle and complied, easing himself into the chair. "Thank you," said a weary Chauncey.

The male nurse wheeled KL along the hospital corridors. Marlene took charge behind the scenes, signing and clearing paperwork and getting KL's prescriptions to be filled from the nurses. With the fist full of papers, she joined Devin and Liz, and Chauncey and Eric, and KL and the male nurse on the emergency room sidewalk in the warm night. The nurse helped KL to his feet. "There you go, sir," he said. "Next time, I'll wear a short skirt, okay?"

Devin watched his father hobble to his feet, then clutch his left side. He felt for him. "Those drugs'll kick in soon, Pops," he assured him. "You'll be fine."

"If I had a wet nose, I'd believe you, son," KL fired back.

Typical KL. Stick and move. Devin merely laughed to mask his pain.

"Feel better, Mr. Rhym," the male nurse said, then waved to every-one. "You folks have a good night."

Everyone thanked him and watched as he entered the automatic double doors. Chauncey immediately took charge. "Okay, Dad, Eric and Marlene and I'll drive you home, since you're practically around the corner," he said. "I'll stay with you tonight."

KL shook his head emphatically. "Chauncey. Go home to your wife and children. I will be fine."

Chauncey opened his mouth to protest, but a look from KL that they all knew well silenced him. Instead, Chauncey turned to Devin. "Dev, you're gonna take Liz home?"

Devin and Liz exchanged glances. "Your car's at Chauncey's?" Devin asked.

She shook her head no. "Eric and Marlene picked me up. My car's at home."

Devin smiled. "Then I'm taking Liz home," he said.

"And he's going to be a perfect gentleman, isn't he?" Eric cautioned through gritted teeth.

Devin gave Liz the once-over, and she did the same for him. He wasn't making any promises.

Devin took the scenic route, driving her in the "penis mobile" along Georgia Avenue in D.C. The bright lights and monuments of D.C. gave way to the suburban sprawl of Maryland. Slow jams played throughout The Quiet Storm on WHUR. Between the music and their light banter, they were soon in front of her brick high-rise on Colesville Road in Silver Spring. He pulled the car up against the sidewalk, put the car in park, and turned to face her. "This is you, huh?" he asked.

She nodded. "This is me," she said. "You want to come up?"

He stared at her in disbelief. After all this time, his pursuit of her was unfolding into success. *What's going on? What am I doing right?* Whatever it was, he didn't care. "Sure," he said, trying to play it cool, but even he heard the wobble in his voice.

She directed him to park in the garage under the building. After a quick elevator ride, they arrived on her floor, a sanitized combination of an anteroom and halls with brown carpet and a cherrywood credenza, upon which tenants put their junk mail to be tossed.

He followed behind her as she turned the key in her lock and opened the door. "This is the inner sanctum," she laughed.

Her crib was small, an efficiency. She gave him a tour, and it was short . . . the living-slash-dining area with a TV and stereo, and an Ikea table in a tiny nook. The kitchen was two walls—one for the stove and under-the-cupboard microwave, the other housing the fridge, sink, and dishwasher. A linoleum floor cut a swath between the two walls. In the back of the apartment were a small bathroom and a closed door. He assumed that, behind that door, was the bedroom. He felt cramped in her space. He could only imagine how her ex-boyfriend, the Washington Wizard, felt.

"Would you like a drink?" she asked, then she called the roll, her eyes darting back and forth as she thought. "Umm . . . I have wine—red and white—beer, Coke, orange juice, water."

He thought. "Juice sounds good," he said.

He rattled around through her CDs while she got the drinks. He was so deep in his examination that he nearly jumped when she returned. "Janet, Mariah, Mary J.," he said, taking the juice she handed him. "You've got good taste."

She laughed a girlish laugh that was a full 180 from the cool, collected Liz who'd been brushing him off from the moment he met her. "My secret passion," she confessed.

They made their way over to the couch and sat. He couldn't resist asking. "What other secret passions do you have?"

Again she laughed. "Music and the law," she sighed. "It's that simple. What about you? What gets your juices flowing?"

He didn't even have to think about it. "My family," he replied. "And my practice. I love what I do."

"I doubt it gets in the way of you having a life," she said. "You found time to go out with Ayanna."

He winced. There was that name again. "Ayanna and I just didn't get along," he stated.

"I liked her," she confessed. "She was fearless. But she was combative just to be combative, and she thought being a lawyer'd justify that behavior. The law is much more than that."

He sipped his juice. "Uh-huh," he said, nodding.

But all he could think about was her rising from the water in that orange bikini. What a letdown, from that to sitting here on the couch with her, waxing poetically about the fucking law. It was like being with his father and brothers, only they were less pretty. "I wonder if I've given up too much for my career, though," she said suddenly.

He raised a curious eyebrow. "Why do you say that?"

"Look around you," she prompted, did the same. "I'm almost thirty.

I'm far away from my family. I live alone, in a small apartment in one of the most dynamic cities in the country. I just broke up with my boyfriend, who accused me of having absolutely no time for him. Which was the truth. I'm starting to question some of my choices."

"That's normal," he assured her. "My stepmother—Eric's mom— she calls it going through your Saturn Return. It usually happens when you're almost thirty. You ask yourself all the same questions you're asking now, and if you don't like the answers, you change your life."

She smiled, nodding, like she was taking the concept in, knocking it around her skull. "Eric's mother said that?"

He nodded, his memories of her warming him. "Daphne," he said. "She lives out in Cali. I used to visit her when I was in college. She's got flaming red hair, and a house in Topanga Canyon where she makes these horrible sculptures and paintings." He couldn't believe he was revealing this. "One night, we got drunk together, and she painted me nude. I was getting into it . . . until she told me that I looked like my father naked."

"Ewww! Oedipal!" Liz laughed.

"I thought so, too!" he exclaimed. "Then I saw the canvas. Double ewww! She painted me with like, three penises. I was traumatized. That ended my nude modeling career."

Liz looked at him, and he could've sworn he saw something raw, sexual behind her gaze. "Well, that's a shame," she commented.

He stared at her. "Meaning?"

She looked him over again, and this time he knew he wasn't imagining this. She was giving him the green light. "Meaning I'd like a copy of that painting," she said.

His stare deepened. He put his juice down on the coffee table. "Okay," he said. "I'm trying to be the perfect gentleman here, but all night—with the exception of my dad falling off the deck, of course— all I could think about is you in that orange bikini. If you want me to, I'll go, and we can play this game for as long as you want. Or we could take it to the next level."

She looked up at him with those huge, dark eyes, and he knew that was the green light. "I don't want you to go," she whispered.

They moved closer on the couch, and in the next second, they were kissing. He was tasting her tongue, sucking her kisses. His heart pounded mercilessly, painfully forcing blood down between his legs. His long fingers found her bra clasp underneath her T-shirt and popped it open. Moaning hungrily, she pushed his shirt up with eager hands, helped him pull it over his head. They stood up, hands working all the fabric that separated them until they were taut muscle against taut muscle, skin on sweaty skin.

He snatched her close to his bare chest. He hunched over and pressed his pelvis against her, ground his rock-hard dick against the triangle of hair between her thighs. His commonsense side remembered the condom he had in his wallet. As if she read his mind, she whispered against his mouth, "I have condoms in the bedroom."

That's so fucking hot! Sistahs today brought their own balloons to the party. Between wet tongue kisses and bare skin caresses, they made it to the bedroom. In the dark, he could see that it was all pink and frilly. She got the strip of condoms from the nightstand, ripped off one, and handed it to him. Even in ecstasy, she was still concerned with order and uniformity.

She watched with rapt attention as he stroked himself until he was so hard that even he couldn't take it, watched as he ripped open the condom packet, pinched the reservoir tip, and rolled the condom on slowly. She looked like she was about to lick her lips, which appealed to his manhood in ways she couldn't even imagine. He joined her under the covers, she lay back, and finally, he was inside her with one explosive thrust that made her gasp out his name.

She ran her fingers along his back, grabbed handfuls of his ass, urging him deeper inside her. He closed his eyes, internalizing every sensation, feeling her grip him and relax, filling his nostrils with her scent, staring down at her contorted face, at her breasts bouncing up and down the deeper he thrust into her. He sucked her flesh, from her pink mouth, to the curve of her throat, to those small breasts and their pinpoint nipples. All of the sights, and smells, and feelings rolled into one massive emotion, drawing sensations seemingly from every cell in his body. And when she came loudly under him and then melted into the sheets, he couldn't hold back any longer. His muscles took over when executive mental functions checked out. His pelvis lurched and released, and he trembled on top of her. "Liz!" he moaned. "Oh, God, Liz!"

Later, in the silence, he looked down at her glistening face. He pushed wet strands of hair from her damp skin. She smiled, exhausted. "Liz," he whispered. *Finally* . . .

He cleaned up in her bathroom, also pink and frilly, then returned to the bed and cuddled close to her. She lay in his arms and stared off out the window across the room. The light from the road and the metro pierced the veil of darkness. Snuggled against her warmth, he felt relaxed, comfortable. His eyelids began to droop. He dropped a kiss in the hollow of her throat. "Can I stay?" he asked.

Under the covers, she folded her arms across her midsection. She felt stiff against him all of a sudden. "I've got to work tomorrow," she said.

He kissed her again. The last thing he wanted to do was leave her, heave on his clothes, and go back to his empty house. "I could take you in," he suggested.

She laughed. "That'd be weird, wouldn't it? I work with your brother."

She had a point. Eric already thought Devin was mining his clerk pool for prospective dates. "Okay," he said. "We could have breakfast, then I could take you to the metro."

Liz turned in his arms to face him. She ran a hand across his cheek. "You're sweet, Devin," she said. "But I have this ritual to get ready to spend long days with your brother."

That stung. He assumed he'd just rocked her world minutes ago. Why was he getting the bum's rush now? "Oh. I understand," he said, though he really didn't.

Under lamplight, Devin followed the trail of clothes. She put on a pink satin robe and watched him as he slowly got dressed. Inside, he felt discarded, like a used-up stud pony on the postcoital walk to the glue factory. It wasn't soon enough that he made it, fully dressed, to the front door. She met him there, wrapped her arms around him, and pressed a slow kiss on his lips. He looked into her flawless face, and instantly forgave her for turning him out in the street. "I'll call you tomorrow," he promised.

She nodded. "I'd like that," she said.

He held her face and kissed her forehead. "You have a good day tomorrow."

Her mouth softened into a smile. "You, too."

She opened the door and let him out. He looked back at the door, took a moment to enjoy his memory of what had happened behind it.

Something about his whole scenario seemed strikingly familiar to him. It was only after he was behind the wheel of his ride that it hit him. This was practically a carbon copy of how his date with Zoe ended. Only this time, he was the one tossed out into the night, because someone had "an early day tomorrow." And it didn't feel good.

Seven

Chaney sat there with the phone receiver clutched to her ear and her mouth wide open. Nothing, not even Al glaring through the glass in her door as he passed by, could counteract the surprise. Besides, staring at people he thought were running up the phone bill was Al's M.O., the hobby of a man with too much money and not enough brains.

"Did you hear me?" D asked happily in her ear.

How could you get married before me? You're my nephew! Then, God help her, she felt crushing guilt for even entertaining the thought. "I heard you," she said. "She isn't pregnant, is she?"

"No, she isn't pregnant," D laughed.

"Because you know that's what your mother's gonna ask."

She heard D suck his teeth so hard that she could've sworn that enamel came off on his tongue. "That's why we won't be telling her," he declared.

Chaney shook her head. Once again, she was caught in the middle. "You're her only child," she reminded him. "And you're asking me to keep this from her. That's not fair to either of us, D."

"You know, Chaney, tell Mom; don't tell mom. Do what you want," he said. "I'm getting married on Friday to Hiriko, and I want you there. Please say you'll come."

Chaney sighed. How could she refuse him? She used to share a bed with him, let him play with her toys, take him to the movies. He was more like her close little brother than a nephew. Though she hated the shitty relationship he had with his mother, she couldn't turn him down. "Okay," she said. "I'll come. But your mother will be heartbroken. And, to quote Forrest Gump, 'That's all I'm going to say about that.' "

"That's the shit, girl!" he said happily. "You're gonna dig Hiriko. I know it sounds corny, but you know what it's like to meet your soul mate?"

Ruefully, she thought of Shane. *Soul mates. What a fucking joke!* "Yeah, I thought I did," she sighed.

It amazed Chaney how intuitive D was. For a guy. "Girl, forget that batty boy. Come to the wedding and wild out. There'll be a battalion of Marines there, any one of them more than willing to put a spit shine on my fine auntie's pussy!"

God bless D. He knew that sometimes, the bullshit sugar coating was totally unnecessary. "When you put it that way, how could I refuse?" Chaney laughed.

"I'll e-mail you all the information," he said. "You know you's my girl, right?"

That was D's ultra-butch Marine way of saying that he loved her. "I love you, too, D," she said.

"See you Friday," he said. Then, in an instant, he was gone.

Chaney replaced the receiver and stared out at Rockville Pike. It was June, and everyone seemed to have a summer love but her. Yesterday, the mail came, and in an envelope were pictures of Daisy and the infamous Ricky who made her drop everything and go on tour. He was as tall as Daisy, with light eyes, a headful of reddish, long, highly textured dreadlocks, and a hard body in a white wifebeater, linen shorts, and Birkenstocks. They were inside the walls of Dachau, the concentration camp that was a present-day museum and showcase of Nazi atrocities. The letter that came with the pictures waxed poetically about Ricky's many positive qualities, how he'd written songs and poetry for her, how he called her "his queen," how he put it down like a champion in bed.

Daisy then talked about how Dachau affected her, how she and Ricky held hands as they stared at the horrors that Nazi hatred of the Jews produced, from photos of Mengele's experiments on twins, to the showers where they gassed people with Zyklon-B, to the massive ovens where Jews were cremated. "I guess this was how you and Anna Lisa must've felt in Ghana, when you visited The Point of No Return, where slaves got on boats bound for the New World, knowing in their hearts that they'd never see Africa again," Chaney had read from Daisy's letter.

Chaney sighed. She tried to see this as the hands of time at work, other than some cruel cosmic joke engineered at her expense. After all, D was thirty-one. He couldn't live the single life forever. He was a career military man, handsome, intelligent, and had a big heart. In the present climate where a good brothah was getting harder to find, it was doubtful that D was going to sit on the shelf forever. But, not only did her nephew upset the matrimonial balance by making it down the aisle before her, he engineered the circumstance in which she was going to have to go dateless to her own nephew's wedding.

Suddenly, she got a news flash. As usual, though, she couldn't, for the life of her, remember the number. She dug her purse out of her bottom desk drawer, then fished out the business card from the pocket where she kept her wallet. She picked up the receiver and dialed his cell phone. After three rings, he answered, and she identified herself. He laughed out loud. "Cousin Chaney!" he said. "What's up?"

He sounded happier than the last time they'd spoken. "Someone took their perky pill this morning," she remarked.

"You got me," he laughed. "How are you?"

"Desperate," she confessed. "My nephew—your real cousin—is eloping next Friday, and I need a date to help me forget how depressing it is. You wanna come with me?"

He sucked in air through gritted teeth, and she could practically envision herself on I-95 heading to the wedding by herself. "If you'd asked me last week, I would've been available to meet him and come with you," he said, "but I followed your advice. I hooked up with Liz the Law Clerk."

To her ultimate surprise, she felt her heart sink. *You and your fucking advice!* So much for her tiny crush on her fake cousin Devin. He'd moved on. To deflect the shard of pain, she made light. "Oh, see, you sleep with a brothah, and they forget about you," she chuckled.

"Well, if you'd let me hit it that night, my answer might've been different," he teased.

Her mouth hung open. "Now who's got jokes?"

"Why don't you ask Randy?" he said, a taunting inflection on Randy's name.

She laughed, but she asked herself the same question. Why hadn't she asked Randy? After the Mystics game, he'd been conspicuously absent from the office, working out of downtown D.C., or going off on events with his children. They'd pretty much just passed in the elevator or joined forces in meetings to keep the evil tag team duo of Callie and Doug at bay.

Deflect, deflect. "So . . . you and Liz, huh?"

She could hear the happy smile in his voice. "Yeah," he said. "Me and Liz."

"You didn't want to be a lawyer. The last thing I thought you'd want to do was date one."

"Me, too. But in my old age, I'm open to change."

She couldn't help but smile at the quip about his age. "I'm happy for you, Devin. You got what you wanted."

He let out a goofy, throaty laugh. "Yeah."

The last thing she wanted to listen to was another person waxing about having made a love match. "Well, since you're taken, I gotta go find a date," she said.

"As hot as you are, cousin? That should take you less than five minutes."

Who were these hypothetical men who thought she was fine, who would, as D said, "put a spit shine" on a certain body part? "Thanks for the vote of confidence, Devin," she said.

"It's all true."

After some small talk, they hung up, and she sighed. *Chaney Braxton: Dateless Spinster.* The upside to this whole thing was that she'd be gone from the office. She'd be hip-deep in Marines. She got up to get things in order so that she could disappear on Friday with a clear conscience.

She walked the halls in search of Coco. As she passed the glass of Lissa's office, though, she saw Lissa, seated on the lip of her desk with her legs crossed. Seated in the guest chair in front of the expanse of her legs was Randy. She was laughing like a giddy schoolgirl, and he was flexing, seemingly pretending not to be flattered by the attention. Chaney herself laughed, shaking her head incredulously. She wondered if Randy was making the same type of calls to Lissa as he'd made to her.

She found Coco in her gray cubicle, which was covered with photos of her husband and children in various stages of their development, as well as certificates of achievement from her Catholic church. Coco sat at her computer, a frown on her face as she stared at a piece of paper in her hand. "What's the matter?" Chaney asked.

"Laura, man," Coco complained. "She calculated my PAL wrong—again. You own twenty percent of the company—can't you straighten her out?"

Laura's fuck-up wasn't on the radar screen just then. Nonetheless, she saw how much it troubled Coco. "Okay, I'll talk to her," she promised. " 'Cause I got a favor to ask you. Can you present the storyboards to Callie and Doug on Friday?" She thought about telling her about D's upcoming marriage, but decided against it. Did Coco really need to know that the official memo stating that Chaney was a hag had arrived gift-wrapped from Quantico?

Coco thought for a minute. "No, I've got something at church that day," she said.

That meant there was only one more person to ask. *I'm screwed.*

Chaney approached Carly's office. She found her, working diligently on her computer to a classical music soundtrack that played from her desk speakers. No doubt fucking up someone's project. Chaney knocked on the doorjamb. "Carly," Chaney called over Debussy's "Claire de Lune."

Carly turned around, and Chaney suppressed a gasp, trying not to stare at the huge, crusty dandruff flakes along her middle part. "Chaney!" Carly exclaimed. "Hello!"

Chaney guessed no one went back there to visit her. Chaney gave a little wave. "Hey, Carly. Can I ask a favor?"

"Sure. How may I help?"

Even as she asked, she sensed doom. She felt her eyes narrow. "Would you be able to present the storyboards to the Navy clients? I have something on Friday that I can't miss."

Please say no. Please say no . . . Just the converse, Carly's gray eyes lit up in her freckled, wrinkled face. "Oh, Chaney," she said. "I'd be happy to help."

Oh, shit. There was no way out now. Chaney put on a brave face. "Thanks, Carly," she said.

Carly clasped her hands together. "No problem!" she squealed.

"Okay then, Chaney concluded. "I'll provide you with everything you'll need, the electronic and the hard copies, and we'll talk later."

Carly nodded, and a few flakes fell into the lap of her too-tight red nylon skirt. Chaney grimaced. "Okay," she said.

Chaney turned on her heel and walked away. Her heart thumped, and suddenly, she felt queasy inside. *I've just handed my project over to Cluster Fuck. What have I done?*

Devin stared out the glass in Eric's fishbowl of an office. From there, he could see Liz, talking to a gaggle of coworkers in the brightly lit hallway. He observed her possessively; she was *his* woman. He looked her over in her very conservative skirt suit and laughed to himself. What would everyone think if they'd seen her wrapped around him like a beautiful, dark boa constrictor on the nights they'd spent together, seen him penetrate that businesslike veil to make her tremble underneath him, in front of him as he gave it to her doggie-style. She looked up at him just then and gave a subdued wave. Grinning from ear to ear, he returned the wave with gusto.

"Devin!" Eric called, his tone scolding.

Devin whipped around to face him and Chauncey. Eric sat behind his oak-and-glass desk, in front of the breathtaking picture-window view of the Washington D.C. skyline, with its buildings that weren't allowed to be taller than the Capitol, with its construction cranes that had jokingly become the unofficial bird of the city. Chauncey, in a rumpled brown linen suit, sat in one of the two guest chairs in front of Eric's desk.

Both brothers stared at him: Chauncey, quizzical; Eric, terse. "Devin, can you mack . . ." Eric did the air quotes ". . . on your own time? Some of us have things to do. You called this meeting."

Chauncey laughed. "Leave little bruh alone," he said. "Boy's nose is open."

"Hello? Billable hours?" Eric said. "I know, the doggies and legal aid don't care about that, but I've got a wife with major plastic to support. Let's get on with it."

With the utmost reluctance, Devin stepped away from the window, made his way to the guest chair, and plopped down. "I'll be quick," he announced. "I'm worried about Dad. He was a little forgetful before, but since he fell on Memorial Day, he's gotten worse."

Eric shrugged, like it was no big thing. "What do you want from him? He's seventy. He's going to forget things."

Devin shook his head. "This is different. I've gone over to the house, and Sadat hasn't been fed, or the door's left open, or the garage."

Chauncey nodded. "He has been acting a little different lately," he said. "I can't put my finger on it. He's just been . . . I don't know . . . different."

Eric threw up his hands. "Well, what are you two suggesting we do?"

Am I crazy? "Of course, I'll have to run this by Dad, but I was thinking I'd sell my house and move in with him," Devin announced.

Eric and Chauncey looked at each other, as if letting it sink in. Devin sat there, too. He'd put it out there in the atmosphere. Now what? Finally, Chauncey spoke. "Dev, you sure you wanna do this?" he asked. "I mean, Eric's right. Dad's seventy, but you're twenty-eight. You want to spend your life playing nursemaid to a cantankerous old Marine colonel?"

Devin shrugged, trying to find the words to explain. Just by virtue of being older, they'd had KL around longer. This might've been Devin's last opportunity to bond with his father before he went off to the great beyond. "He's my dad," Devin said finally. "I want to get to know him while I still can."

Eric and Chauncey were silent, like they were thinking. It seemed like forever, but then Eric spoke. "Well, that's laudable, Devin," he said.

I'm not looking to be lauded, E," he declared. "This is totally selfish for me."

Chauncey smiled at him, and Devin felt a glow all over. "I hope to be as selfish as you one day, li'l bruh," he said.

"I agree with Chauncey," Eric said. "And I want to help. I have a friend who's a real estate agent with Long and Foster. Why don't you give me a copy of your house key? I'll give it to her and see if she can do something with her fee on your end."

Devin took out his key ring and picked out his spare house key. With some difficulty and chipped nails, he wound the key off the ring and handed it to Eric. "Have her call me when she's showing the house, and I'll leave the alarm off," he announced.

Eric nodded.

"So, you guys are down for this," Devin concluded.

Both Eric and Chauncey nodded. Devin sighed. He wanted to hug them both. The good feeling ended, though, when he thought about surmounting the final hurdle: KL himself.

Thank heaven for Fluexa.

The chapel at Quantico was serene, sunlight pouring through

Marine-themed stained-glass windows onto the small crowd of D's friends who occupied the pews inside. Chaney sat among a throng of Marines in dress blue uniform with white slacks, watching as D, looking so serious and dapper in his dress uniform, held hands with Hiriko. She looked serene in a cream-colored lace confection with flowers in her frosted waves of dark hair, in front of a berobed priest before a simple altar. Chaney marveled at D's reverence, considering that they'd both run screaming from the Espicopal church the minute they'd escaped Anna Lisa's roof. At the altar, though, D and Hiriko exchanged vows with the gravity that the event required. Suddenly, it hit Chaney. *D's really in love with her.*

After the ceremony, Chaney stood on the sidewalk and watched in awe as a guard of eight Marines held swords aloft, and D and Hiriko rushed out under the swords amid a flurry of thrown rice. Midway through the arch, two Marines brought their swords down. "Kiss to pass," they commanded, and D and Hiriko gleefully complied. Then the last Marine, closest to Hiriko, swatted her on her behind with the sword. "Welcome to the Marine Corps, Mrs. Hall!" he said.

It was official. Her nephew was a married man. And Anna Lisa wasn't there to see it happen. The bittersweet factor heightened for Chaney.

She approached the couple and waited until D looked up from his group of well-wishers and saw her. His eyes widened. He rushed toward her and crushed her close. He smelled of cologne and navy blue wool. "Look at you!" he laughed. "You came!"

Chaney rose on tiptoe to his height and kissed his smooth cheek. She'd never seen him so happy. "Of course I came," she said. "Had to make sure."

D ended the embrace and pulled Hiriko close. She looked prettier in her picture, obviously a mix of Black and Asian. She was tall and statuesque, working every inch of her dress. For a brief second, Chaney thought about Devin. "Hiriko, this is my Auntie Chaney," D announced.

Chaney rolled her eyes. She already felt as old as Methuselah; the last thing she needed was this big, hulking Marine referring to her as *Auntie.* Hiriko's dark, almond-shaped eyes widened. She kissed Chaney on both cheeks. "Yes!" she cried.

Chaney held her hands and gave her dress the once-over. "No white?"

"Not after being fucked ten ways from Sunday by this guy here!" Hiriko laughed, then winked at D.

Chaney blushed. *T.M.I.!* Just the thought of D getting busy . . .
"Okey-dokey," Chaney commented.

D just laughed and kissed his bride's dirty mouth. "Come on!" he
said. "To quote Mike Myers, 'Let's get pissed!' "

D and Hiriko had rented out a bar in nearby Woodbridge, near the
Potomac Mills shopping complex. All of the Marines, including D,
had changed into civilian clothes on the way to the reception. There
would be no desecrating the uniform with the drinking and debauch-
ing that was about to take place. Plus, Chaney assumed, all that wool
in June was bound to give someone heatstroke.

Chaney sat by herself on a lumpy couch, nursing a Coke with ice
while she watched all the mirth and frivolity. D had hired a deejay,
who spun the day's Top 40. A bunch of drunk white Marines with
milky faces and severe crew cuts were doing the kick dance, off beat,
to N.O.R.E.'s "Nothin'." D and Hiriko slow-dragged to the rhythm
like they were about to get their honeymoon started right on the
hardwood floor. D, typical West Indian man, held his icy drink as close
as he held his wife.

Chaney stared at Hiriko. *My new niece-in-law.* Chaney thought Hiriko
resembled Kimora Lee, Russell Simmons's wife. Hiriko looked like
she'd be the life of any party she'd attend. Her clothes left little to the
imagination, revealing a hard body that looked like she'd spent her
share of time in the gym. She was way too pretty to be very smart, and
her mouth seemed to have no filter. In short, she was everything that
Anna Lisa would've hated in a daughter-in-law.

A Marine slid next to Chaney. "Hello, ma'am," he said, the expression on his face suggestive.

Chaney stared at him, willing herself not to laugh. This young
brothah was supposed to be one of the Marines who was going to put
a spit-shine on her pussy? *I'm not drunk enough!*

Suddenly, she looked up. D had come to her rescue. Her goofy
nephew pulled rank, right before her eyes. "Get up, Richardson," he
commanded.

The young Marine looked up, sobering suddenly. "Yes, Sergeant
Major," he said, then snapped to and disappeared.

D laughed as he plopped down in the space Richardson had va-
cated. Chaney punched him in a hard bicep. "You know you're wrong,"
she said.

D slipped an arm around Chaney's shoulders and pressed his sweaty head against hers. "Rank has its privileges," he declared. "You know, I meant to ask you—you know Dad's second cousin, Devin Rhym?"

Chaney's brows flew north in surprise. "Yeah. Nice kid. He's Daisy's dog's vet." He was becoming a little more than that to Chaney, but there was no need to tell D anything about that.

D raised and lowered his brows. "Nice kid, huh?"

"Yes. Nice kid," she repeated, effectively shutting him down. "Why'd you ask?"

"He sent me and Hiriko an espresso machine. At the base. That was nice of the brothah."

Chaney smiled. That did sound like something Devin would do.

"Why are you sitting over here all by yourself?" D asked. "You not having fun?"

She couldn't explain to her nephew that his wedding revealed to her suddenly how lonely and vulnerable she felt, that she would have dissolved into a puddle of tears by now, if it hadn't been for her anti-depressant. *Deflect, deflect.* "I would feel better if I weren't lying to my big sister who spent her youth raising us both," Chaney declared.

D sucked his teeth. "I've been hearing my mother's mouth for thirty-one years," he said. "I spent my teen years on the chronic 'cause I couldn't live up to her expectations, her trying to make up for the fucked-up hand she got dealt."

Chaney felt a twinge of guilt that surfaced every once in a while, when she remembered everything Anna Lisa had sacrificed for her. "Hey, taking in me and Daisy was part of that fucked hand she was dealt, thank you very much," she reminded him. "Anna Lisa just wants the best for you."

"And I have it, Chaney," he insisted.

Chaney followed his gaze to rest on Hiriko, at the bar with a diverse group of young women. She smoked her cigarette and sipped her Cosmopolitan like she was the Black-Asian Carrie Bradshaw at some New York City watering hole. "I have everything I ever wanted," D said. "And I just want one of you guys to be happy for me. I ain't gonna get it from Moms, and Daisy's off in Europe getting that ass tapped. So that leaves you, Auntie."

Chaney looked at his face, so handsome and hopeful. "As long as you're happy, then I'm happy," she said.

D sighed with relief. Chaney closed her eyes as he pressed a kiss into her hair. "I want you to take care of her," he said in her ear.

Chaney stared at him quizzically. "Where are you going?"

"Chaney, I'm a Marine," D reminded her. "We're already in Afghanistan. I'm sure you've heard rumblings about us invading Iraq. I just want to make sure we're all prepared."

Chaney's stomach sank . . . the same feeling of impending doom she'd experienced eleven years ago, when he'd gotten called up for Desert Storm. "No," she gasped.

He squeezed her closer. "Just in case," he said. "If, God forbid, anything happens, just don't let them send me to Walter Reed. They'll perform an addadicktomy."

Despite the shitty news, she took the bait. "What's an addadicktomy?"

D just laughed, the puckish laugh that preceded a blistering punch line.

It was real. The ambient noise of the Route 1 late-afternoon traffic washed over them both, functioning like the soundtrack to crushing failure. Devin and Jamal stood in the expansive parking lot and stared at the warehouse-sized building with the gaudy marble façade and the Doric columns that made it look like a knockoff of the Parthenon. They looked at the balloons floating in the air, at the people streaming into the double doors with leashed dogs and cats in carriers. "It's ahead of schedule," Devin mumbled.

"They have an animal hospital inside, too, don't they?" Jamal asked.

Devin nodded. Inside, he was kicking himself. Didier had warned him, alerted him to this impending development. They had done everything they could have to find a way to peacefully coexist with this independent-veterinary-hospital-devouring behemoth. Now it was here, practically in their backyard. Suddenly, Didier didn't seem like such a reactionary.

"Dev, what's the plan?" Jamal asked.

Devin shrugged, genuinely at a loss. "I don't know, Mali," he confessed. "I guess Didier and I'll have to meet again with the business advisor."

Jamal looked over at him, a look that was a mixture of sorrow and pity. "I'm sorry, Dev," he said.

The constant flow of customers made Devin physically sick to his stomach. "I gotta get out of here," he said, looking over his shoulder at the ride he might not soon be able to afford. "You coming?"

Jamal nodded, getting into the Navigator on the passenger side. They rode back to Rosslyn in silence. Devin was thankful to have him there. A friendship of twenty-three years meant that they could sit there together, not say a word, and still be a comfort to each other.

Devin stopped on Wilson Boulevard, across the street from the Rosslyn metro station. He slapped on the hazards and turned to Jamal. His face said everything. "Call me tonight," Jamal said. "I'm off. Maybe we can get the fellas and go for drinks, okay?"

Devin nodded, though secretly, the last thing he was up for was hunting honeys in a bar. He just wanted to go home, have a shower, and escape into his big-screen TV. "Okay," he said. "I'll call you."

Jamal got out and blended into the pedestrian traffic crossing the street. Devin watched as Mali disappeared into the metro station. Devin sighed, then headed to the next traffic light, hung a left onto North Lynn, then headed for the Key Bridge and home.

The drive home was a complete blur. Before he realized it, he was pressing the remote to open the garage door at his town house. He was going to have to sell this, too. He was going to be ruined. He was going to have to move in with KL, not out of generosity, but out of necessity. And Bill . . . what was he going to tell Bill, who'd invested every penny he'd had into Devin and his dream of a veterinary practice?

Devin entered the kitchen and tossed his keys onto the counter. He looked around the open space of the town house, the drawn blinds darkening the space, shutting out the outside world. He felt just like that house . . . dark . . . empty.

He hated having to have to be the bearer of bad news, but he moved over to the phone on the kitchen wall. He was going to have to call Didier and tell him that, basically, he was right; they were fucked. He picked up the cordless and speed-dialed the office. While he listened to the rings in his ear, though, something caught his eye. He hung up, moved over to the sink, and leaned in closer to get a better look. In the porcelain sink, there was a round, gold plastic strip and a champagne cork. He picked them up and examined them further. *What the . . . ?*

Devin suddenly remembered that he told Eric to have his realtor friend come over to look at the house. That was why he'd left the alarm off. But why would the realtor need champagne?

Devin put the phone back in the rest on the wall; then he walked through the lower floor of the town house to make sure his belongings were undisturbed. Slowly, he realized that his stereo, records, and CDs were intact and in order. His computer, monitor, and peripherals were all there, as were his TV and DVD system. He sighed, relieved. *Am I crazy?*

Then, from the foot of the stairs, he heard it. Laughter. Coming from upstairs. Peals of girlish laughter, like a woman being tickled. Or something more sexual.

Devin moved up the stairs, his heart thudding with every step. As he reached the top of the stairs, the woman's laughter evolved into moans of ecstasy that seemed eerily familiar. The moans mingled with those of a guy to produce a duet of raw sexual expression. Devin went from curious, to warm inside, to heated with fury in a matter of seconds. *No, this realtor isn't fucking in my house!*

He followed the moans, which predictably grew louder and more frenetic, the closer he got to his bedroom. He stood in the doorway to the room and came upon the spectacle unfolding in front of his eyes. His pulse raged in his head so hard that he would've keeled over if he hadn't clutched onto the doorjamb.

Liz was stark naked, drenched in sweat, pert nipples hard, breasts moving rhythmically up and down. Her eyes were closed, her hands in her hair, her head jerking in a circle on her neck. She undulated her body slowly on the dick inside her, her face stretched in an expression that said she clearly was having a good time.

Devin, unable to move, stared with his mouth gaping open. His woman was fucking in his bed; what made the picture not quite right was the fact that she wasn't fucking him! All Devin could see was the swell of a chest, legs with curly red hair, and a head of slack reddish curls, covering an emerging bald spot in the guy's crown. The guy's hands came up to clutch Liz's tiny breasts, and Devin saw the wedding ring. The picture was complete. Devin realized that Eric, his own brother, was the one fucking his woman.

He couldn't look away. Every once in a while, tears blurred his vision, and he angrily blinked them away. He wasn't going to be weak; he was going to look directly at betrayal and pain, like looking full-on into a lunar eclipse, even though the shit hurt like someone kicked him in the balls.

Suddenly, Liz opened her eyes. Devin witnessed the look on her face go from pleasure to pain in an instant. She stopped dead on the dick. "Devin!" she gasped.

Eric laughed under her. "Now you're hurting my feelings, baby," he whispered.

Liz slapped him on his arm, looked down into his face. "Devin!" she repeated, then angled her head toward the doorway.

She leapt up off Eric. Devin got a glimpse of his brother's erection, sheathed in a milky white condom, as it came out of her, and he wanted to puke. Eric turned onto his side, came face-to-face with Devin. He closed his light eyes and shook his head. "Devin," he sighed.

Guiltily, they covered themselves in his white sheets, made out of T-shirt material, that he bought at Bed, Bath and Beyond. He clenched and unclenched his fists, breathing in and out, vacillating between wanting to hear what they had to say and beating the shit out of them both. He focused on Liz, who sat cowering on the side of the bed. "Why don't I call Chauncey over?" he asked. "That way, you can see all three Rhym dicks before you decide which is biggest."

Eric stood up, all pale, hairless, and doughy, his dick going limp right before their eyes. "Don't you talk to her that way," he commanded.

Devin stared at him in disbelief. His inner, foul-mouthed thug was reborn, bubbling violently through to the surface. "You're fucking *my* woman in *my* bed, and you have the balls to be giving me orders? You shady motherfucker!"

Eric held up a hand. "You're right," he said. "Be mad at me. Just leave her alone."

Fuck you! "Just how long have you two been fucking each other?" Devin asked.

Eric sighed. He held his hands akimbo at his love handles. "A year," he confessed.

Devin's pressure spiked. He raked them both with a glare of raw contempt. "A year?!" he roared. "You've been cheating on Marlene for a whole year? You brought Liz to your house! To Chauncey's house! You let Marlene fix us up! All the while you were tapping her. You heartless motherfucker! You lied to me about helping your own father so you could shit on my home like this."

Eric rolled his eyes. "What home, Devin? You don't even have any furniture."

There was no talking to him; he so missed the point. After all, he was Big Tort. He made a nice living shitting on people's feelings. Instead, Devin focused on Liz, and his heart squeezed in agony. She sat there cowering, her nakedness draped in his sheets. "Why?" he asked her.

That simple question encapsulated everything he wanted to ask but couldn't find the words: *Did I mean anything to you? How could you do this to me? What kind of heartless bitch fucks two brothers at the same time?*

Liz looked up finally, and he saw a lone tear trickle down her face. "I'm sorry," she whispered.

That's it? You're sorry. If he was into hitting women, he would've ground his clenched fist into her tear-streaked face. Before he changed his mind about that, he opened the door wider and stepped aside. "You two. Get out," he said.

Liz immediately got up, and with rounded shoulders, she scrambled to retrieve her clothes. Eric, on the other hand, came closer to Devin. For the first time ever, since Devin had known him, he had a pleading expression on his face. "Umm . . . Devin," he began. "Can I please take a quick shower? I can't . . ."

Devin looked him over scornfully, with the condom wilting on his dick smothered in Liz's juices. "You're gonna have to go home and explain to your wonderful wife who loves you, as fucked-up as you are, why you smell like some other woman," Devin declared.

Disgraced, both Liz and Eric broke the land-speed record for getting dressed. Eric stopped only to flush the evidence of his indiscretion down the toilet in the master bath. Devin then escorted them to the first floor, resisting the compelling urge to kick them both down the flight of stairs. He held the front door open and slammed it pointedly behind them as they left.

Envy settled in his gut as he parted the blinds and watched them through the window. They held hands as they descended the concrete stairs and made their way to Eric's black Beemer. Devin could've kicked himself; he was so focused on his own financial ruin that he didn't even see it parked at the curb when he'd come in. At the car, Eric pulled Liz close, and she melted in tears against him. Devin slapped the blinds shut and bounded up the stairs.

Furiously, he lunged at the bed. His breathing was labored, vocalized in groans, his chest heaving as he clawed at the sheets, as if stripping them off could erase what had just happened there. He stared at everything in a dirty heap on the floor, self-loathing filling the emptiness inside him. *You fucking chump!*

He was about to ease down on the bed, but in his mind, he saw Liz's contorted face as his brother was giving it to her. Right in that very spot.

Instead, he reached for the phone next to the bed. He hit Jamal's cell number on the speed-dial panel. After two rings, Jamal answered. "What's up?" he shouted from the other end.

Devin heard the ambient noise of traffic under Jamal's voice. "Mali, where are you?"

"In front of the HUB on Georgia Avenue," Jamal shouted.

Devin knew just the spot; he was at the Howard University Bookstore, just up the street from the hospital where he worked. "Stay there," he said. "I'll come get you."

"What's going on, Devin?"

With his free hand, Devin balled up the soiled sheets and headed downstairs toward the kitchen trash can. "I need to buy a new mattress," he announced.

Chaney wore a sky-blue tailored blouse, black Capri pants, and black strappy sandals that showed off her gold toe rings and newly-minted manicure. She stared in the well-lit bathroom mirror and put the finishing touches on her makeup, fluffed the tiny pick through her curly 'fro. She looked down at Tony, who sat in the doorway to the bathroom. "What do you think?" she asked.

Tony got up, turned slowly on all fours, and walked pointedly away. Devin's words echoed in her head. *I'd trust Tony. Dogs have good instincts.*

But then, how could Tony know that she was going out with Randy that night? For him to know that, he'd have to have instincts that bordered on clairvoyance. He was a dog; he couldn't have known that she'd stopped by the office after D's wedding. Her nephew, her ace boom coon, was a married man now, headed off to Virginia Beach for a makeshift honeymoon. And, alas, no Marines had offered to spit-shine her pussy. She was thirty-six and all alone. She realized that all she had was her twenty percent of Autodidact to keep her warm.

She'd gone into her office and found darkness. Of course, everyone else had lives and wouldn't be in the office on a Friday evening. She entered her office and found Carly's notes from the meeting. Chaney was pleasantly surprised. So she was the one person that Cluster Fuck didn't fuck over after all.

She logged on, checked her e-mail, and decreed that everything could wait until Monday. She was about to log off when she looked up and saw Randy in the doorway of her office. A confluence of emotions assailed her. She didn't know whether to be happy to see him, or to be pissed about the little demonstration in Lissa's office earlier in the week. But when he smiled at her, her heart melted. He leaned his long body against the doorjamb and looked her up and down. "Hi," he said.

She looked him up and down, too, but feigned disinterest. She logged off her computer and started getting her belongings. "Hello," she said.

"How've you been?"

"Fine," she said. She wanted to ask, *What's up with you and Lissa?* Instead, though, she asked, "How've *you* been?"

He shrugged. "Been," he said simply. "I'll cut to the chase. My favorite local jazz group's playing at Takoma Station tomorrow. Wanna come?"

Her mind and body screamed, Yes! But she didn't want him to think he was in there that easily. "I don't know, bruh," she said, shaking her head. "I'm a *Rules* sistah. According to that book, if you don't ask me by Wednesday, all bets are off."

He came closer, and her heart lunged against her ribs. "I get it—you're playing hard to get," he said.

"I don't play games," she declared.

He didn't say another word. In seconds, he was in her face, and his mouth was on hers. Chaney realized right then how horny she was. Just as she was getting into it, he pulled away. "Pick you up at eight?" he whispered against her cheek.

That's how she ended up checking herself out in the mirror and getting fever from the dog.

She glanced down at her watch; it was 7:30. She ran the mental checklist. She'd eaten. She'd fed Tony. She'd promised to print off the directions from her house to the club.

She logged on, did a Mapquest, and printed the directions. She started to check her personal e-mail when she heard the familiar digital tone coming from the computer and saw the tiny screen on her monitor.

D-Riddim: Chaney. Wazzup?

Chaney smiled. *Devin.*

SYRAQQ: Hey. I'm good. Wat r u doing alone on a Sat nite?
D-Riddim: TV.
SYRAQQ: No Liz?
D-Riddim: That's done.
SYRAQQ: That was quick! What happened?
D-Riddim: Wasn't the person I thought she was. That's life, right?

Chaney sighed. They seemed to always be on different pages. Just the previous week, she was envious that he had someone while she was all alone.

SYRAQQ: I'm sorry, Dev. Breakups suck.
D-Riddim: Wat r u doing tonite?

Chaney winced. There she was, off on a date while he was licking his wounds over his flameout with Liz. Nonetheless, she typed.

SYRAQQ: Actually, going out with Randy.
D-Riddim: u r dating? That's good, right?
SYRAQQ: Don't know. Not very good at this. Haven't dated in so long. Opened my drawer and found that all the condoms in there had expired. I 4got 2 get laid, cousin! ☺
D-Riddim: ROTFLMAO!!!!
SYRAQQ: Glad my pain amuses u, Devin.
D-Riddim: Sorry!

The doorbell rang just then, and Tony began barking like a maniac. He bounded down the stairs with a thick, thudding sound. Chaney's heart leapt. *Randy!* But then, she was torn. On the other end of the broadband cable, Devin was obviously hurting.

SYRAQQ: Got one of your brother's jokes 4 u. What do u call
the process of sewing a penis to someone?
D-Riddim: ???
SYRAQQ: An addadicktomy.
D-Riddim: LMAO!!!

The bell rang again, and Tony began to howl. She could hear his
nails on the glass windows in the front door.

SYRAQQ: Gotta go. R u gonna be ok?
D-Riddim: Yeah. U have a good time. With fresh condoms.
SYRAQQ: We'll see. C U l8tr.
D-Riddim: L8tr.

Chaney logged off, then rushed down the stairs. As she'd guessed,
Tony was up on his hind legs, barking at Randy through the gauzy material that partially obscured the glass windows in the door. Through
the material, she could see by the look on Randy's face that he wasn't
amused. So clearly not into dogs in general and a behemoth like Tony
in particular. She figured she'd put him out of his misery.

She shooed Tony away from the door, then opened it to get the full
view of Randy, rocking a dark shirt, tan slacks, and loafers. "Hey," he
said.

Chaney smiled brilliantly. "Hi."

Chaney held Tony by the collar and stepped aside to let Randy into
the anteroom. "This is Tony," she announced.

Randy looked down into Tony's doggie face. "Hello, Tony."

"Wuh!" Tony barked.

Chaney let Tony's collar go, and Tony proceeded to leap up on his
hind legs and press his paws against Randy's dark shirt. "Oh, shit!"
Randy exclaimed, looking down as Tony's nails raked his chest.

Chaney stared as Tony slid down to all fours, leaving a trail of light
hairs on Randy's shirt. She clapped her hands. "Tony!" she scolded.

Randy smiled sheepishly, brushing the hairs from the front of his
shirt. "It's cool," he assured her, but Chaney knew full well it wasn't,
that you didn't mess with brothahs and their clothing.

"Want a drink before we go?" Chaney asked.

"Sure," he said.

Chaney entered the kitchen, and Randy followed, with Tony close behind. She took out a chilled glass and a bottle of merlot from the freezer. She held it up for his approval, and he nodded. She poured him a drink, then handed it to him. "Cheers," she said.

Randy wrapped those long fingers around the body of his glass and sipped, all the while staring at her over the rim. "That's good," he remarked. "None for you?"

Chaney stared longingly at his drink. *Fucking Fluexa.* She held up a hand. "Naw, I'm good," she said.

Chaney led the way to the couch, and again, he followed. "Your house smells delicious," he commented.

She'd tell him about her creams later. For now, she said, "Thank you."

He set his drink down on a coaster on the coffee table. "Now, how about a proper welcome?" he said.

"What do you mean?" she asked.

He moved closer to her. She just sat there, put up absolutely no protest as he brushed his mouth against hers. She closed her eyes, tasting him and the wine on his lips. She opened her mouth, as if doing that could enhance the deliciousness of him. She felt his tongue against hers, snaking with hers. Everything in her body rose up. The nerves in her skin stood up on edge. Nipples formed hardened buds inside the silk of her bra. Her crotch throbbed like a mini heartbeat inside her panties. She ached when he moved away suddenly. "I don't think we're gonna make the show," he gasped, stroking her face in his hands.

Oh, God, finally! She thought of all those brand new condoms she had upstairs in her underwear drawer, next to her overused vibrator. "I don't think so, either," she panted.

They parted and were about to get up when Tony leapt clear across the coffee table and landed between them on the couch. He sat proudly upright and looked at both of them. "Wuh!" he barked.

What the hell? Tony knew that, after that horrible first night, he wasn't allowed on the couch. And if dogs had such good instincts, couldn't he tell that he was getting in the way of her finally getting some? "Tony, get down!" Chaney ordered.

Tony sat there defiantly between them. Chaney stared at the dog in awe. "Tony, get off the couch!" Randy roared.

There must've been something to a man's voice, because Tony, albeit spitefully and slowly, jumped down from the couch. Randy and

Chaney exchanged glances, their heated minds in synch. "Let's go upstairs," she suggested.

He smiled confidently and nodded, then picked up his wineglass and followed her as she led the way.

He was smooth and calm, the perfect contrast to her. She wanted to tear her clothes off and impale herself on his dick. In the bedroom, the light from both the full moon and the traffic lights on Harrison Lane sliced through the open blinds. He sipped his wine, watching her with pure sex in his eyes, and she basked in his gaze. "Damn, girl, you're so fine," he said, his voice husky.

She came up to him, boldly unbuttoning his shirt to reveal his beautiful brown chest. She ran her fingers against his soft skin, feeling his muscles clench under her fingertips. "You're not so bad yourself, Temple, Class of '78," she whispered.

Randy put his glass of wine down on the dresser and slowly tackled each button on her blouse. He revealed her bra, then looked up at her and smiled. "Front clasp," he laughed.

"Go for it," she said.

He worked the clasp, and Chaney gasped as her breasts spilled out. She relished the expression on his face; after all, she knew one of her best features—even for a smart girl—was her nice rack. He bent his bald head, and Chaney swelled with anticipation. He caressed her left breast in his large hands, and she gasped as his mouth found the nipple and sucked deeply. A full-scale riot erupted below her waist, escalating as he gave the same treatment to the right breast, kneading her flesh . . . sucking her flesh . . . massaging as he sucked. *Oh yeah!*

Then she heard clinking, totally ruining the moment. She looked up and saw Tony, sprawled out in the bedroom doorway, his metallic ID and rabies tags clinking as he scratched his neck with gusto. Even Randy looked up from what he was doing. "Chaney," he moaned. "The dog!"

"I know, I know," she sighed.

She rushed over to Tony, shooed him from the doorway, and shut the door closed. Eagerly, Randy came up behind her, wrapped his arms around her waist, and slowly worked the zipper on the side of her capris. She could feel every inch of him pressed against her ass. She cried out as he reached into her bikini briefs, scooping a hand between her legs. He slid long fingers inside her, thrusting them in and out. "Oh God!" she cried out.

She wanted to sob as he slipped his hand out of her. *Don't stop!*

He turned her in his arms to face him, and she realized that, save for his shirt, he was naked in front of her. It was everything she'd imagined, helped along by that photo of him in the Miami surf, in nothing but that swimsuit. The swimsuit was gone, and he proudly sported a rock-hard dick that lay pointed to the left. "I wanna fuck the shit out of you," he said in her ear. "You want that?"

"Yes," she moaned. "Yes!"

"Wuh!" she heard through the door. "Wuh!"

What the . . . ?

It was ugly to watch how quickly Randy's majestic erection deflated like a tire with a nail puncture. That long, thick, beautiful dick drooped like a fleshy balloon. She wanted to cry. She looked up at him. He was crestfallen. She reached out and took him into her hands, massaging him feverishly while she kissed his face, his mouth, his earlobes, ran her tongue down the length of his dome.

Nothing seemed to work. Frustrated, he pulled up his pants and plopped down onto the bed. "Wuh!" Tony barked through the door.

Chaney pulled up her capris and zipped them. She opened the door, and Tony came bounding in. She glared at him. *I'm being punished for taking you in!*

She eased down on the bed next to Randy and sighed. The look he gave Tony, too, would also ice the dog if looks could, indeed, kill. "I'm sorry," she said.

He furiously buttoned his shirt. "I'm sorry, too, Chaney," he declared. "Your dog is throwing salt on my game."

She looked at Tony. He sat looking from Chaney to Randy, his expression like, *what did I do?*

Chaney snuggled close to Randy, danced her fingers along his thigh . . . down between his legs. Still limp as wilted lettuce. "I want you," she whispered in his ear.

Randy turned his head, softly kissed her mouth. "I wanted you the second I saw you in that meeting."

"We could go to your place," she suggested.

Suddenly, his eyes glinted in the semidarkness. "I want to share something with you," he announced. "Something I'm into."

Curiosity was on overkill. "Something like what? You're not going to try to tie me up or anything like that, are you?"

He laughed, shaking his head. "Come with me," he said.

She looked him up and down. Her instincts told her that she wouldn't wind up in some harness, being anally intruded. "Okay," she said.

Minutes later, they were rolling in his air-conditioned silver Nissan Murano, going west up Route 1. She watched chain restaurants, banks, and bars flash by through the passenger-side window. "Can I ask where you're taking me?" she finally said. "Takoma Station's the other way."

He smiled cryptically. "Just wait," was all he volunteered.

About twenty minutes later, they turned off Route 1 and onto the darkness of Fairfax County Parkway. Chaney's senses heightened. This resembled dark roads from horror movies, just before Jason and Michael Myers emerged from nowhere to slice and dice horny black people just like the two of them. "What is this place?" she again asked.

"Baby, just wait," he repeated.

"Okay . . ."

Soon, she saw signs of civilization in the form of an Exxon station to the right, which was lit up like a Roman candle. She suppressed a sigh of relief. A few feet after the service station, Randy moved into the leftmost turn lane at the traffic light. The blue lead light appeared in the traffic light, and Randy hung the left onto Terminal Road.

More darkness, and Chaney's recently resuscitated relief died another death. Randy rambled past huge gas tanks and industrial-sized service stations by the light of his high beams and the moon overhead. Chaney looked over at his profile. *Are you insane? What do you really know about this man?*

Before doubt could set firmly in, though, Randy turned into the parking lot of what looked like a converted warehouse. Lights blazed in the parking lot and atop the building. A red neon sign in front of the building blazed out the words *Club Pendulum.* The lot looked harmless enough to Chaney. There were many cars, but, suspiciously, no people. Usually, when she used to go to clubs in New York and Jersey, like The Garage, or Cheetah's, or Zanzibar, there used to be horny, underage-with-fake-ID folks like her, milling about, with Last Call Louies trying to score, even in the parking lot.

Randy drove up in front of the club, and a red-jacketed valet came up to the car. "Valet," Chaney commented. "Classy."

Randy merely smiled, further adding to the mystery.

They entered the lobby of Club Pendulum. It resembled the lobby of a business complex. The only thing that gave away the fact that they were, indeed, about to enter a club was the muffled thumping backbeat of music coming through the walls. Behind the high, oval-shaped desk stood a white man with long hair, a scraggly soul patch, and a pierced tongue that showed when he asked Randy for his credit card.

Randy handed it over. While he and the white guy transacted business, Chaney looked around the lobby. At her right, a simple white vinyl sign stated the rules for entering the club. *No drugs. No offensive behavior. No violence.* Another side next to it delineated the dress code for the club. For men, it was a list of No's: *No shorts. No T-shirts.* No this, no that. Conversely, the dress code for the ladies was one line: *Always sexy.* Chaney looked down at what she was wearing: the blue blouse, black capris, and black sandals. Far from sexy, it was what she would've worn to the office on business casual Fridays.

Randy's card went through, and he signed the slip. Then he took her hand and led her toward the frosted glass double doors. On each of the doors, stenciled into the glass was a STOP sign, followed by the words: IF NUDITY OFFENDS YOU, DO NOT ENTER!

Chaney's radar went off, her fight-or-flight instinct telling her that either of the two would probably be a good option. Too late. Randy took her hand and led her through the double doors and into a whole other world.

A nubile stripper in a slutty Catholic schoolgirl outfit and high-heeled stiletto pumps worked a metal pole in the middle of a wooden dance floor, slithering and writhing to Rick James's "Superfreak." She did a handstand on the pole just then, and her black thong showed her ass and the black fabric that cleaved her glistening pink labia and ass cheeks in two. Chaney recoiled in scorn and revulsion. Randy, on the other hand, gripped her hand tighter.

At tables next to the wooden dance floor, where the stripper danced, both men and women glared appreciatively and threw dollar bills. To the stripper's right, there was a deejay booth, with a white middle-aged guy on the wheels of steel. By contrast, the tables where people sat were café style, intimate. People also sat at the fully stocked bar, watching the show on the dance floor. And a full buffet that spanned the far wall held a spread of food and desserts, served and carved by a chef with a large hat, that one would expect to see at a swanky wedding, not at some seedy strip club.

Then Chaney looked up. On each of the four big-screen TVs on the walls of the club, varying shades of hard core porn played. Women were being intruded vaginally, orally, and anally by buffed naked studs, or by other women with sex toys of all kinds of shapes and sizes. *Okay . . .* She'd enjoyed her share of adult entertainment, but always with her man, in the privacy of her own home, not in a room full of strangers. This shit tested the limits of her tolerance. *Okay . . . what do I do here?*

Chaney looked over at him. So, this was entertainment for middle-aged men. By his glassy-eyed stare and goofy smile, he looked like he was safely ensconced in his own wet dream. Was she going to be the uptight prude to ruin the night? "Let's find a table," he suggested.

Over KC and the Sunshine Band's "That's the Way I Like It," Randy escorted her to a table in the back of the club that afforded them a 180-degree view of the bar, the buffet, the dance floor, and the deejay booth. "Want a drink?" he yelled over the music.

She shook her head no. If this was what he was into, she didn't put it past someone to slip her a roofie, having her end up violated and in a Dumpster out back. Randy flagged down a waiter in black slacks and a black T-shirt and asked him to bring over a Scotch.

She stared incredulously at him. For him, this was just chillin', having a drink at the club! She leaned in toward him as he moved in his chair to the music. "*This* is what you're into?" she asked over the music.

He kept dancing in place in the chair. "I get here on one date what'd take me about ten dates at other clubs to get," he declared. "And I don't have to bring flowers and candy. There's no mystery."

Chaney looked him up and down. It was official; he was a full-on asshole.

The dance floor opened up, and couples, both black and white, headed to the floor, dancing like they were taking out billboard space to Chic's "Le Freak." *Super Freak. That's the Way I Like It. Le Freak.* In the back of her mind, Chaney noticed a running theme there. Her mouth flew open, telegraphing her astonishment, as the couples started jettisoning clothing. The women tossed tops to reveal breasts that had been perkier back in the day, but were now freckled and saggy. Men in couples traded off with the women from other couples, dancing in front of them and behind them, forming a saggy tit sandwich. Men kissed each other, with the woman in between them, writhing as they fondled breasts, raised skirts, slid hands into thongs. And people rode her about living in George-W.-Bush-loving, conservative-ass Virginia. *This must be where all the Democrats in the state hang out!*

Randy gazed at her, looked her up and down. "Wanna dance?" he shouted.

"Not like that!" she countered.

He made a face that told her everything. She was ruining his good time.

The deejay mixed the cut into Culture Club's "Do You Really Want to Hurt Me?" Chaney grimaced. *This must be the S&M cut.*

An older sistah sidled over to the table. She was pretty, dressed in an understated black spaghetti strap dress and pumps. She smiled at Randy. "Hello," she said.

Randy's gaze shifted; he appeared to like what he saw. Chaney, though, stared pointedly at her, hoping her eyes said what she didn't want to. *Can't you see he's with someone?*

The sistah looked over at Chaney. "You're very pretty," she said.

What the fuck is going on here? "Umm . . . thank you," she returned. "So are you."

The sistah focused on Randy once more. "Would you and your woman like to join me in the back?" she asked, her tone unwavering.

Randy's eyes lit up. He turned to Chaney. "I don't know," he said. "Would my woman like to join me and her in the back?"

Chaney stared at them both, her brows knitted. *What's going on in the back?*

She turned in her chair, facing in the direction where Randy and the woman were looking. At the back, there was an unassuming white door. People Chaney recognized as couples who'd been making dance-floor sandwiches were either going into that back door some-what clothed, or coming out wearing nothing but antacid-green towels. At that moment, the penny dropped. This was no run-of-the-mill tittie bar. Randy Tyree had taken her to a swing club and was now negotiating to share her black ass with the comely woman before her. Suddenly, being a prude seemed the appropriate course of action.

She stood up. "I'm so outta here," she declared.

She headed for the door, picking her way through waiters and peo-ple finding their tables. She was nearly to the lobby before she felt someone grab her arm. She turned to face Randy, and he looked pissed. "What the hell is wrong with you?" he yelled over the music.

"I am uncomfortable here, and I want to go," she yelled back, which she realized was an understatement. "Now!"

"You've got to be the most uncomfortable sistah on this planet, Chaney!" he stated. "You're uncomfortable talking to me on the phone. You're uncomfortable with this. Just what the fuck are you comfortable with?"

She snatched her arm out of his grasp. "I'd be comfortable with getting the fuck out of here!"

She headed out into the lobby, and he followed. "Well, I'm not," he said.

The white guy behind the desk in the lobby turned away, averting his eyes. Chaney guessed that was probably his M.O. *See no evil, hear no evil . . .*

Oh shit! She realized she couldn't go anywhere; he was driving. "I want to go home," she said.

He folded his arms across his chest. "Then go," he said simply. "I'm going back in."

She could feel her unmitigated fury . . . somewhere in her body. Unfortunately, the Fluexa kept it firmly in check. The old Chaney would have let loose the Brooklyn and cursed him into oblivion. The new Chaney was mentally backtracking, thinking about how they'd gotten to the club, about where she would be able to go to get away from him. "You go back in then," she said. "I hope somewhere in that back room, there's a place for you to go fuck yourself!"

Chaney headed toward the front doors. "Chaney!" Randy called after her.

She turned and glared, but secretly, she'd hoped he'd come to his senses. "What!" she yelled.

He waved his hand dismissively at her, then turned his back on her and headed back into Sodom and Gomorrah. Chaney stared at the swinging doors in utter disbelief. *This motherfucker!*

Chaney noticed the guy behind the desk, who finally regarded her as someone occupying his space. "Can I get a cab somewhere?" she asked.

He shook his stringy, dirty-blond hair. "Lady, cabs don't come here," he said.

Shit!

Chaney stared at the double glass doors, with the STOP signs stenciled on them. The choice was humiliation and discomfort on the other side of those doors, or outright danger and uncertainty on the other side of the ones they came in through.

Are you crazy! She cursed her pride for making her think that trekking back to the Fairfax County Parkway in the pitch blackness was her feminist stance, her I-am-woman-hear-me-roar. About a mile later, covered in sweat, her sandals pinching her tender feet, she wondered whether this was such a good idea. She was in pain and in danger, because she wanted to teach Randy Tyree a lesson.

Still, she trudged on, jumping practically out of her skin at every car that zoomed past her. To keep focused, she tried to think about things she should be thankful for at that very moment. It was June, not too hot, not too cold, a nice night to ditch your date at the swing club. She was rocking sandals, not high heels; her shoes hurt her feet, but they sure didn't hobble her. She wore sensible clothing, so she wasn't going to attract much attention; she could blend in, in black capris and a blouse, better than if she'd been wearing the come-fuck-me club finery.

Just as she was about to abandon hope and give in to the fear forcing her heart to beat like a drum, she recognized the entrance to the Fairfax County Parkway, saw the Exxon station that was still the brightest thing on the strip. Single-mindedly, she tore off her sandals and sprinted toward the light, bare feet slapping against the asphalt, the skin tender, her chest heaving.

Chaney crossed the Parkway and staggered the rest of the way to the station. A couple of motorists, filling up their rides, stared at her like she was a mental patient. She probably did look like one—drenched in sweat, clutching her shoes in her hands, panting like she was one second away from a full-blown heart attack. She could've cared less. She was safe in this island of civilization. Then she remembered. She was still stranded.

She put her shoes down and winced as she slipped her raw feet into them. Then she reached into her purse and took out her cell phone. She searched through the numbers, doing a mental inventory of who she could call, who would come get her, no questions asked. Then it hit her—the perfect person to come to her rescue.

She speed-dialed the number. After four rings, there was an answer on the other end. *Thank God!* "Hey," Chaney said. "I need help. Can you come get me?"

Chaney waited for over an hour, staring hopefully out at the Parkway.

Her heart thudded at every car that slowed down or stopped. Finally, the big blue Ford Explorer pulled up. The driver's-side window rolled down, and Dani appeared. At first, she seemed concerned as she looked Chaney up and down. Though Chaney called her because she was the friend least likely to moralize, Chaney expected a speech, an I-told-you-so continuation of the discussion on the metro platform. Then Chaney saw a subtle smile on her face. Chaney recognized it instantly—relief. Chaney sensed she'd be spared from having to hear shit. For now, at least. "Hop in, Chaney," Dani said.

Chaney, for once, did as she was told, leaping up into the passenger seat and shutting the door solidly . . . shutting out Randy Tyree, and Club Pendulum, and her long, dark Walk of Shame in the Virginia night. Dani watched as Chaney belted herself in. "Where you wanna go?" Dani asked.

"Home," Chaney sighed.

Dani nodded, then hung a left and headed toward Alexandria.

Eight

The minute Chaney saw Al pulling up a chair in the conference room, she sensed that the meeting concerning the first draft of the storyboards was not going to go well. Al almost never concerned himself with the day-to-day operations of Autodidact. Lissa sat next to Al, her face also reflecting displeasure. Callie's face looked like she'd just spent an hour chugging lemon juice, and Doug kept sighing and running his hands over his receding hairline. The door opened just then, and Randy breezed in. "Good morning, all," he said.

Chaney resisted the urge to look at him directly. Instinctively, though, she knew he was GQ'ed down from head to toe in the fashionable suit, tie, suspenders, and shoes. She doubted that anyone in the room would've believed her if she'd told them that about two weeks ago, before he'd left for summer vacation and the July fourth holiday with his kids, he was trying to get her into a threesome in the back room of a swing club. They would've thought she was crazy . . . or getting revenge for having had her advances spurned.

Coco sat next to Chaney, behind the laptop on the conference room desk. "Look at these *pendejos'* faces," she whispered in Chaney's ear. "Something's up."

Chaney stared around at the cast of characters at the table. Coco was hardly ever wrong. "I know," she whispered back.

"Let's start then, shall we?" Lissa said. "I'll yield the floor to Callie."

Callie's gaze darted around the table, coming to rest on Chaney. "Okay, I'm going to be blunt," she declared. "After I reviewed these storyboards . . ." she waved a stapled stack of paper in her hands ". . . I decided to have OPM issue a stop-work order on this project."

Chaney's heart thudded so hard in her chest that she could've sworn everyone in the room could hear it. In the world of government contracting, a stop-work order was one step closer to being fired off a project. Her mind ran through all the horrible scenarios of how this was going to play out. The last thing she wanted was to be the partner who lost Autodidact six million dollars. They wouldn't be ruined, but their name would be close to mud in the close-knit D.C. contracting community, especially since OPM was reviewing their proposal to be eligible for government work for five more years. In the incestuous instructional design community, everyone would be privy to the knowledge that Autodidact had lost a six-million-dollar project. Personally, she had sunk what had remained of her inheritance, which Anna Lisa had so patiently invested, into this company. A loss of that magnitude would bankrupt her.

Thank heaven for Fluexa. Chaney's external demeanor did nothing to betray her brewing inner storm. She focused like a laser beam on Callie. "When did you consider that course of action, Callie?" she asked, her tone even.

"After Doug and I read the storyboards you submitted," Callie announced. "Then yesterday—Monday—I spoke with Al and Lissa about it."

Chaney looked over at Al and Lissa across the table. Al returned the look with his beady gray eyes deeply set in his chubby face. Lissa looked away. *Fuckers!* They knew about this for over twenty-four hours and let Callie ambush her like this. "Ah," Chaney said aloud. "Perhaps if we had talked, you probably would have gotten a better quality of information, as I am the lead on the project."

"I wanted a different perspective," Callie announced.

"Hopefully you have it now, then," Chaney returned. "My partners can be very thorough. But back to the issue at hand. Why are you contemplating the stop-work order?"

"We spent months going over the management plan and the design document," Callie declared. "Well, your storyboards don't seem to reflect any input from those meetings, other than a tenuous connection to the content," Callie announced. "The objectives were not the ones we agreed upon. Even though I didn't care for them, we agreed on them as a team. As a result, the test items don't match, either."

Doug piped up. "A delay of this sort can conceivably cost us more money down the line, Chaney," he declared, then took on a paternal tone. "We're very disappointed in Autodidact."

Cluster Fuck strikes again! The old Chaney would've delighted in visions of striking Carly about the head so hard that the blow would dislodge her perpetual dandruff flakes from her part. The Fluexa-induced break in her anger, though, allowed her to see the error of her ways in this situation. She should have triple-checked the work before handing it to the cross-functional team for review.

In other meetings, this would've been the time for Randy to speak up and come to the rescue by neutralizing the petty grievances of his colleagues. She did look over at him, and he shot back a venomous, self-satisfied gaze.

"What are your thoughts concerning this matter, Randy?" she asked, her eyes unwavering.

He shrugged, his gaze equally implacable. "For once, Chaney, this time, I'm on the same page as Doug and Callie," he declared. "Usually, I've championed Autodidact's work from my position as SME, but this time, I can't, in all good conscience, do that now."

This man once had his fingers inside her. There he was again, trying to fuck her, but in a more insidious way. "Ah," she commented. "Well, it's unfortunate you feel that way."

"Guys, as I said yesterday, of course, we don't want you to issue a stop-work order and get OPM involved in our process here . . ." Al began.

Chaney wasn't relinquishing her project without a fight, albeit a very polite one, courtesy of her antidepressant. ". . . and you shouldn't have to," Chaney said, cutting Al off at the knees. "When it comes down to it, you guys are the client. You're the ones spending the money. It's our job to make you happy."

Doug harrumphed, a sound that, if he were hip, would've meant *Damned skippy!* Chaney addressed him first. "Doug, I'm sorry that you feel the storyboards are substandard," she said. "That's fixable. By us, the vendor you already have. Understandably, you're concerned with delays and waste of money. Well, you're probably going to get both if you start searching for another vendor this late in the game. We're this close to programming your lessons. It's most likely more fiscally responsible to fix any issues we may have now with the storyboards than to throw the baby out with the bathwater, don't you think?"

Doug's gray eyes darted thither and yon, and Chaney sensed she had him. That was until Callie spoke up. "I disagree," she declared. "I don't think this is fixable."

Bitch! Chaney smiled sweetly at her. "Callie, I understand your frustrations," she said. "I sense that change is a big issue for you. I can be the same way, too, sometimes."

Callie soldiered on. "It's not just change," she said. "It's change without checking with the team first."

Chaney shrugged, making it seem as blasé as she could. "Callie, we tried something different; it didn't work," she said simply. "What I can promise is that, in the next four days, I will personally take responsibility for the creation of the second draft of the storyboards. We'll even rapid prototype it."

Callie's face drew a blank. *Typical.* Chaney should've known her online instructional design certificate program from Generic U wouldn't have spent much time on rapid prototyping. Chaney felt a tremendous sense of satisfaction in breaking it down for her. "You know . . . everyone on the team is involved in all phases of the creation and review cycles of the new 'boards'. Everyone on the team will have a final draft by close of business on Friday. Look 'em over on the weekend, and we'll come back together on Monday. If you're still unhappy, then I would personally help you file your stop-work order with OPM. How does that sound to everyone?"

Everyone at the table said nothing, as though they were all mulling over the proposition. Finally, Chaney asked, "Am I to take silence as tacit agreement?"

"In the absence of a better plan, yes," Randy stated.

His and Chaney's eyes locked. *Dick!* "Duly noted, Randy," she said aloud.

Chaney stood up. The desire for fresh air was overwhelming. "Please, give me the marked up copies of your 'boards,'" she said. "I'll go to my office and review them with a fine-tooth comb."

Two copies of the storyboards—from Callie and from Doug—

found their way around the table to Chaney. Each looked like it was hemorrhaging red ballpoint pen ink. *Shit, there goes my social life!* "Thanks, everyone," Chaney said.

"I'll bring my markup by later," Randy said.

Motherfucker! She smiled sweetly. "No problem," she said.

With that, she turned on her heel and headed in the direction of her office. Just as she got there, her phone began to ring. She snatched up the receiver. Before she could say hello, the person on the other end said, "I wish to speak to my sister, the quisling."

Oh shit! Anna Lisa.

Anna Lisa continued. "I opened yesterday's mail this morning and got wedding photos from my new daughter-in-law," she declared. "I especially found it interesting to see my sister in one of them . . . my sister who didn't tell me that my only child was getting married!"

Chaney mentally prepared herself. She knew this moment was going to come; she'd just hoped it would've been later than sooner. "He asked me not to, Anna Lisa," she said. "Hell, I didn't get much notice. He called me on Monday; they got married on Friday."

"That's more notice than I got," Anna Lisa said.

"I told him you'd be hurt," Chaney said. "But he's a grown man, and as we both know, men are gonna do what they want to do, regardless of what we think."

"I don't understand that boy," Anna Lisa declared. "How would he think this would be okay? How could he be fine with neither his father nor me being at his wedding? To this girl neither of us knows anything about."

Chaney was torn—stand up for D or cause her sister further hurt. It was so hard to find middle ground. "I guess he didn't want a lecture," she said. "He says he loves her, and that's all that matters."

"Hiriko," Anna Lisa spat. "Hiriko Hall. Sounds like the name of a porn star."

What on earth do you know about porn? Anna Lisa put the "straight" in straightlaced. "Who are her people?" Anna Lisa asked.

That was so Bahamian. In a country with less than a half a million people, your lineage still made a difference in personal relationships. "She seems nice enough," Chaney said. "Her dad's a Black Marine, and her mom was his Japanese war bride. The only contradiction about her that I see is that she's a personal trainer at the local Gold's, but she smokes and two-fists martinis."

"How could you not tell me about this?" Anna Lisa asked. "How could you keep this from me? I'm your sister!"

Typical—all roads led back to Chaney. "Anna Lisa, this isn't about me," Chaney declared. "This is about you and D. Frankly, this shit between the two of you has gone on long enough. Instead of blaming me, why don't you reach out to your son so both of you can squash this?"

"Oh, I forgot, Chaney, you have all the answers in that foul mouth of yours," Anna Lisa snapped. "What do you know? The closest you've got to mothering is watching Daisy's high-maintenance dog!"

Pre-Fluexa Chaney would've let loose her temper, reminding Anna Lisa that giving birth didn't endow women with the inalienable right to shit on someone who pointed out the flaws in their relationships with their children. Post-Fluexa Chaney took a deep breath and counted to ten. "Anna Lisa, I understand you're hurt," she began. "When you find a civil tongue, feel free to call me back."

Then Chaney did something she had never done to her older sister: she hung up on her. She was sure she could picture Anna Lisa's shocked face when she heard the dial tone buzz in her ear, that the baby sister had the audacity to end the conversation in such a dramatic fashion. But Chaney had other fish to fry. Namely the tall fish that materialized in the office doorway.

Randy regarded her with a coldly professional look, and she returned the favor. "Come in and shut the door, please," she said, and he complied.

He handed her the marked-up copy of the storyboards. "Here you go," he said.

She let him have it. "What was that about in the conference room?" she demanded.

He feigned ignorance. "I don't know what you mean."

"The hell you don't," she declared. "We were on the same page during all of those meetings with your cohorts. Then, after I refuse your invitation to a three-way, you're suddenly displeased with the way the project is going."

"I'm not comfortable with the direction of this conversation," he declared.

Cute. There he was, using her words against her. "What is this, the embodiment of that Robin Williams quote about men: 'If they can't fuck it, they'll kill it?' "

He was as cool as a northern breeze. "Maybe I let my feelings for you cloud my perceptions of your abilities," he mused. "I'm starting to think that maybe Callie and Doug were right after all . . . about the instructional goal, about the objectives, about everything."

Chaney took a deep breath, letting the Fluexa do its work. She looked him up and down as she wondered what she ever saw in him. His strong-arm tactics suddenly made him the most unattractive man on the planet. Finally, she laughed, shaking her head. "Well, then," she said. "That is your prerogative. But I will say this, Randy. You think you're uncomfortable now? If you negatively affect my livelihood with your petty little masculine agenda, you will be intimately familiar with discomfort."

He laughed, too. But Chaney could see a tinge of fear in his eyes. "Are you threatening me?"

"Naw, man," she said. "Just putting some brand new flava in your ear."

Randy headed toward the door and threw it open like he had to be somewhere else immediately.

Chaney eased into her chair. She never thought she'd admit it to herself, but she felt long overdue for an appointment with Tolochko. She unclasped her Blackberry from the waistband of her trousers, and with its stylus, she began checking her calendar when the contraption beeped in her hand. She looked down, and the mailbox icon was lit up, indicating that she had a text message waiting. She tapped the icon, and read the message:

D-Riddim: Hey. Busy?

She smiled. After the shitty beginning to the day, his timing was right on the money. Her mind immediately flashed on the Kenny Lattimore joint that she and Shane used to slow-drag to. She began to type.

CBraxton: Never 2 busy 4 u, babe. Wazzup?
D-Riddim: Wanna hang l8tr?

What's this about?

CBraxton: Wat? No honeys riding your jock? Studly do right like u?
D-Riddim: Wanna spend time with my old wise cuz.

Chaney laughed. *Fuck you!*

CBraxton: Dunno. Might b soaking my teeth in a glass of Efferdent.
D-Riddim: LOL!!! C'mon. I'll even make you dinner . . .

Chaney looked out her now-open door at the poisonous alliance of Al, Lissa, Callie, Doug, and Randy hovering near the copier in the hallway. *Do I have time to hang out?* Then she sucked her teeth. *Fuck them!*

CBraxton: OK. My place? 6?
D-Riddim: K. C U then.

Chaney ended the messaging and suddenly stared off into space. *What was I doing before?* Then she looked down at the Blackberry in her hand and remembered. She entered her address book and pulled up the number for Sean Tolochko.

Devin sat in his ride in the parking lot of 3702 Suffolk Court. He had the windows up, the air blasting, and Jagged Edge's "Where the Party At" booming in the speakers. Nelly's voice practically made the cut as he rapped over the Latin-sounding piano and the fellas' harmonies. It was the perfect antidote to the shitty day he'd had.

He'd actually been sitting in his ride, in front of Chaney's house, since 5:30. He hoped nobody had called the Fairfax County police to report a suspicious Cablanasian lurking in a Navigator.

It was ugly how suddenly business had taken a nosedive at the office. He and Didier used to have to plan bathroom trips so they could accommodate their heavy load of patients. Now hours yawned between appointments. Devin could go to the bathroom whenever he liked. He could leave, take two-hour lunches, and return to find a practically empty waiting room. He and Didier even entertained the thought of putting Maria on a half-time schedule to avoid having to dip into the practice's monetary reserve. He wasn't above selling his body . . . anything to avoid having to tell Bill that he'd failed him.

Mercifully, Chaney pulled up in the Altima just then, sparing him from his thoughts. He glanced down at his watch. Six on the dot. He saw her face behind the windshield of the car and guessed that she hadn't had the best day, either. *Misery loves company.*

Devin got out into the July heat. There, again, was one of the things he missed about Seattle. The summers there were moderate, not anywhere close to Virginia's oppressive heat and humidity. He, toting his bags, met her on the sidewalk as she locked the car with her remote. Behind his sunglasses, he looked her up and down. She looked cool in a white, short-sleeved cotton turtleneck and creamy-colored slacks. She held a matching jacket over her arm. "Hey," he said.

She shielded her eyes from the sun with her hand and flashed him a smile. "Hey, Dev."

On impulse, he hugged her, and she gasped. He could tell she wasn't expecting it. As usual, she smelled delicious, this time edible, like citrus fruits. "How you doin'?" he asked.

"Slaving to the rhythm," she sighed against him.

Before she thought he was truly trying to cop a feel, he got up off her. They stood in place, checking each other out and smiling. In that moment, he could feel the dynamic of their relationship shift to the other end of the spectrum. Yes, she was pretty and she had a beautiful pair of titties and an ass he could set his drink on, but the other reason why he found her so hot was the fact that he could tell her anything. He could be himself when he was with her.

She was feeling something, too. He could tell, because she laughed strangely. "Umm . . . shall we go inside?" she asked.

He nodded, following her into the house. He watched as she performed her ritual, turning on the lights, turning off the alarm. He let the exotic smells in the house—scents of spices and citrus and flowers subtly intermingling—wash over him. Then she turned to him, and his gut seized. *Those eyes.* He hadn't realized how large her eyes were . . . like Speed-Racer-Japanese-amine large. With long lashes. "It's, like, dress-rehearsal-for-hell hot out there," she laughed.

He laughed, too. "Yeah, that heat is no joke."

She rubbed her hands together and focused on the bags in her hand. "What ya gat?"

Oh yeah. He opened one of the grocery bags in his hand from the Giant. "Umm . . . I figured we could do burgers. You have a grill, right?"

They went into the kitchen. She pointed to a white contraption on the countertop. "George Foreman," she said, then shrugged.

Worked fine for him. He didn't think she was ready to see him all unattractively sweaty, like he was at Chauncey's on Memorial Day. "That's cool," he remarked.

She tugged at the Blockbuster bag. "You rented something?"

Devin looked inside. He truly didn't know what her taste in movies was like. "Yeah, I got *Booty Call, The Sixth Man, I Got the Hookup* . . ."

"So, it's gonna be neo-blaxploitation night."

He could tell she didn't much care for his choices. "Jamal calls these types of movies 'niggeos,' " he sighed.

Chaney burst out laughing until tears came to her eyes. "Niggeos!" she hollered. "That's hilarious!"

He laughed, too. More than that, though, he'd made her laugh, which made him feel all warm inside. "That's Mali," he chuckled.

She pointed over her shoulder across the room at the drawn vertical blinds. From the last visit, he remembered that there was a glass sliding door behind them. "Speaking of ma man, let me get Tony inside," she said. "Poor dog's probably melted by now. Put your stuff in the kitchen."

She headed for the doors. Meanwhile, he went to the neat eat-in kitchen and began unpacking the grocery bags. Peripherally, he heard her open the blinds, heard her exclaim, "What the . . . !"

Devin looked up over the counter and saw the back of her as she stared out into the backyard. "What?" he asked.

Nothing.

Devin crossed the expanse of the living room in quick strides until he stood next to her. He followed her gaze into the yard. Just like her, he examined the evidence. Tony's gray metal water dish sat half-full next to the red wooden swing on the deck. The door to the brown picket fence swung ajar, the wrought-iron lock in the middle of it hung limply on its last rusty screw. Tony was nowhere to be seen. "He's gone!" Chaney gasped.

She threw open the sliding glass doors and ran onto the deck. He could see the fear in her eyes. "Tony!" she yelled, a cry in her voice. "Here, boy!"

Nothing.

The cool customer inside him made him take charge. "Okay," he said. "Calm down."

She whirled to face him. "Calm down?!" she cried. "The dog is missing."

"Hey, we don't know that yet," he insisted. "Let's just go out the door, follow his tracks, and see if we can find him, okay?"

She looked like it sounded like sense to her. She nodded. "Okay."

She descended the deck stairs and walked on the cobblestones that led to the open back gate. He followed behind her as they left the yard and walked along the grass just outside the wooden fences that separated the backyards of the town houses from the common areas. Even though he was focused on trying to help her find Tony, he did notice that the landscaped space was beautiful, wide open and green, with strategically placed trees. Some homeowner's association lovingly tended to this yard.

"First I almost kill him, now I lose him!" she sighed as she walked, her head darting all around. "Why'd he run? Doesn't he have it good here?"

Devin looked around, too, particularly at his left in the high grass. He prayed Tony didn't go in there. The area looked to be rife with poison ivy. "He's a dog, Chaney," he explained. "They run off. It's not about how much he might or mightn't love you. It's about freedom."

"Sounds just like a man," she commented.

He laughed, thinking a second about his dad. "Yeah, I guess you're right."

They walked through the vast expanse of field, both of them calling out Tony's name periodically. Soon, though, the field grew bigger and wider. Even Devin began to wonder if it was hopeless. They parted, standing back-to-back in the field. "Tony!" he heard her call behind him.

Is that . . . ? Devin walked further ahead, stalking closer to a stand of trees. Yup, it was. "Chaney," Devin called over his shoulder. "I think we found him."

She came up behind him and he pointed over by the trees. "Oh my God!" she cried.

A chocolate lab looked straight ahead with a vacant stare. Her body shook rhythmically forward and backward. Tony had mounted her from behind. The expression on his face, on the other hand, appeared to be one of extreme satisfaction as he gleefully gave it to her. She seemed to be stanching against him, but he had the nails of his front paws dug into her hide, his feet firmly rooted onto the earth as he drilled his partner. Next to them, a kid—Devin guessed he was in his teens—lay sleeping, propped up against a nearby tree.

Devin studied Chaney; she had her hands clasped to her mouth. Then they looked at each other and burst out laughing. "I'm worrying about him, and he's all up in Hershey's ill nana," she giggled.

He studied the two dogs. He remembered the last time he'd given it to someone doggie-style. In the mirror, Liz looked about as bored as Hershey did. Now he knew why.

"What should we do?" Chaney asked.

Devin shrugged. "We don't know how long they've been at it. I'd say let him finish. Any damage has probably already been done."

"Damage, like pregnancy?"

He nodded.

Chaney watched them, her head cocked to one side. "Hershey doesn't look too happy," she observed. "What's the matter, my chocolate sistah?"

Devin laughed. "For her, it's more . . ." what was the word? ". . . perfunctory."

She sighed. "I'd take some perfunctory action right about now."

He stared at her. From that remark, he assumed Randy didn't hit it after all. God help him, he was relieved. He looked her up and down. She looked like a long, delicious creamsicle, something he sure would enjoy on a hot day like that one. Off the cuff, he laughed. "I could help you out, if you'd like."

She stared at him; she looked like she was trying to gauge whether or not he was serious. "Oh, Devin, you and your big heart!"

So, that's a no, then. He shrugged. "Well, you know, anything to help," he said.

She persisted. "Plus, aren't we cousins or something?"

He laughed. "We could conceivably get busy and not have flipper babies."

Chaney looked him up and down, checking him out in his white polo shirt with *Rosslyn Veterinary Hospital* on the breast pocket, and his brown cargo pants, and his brown lug-soled shoes. To punctuate it, he folded his arms and posed like a b-boy. But inside, his heart thumped. *She's actually considering it!*

Unfortunately, though, he and his dick wilted at the sound of a scream from behind them. He and Chaney turned and saw an older woman in a housedress, crying as she rushed toward them. She was followed by an equally old and pasty man with thick glasses and wearing polyester slacks and a T-shirt. At that moment, the kid under the tree woke up and rocketed to his feet. He stared at everyone in front of him, followed their gaze to the two dogs . . . just as Tony busted his nut and then climbed off Hershey. "Holy shit, man!" the kid moaned. "You fucked my dog!"

Devin took one look at him. *Stoner.*

He and Chaney joined the fray, running over to the scene of the crime. "Come here, Tony!" Chaney called.

For once, an obedient Tony did as he was told. Chaney held him by the yoke of his collar, as she, the old folks, and the kid faced off. "Oh, Hershey," the old lady said in an English accent. "Come here, darling."

Hershey took her own sweet time, but she approached the white folks. The old lady inspected Hershey's rump, and Hershey looked quite satisfied. The old lady then turned on Chaney. "That hound has defiled my beautiful show dog!" she hissed

"I'm so sorry, Mrs. De'Ath," Chaney said. "Somehow, he got out of the gate."

"Pets only run away from bad owners," the man said, his accent English, too.

Devin piped up. "That's really not true," he said. "As I was telling Chaney, dogs run off. It's in their nature."

The couple looked at him, like *who the fuck are you?* "We've raised show dogs for thirty years, young man," the woman, Mrs. De'Ath, declared. "Who are you to tell us our business?"

He was about to explain his occupation when Chaney leapt to his defense. "He's a veterinarian, that's who," she declared, then pointed a finger at the kid. "Maybe if Johnny Blaze over here hadn't been toking up while he was supposed to watch Hershey, none of this would've happened!"

The kid's face turned ten shades of red. "Hey, man, I was just sleeping 'cause it's, like, hot!" he insisted.

"You're not going to hear the end of this, Miss Braxton," the man stated.

Devin held up a conciliatory hand between the two parties. "Hey, this isn't life or death, people," he reminded them. "If it would help, I could take Hershey to my office, examine her, and give her a morning-after injection for free."

Mrs. De'Ath wasn't buying. "You two've done enough for one bloody day!" she declared. "We're taking her to the Pet-Thenon."

Devin felt as though he'd been slapped across the face. All roads to his ruination led to the Pet-Thenon. Without a word, he stepped aside and watched as the three of them led Hershey away by the loop of her choke chain. For a second, Hershey looked back at Tony, and he looked back at her, like two star-crossed doggie lovers.

Chaney touched his arm. "Hey," she said, her tone soothing. "You okay?"

He looked down at her. She couldn't know that she was actually making life a bit better. "Yeah," he said. "Let's go inside."

This is nice . . . They made the long walk back to the town house in silence. Once inside, they washed up. While Chaney fed Tony his special food, Devin searched through her CDs. Immediately, he recognized some of the same cuts he had at the crib in Georgetown. Though her taste in rap was old school . . . Tribe Called Quest, Public Enemy, Gangstar, Smif-N-Wessun . . . This probably wasn't the right time to plot the revolution, anyway.

Instead, he went for a softer vibe. He put in the new Mary J., the new Janet, both CDs of Whitney's greatest hits, and "Butterfly," Mariah's joint from 1997. He hit Shuffle, then Play. Instantly, Raphael Saddiq's guitar from Whitney's "Fine" blew up the room. Chaney's head shot up from behind the bar. "Nice!"

They each took control of their cooking apparatus of choice, with him on the George Foreman grill and her at the stove. In a little over an hour, they were finishing up a meal of burgers, potato salad, and a green salad in the nook of the eat-in kitchen. Tony sat upright at their feet, ears perked up. Chaney sipped her Coke. "Look at him," she said. "He's like, 'Which one of you's gonna give me some?' "

"We shouldn't give him table scraps," Devin said.

Nonetheless, Chaney broke off the last piece of her burger and handed it to Tony. He nipped it out of her hand. *Oh well, so much for my professional advice* . . .

"You should've brought some *kimchi*," she insisted. "I never would've thought you, Doogie Howser, D.V.M., would be introducing me to new things."

He smiled, looking her up and down. Girl could cook, had excellent taste in music, a sympathetic ear, got along with his father, and most importantly, loved *kimchi*. She was this close to being wifey. He held his chin in his hand and studied her. Unlike Memorial Day, now it was the big head saying, *Liz* who? "To quote Aaliyah, age ain't nothin' but a number," he declared.

"That was her justification for marrying R. Kelly," Chaney said. "When it's reversed, though . . ."

". . . younger man, older woman . . ."

". . . then society flips."

All he knew was that he could look into those eyes all night. He wanted to hug her and inhale her until he was all filled up. "As long as two people are compatible, then society can go fuck itself," he said. "What happens between two consenting adults is no one's business but their own."

She seemed to be choosing her words carefully. "I think the fear with older women is that the younger man is in it for the curiosity factor, the experience. When he's learned all he can from her, he drops her for someone more age-appropriate. Bahamians call it 'fattening the frog for the snake.' "

The fear with older women . . . She couldn't have been more obvious that she was talking about herself if she'd used her own name in the sentence. He looked her directly in the eye. "If one of your personality traits is to be an asshole who can't commit, then you're an asshole first, then a young asshole second, Chaney," he said.

"That's one theory, Devin," she conceded. "Some people just aren't cut out to take the risk."

Was she 'some people?' He was going to open his mouth to make his case, when Mariah Carey's voice swelled from the speakers, urging a woman to spread her wings and prepare to fly, with the promise that she, too, would become a butterfly, able to fly into the sun. He merely sat back, watched her, and let the lyrics sink in.

It seemed like hours later when he pried his gaze away from hers and looked down at his watch: *9:30. Shit!* "Unfortunately, Chaney, I have to go," he announced. "I promised Pop I'd come over and check on him. What are you doing tomorrow after work?"

She blinked, like she was shocked there'd be a return engagement. "Tomorrow? Work, the usual. Why?"

"Wanna hang out?"

"Sure, but somewhere down the line, all this hanging out's going to evolve into a date."

He laughed. "Okay. A date. You choose."

"Can I think about it and call you?"

He nodded.

They got up, and he stretched his legs. "You've got to take your dad a plate," she insisted.

He watched as she lovingly prepared a plate for KL, with burgers and buns—with condiments—on one plate, and potato and green salad each in two separate Gladware containers. He wondered what it was about his father that made women want to care for him. He was a career Marine; he certainly didn't give off an air of helplessness. "He's gonna love that," Devin said as Chaney stacked everything with precision in a plastic Giant bag.

She snapped her fingers. "Oh, there's something else." ·

Curiously, he watched as she headed out of the kitchen. "Where are you going?"

"You can come, if you like," she said.

Warily, Devin approached and Tony followed as she headed toward a white door. He followed behind her down a flight of carpeted stairs. The cool dampness told him that he was in the basement. He followed her and his nose toward scents that became more pungent. Finally, they stood in the doorway of the unfinished section of her basement. There were amber apothecary jars and bottles on numerous shelves nailed into the concrete. On another set of shelves sat jars and jars of products, with labels put on with a Brother P-Touch. At his right sat a wooden workbench with a six-quart mixer, amid jars of products, he guessed, she must've been working on. "This is where you do it," he said.

She nodded, surveying her surroundings with her hands akimbo. He looked at yet another shelf, replete with small white candles and tealights in glass holders. "You make candles, too?" he asked.

She nodded. "Yup," she said. "Soy candles. Pour 'em myself. They burn cooler and more evenly than products like beeswax and paraffin."

She walked over to the products. "I wanna use you as my guinea pig," she said, picking out creams from the shelf and tiny, pocket-sized jars. "These are shaving mousses and lip balms. For you and your dad. Use them; let me know what you think."

He stared at her in admiration. He already knew what he thought: *You're the shit, girl!*

Minutes later, they were upstairs again. He was gathering up his dad's food in one bag, and the mousses, lip balms, and candles in another.

They stood in the awkward moment, facing each other, waiting for the other to make the first move . . . any move. So, he played his guy card, took the initiative, and pulled her into his arms. He buried his nose in the hollow of her throat, inhaled the scent at the point where her carotid artery beat against her soft skin. "Candles, food—I gotta come over more often," he said, but meant every word.

She pressed her head into his chest, held her arms slung low in the small of his back. "Just say when," she said.

He moved away, found himself staring into her face. He meant to just give her a quick kiss. After all, he didn't want to take advantage of her ambivalence about getting with a young 'un like him. But when he touched his mouth to hers, the feeling of softness against his hardness, along with the taste of her flesh, overtook him. He closed his eyes, kissing her again and again . . . until she pulled away, gasping for air. She looked hot and bothered and confused, all at the same time. She leaned her forehead against his, her eyes closed. "Just so you know," she whispered, her breath fresh on his face, "I'm not trying to be someone's transitional babe."

Liz who? "I'm done with my transition," he declared.

They stayed like that for some time, head to head, hand in hand. Through the corner of his eye, he saw Tony circling them. Finally, though, she wriggled from his grasp. "Umm . . . your dad's probably starving," she murmured.

"Yeah," he mumbled. "Dad."

Devin said 'bye to Tony, took his bags, and headed for his ride. He could still feel the kiss on his mouth as he took the George Washington Parkway from Old Town, Alexandria, with its cobblestoned majesty and its brick buildings from colonial times, to Route 50 and the skyscrapers of Rosslyn in Arlington. He zipped up Wilson, then turned onto North Garfield and parked in front of KL's house. Secretly, he wondered what he was going to find there that night. In two months, KL's behavior had gone from the usual hard-to-please spikiness that Devin remembered from his youth to outright hostility sometimes.

He let himself in with his key and found his dad, sound asleep in his wooden, hand-carved chair, strategically placed in front of the TV. Sadat, the embodiment of loyalty, lay curled up at KL's feet. He looked up at Devin and gave his tail a slight wag of recognition.

In his sleep, in the cathode-ray-tube glow of the TV, KL looked peaceful. He didn't look like the grandson of slaves, the son of Bible-thumping sharecroppers trying to raise their only child under the strangling yoke of Jim Crow, like the Marine who'd seen all kinds of combat and inhumanity, like the attorney who once defended the system, then railed against it to protect brothahs who got caught up in the machine. Devin took a blanket off the nearby sofa, unfurled it with a snap, and tucked it around his father. He was about to slowly pinch KL's glasses off his nose, when KL opened his eyes. Shock of all shocks, he looked in Devin's face and smiled. "Devin," he murmured sleepily.

"Hey, Pops," he said. "You hungry?"

KL's eyes lit up. Devin took that as a yes.

Devin set the table in the dining room, warmed up KL's burgers, then set a place for him. KL took one forkful of the potato salad and closed his eyes. "Damn, that's good!" he exclaimed. "Who made this?"

"Chaney," Devin announced.

KL looked him up and down, a satisfied smirk on his face. "Chaney, huh?"

Devin knew what he was thinking. "Yes, Chaney," he repeated.

KL grunted, then returned to his plate. Devin produced the other bag, with the candles, creams, mousses, and lip balms. "She gave us this stuff, too," he said. "She makes it at home."

KL held up one of the bottles. "Shaving mousse. 'Combats razor bumps,'" he read, through the lenses of his glasses. "So, she's easy on the eye, she can cook her ass off, and she makes skin care products for her people. Why's she wasting her time with you?"

Devin laughed, shaking his head. KL was back, with a vengeance. "We're just hanging, Dad," he said.

KL stared at him, looked him up and down with that all-seeing, all-knowing gaze. "Don't let what happened with your brother cloud your judgment, Devin," he finally said.

The mere mention of it nearly erased the weeks of trying to distance himself from what he'd seen with his own eyes. He regretted telling his dad about the whole episode. Strictly to have something to do with his hands, he opened one of the jars of lip balm and sniffed it. *Chocolate.* "I don't wanna talk about it," he announced.

Apparently, KL did. "The girl had been fucking your brother for a whole year," he reminded Devin. "That had nothing to do with you, really."

"They involved me in their shit to stop Marlene from being suspicious," he declared. "It has everything to do with me. And what about Marlene? He's been with her, like, forever. Is that how you treat someone you love?"

"The heart has absolutely nothing to do with the penis," KL stated with conviction.

Devin thought about that pearl of wisdom for a minute, along with all the women he'd run through when he was in college and veterinary school. Not one of them had captured his heart like Kimmy had. But he imagined if one of them had, that he would've stopped fucking around. He saw the hurt infidelity brought to a relationship every time he stared into his mother's eyes. He looked at his father, who was again focused on his plate. *That's what makes me different from you . . .*

Devin looked down at his watch. The hands pointed out eleven o'clock. Suddenly, he was very tired. "Listen, Dad, can I crash here?"

KL looked up in mild surprise. "You actually want to stay here, instead of at Mt. Olympus?" he teased. "With your view of the Potomac?"

What he didn't want to tell KL was that, even with the new mattress, he still couldn't bring himself to sleep in the bed where Eric fucked his woman. For weeks, he'd sacked out on his couch, in front of the big-screen TV. "I've got an early day tomorrow, and I don't want to have to make that drive when the office is just up the street," he explained, which was partially true.

KL ate the last forkful of potato salad, and Sadat, who'd been sitting at his feet hoping for scraps, lay back down. "The sofa bed in the basement's all made up, son," he said. "It's yours."

Devin stood up. "Thanks, Pops," he said. "Good night."

" 'Night," KL called after him.

Moments later, Devin touched both the wooden paneling and the railing as he descended into the subterranean darkness of the basement. It held the personal effects of three children, three wives, and almost forty years of life at the house on North Garfield. The place was its own self-contained living space, separate and apart from the other floors of the house. It had its own facilities, even though the sink and toilet were in one sliver of a room, and the shower was in another clear across the space . . . both separated from the open area by dry-wall and a door.

Devin saw old schoolbooks, board games, and records on book-shelves that were nothing more than sagging plywood and cinder blocks. He saw old appliances, like his first transistor radio, along with his first black-and-white TV, and his first set of turntables. KL had added some new touches, like a 36-inch color TV in front of the new couch that folded out into a queen-sized bed. The washer and dryer in the far corner were also new additions, as was the table and four chairs just behind the couch. Only windows in the bathroom and above the table let in any kind of natural light from the street.

He stood there and let the memories wash over him . . . watching TV and getting stoned for the first and last time with his boys, mixing and spinning 12-inch records on his turntables, doing homework away from his parents' incessant fighting, making love with Kimmy, con-centrating hard as his mother was banging on the door, disrupting his flow.

Right then, he realized that everything he loved about being home was not in some town house in Georgetown. It was not in the practice up the street. All of his best memories lived right in the little room be-neath this house on North Garfield Street.

This was your dumb-ass idea . . .

Even though the hot July sun was fading fast, taking its heating rays with it, it probably still was not the best idea to suggest watching a flick *al fresco* on the National Mall. Every year, HBO and AOL sponsored Screen on the Green. She'd missed it the year before. That day, they were showing *The Maltese Falcon* on a massive silver screen at the far end of the grassy mall. When she'd called Devin with her suggested activity, she'd thrown this out for consideration, even though she didn't think watching Humphrey Bogart flex was on the top ten outings for twenty-eight-year-olds in D.C. To her surprise, he said yes.

So, that's how she ended up, sitting on a blanket among the thou-sands of sunbaked bodies on blankets as she waited for him to come. She looked down at what she was wearing. The white blouse and floral skirt were okay, good from work straight to fun. The black Steve Madden high-heeled mules with the buckle on the side were another story. Already she saw clumps of dirt and grass from the mall collecting at the tips of the heels, along with dirt streaks on the shoes themselves. *Inappropriate footwear for your inappropriate date? What are you doing, girl?*

The Blackberry clipped to her waist rang. She snatched it off and looked down at it. *Please don't be the office!* She put it to her ear and said hello. "Where are you?" Devin asked.

She stood up and looked, in awe, at the thousands upon thousands of people either standing up or stretched out on blankets, as they waited for the movie to start. She looked for landmarks. "Stay on the Constitution Avenue side," she instructed. "I'm wearing a white blouse and a red skirt. I'll wave so you can see me."

Chaney waved at no one in particular, feeling like a world-class bonehead . . . that was, until she saw him. He was gingerly picking his way through the supine crowd. He was dressed like he was yesterday, only today, he wore sunglasses and carried a backpack across his shoulder. He saw her and smiled, then picked up the pace until he was standing right in front of her. "Hey," he said.

"Hey," she giggled. *What is wrong with you, girl?*

He bent his head and kissed her, and she tiptoed and returned the favor. "Get a room!" someone shouted from somewhere behind them.

They laughed as they sat down on the blanket and made themselves comfortable. Immediately, she handed over the folded cardboard box that she'd gotten from the vendor on Fourteenth Street. "Here," she said. "I knew you'd be starvin' like Marvin."

He looked down at the two hot dogs, a bag of Lay's Original Potato Chips, and a Coke on the inside of the box. He looked up at her, unvarnished gratitude on his face. "You think of everything," he said. "What about you?"

She thought of the huge lunch she and Coco had shared from the Fuddrucker's on Rockville Pike. It was still sitting in her stomach, about to migrate to her thighs, no doubt. "I'm good," she assured him.

They talked as he devoured his dinner, as the hot sun dipped below the horizon and makeshift lights set up across the mall flamed on. When it was dark enough, the HBO introduction that usually opened the Saturday-night movie began playing both on screen and through the speakers, also strategically placed across the mall. Two hippies in front of them got up and danced, and they looked at each other and laughed. She suppressed a gasp as he slipped an arm around her shoulders and pulled her close. She looked up at him in surprise. The whole scene reminded her of high school, going to the movies with boys at the theater at Kings Plaza and snuggling with them in the dark. *I'm thirty-six years old and regressing to my teens!*

When Chaney began to watch the first frames of the flick, though, she could hardly contain herself. Humphrey Bogart was punishingly kissing a weepy woman, and Peter Lorre's effete performance as the guy in search of the Maltese Falcon statue made her want to laugh outright. *This shit is an American classic?*

Chaney looked at Devin, and Devin looked at her. They both laughed hysterically. "Let's go," he suggested.

"Okay!" she giggled.

They folded up the blanket, then picked their way through the folks on the mall until they made it to the sidewalk. He held her hand, lacing his fingers through hers as they ran across the street, evading oncoming traffic. That was how they walked—hand in hand—to the Smithsonian metro station. She looked up at his profile. She couldn't remember the last time she'd held hands in public. She imagined it was the night at The Blue Mountain Restaurant, when Shane changed her life forever.

As they waited for the Blue Line train on the crowded platform, he slipped his arm around her waist. *Get into it, girl!* She rested her head on his shoulder and sighed. "Bogart should try dating some of these women today," Devin commented. "One of these women who take Pilates would mess him up."

"Women actually liked that stuff back in the day," Chaney laughed incredulously.

"You wanna do something else?" he asked.

Chaney looked up at the digital clock on the platform's announcement board. The dots winked out 9:30. "As much as I hate calling it a night, I can't party during the week like you young 'uns," she laughed. "By the time I get home, it'll be almost 11:00."

He nodded, seemingly understanding. "Another night, then," he said. "I'll see you home."

The lights on the platform blinked, and the air shifted as the train pulled into the tunnel. They got on amongst the crowd, the doors closed, and the train shot like a bullet through the tunnel. At National Airport, they got off to switch lines. Aside from the odd cop that patrolled periodically, there was no one on the platform. They sat on the metal bench and watched as the planes took off into the hot, starry night. "Me and the fellas used to come here," he said. "What else could we do? We didn't have any girls . . . couldn't drive. We'd just sit here and listen to hip-hop." He shook his head. "That shit spoke to us. It still does."

Chaney stared incredulously at him. "Hip-hop today speaks to you?" she asked. "Ludacris screaming at bitches to get out the way. That speaks to you?" she asked. "Luda threatening to spray haters like Afro Sheen? Biggie telling sistahs he wants to lace some lyrical douches in their bushes? Him telling playas to rub their dicks if you love hip-hop?' That speaks to you?"

He colored. "Naw, man, that stuff's just fun," he laughed. "Playful."

"Young brothahs could take a page from the rhyme books of Chuck D.," she insisted. "Guru from Gangstar. Q-Tipp. Even Queen Latifah and MC Lyte."

He looked her up and down, with admiration. "Listen to you, Sistah Souljah," he said. "Maybe you need your own hip-hop name."

Chaney laughed. "You know, I was asking myself the other day just what I needed, and a hip-hop name didn't even make the cut."

"No, seriously," he insisted, totally not serious. "You could be like . . . Chay Brax."

Just the thought! This was different. No man had ever given her a hip-hop name before. "Don't make me holler, boy!" she laughed.

He played on. "I could call you Chay Breezy," he insisted. "Or Chay Brizzle, my nizzle."

"Stop!'

"Chay Brax in the wheels of steel. I could even teach you how to break dance."

This was getting funnier by the minute. She looked down at what she was wearing. The last thing the world needed was an eyeful of her ass. And her shoes were already a mess from the mall. "Not in my good Steve Maddens!"

Her mouth widened as he dropped to the ground and began spinning like a top . . . a top with spindly, long legs, whipping around. She hated to admit it, but the boy did have skillz. He was better than shell-toe-wearing b-boys she used to watch breaking in Washington Square Park in the eighties. She looked around; the platform was still, mercifully, empty. "Get up!" she giggled.

He lay on one side, with one leg over the other and posed . . . just as a middle-aged, white, uniformed cop came that way on his rounds. *Oh shit!* The cop stared at her, then at Devin, still posed on the ground. Devin suddenly untangled himself and jumped up to his feet. A sheen of sweat glimmered on his face; his chest heaved up and down. "Officer," he gasped.

The cop studied him. Just as Chaney thought they were doomed, the officer smiled . . . a slight smile but a smile nonetheless. "Son," he said, then doffed his cap at Chaney and moved on.

Chaney giggled behind her hand as Devin sat back down beside her. She took a handkerchief out of her bag and handed it to him. He dragged it across his face, then wiped his hands. "Are you trying to get profiled?" she asked.

He winked at her. "Well, you were the one who asked what you won't do for love," he said.

Before she could ponder what he meant, he moved closer, like he was going to kiss her. She knew there were so many reasons why she should have backed away and played the role of the adult. They were out in the open; she'd never been one for public displays of affection. Randy Tyree had so reinforced her mantra of No plants, no pets, no men. And he was a kid . . . a wonderful, open, impetuous kid, but a kid nonetheless. With all those reasons resonating inside her head, all she saw was him breakin' for her, him holding her hand, him hugging her close, him giving her affection she so desperately craved. So, she didn't move away as he touched his mouth to hers once . . . twice . . . She held his face in her hands. His tongue found his way into her mouth. Greedily, he sucked her tongue, the softness of her lips, as if he wanted to devour her right there on the bench. A riot ensued inside her panties, her groin contracting and throbbing violently. *God help me, I'm so fucking hot for this kid!* But if he'd gotten a stern look for break-dancing on the platform, she could only imagine what would've happened if she stepped out of her drawers, mounted him, and rode him like he was Seabiscuit right there on the platform, as the planes blasted into the heavens in Freudian fashion.

The Yellow Line train chugged onto the tracks just then. Lazily, they separated. He smiled, mischief in his eyes. Blushing, she looked away, taking his hand as he helped her to her feet and onto the train. Instead of sitting, they held onto the pole at their end of the car. He brushed a kiss against her lips, and Chaney gasped, looking around at the many people in the car, some of whom were looking at them. "Devin," she whispered.

He laughed and shrugged, like, so?

So indeed! These people didn't know her from Eve's housecat, and she'd probably see none of them ever again. He kissed her again, and she reciprocated, darting tongue and all, with the only thing separating them being that hard metal pole. The forced restraint, along with the voyeuristic eyes of passengers, only heightened her feeling of liberation, of thumbing her nose at established mores that used to bind her up tightly. She just knew she felt like Halle Berry in *Monster's Ball*, wanting him to make her feel good, and supposed common sense, along with everything else, be damned. She kissed him as if the feel of it sustained her right down to her soul.

He held her close, the metal pole strategically between them, as the train lurched into Huntington station, the last stop. He slipped his arm around her waist as they walked down the escalator to the parking garage. Chaney made this journey every day, and every day, the commuters jostling her and the long walk pissed her off to no end. That night, though, the only thing she was aware of was his protective arm around her waist, his body pressed against hers. She clung to him all the way to the Altima, parked on the second level of the structure on Huntington Avenue.

He helped her into the car, and she started it up and turned down the window. He touched her nose, and she laughed. He kissed her, and she involuntarily clutched the steering wheel. "I had fun tonight," he said.

She grimaced. "Even though it was hotter than Hell on the mall and the movie sucked?"

He kissed her again. "I had fun tonight," he repeated. "Chay Breezy. Wanna hook up tomorrow?"

She laughed, shaking her head. How could she fight it, especially when he'd made a special hip-hop name, just for her? "Okay," she relented. "Meet me tomorrow at seven at the Twinbrook metro platform. Then we can decide if we both need to have our heads examined!"

Chaney watched him wave to her through her rearview mirror as she left. She could feel herself beginning to melt. It excited her and terrified her at the same time.

* * *

Devin sat in his office, bouncing a whiffle ball against the wall and catching it as it bounced off. He looked at his watch. Five more hours until he was supposed to meet Chaney at the metro for an actual date. The anticipation of seeing her again helped to take the focus off the fact that it was two o'clock in the afternoon, and they had had more cancellations than patients come through the door.

He heard the office door creak open wider, then caught the ball and turned to see Maria coming in. Her face was grave. Had Didier told her she was one month's receipts away from going half-time? "Let me guess," he said. "The Levinsohns have cancelled Fluffy's two o'clock spaying."

"Yes, the Levinsohns have cancelled," she confirmed. "But also, there's a woman here to see you, and she's got two kids with her. She says her name's Kimmy. She's not looking good, Devin."

Oh, shit. He shot to his feet. "She can come in," he said.

Maria stepped aside and opened the door wider to make room. Kimmy entered, and Devin swallowed a gasp. She had Denis by the arm, and clutched a swaddled Dante with her free hand. She wore a baseball cap and shades, but Devin could see a reddened nose and a scab-encrusted lip. In his mind, he drew the most logical conclusion: Don got tired of beating up on the furniture and turned his anger on her. "Devin," she said, her tone nasal, like she'd been crying.

"Hey, Kimmy," he said, trying to sound casual. "What's up?"

Maria looked at Devin, then Kimmy, then back at Devin. "Umm . . . I'll leave you guys alone," she said, then walked out, closing the door behind herself.

Once the door was closed, Denis broke free from his mother's grasp and rushed toward Devin. On cue, Devin scooped him and held him close. Denis sobbed into Devin's shoulder with such force that his little body quaked. Devin's heart squeezed tightly, and he fought back tears of his own. He cradled Denis's little head. "Hey, what's wrong, little man?" he asked, his tone gentle.

Denis could only cry, as if the load he was carrying was too big for words that a four-year-old knew. Devin looked up at Kimmy. She took off her shades to reveal a bruised left eye, the black of her wounded flesh blending with the blue of her eye. Her contorted face revealed how hard she was fighting to maintain control. "I left him," she announced. "I need your help."

The part of his heart over which Kimmy still held sway filled up and overflowed. "What do you need?" he asked.

3:30 . . .

Chaney entered one of the empty offices and stared across the street at the Twinbrook metro. Three and a half more hours, and she was going to meet him right there on that platform. She'd done everything to make the best impression possible. She'd taken a lunch hour from the office, away from her steaming-hot project, to visit her hairdresser, Olivette, the Jamaican babe with the overcrowded salon in Southeast. She ran her hands through Chaney's hair. "Gyal, when you gwine let me get rid of dis gray?" she asked.

Chaney looked in the picture mirror, from profile to profile, as Olivette held her hair away from either side of her face. She was right. Gray didn't go with the hot, young boyfriend. The last thing she needed was folks thinking she was Devin's mother. So, she said something she'd never thought she'd say to a hairdresser. "Do what you feel. I trust you."

In between Olivette talking about having read Dani's book, about Clinton and the "*D-N-hay* on de dress," she dyed Chaney's hair a cinnamon brown, washed and conditioned it, and did a straw set with some setting lotion to augment her natural curls. Chaney studied her shadowed reflection in the plate glass window and liked what she saw. *Will he like it, too?*

She felt her Blackberry buzz against her waist. She unclipped it and looked at the face. She looked down and saw the lit mailbox icon. She tapped the icon, and her heart practically leapt. *Speak of the Devil.*

D-Riddim: Hey, Chay.

She remembered the moniker, remembered him break dancing on the metro platform at National. She laughed out loud as she typed.

CBraxton: Hey! Wazzup?
D-Riddim: Gonna have to postpone tonight. Have an emergency. Rain check?

The heart that had leapt now sunk. All the imaginable scenarios ran through her head. Part of her worried; what was his emergency?

Was he hurt? Was KL all right? The other part of her that was used to being disappointed by men, though, predominated. He didn't mean anything he'd said the night before. He'd met someone else. He'd changed his mind. Either way, it was another guy, another disappointment. *You're better off being frozen, girl!*

CBraxton: Sure, Devin. Rain check.

In a nanosecond, he was gone, disappeared into cyberspace. She stared down at the Blackberry. *Rain check, my ass.*

The house had never felt so alive. Devin brought in the Wal-Mart bags, which held everything that Kimmy and the boys would need for their lives without Don. In the shadow of the big-screen TV blasting the Cartoon Network, Devin made hot dogs. He sat on the couch and stared as Kimmy and Denis ate, while Dante sucked gleefully on a frank. Devin marveled at how much he'd grown since Kimmy had told him to get out of her house, to mind his own business.

She looked like a losing prizefighter. He could only imagine the strength it took to leave with only her children and the clothes on their backs. "Where are you gonna go?" he asked.

She looked up. "I called my aunt, the one in Manhattan," she said. "She said I could come stay with her."

"That was the plan," he reminded her.

She smiled wryly, then winced and held a finger to her split lip. "Yup, that's me. Supermodel Mommy."

"Baby steps," he said. "Baby steps."

Denis looked up at him. "Baby steps, like Dante?"

Devin smiled and ran a gentle hand over Denis's unkempt head. "Just like Dante," he said.

Kimmy smiled at her little angel. "Better pack," she said. "But first, Denis, bath time!"

Devin stared at the little fellas, then at her. She needed someone to help make her life easier. "You pack," Devin said. "I'll bathe them."

Kimmy was leery. "Really?"

"Stop looking at me like I'm Michael Jackson," he laughed. "Really."

Devin ran a bath in the tub in the master bathroom. He poured a liberal dollop of Mr. Bubble into the tub and watched Denis's eyes widen as it frothed up mightily. He laughed, and put more in. It made a nice mountain of bubbles. Kimmy helped to undress Denis and Dante. Denis leapt into the tub. Kimmy put the baby bath seat they'd gotten from Wal-Mart into the tub, then set Dante into the tiny seat. He watched, grinning from ear to ear, as the boys played with the bubbles. Denis laughed, and Dante gurgled happily. For a second there, Devin imagined that they were a family, that Kimmy was his wife, and these two boys were his sons, and they were bathing them after a long, hard day. Then he looked at Kimmy's battered face. *Focus, Devin . . .*

Still, though, he knew he could get used to this . . . preparing the bed for the fellas and powdering them both down. He helped Denis into his new Spiderman pajamas. Devin looked at Dante's bare bottom and grimaced. *Please don't shit or pee on me!*

It was a struggle, but Devin actually diapered Dante. It was Denis, though, who helped Devin wrestle the squirming baby into a blue cotton unitard. While Kimmy headed to the master bath, Devin used the full body pillows to make supports so the boys wouldn't roll out of the bed, then he tucked the boys in between them. Devin leaned over and tickled Dante in his chubby little tummy. Dante giggled, showing off his pink, toothless grin. "Good night, little boy," he whispered.

Dante emitted a loud sound that Devin could only imagine was pure joy. He wondered how a man could look at these beautiful little boys and then haul ass out of their lives. Devin then focused on Denis, who was smiling sleepily. Devin bent over and plopped a kiss on his forehead. "'Night, little man," Devin said.

"'Night, Uncle Devin," he said. "Are you coming to Manhatma with us?"

Manhatma. Devin chuckled. "Naw, dude, I gotta stay here."

His eyes were wide as saucers. "Am I gonna see you again?"

Devin felt the tears before they blurred his vision. He knew that this was probably the last time he was going to see Denis. But the kid's world was coming undone; why add further to the disillusionment? He blinked the tears away. "'Course we're gonna see each other again," he said. "I'll make sure of it. Now go to sleep. You've got a big day tomorrow."

Devin watched as Denis drifted off to sleep. After he was sure it was okay to leave, he got up off the bed and reached for the cordless phone. It had been hard, having to choose between sharing the evening with Chaney, or making sure Kimmy and the fellas got squared away. But, given that his father had helped her and her sisters also escape to New York, he was sure she would understand once he'd broken it down for her.

He dialed her home number. After three rings, she picked up on the other end and said hello. He closed his eyes, savoring the sound of her voice. "Chaney, it's Devin," he said quietly, then looked over his shoulder. The boys were still asleep.

There was a pointed pause on the other end. Finally, she said, "Hello, Devin."

"I just wanted to call in person to apologize for tonight," he said. "I'm gonna make it up to you."

"It was a first, being blown off by text message," she declared.

He could feel the frost from her end. Clearly, she wasn't feeling him. "I didn't blow you off," he explained. "Like I said, I had an emergency."

"Is your dad okay? Your brothers? Renee? Marlene? Your practice?"

"They're all fine. I'll tell you when I see you."

Just then, he felt Kimmy come up from behind and touch him on his shoulder. "Devin, the shower's all yours," she announced.

He covered the mouthpiece with his hand and turned to see her in nothing but a towel that left little to the imagination. Milk-filled cleavage spilled out over the top, and the slit in the front gave him a long look at her thigh. Surprisingly, he felt nothing but pissed off. *You have the worst timing.* "Thanks," he said nonetheless.

She walked away, and Devin turned his attentions back to the conversation. "Hey, I'm back," he said. "So, when can I see you again?"

The frost on the other end thickened. "You keep handling that emergency," she stated. "I'll call you."

He sighed. "It's not what you think, Chaney."

"Devin, I'm not your woman. You don't have to explain anything to me. You have a good night, okay?"

In his dealings with women, he'd learned that things like this tended to smooth themselves out in the cold light of day. Kimmy would be on her way to New York, and he would be able to handle this in person. "You, too," he said.

Abruptly, he heard the dial tone droning in his ear. He looked down at the phone. *That went well . . .*

* * *

Union Station was a mass of frenetic activity. In the majestic marble structure, people were either shopping at the high-end stores, or grabbing a cup of coffee and a pastry at the Au Bon Pain, or rushing to catch their movie that was just starting at the theater. Other people were leaving D.C. by train to spend the weekend in some other part of the country. Travelers blocked the Amtrak kiosks, and crammed the terminals and took up all of the chairs in the waiting areas. Devin was just able to get tickets on the Acela train to New York City before Amtrak closed out the booking.

He joined Kimmy, Dante, and Denis on the line, with duffel bags carrying all their new belongings. Reflexively, Denis took Devin's hand, while Kimmy tended to the baby. She looked nervous and excited at the same time. Her eyes darted around the crowded-to-bursting terminal, and he instinctively knew who she was looking for. "He's not here," Devin assured her. "You're safe."

Just then the line started moving slowly, lurching up to the open door, which led to the trains. "I'll stop worrying when we leave the station," she announced.

Devin reached into his jacket pocket and pulled out a thick white number ten envelope. It contained the most cash he could get his hands on in such short notice—five thousand dollars. He tucked it into her shabby black pleather purse. "To get you started," he said.

She looked up at him and sighed. Tears rolled unabated down her bruised cheeks. Denis protectively patted her thigh. "Don't cry, Mommy," he pleaded. "It's gonna be okay."

Devin had to look away, lest he dissolve right there along with her. *She's going off to something better.* He took a handkerchief out of his pocket and handed it to her. "Hey, hey, hey," he said. "Wait until you see they don't have any Utz chips up there. Then you'll cry!"

She smiled through her tears, despite herself. "Why didn't I wait for you?" she asked.

"That's all history now," he insisted. "You're gonna do great things, Kimmy."

She looked so beat down by a hard life, bad men, and dumb life choices. She looked up at him, her eyes hopeful in her wounded face. "Really?" she asked, begged.

He nodded. "Really."

At the door to the train, a brothah in an Amtrak uniform announced, "Only ticketed passengers beyond this point."

Devin's heart sank. It was real; they were actually going. "This is where I get off," he said.

Kimmy sat Dante on her hip and hugged Devin tightly. "Devin," she wailed. "Thank you so much!"

He squeezed his moist eyes shut, taking a moment to smell her hair and her skin, to feel her against him for probably the last time for a long time. "Love you, girl," he said, his voice thick with emotion.

"I'm scared," she whispered in his ear.

"You're gonna be just fine."

She let him go. He tucked her hair behind her ears and kissed her pink mouth. "You're gonna be fine," he assured her again. "Call me when you get there. If you need anything, let me know. Anything. Okay?"

She locked eyes with his and nodded.

Dante squealed just then, lightening the mood. They both laughed, and Devin dropped a kiss on the crown of his head. Dante laid a chubby hand against Devin's cheek, and he kissed that, too. " 'Bye, Dante," he said, his voice rising a bit in pitch. "You be a good boy."

Devin then looked down at Denis. Devin knew that expression on the boy's face: false bravado. It was his mask, too, when he tried to protect his mother, at the same time trying to hold fear at bay. The knot that throbbed in Denis's cheek betrayed the fact that he was biting the flesh inside. " 'Bye, Uncle Devin," Denis said.

Devin picked him up and held him close. That was when he lost it. Tears flowed down his cheeks unchecked. "I'm gonna miss you, Denis," he sobbed.

Denis crushed his face into the hollow in Devin's neck. "Gonna miss you, too, Uncle Devin."

Devin opened his eyes and saw the line of people waiting for the train growing fitful and impatient. He put the boy down and brushed tears from his eyes. "You protect your mommy, okay?" he said.

Denis puffed out his tiny chest. "Okay."

"I love you, boy."

"I love you, too."

Devin watched, his face pressed against the glass, as Kimmy and the fellas headed toward the train waiting on the track. She didn't look back, and Devin didn't blame her. He guessed if she'd looked back, she would've lost her courage and gone right back to Don and his abuse.

Devin imagined that his father probably stood in that same spot over thirty years ago, watching as Chaney, her two sisters, and her nephew headed off for a better life. Just like KL had done for someone else, Devin had saved Kimmy and her sons. Then it hit him. Maybe in the best way possible, he'd become his father.

Devin looked around at the Friday-night crowd at the bar in Clarendon. There were the usual college girls who dressed like they were taking out billboard space that screamed "FUCK ME!" There were the horny white boys who stared at them, tongues practically hanging from their mouths. Then there were the jaded types who just held their drinks and leaned against the wall or the bar. Then there were the women who'd come with their girls whose billboard screamed to the men in attendance "FUCK OFF!" "N 2 Gether Now," Limp Bizkit's collabo with Method Man, was coming from somewhere, and those L.L. Bean and J. Crew gangsters nodded their heads off time to the beat. Just another Friday night in "The New Georgetown."

His boys sat with him at the round table. Jamal looked bored, nursing a Red Stripe straight from the can. Ryan opted for the ever-favorite Heineken, as did Andre. Devin was on his second Scotch. His father liked to pound Scotch as his drink of choice. Unfortunately, after finishing number two, he was still stone cold sober.

Andre homed in on him. "Hey, everyone," he said, over the ambient music and crowd noise. "Let's play 'Spot the Humorless Fuck; Win a Prize!' "

Devin glared at him, letting him know he wasn't in the mood.

"Stop it," Ryan said.

Even Jamal eyed Andre disapprovingly. "Bruh. Why?" he asked.

" 'Cause he's bringing me down," Andre complained. "All this pussy 'round here, and he's moping over the baby mama and the bitch who fucked his brother."

Devin shifted the glare to Jamal, and Jamal cowered in his chair. Devin had sworn him to secrecy at the Mattress Discounters after he explained why he was tossing a perfectly good Sealy Posturepedic. "Nice," he spat.

"Don't be mad at him," Ryan said. "You should've known you couldn't keep that from your boys."

The hurt intensified. He felt exposed, like he had no skin to protect him from the slights. He got up, reached into his pocket, and tossed a twenty onto the table. "I'm gone," he announced.

"Go on, then," Andre said. "You ever stop to ask yourself if this sulky, intense, brooding shit you got goin' on could be the reason why your girl got tired of you and fucked Eric?"

Twenty-three years of Andre riding him unleashed the mother of tempers from inside him. "What the fuck do you know about anything?" Devin roared. "Have you *ever* had a relationship with a woman that lasted more than fifteen minutes and produced more than a used condom?"

"Yeah, a half-hour and *two* used condoms," Andre retorted.

Devin raked him with his gaze, shaking his head. "What else should I expect from a man who thinks that pussy is the answer to life's greatest questions?"

Andre smirked. "All the good questions, anyway."

Devin turned, pushing his way through the denizens of the New Georgetown until he found himself outside on the sidewalk. The sound of traffic replaced the music and chatter from the bar. He turned to see Jamal and Ryan come out of the door behind him. He pointed a finger in Ryan's face. "You better school your brother," he declared. "There isn't much more of his shit I'm gonna take."

"You know my brother," Ryan said. "Small doses."

The door opened again, and this time, Andre came out. "All right, all right, Dev," he said, laughing. "My bad. Come back inside. I'll buy you a drink."

You think it's that easy? "Fuck you, Andre," Devin said.

"Yeah, yeah, yeah, fuck me," Andre said. "Just come back inside. I feel bad."

Devin jingled his keys in his pants pocket. Home to the basement, or back into the bar to play more sexual games? Before he could make up his mind, though, a shiny blue Ford pickup stopped abruptly in the left lane, close to the sidewalk. Behind the truck, motorists who had the misfortune of having been stuck behind him in that lane honked their horns furiously, then waited until drivers in the other lanes would let them go around the truck and into their lane.

Devin and his boys watched as a white man in a navy blue maintenance man's uniform, with an American Red Cross patch on his left
pec, and the name tag *Don* sewn over the pocket on his right stormed
toward them. His face was screwed up in pure anger, veins in his neck
poked out against the collar of his uniform. It took Devin a second,
but he recognized him.

Don pointed an index finger of one of those worn hands Devin's
way. "There you are!" Don said.

Devin sized Don up. Between his height and weight, along with the
fact that he had three other very fit black men on the sidewalk with
him, Devin guessed that he had the advantage. "What do you want?"
Devin asked.

Don came closer, and Devin could see that his gray eyes were
hooded, with a network of capillaries showing through the whites.
Don was fucked up. "Where's Kimmy?"

Devin wanted to laugh in his face. "You mean your woman that you
beat like a dog up and left you? I'm shocked!"

Don busted into chest-heaving, manly sobs right then. "I want
Kimmy!" he shouted. "You know where she is, and you're gonna tell
me."

Devin would've been moved if he hadn't, just the night before,
seen how Don had used Kimmy's face as an Everlast heavy bag. He
wasn't about to tell him that Kimmy had phoned to say that she and
the boys were safely at her aunt's. "Don, go home," Devin said. "Sober
up. You lost her. Take the hit."

Don probably meant to get up in Devin's face. However, since he
only stood at about five-foot-ten at the most, he only reached as high
as Devin's chest. "Listen here, you Chinese nigger," he snarled. "You
better fucking tell me where she is, or you'll be the sorriest boy in the
whole state of Virginia. You hear me?"

At the resounding dropping of the N-bomb, Ryan, Jamal, and
Andre came over to have Devin's back. The wild grief in Don's eyes let
Devin know that the man didn't have the good sense to realize when
he should let it go. "You better back the fuck up just a taste, son,"
Andre declared. "'Cause that shit'll get you hurt."

Devin felt himself giving Don the benefit of the doubt. God only
knew that he'd spent many sleepless nights mourning for the sunshine that Kimmy had brought into his life. "I know you fucked up

and lost your woman," he said gently, "so I'm going to cut you a whole heap of slack. Just get into your truck and drive off."

Don's response was immediate. Before Devin could move out of the way, Don had made a fist with those huge laborer's hands, swung mightily, and ground it into Devin's nose. The pain seared through his head. His vision blurred for a second. His eyes began to water. Rivulets of blood cascaded from his nose. "Shiiitttt!" he cried, dragging out every syllable.

"That's what I think o' your advice," Don declared.

That was the last shot Don would get off. Devin shook his head to recover and saw that Andre, Ryan, and Jamal had a hold of Don, who squirmed his wiry body against the big, restraining hands. Kimmy's shattered face came to Devin's mind, along with Denis's abject terror. Devin made a fist and punched Don squarely in his midsection. Don made an *oooof* sound. When he doubled over, Devin caught him with a left jab across his chin.

The fellas let Don go, and he slumped to the sidewalk. "That's for Kimmy, and Denis, and Dante," Devin shouted at Don's dirty-blond head.

Typical Arlington County style, a police cruiser, with lights spinning and sirens blazing, sped up, way after the fact, and two white officers with buzz cuts got out. "Hold it!" one of them commanded.

"I'm a cop!" Ryan called.

"Slowly reach into your pocket and pull out your badge," the other officer instructed.

Ryan complied, pulling the chain out from his shirt to reveal his detective's shield. One of the officers came closer and studied it. "You're a D.C. cop," he said. "This isn't your jurisdiction."

Ryan pointed to Don, kneeling on the sidewalk. "When this man decided to assault my friend, my juris*dic*tion was all up in dude's face," he declared.

The other officer went over to help Don up. He didn't seem to care about Devin, who held his head back and pressed his hanky to his face in an attempt to stop the blood flow from his nose. "Are you all right, sir?" the officer asked Don.

Don, now upright, snatched his arm away from the cop. "Leave me alone," he wept.

The officer who inspected Ryan's badge relaxed, as did his partner.

"Fellas, go home," he commanded. "Call it a night. Or next time, we won't be so forgiving."

The officers disappeared as quickly as they appeared. Don staggered over to his truck. He gave Devin a hateful look as he got behind the wheel and sped off into traffic. Devin and the fellas stared after him, then Jamal examined Devin's nose, which had suddenly stopped bleeding but still hurt like hell. "Ridiculous!" Jamal commented. "That asshole started it, and he gets the preferential treatment from those fucking Nazis while you hemorrhage to death! This is why we in D.C. hate Virginia."

We in D.C. Like he didn't spend his formative years, just like they all did, practically right up the street.

Devin unbuttoned his polo shirt, saw tiny drops of blood from his nose forming on the front. Suddenly, it felt like the whole world was suffocating him. "I gotta go," he declared, then fished into his pocket and pulled out all the bills he had and handed them to Ryan. "You guys go back in. Have drinks. On me. I just . . . I gotta be somewhere else right now."

Andre nodded, as did Jamal. "Go on," Ryan said. "Give us a call later."

Devin sighed. He knew they would understand. He turned and headed toward where he'd parked the Navigator. Moments later, he was speeding along the George Washington Parkway. The well-lit monuments to American democracy zipped by at his left, exits for National Airport at his right. Some arcane instinct was propelling him toward Alexandria, and he didn't have the energy to question why.

Chaney sat hunched over the keyboard, while she cradled the phone in the hollow of her throat. Lissa and Callie were conferenced in on the phone. Chaney looked at the clock on the status bar of the monitor. Ten o'clock on a Friday night and three revisions later, Callie was still attempting to assert her will concerning the storyboards. Lissa, just as blinded by her twenty-one percent of six million, was humoring her to the point of being her sycophant. "Okay, ladies, I've just e-mailed everyone on the team the boards with the changes we discussed incorporated in them," Chaney said. "You both got 'em?"

There was a lull over the phone as, Chaney assumed, they checked their e-mail boxes. "Got 'em," Lissa announced.

"Got 'em," Callie said. "I'll call Doug and Randy, and we'll look them over this weekend."

Probably can find Randy at the swing club. Aloud, though, Chaney said. "Okay. Shall we meet on Tuesday in our offices?"

"Sounds good to me," Lissa said.

"That's fine."

"Well, ladies, good night," Chaney said. *Fuck off.*

Lissa and Callie chorused their good nights and hung up. Chaney looked down at Tony, who lay patiently at her feet. "Don't ever sell your soul, dog," she said.

Tony's tail thumped mightily as he stared up at her with those all-knowing brown eyes. "Oh yeah, that's right. You don't have a soul," Chaney laughed. "Kind of like our client."

Chaney was about to shut down her system when the phone rang. She looked in the caller ID; the green screen showed a 301 area code and the name *Lissa Janus.* Chaney swore, scaring Tony. She was just minutes away from her Spinster's Friday night of a pint of Ben and Jerry's Chocolate Chip Cookie Dough and the DVDs she'd rented at the Blockbuster up the street. Chaney composed herself and pressed the TALK button on the cordless. "Hi, Lissa, what's up?"

"That woman!" Lissa exclaimed. "Could she be more difficult?"

"You created the monster—now you hate it?"

"What do you mean?"

"You and Al have given her candy for being difficult, Lissa," Chaney stated. "That meeting on Monday was just the tip of the iceberg. She wants a suite of offices, you give it to her. She adds needless review cycles to the process, and you sit there and allow it to happen. She maligns my credentials, and you say nothing."

Silence. Chaney knew Lissa, knew she was probably wondering how Chaney had heard about the Chaney-doesn't-know-anything-about-instructional-design meeting in Al's office. *Thank you, Coco!*

"Maybe Al and I thought that you could handle yourself, Chaney," Lissa finally said, as if what Chaney had said had hurt *her.* "We don't know who this kinder, gentler Chaney is."

Lately, Chaney didn't know who she was, either. Initially, the Fluexa had helped her to focus, to stay on task, and to filter out the distractions, like Callie and Doug. But she felt the drug changing her personality. Maybe, if the old Chaney had lost it and spanked Callie and

Doug when they'd begun to act up at the inception of the project, then all of the flexing at the back end now probably could've been contained. "Do I need to be a pit bull in a skirt and lipstick to make my point, Lissa?" she asked quietly.

"Sometimes, that's what people respond to best," Lissa said.

"I did think I was handling myself and my business, Lissa. What I had expected was more support from my friend." *That would be you . . .*

"And you have it," Lissa declared. "But there are issues here that are much bigger than our friendship, Chaney."

Issues much bigger than our friendship? Chaney stared at the phone, wanting to kick herself for her initial dismissal of Coco's conspiracy theory. Had she not been sucking down Tolochko's feel-good-when-last-have-you-had-joy pills, she probably would've been able to see all of this coming.

The doorbell rang right then, and Tony pitched up and ran down the stairs, barking his head off. "What, you got Cujo over there?" Lissa laughed uncomfortably.

Chaney followed Tony down the stairs. Tony had leapt up on his hind legs and was staring through the glass. He'd stopped barking. His tail, though, whipped around in a circle. Through the window treatment, Chaney saw Devin's silhouette. Her heart raced. "I gotta go—there's someone at the door," Chaney announced.

"We'll pick it up on Monday," Lissa insisted.

And monkeys'll fly out of my ass. She pressed the TALK button to end the conversation, then set the phone on the bar.

She wondered how to play this. She could take the spiteful road. After all, he'd cancelled their date by text message! That was almost as bad as blowing someone off by e-mail . . . or voice mail. And then the showering at his home with another woman was just the limit. But she liked him so much. And after dealing with Callie for over twelve hours, she could've used a hug from him, one of those hugs where he wrapped those long arms around her and dug his chin into the crown of her head and tickled her.

Holding Tony back, she opened the door and instantly recoiled. He looked disheveled, his face swollen around the nose. Then she saw the blood contrasting starkly with the white cotton of his polo shirt. "Jesus!" she cried. "What happened?"

He sighed wearily. "Can I come in?" he pleaded.

She ushered him in and shut the door. Tony happily ran rings around him. In spite of himself, he laughed. "Hey, boy," he said, stroking Tony's head.

She led him into the kitchen and pushed him into one of the chairs at the table. She stood in front of him, gently held his face in her hands, and surveyed the damage. She touched her index fingers to the bridge of his nose. He winced, but she couldn't feel anything broken. The blood under his nose looked like that of a nosebleed that had scabbed up. It looked worse than it actually was. She'd seen more damage after D and some tough thug *du jour* had gotten into it on the high school playground. "What happened?" she asked again.

"I got into a fight," he announced.

"No shit!" she said sarcastically. "With who?"

"My ex-girlfriend's man rolled up on me on the sidewalk."

She couldn't resist. "This is the babe you were in the shower with last night?" *When you should've been with me.*

He looked like he wasn't in the mood. "She showered at my house," he explained tersely. "I wasn't *in* the shower with her. Big difference."

She pressed an index finger in the middle of his forehead. "Hold your head back," she commanded, and he complied.

She washed her hands, then took a zippered plastic bag from the pantry and filled it with ice. She wrapped the bag in the closest dish towel she could get her hands on. "This is gonna be cold," she warned.

She laid it across the bridge of his nose, and she could see every muscle in his body tense. Part of her felt sorry for him. The part of her that spent the better part of Wednesday dyeing head hair and waxing body hair, though, was still pissed. "Men," she spat. "Why don't you guys just take 'em out and measure 'em and stop with the ridiculous flexing?"

"I really don't need this," he declared. "Not tonight."

"Then why *are* you here, Devin?"

He snatched off the makeshift ice pack and tossed it onto the table. Even Tony jumped and skulked away out of the kitchen. Devin looked angry and hurt, and he directed both emotions at her. "Because I almost got my ass beat tonight, and I thought I could come here for some TLC," he explained. "Guess I was wrong."

"Guess you were," she retorted.

He got up, more pain than anger in his beautiful eyes, and immediately, she felt like the biggest bitch on the planet. "I know you've been hurt—we both have," he said. "That doesn't give you license to shit on me and try to fuck with my head."

A part of her wanted to lunge for him and scratch his eyes out. Fluexa kept that part of her in check. "I don't have time to fuck with your head, Devin," she declared, her tone surprisingly calm. "Trust me—I have better things to do."

"Well," he said, "I don't want to be accused of wasting your precious time, Chaney. I'm gone."

She didn't even stop him. She just watched the back of him as he headed toward the front door, giving Tony a pat on the head as he left. *Good riddance.*

After he'd left, she did the usual things she did at night. She shut down her computer system upstairs. She cleaned Tony's ears, which, with him squirming and rebelling against a gloved finger in his ear canal, was a workout in itself. All the while, though, she ran the conversation she'd had in her kitchen over in her head on a constant loop. The more she thought about it, the angrier she got. *This brothah's trying to flip this thing onto me!*

She stashed the videos and the ice cream that she'd taken out, then picked up the cordless. She speed-dialed his cell phone number. After two rings, he answered. "Where are you?" she asked.

"At my dad's," Devin answered.

"Stay there—I'm coming over to talk to you."

Chaney put Tony and his water dish onto the deck, then, with just her wallet and keys, she got into the Altima and hit the road. She took the GW Parkway, instead of Route 1, and stepped on the gas. On the radio, Faith Evans was cussing some brothah out in her funky cut, "You Gets No Love," and that functioned as Chaney's angry soundtrack as she, oblivious to the monuments lit up like Roman candles, headed toward Arlington.

When Chaney parked in front of the house on North Garfield, she saw him standing under the porch light. Gone was the bloodstained polo. He wore a white wifebeater, his cargo pants, and Adidas sandals. She locked the car with her remote, bounded up the concrete path, and took the steps two at a time. *Anger-induced physical exercise.* He looked a tad peeved as well. "You gave me my orders," he said. "I'm here. What do you want?"

"You come over to my house, mooning over some bitch, and I'm

supposed to be open like 7-Eleven?" she demanded. "Are you insane?!"

He opened the glass door, and she could see the darkened anteroom. "Let's take this inside," he said quietly. "Unless you want the
whole neighborhood to hear us."

Chaney thought about it for a second, then stepped into the house.
He closed the glass door and the front door, leaving them both in the
dark. Her heart thumped as her eyes adjusted to the darkness. "Can
we shed some light on the subject, please?" she whispered.

"Come this way," he said.

Obediently, she followed him, all the while looking around for
landmarks. She was doubtful that he'd physically hurt her, but she was
leery nonetheless. He led her into the kitchen, and she remembered
helping him clean up that night he'd had her over for dinner. For a
second, she regretted allowing romantic feelings to cloud her judgment where he was concerned. Despite all of this, he'd been a great
friend to her.

He opened a door at the far end of the kitchen. A sliver of light
from the basement cut the darkness in the kitchen. "Go on," he said.

She hesitated briefly, feeling any control she'd had over the situation ebb away. She descended the wooden stairs one at a time. Behind
her, she heard him close the door, heard him on the stairs behind
her. A few more steps, and she entered a whole new world. It reminded her of her basement at the house in Brooklyn . . . space filled
with memories of lives lived well in a home. A sofa bed lay turned
down in front of a 36-inch color TV. He had the TV tuned to BET; the
logo was visible in the corner of the screen, and the video for remix of
Craig Mack's "Flava in Ya Ear" played at low volume.

He came around her and shut off the TV. They stood there in silence in the subdued lighting. "First of all, she's not a bitch," he announced. "Her name's Kimmy. She fucked up her life by having two
kids for two different men, and then hooking up with some insecure
redneck who beat her like a rented mule. She needed my help getting
out, and that seemed more important than our date. I thought you'd
understand that."

Oh, shit! She felt like such a drama queen all of a sudden, railing
about her hurt feelings while he was helping out a battered woman.
After all, his father had done something similar for her and her fam-

ily. But still, her pain spoke. "And how would I have known that, Devin?" she asked. "From your oh-so-personal text message?"

"I couldn't talk, Chaney," he explained. "I was holding a baby in one hand while trying to stash about twenty shopping bags into the ride. You know, I could've just been a dick and stood you up."

"So why did you even bother with texting, Devin?"

He shook his head. "More degrees than a thermometer, and you don't know anything. Why did I bother? Because I fucking like you, okay?!"

Chaney stared at him in shock, her mouth hanging open. It was out there, in the open. She clutched at the front of her velour sweats. *What do I do? What do I say?* Finally, she found her voice. "And that's how you think I want to hear it?" she croaked. " 'I fucking like you?' "

He sighed. "Chaney, I'm tired, and my head hurts," he said. "I don't have time for the sugar coating. I like you. We have a lot in common. Even my dad likes you. But this age thing with you is like pushing a rock up a hill."

"So, I'm the one with the problem . . . again."

He shrugged. "Well, yeah."

This was too much. She had to get away, think this through like the levelheaded older woman that she was. "I've said my piece," she announced. "I'm going home."

He threw up his hands. "Wha . . . ?"

She headed toward the stairs like a caged bird. "I'm going home."

He was behind her like a shot. "Wait!" he commanded.

She turned around to face him, her face practically in his chest. "What?!"

He took her hand in his. She looked down and saw the cuts and bruises on his knuckles. "Wait," he pleaded.

She looked up into that face that was mere inches from hers. Her heart squeezed in her chest. He wrapped his arms around her and held her close. A contented sigh rumbled from his chest to hers. He felt so good, so hard, so close. Slowly, she relaxed into him, opening the fists she'd made and pressing her hands against his broad back. *Let it go, girl . . .*

"Baby," he whispered.

It had been so long since she'd been anybody's baby. She lapped up the affection, like a cat with cream on its tongue. She stood on tiptoe and held his face in her hands. She brushed kisses on each closed eye, on his wounded nose, and, finally, on his full mouth. He laughed softly.

She shifted in his arms and suddenly felt him pressed against her thigh. It felt more than adequate to the task. He played in her hair, his long fingers threading through the curls. He kissed her slowly, deliberately, until she was dizzy and breathless. "Stay over," he moaned.

What are you saving yourself for? He was hot. He was straight. He was open like 7-Eleven. Then she remembered; she didn't come prepared to party. Mentally, she kicked herself, practically envisioning all those brand new condoms tucked safely in her nightstand drawer at home. She pressed her forehead against his, her fingers stroking the nape of his neck. "If we're gonna do this, sweetie, we need protection," she said softly.

"We're good," he assured her.

They moved slowly into the room, tossing clothes as they went. Chaney stared, awestruck, as he peeled off his wifebeater. Her eyes took in ripped abs and pecs, biceps and triceps. Chaney doubted he had any body fat whatsoever. *Boy's got the* Men's Health *chest!*

Tentatively, she unzipped her hoodie, revealing her lacy black bra. His eager fingers manipulated the front clasp, then it was his turn to be awestruck at the sight of her bare breasts. Brothahs always did love her chest. She was doubtful about the rest of the package. She hadn't been to the gym in ages, had consumed her share of Rockville Pike lunches. Instead of volunteering to go first, she watched as he chucked his pants and briefs in one swift motion.

Every cell in her body stood at attention after the reveal. He stood before her, hands akimbo, proudly showing off a long, dark, thick, deeply veined dick that stood straight up and seemed to salute. It looked like a delicious brown Sugar Daddy that she could wrap her tongue around and enjoy for hours on end. Her hands, seemingly with a mind of their own, searched him out, took a hold of him. She relished the feel of his hard flesh against her palm. She kneaded and massaged, with just the right amount of pressure. She ran her hands down the length of him. She didn't think it was possible, but he got harder still, right in the palm of her hand. He moaned her name, his head revolving furiously on the base of his neck. "Condom," he panted.

While he foraged for his wallet on the floor, Chaney turned away from him, attempting to hide her flaws as she kicked off her shoes and shimmied out of her velour sweatpants. The damp air in the basement hit her naked body, and she trembled a little. She was about to hug herself to keep warm when he came up behind her. He wrapped his arms possessively around her, and she could feel him, now gloved in latex, pressed against her ass. He nuzzled her neck, kissed and sucked the tender hollow, extracting a cry from her mouth. He turned her head and greedily sucked her mouth, and the cry morphed into a groan as his hands found her breasts. *Oh yeah!* His fingers became gentle, like flower petals, teasing rock-hard nipples and inducing goose bumps across her flesh. She reached up and wrapped her arms around his strong neck. Those hands traveled the length of her body . . . her navel, her thighs. His hands darted between her legs. Fingers found their way inside her, stroking her until she thought she'd float away on her own wetness. "Devin," she moaned.

She bent over the back of the couch. He grabbed handfuls of her ass. Before she could prepare herself, he thrust himself inside her, filling her with that delicious, long thickness. She cried out loudly, her fingernails digging into the fabric of the back of the couch. He worked it slowly, deliberately, straight in and out, in circles, then in and out again. He held her close. His mouth found her earlobe and sucked.

He thrust deep inside her, and sucked her flesh, and tweaked nipples, and massaged cleavage. And it all blew her mind, but she realized that by this time, she would've been lying in bed, a twitching wreck. Briefly, she wondered what was different, until her feverish mind delivered the answer. *Fluexa*. One of the famously touted side effects of selective serotonin reuptake inhibitors was sexual dysfunction. She had the hot brothah who fucked like a champion and filled up her dusty, empty affection tank, and some chemical prevented him from getting her off. Someone had a sense of humor.

She pulled away from him, feeling him leave her inch by stout inch. She turned in his arms to face him. He regarded her with hooded eyes, looking at her like she was all he needed in the world. If she couldn't enjoy it, she could make him feel good. "I wanna see your face," she whispered.

They took it to the sofa bed. She lay against the crisp, cool sheets, giggling as he slowly climbed atop her and kissed a trail from her navel, to her breasts, to her mouth. His expression, though, went from happy and goofy to serious as he entered her. She arched her back up, and their pelvises touched. He thrust in and out, his gaze on her face unwavering. He touched her face. He ran his fingers across her mouth, and she took them into her mouth and sucked furiously. He tasted like salt, and sweat, and her. "Chaney," he whispered.

"What," she moaned.

"I'm close," he panted.

She had a tried and true method of sending him over the edge. She rolled him onto his back. He grabbed her hips as she mounted him and helped him inside her. She moved her hips in a circle, then up and down, tightening and relaxing around him. He ran his hands along her back, up and down, from the base of her skull to the small of her back. All the while she watched his face, looking for the telltale sign that he was nearing total release. He dragged his teeth over his bottom lip so hard that he left a white, bloodless trail. The long vein that snaked the length of his forehead bulged against his skin. But he fought it. "Gotta . . . wait . . . for you," he gasped.

She leaned in closer, the angle of her body seeming to intensify the sensation of each thrust. "Go on, sweetie," she whispered in his ear. "Go on."

So, he did. She felt him tense under her. His grip on her ass released. And he let out an explosive sound, like *argggghhhhhh!* For a good minute. Chaney wondered if KL could hear them going at it in his room two floors up. Shattered, he let his muscles release. He lay limp under her. He looked so adorable, lying there with his eyes closed. She leaned in further, dropping kisses on his mouth, kisses he lazily returned. "Chay Breezy," he sighed, then laughed deep in his throat. "You rocked my world!"

She kissed him again. "You didn't do too bad yourself," she said.

They stayed like that, sweaty limbs intertwined, for what seemed like hours. She languished there, with his arms around her. Finally, he'd satisfied her need for sex and affection. She would've purred if she'd been the right species for it.

Soon, though, he held the condom in place, and she rolled off him and to the side. Chaney watched as he got up and headed to the back of the room to, she assumed, the bathroom. Despite the fact that, mere minutes ago, he'd been inside her, she was able to study him clinically, appreciate his aesthetic . . . his strong back that tapered to a thin waist, his absolute lack of ass for a brothah. She laughed. She had enough ass for both of them.

She heard him pee like Niagara Falls, then flush. She then heard hands being washed. Then, minutes later, he was climbing back into bed with her. He propped himself up on his elbow, watching her as she lay on her stomach. She leaned into it as he kissed her forehead, shivered as he ran a still-moist hand down the length of her spine, to her substantial ass. He stared at it. She giggled as he ran his hands over the swell of each cheek. "That's the hotness, girl," he decreed.

He even loved her fat ass. He was a keeper. "Bless your heart, Devin Rhym!" she laughed.

They lay facing each other, her on her stomach, him on his side. He stroked her face. "Hey," he said, tentatively. "Did you . . . you know . . . ?"

Deflect, deflect. "What . . . come?" she asked. "Did you?"

"I just flushed the evidence," he said, "but you're just going to have to believe me when I say hell, yeah!"

Chaney looked him up and down. *Can I trust you?* "I guess I should tell you," she said. "After all, I let you put your dick in me."

He threw his head back and laughed. "And I can't thank you enough!"

"I'm taking an antidepressant," she announced. "That's why I can't drink."

She lay there and waited for a reaction . . . any reaction. He studied her curiously, his brows knit, as he played in her hair. "You're depressed?" he finally asked.

"Apparently, I am . . . mildly," she said. "The pill helps me focus, you know, chills me out so I can deal."

"Deal with what?" he asked.

He's genuinely interested. "With difficult clients, with this partnership that's been feeling like a bad marriage for a long time," she replied. "But unfortunately, I just found out what one of the side effects is."

He furrowed his brows. "I can't make you come," he concluded.

How can I explain it to you? She reached out for him. "It's okay," she assured him. "Let's keep some perspective here, sweetie. My vibrator can make me come. Not making me come is not a deal breaker, Devin. I'm happy being with you."

He leaned and kissed her on the mouth, and she returned the favor. "You're a special lady," he whispered.

She felt a warm glow all over. *He thinks I'm special!*

"You're gonna stay over, right?" he asked.

Reflexively, she began to think of reasons to go home. After months of jousting and parrying, they'd just made love. That was a big enough step for now. But she didn't want to put it that way. "What about KL?" she asked.

Devin made his case like he was Perry Mason. "He sleeps in on the weekends."

"And Tony? I left him in the yard."

"You fixed the latch on the gate. He's a dog, Chaney. He'll be all right spending one night outside."

"I want a shower!"

"There's one right down here. We could even take one together."

Chaney shook her head. "You've thought about everything," she concluded.

He moved in closer to her, wrapping his arms around her. He rubbed his chin on the crown of her head, and she giggled. "I wanna wake up with you next to me," he said simply.

To feel those arms around her, Chaney probably would've given him whatever he wanted right then. "Okay," she relented. "But you've gotta wake me early. I don't wanna have to explain anything to your dad."

He pulled her closer still, interlocking his legs with hers. He buried his nose at the base of her neck. He settled in, and Chaney could see his fatigue overcoming him. "Okay," he promised, but Chaney sensed she was talking to herself.

Devin woke up to feel her getting up from the bed. He watched as she tiptoed toward the bathroom. He stared particularly at the outline of her left breast, his gaze lingering on the slope of her spine that led to the deliciously full ass. His smitten heart and well-fucked body practically sang. His mind flashed on early morning quickies, as he put it on her in the light of the sun coming through the slivered windows.

It hit him that he'd never woken up with someone he'd wanted there. He'd either been partying after a game or a swim meet, taken somebody home in a drunken haze, and then woke up the next day, engineering her awkward dismissal or his hasty retreat. What he was feeling was a full 180 from those days. He wanted her to stay there with him all day . . . talking, laughing, making love . . .

Devin slowly got up and yawned, scratching his balls. He headed to the bathroom. He arrived just as she was done brushing her teeth. He looked over at the sink. She'd availed herself of the toothbrushes, towels, and soaps that he'd set out the night before.

He leaned against the doorjamb. He could actually see everything in the light of day. The combination of soft curves, sleepy face, full mouth, and disheveled hair made him want to take her back to bed. " 'Morning," he said.

She looked over at him, and he basked in the glow of her appreciative gaze on his body. He held his hands akimbo, purposely calling attention to the beginnings of a morning erection. She laughed and rolled her eyes, as if asking herself, *what am I doing here?* " 'Morning," she returned.

He went over to her at the sink and swallowed her up in a hug. She smelled like she'd just gotten up; he was sure he did, too. He'd always found a woman's pre-shower scent delicious in an animalistic way. He caught a glimpse of himself in the mirror, saw the happiest, goofiest grin on his stubbly face. "You're a bad man," she mock-scolded him, her voice reverberating into his chest. "You were supposed to wake me up."

He kissed her neck, making her giggle. "I did," he said. "Three times this morning."

"What's that, your alarm *cock*?"

He laughed. "Cute."

She wriggled out from his embrace and slapped him on the arm. "I gotta go!" she insisted, trying to hold back a laugh but failing egregiously. "Tony's probably starving to death, and your dad's gonna think I'm a whore."

"Okay," he relented. "Let me get cleaned up, and I'll get you out to the car."

She left the bathroom, and he watched the back of her. *Damn!*

She got dressed in her sweats. He threw on a T-shirt and the cargo pants from last night. He held her hand and they tiptoed up the basement stairs and into the kitchen. *Nothing.* No KL, no Sadat. "The coast is clear," he whispered to her over his shoulder.

They were in the anteroom, inches from the front door, when KL appeared in the arched, open doorway to the living room. Chaney gasped loudly, and Devin saw the blood run from her face. Devin just stood there, shielding her. *Busted.*

" 'Morning," KL said, with a self-satisfied smirk.

Guiltily, they mumbled back the same. Belatedly, Devin realized KL was holding a packet of bacon in his hands. "I was about to make some breakfast," KL announced. "Would you two like to join me?"

In the most unreal of scenarios, Devin was in the kitchen with his father and his lover, making bacon, toast, and scrambled eggs. KL acted like this was the most natural thing in the world. Once the novelty wore off for Chaney, she took over coffee and table-setting duties. She and KL talked like old friends. Devin stood in the wings with Sadat and watched. Something was happening to his father . . . something good. She brought out a side of him that Devin had never seen.

They were done with breakfast and were lingering over coffee when KL said, "I was hoping to thank you for dinner the other night."

Chaney smiled. From across the table, she covered Devin's hand with hers. "Mr. Man here cooked," she said. "I just did the salads."

"Thank you for thinking about an old man," he said. "Now what about these products you sent?"

"I make 'em at home," she announced. "Keeps me from losing it. I've been making a lot lately, so that's pretty telling!"

KL looked down at her over the top of his glasses. "You really should start your own business," he said. "That stuff is excellent. Especially that shaving mousse. If you need investors, I know more than enough men with razor bumps and fat military pensions. I'll lead the charge myself."

Devin tempered his envy. A year ago, KL wouldn't even lift a finger to help him. Now he was practically throwing money at Chaney. "You'd better take advantage of this rare opportunity, Chaney," he said. "Dad didn't even invest in my business."

"You didn't ask me, son," he said simply. "You and Bill had that worked out on your own, didn't you?"

Devin could feel his good feeling evaporating. He should have woken Chaney up early, like she'd asked. He could've at least avoided another altercation with his dad.

Chaney sensed it, too. Mercifully, she shut it down; he loved her for that. She went around to KL's place setting and kissed him on the forehead. "Fellas, I hate to eat and run, but if I don't get home, Tony's gonna die of hunger!"

KL stared up at her, the charm on overkill. "You come back any-time," he said.

"I will, thanks," she said, then waved at Sadat in the corner. Her voice went up a couple of decibels. " 'Bye, Sadat!"

Sadat stared straight ahead. He was as irascible as his old master.

Devin took hold of Chaney's hand and walked her out to the Altima, so angrily parked out in front of the house the night before. In the light of day, Chaney could see the back of it jutting out away from the curb and into the street. "Nice parking job," Devin teased.

"I wanted to strangle you last night," she confessed. "The last thing on my mind was the parallel parking section of driver's ed."

They kissed, and with the utmost reluctance, he watched as she got into her car. She started it up and waved to him before she drove off. He watched her car until it turned onto Wilson Boulevard and was gone. He was surprised at how bereft he felt. Already.

Nine

His dick had been up a good five minutes before he was. Devin rolled over in his bed in Georgetown, and his fingertips found Chaney. He followed his nose to her morning, pre-showered scent. He spooned with her, kissing her throat until she stirred in her sleep. Hands found nipples. Fingers explored between her thighs until she moaned her approval. Half-asleep, he managed to retrieve a condom from the nightstand, rolled it on with a free hand, and turned her over to face him. With one hard thrust, he was in soft, velvet heaven. She cried out, now wide awake. "You feel that?" he whispered in her ear.

"Uh-huh," she slurred.

He slipped one arm under her leg, the other, behind her head, scooping his pelvis into her, lazily, deliberately. He relished the sensation of her hands at the base of his neck, at her fingernails running along the skin of his back.

Suddenly, he felt the immeasurable pleasure of sensitive skin on skin as her body gripped him and relaxed, gripped and relaxed. He moved deeper and deeper inside of her, sweat raining off him like Shaq just before the final buzzer. "Oh God, Chaney!" he roared. "Oh, God!"

He twitched, and shook, and writhed atop her, all the muscular coordination he enjoyed as an athlete gone . . . evaporated. He melted on top of her, nuzzling her neck. He laughed lazily, his breathing slowly going from seriously labored to normal. She wrapped her arms around him, stroked his head. "You're a happy boy, aren't you?" she whispered.

He pulled her up against him and held her close, running his fingers through the hair at the base of her neck. *Damn, girl. I fucking love you so much.*

Unfortunately, on its way through his manly filter, his declaration came out differently. "I love fucking you so much!" he cried.

She uttered a breathy laugh in his ear. "Thanks for the endorsement, sweetie," she panted.

Devin, you're such a fucking bonehead.

They lay together for what seemed like forever. Finally, he rose up on shaky elbows, then reached down to hold the condom in place as he pulled out. Uh-oh . . . He sat back on his haunches. "Umm . . . Chay," he began.

"Hmm?" she sleepily groaned.

He touched her leg and shook her. "Sweetest," he said, more urgently.

Chaney eased up against the pillows and stared between his thighs. Her eyes widened as she saw what was left of the condom, a pale, rubbery ring around the base of his wilting erection . . . everything else, reservoir tip included, gone. Her hands flew to her mouth. "Oh, shit!" she gasped.

The eyes met and held. Devin guessed the same implications of what just happened were running through her mind as well. "No shit," he remarked.

They sat in the restaurant, in front of the picture window where M Street met Thirty-first. Devin stared covetously at the remains of Chaney's pecan Belgian waffle. He looked up at her with the cutest face he could make. "Are you gonna eat that?"

Chaney shook her head in awe. "Devin, you just had pancakes, eggs, bacon, toast, juice, and coffee," she reminded him.

He winked at her. "Sweet lovin' makes me hungry," he said, invoking the Chef on *South Park*.

She took her fork and knife, picked up the waffle, and eased it onto his plate. "Here."

"Thank you, baby."

He polished that off, too, then reached under his black Adidas sweatshirt and rubbed his tummy. Mind-altering sex, good company, hearty breakfast. He remembered what she'd said that morning, while he was coming down off a blistering orgasm. *You're a happy boy, aren't you?* He couldn't ever remember being happier.

Devin scraped his chair on the old tile floor until it was next to hers. He slipped his arm around the back of her chair. She giggled behind her hand, looking around at the patrons in the restaurant. "Devin," she whispered.

He stared at her, trying to commit her face to memory, so that, when he went to sleep that night, he'd remember exactly what she looked like. "What, baby?"

"We should talk," she said. "About the condom."

Oh, yeah. The condom. "Let's *tawk*," he teased. "Should we be worried?"

She looked away. "Stop me if this is T.M.I., but I've got fibroids," she announced. "I probably couldn't get pregnant without having them taken out."

He knew he should've been breathing a sigh of relief right then. But strangely, he felt conflicted. She must've noticed the look on his face. "You want to have children?" she asked.

He listened to the inflection in her voice, to whether or not she was asking if he wanted to have children . . . *with her.* He realized her question was asked for the purpose of gathering information only. "If you'd asked me before, I probably would've said no," he finally said.

Her eyebrows flew up. "Why?"

"My dad wasn't exactly Father of the Year, Chaney. Let's just say I have my own daddy issues that I'm trying to squash while he's still here. Plus there's the whole biracial, freak of nature thing. I didn't have the best childhood."

She touched his cheek, and his heart shuddered inside his chest. "You're a beautiful person, Devin," she declared. "Inside and out."

He looked away, and God help him, heard himself actually guffaw. He changed the subject. "What about you?"

Suddenly, she seemed sad, distant. "My anal-retentive sister raised me since I was five," she said. "I wouldn't know how to begin to parent a kid." She laughed—forced, he sensed. "I can barely keep track of Tony!"

"Well, what do you want from this?" he asked. "From me?"

"Dev, I'm not chasing the white dress," she said. "I already dodged that bullet. If it doesn't happen again, it's not the end of the world for me. I'm not looking to be your baby mama, either. I just like being with you. Two HIV-negative . . ." she looked at him questioningly.

He remembered the AIDS test he took for the insurance policy on the practice. "Yes."

". . . adults enjoying each other's company. Exclusively. If you decide that being with an older, reproductively challenged woman's not what you had planned, then we'll just say thanks for the memories and bug out. Cool?"

The script had officially been flipped on old Dev. Usually, he was the one setting the ground rules. He was the one hauling ass from commitment. Now, he wasn't going to have to wait for the issue of commitment to rear its ugly head. It had just been handled, and they both knew where they stood. He could literally feel himself unclench. He pushed hair from her face and kissed her cheek. "Cool," he said with a lopsided smile.

Chaney closed her eyes as the kinder, late-afternoon August sun warmed her skin. A gentle breeze blew across her body, ruffling the flowing skirt of her sundress around her freshly shaved legs. She smelled a teasing whiff of her peppermint body cream on the currents of air as she ran down the steps of her house to the Altima. She was about to unlock her door when she saw Jon in his usual grungy attire, coming toward her across the grassy field. He had Hershey on a retractable leash. Hershey practically glowed, what passed for a smile on her doggie face. Then Chaney saw the heaviness in her belly and the enlarged teats pointing toward the ground. *Hershey's pregnant!*

Chaney grinned from ear to ear, feeling a surge of pride. She was going to be a grandaunt. She waved broadly at Jon. Jon, on the other hand, rushed to the door of his grandparents' house and hurried inside. Chaney guessed they hadn't forgiven her or Tony for Hershey's condition.

She could pinpoint the exact time when she'd last felt this way: 1997. Five years since she literally floated on air, laughed privately at the thought of a lover, ached for the time they could be together again. That time, it was Shane. This time, she was shamelessly, hopelessly feeling Devin Rhym. She drove toward Georgetown, in her own world of her memories of their weekend together. She shuddered at the memory of every line of that beautiful, long body and what someone as young as he was could do with it. Even though she couldn't fully enjoy him sexually, it was the little things, like holding his hand, like his brief kisses on her forehead, like his text messages to let her know he was thinking about her . . . all of this was melting the ice around her heart. After Shane and his ultimate lie, after Richard and his inability to commit, she knew what she'd said over the breakfast table that morning was true. If things soured between her and Devin, she knew she'd be all right. She sensed, though, that the recovery time wouldn't be as short as she'd led Devin to believe.

The drive to Nathalie's Georgetown crib, which usually took about a half-hour, seemed as short as if she'd traveled by transporter. In seemingly no time, she'd been buzzed into the wrought iron gate and was making her way up the winding cobblestone driveway of the sprawling Foxhall Road all-brick Tudor, with manicured lawns that Craig kept a lush green, even in the heat of summer.

She got out of the car with her goodie bag of creams and candles and was headed toward the huge, wooden red front door when she heard her Blackberry bleating in her purse. She sucked her teeth. *Please don't be anyone from work . . .*

She looked at the Blackberry face. A 305 number showed up on screen. *Miami?* She answered the call. "Hello?"

"Hey, Chanes, it's me."

She didn't sound like her annoyingly happy self, like Ricky was putting it down. She sounded like a woman fast coming to her senses. Nonetheless, Chaney was happy to hear from her sister. "Daisy!" she cried. "What's going on? Where are you?"

"Do you even read the tour book?"

"No, your dog keeps me plenty busy."

Daisy sighed, a world-weary sigh, over the digital network. "We're stateside. In Miami," she announced. "Thank God for air conditioning, 120-volt plugs, and big portions. This shit is getting old. Like Daddy used to say, 'I think I done stayed too long at the fair.' "

Chaney didn't remember Reggie Braxton saying that. She hated how, the older she got, the memories of her parents started to become faded, gauzy.

"How's my baby dog?" Daisy asked. "Does he miss me?"

Chaney decided to wait until they saw each other to tell her about the destructive behavior, the drug overdose, and how Tony knocked up the neighbor's dog. "He's good," she said, which wasn't a lie. Tony was thriving. "The question is, how are you? You sound so down."

Daisy sucked her teeth. "Ricky and I are on the rocks," she sighed. "Brothahs. What can I tell you?"

Plenty! From the time she'd developed into this long-legged goddess, Daisy'd been around, had her own case of Mad Cock Disease.

"If you'd read the tour book, you'd know that I'll be seeing you next month," Daisy said. "The star's playing the Nissan Pavilion in someplace called Bristow, Virginia. Can you just hear the banjoes!"

Chaney laughed, but still rose up in defense of her adopted home state. "Don't sleep on Virginia. It's a wonderful place. You'll never see me back in Brooklyn again."

Daisy sucked her teeth. "Speaking of home, I spoke to The Judgmental One," she announced, her code for Anna Lisa. "She's mad at you because you didn't tell her that D ran off and married some porn star?"

Anna Lisa. Chaney was too busy getting her own dose of Vitamin F to realize how much she missed her . . . and her judgmental nature and misdirected anger. And typical, Daisy got it all wrong. She used to suck at *Pass a Secret,* too, when they were kids. "She's not a porn star," Chaney insisted. "Girl, call your nephew yourself. Get the story from the horse's mouth."

"Well, I gotta go," Daisy said. "We're all having dinner at the house of one of the Miami Heat players. On Star Island, girl. Right next to Gloria and Emilio!"

This shit was getting old, my ass! Daisy was having far too much fun to leave the fair just yet. Chaney reached Nathalie's massive, wooden red door. For once, her evening was going to be almost as tony as Daisy's. "Haven't you done enough ball handling of your own, my sistah?" Chaney teased.

Daisy giggled. "I love you, Chanes. I'll see you, in the flesh, next month."

"I can't wait," Chaney said. "Love you, too."

Which was true. Sisters were sisters. Even though Daisy used to terrorize her when they were kids, took advantage now that they were adults, and got her into all kinds of situations that defied common sense, she still loved her sister dearly . . . passionately.

Chaney hung up, then rang Nathalie's bell. Almost instantaneously, the door opened. Nathalie was standing there, wearing a dress made of lavender-and-white African cloth. "Hey, girl," she greeted Chaney, and they kissed on both cheeks. "Late, as usual, but we forgive you."

Chaney looked her up and down. "Is it just me, or are you glowing?"

Nathalie laughed, all evasive. "Am I?"

They went inside. Nathalie led Chaney down a marble hallway, past an expansive sunken living room decorated with African artifacts, to the huge living room with windows that looked out on what seemed like all of D.C., with a view of the Georgetown University Hospital at the right. The house that pricey legal advice built.

Dani and Coco were setting places at a table that looked like something out of *Martha Stewart Living*. They looked up. "Look who's here!" Coco laughed.

Dani winked at Chaney and flashed her a smile, one which Chaney returned. Nathalie and Coco seemed oblivious to their private moment. Chaney realized why she was such a good friend. Good friends kept your secrets until you were ready to tell all. "About friggin' time," Dani declared.

Chaney complemented the table setting with three of her own cinnamon-scented pillar candles. They feasted on spicy seared salmon, asparagus tips, and new potatoes. Chaney shared samples of new creams and lip balms with them. They talked about everything and nothing. Nathalie glowed in the candlelight as she held court over her table, as afternoon turned to evening through the picture windows.

They took their dessert—Nathalie's grandma's peach cobbler—and coffee—a dark Ethiopian blend—to the pool area. Nathalie lit an insect-repellent coil. They sat there, listening to the lapping water and the sound of the city outside the gate.

Coco turned in her chaise to Chaney. "I didn't know you had a man," she said. "I had to hear it from Nathalie that you were seeing the vet. The *younger* vet. And you only told her because you blew her off for the movies."

Chaney blushed. Well, that secret was out. "You know, can I, for once, be that friend who forsakes her friends 'cause *she's* getting some?" she asked.

"How is the Dog Whisperer?" Dani laughed.

Chaney grinned from ear to ear. Immediately, her time with Devin played over in her mind, every sense being catered to. She remembered how he looked, stark naked, as he reached for her, how he smelled as they lay together after making love, how his kisses tasted, how affectionate his voice sounded when he called her by that goofy hip-hop name he'd given her. They didn't need to know all that. They would have to settle for a guarded, "He's good."

"I'll bet he is," Nathalie teased. "Look at that smile. I've never seen that. And I knew you back in the day at 'Cuse."

"But, irony of all ironies, I get the hot man at the same time I . . ." how could she say *I can't come* in polite company? ". . . lose my ability to fully enjoy him."

Dani sucked her teeth. "You need to get up off of that antidepressant, girl," she declared. "I told you that since Day One."

Coco looked shocked. "You didn't tell me you're taking an antidepressant!"

Coco sucked at keeping a secret that way Daisy used to suck at *Pass a Secret*. "It's not something you want to broadcast, Coco," she explained. "Autodidact hasn't been the easiest place to be lately."

Coco shook her head, like she was trying to process the latest development. Finally, the expression on her face looked like she understood. "Shoot, I may need to borrow a couple from you myself."

Nathalie held up the jar of plum lip balm that Chaney had shared over the dinner table. "You should start your own business," she said. "This is your gift, Chaney. You need to share it with our people. With the world."

Nathalie sometimes had a way with hyperbole. But the fact that two people in the know made the same informed recommendation to her within a space of a couple of weeks made Chaney sit up and take notice. "Devin's dad said the same thing," she said. "He said he could help me find investors."

"You have two right now," Nathalie announced. "Me and Craig."

"And me and Sandy," Dani piped in. "We could also help you with the articles of incorporation."

Coco shook her head. "I don't know about investing, but you get it off the ground, and I'll come work for you," she said. "I'll be, like, your Dorothy Boyd from *Jerry Maguire*."

Damn! The rubber was really hitting the road. "Just like that?" Chaney asked, surprised at how easy getting a commitment was.

"Just like that," Nathalie declared. "Stop tilling that Shanty Irishman's field and leaving yours eighty percent barren."

The prospect of jumping ship sent her dangerously close to the line of her comfort zone. Taking the younger lover was as daring as she would commit to being right then. Starting up her own company was a commitment of the head, one that required some more homework on her end. "I will seriously think about it," Chaney announced.

They all sighed and rolled their eyes. "Well, don't take too long," Nathalie commanded. "This offer of investing has a freshness date of exactly seven months. After that, Craig and I are putting all of our disposable income in a 529 account."

All eyes shifted to Nathalie. "Wait a second," Dani said. "Only parents put away college money in a 529."

Nathalie beamed as it gradually sank in. Chaney gasped. "You're pregnant!" she cried.

Nathalie cradled that big dress against her midsection. "I'm gonna be a mommy!" she giggled.

Chaney's eyes misted. She knew she would've been bawling ordinarily, but that was all the emotion the chemical in her system would allow. She'd seen firsthand everything that Nathalie and Craig had gone through to be parents . . . the hormone shots, the in vitro, the endless temperature-taking and plotting fertility dates on calendars. A couple so deserving had put in the work and were going to get what they wanted.

Chaney got up, eased her arms around Nathalie, and held her close. Tears of joy spilled down both their faces. "Congratulations, girl," she whispered in her ear. "You're gonna be a great mommy."

Coco came, and then Dani. They all embraced Chaney and Nathalie, creating a group hug. A new sound intermingled with the lapping water and the noise from the city . . . happy sobs.

Lissa knocked on Chaney's office doorjamb just as Chaney was finishing up an e-mail to Callie. Chaney looked up at her and felt a wave a sadness wash over her. *There are issues here that are much bigger than our friendship.* "Hey," Chaney said.

"Hey," Lissa returned, all perky.

She came in and handed Chaney a small bubble envelope. "A courier just brought this over for you," she announced. "Related to the project?"

Chaney examined it. The return address told her that it was from the Rosslyn Veterinary Hospital. She smiled broadly. The contents of the package, Chaney guessed, were the antidote to the project.

Lissa stared curiously at her. "What?" she asked.

Chaney stashed it away for later in her top desk drawer. "Nothing," she said. "What's up?"

"You get my e-mail?" Lissa asked.

Chaney nodded. "Yes, OPM gave us another five-year contract," she said. "That's excellent news. I see we're having pizza and cake in the big conference room to celebrate."

Lissa helped herself to one of the guest chairs in front of Chaney's desk. "We couldn't have done it without your input, Chaney," she said. "That section you wrote really crystallized instructional design and the systematic and systemic nature of the process. You broke down what we do for the layperson. I personally think that's what helped people to see that there's a methodology to what we do, not just dream up some test questions and call it training."

Months ago, Chaney would've thought her genuine. This was before all of the water that had raged under the bridge between them. Nonetheless, she said, "Thank you."

"Well-deserved high praise," Lissa declared.

Am I nailing my own coffin shut here? Nonetheless, though, she went for it. "I have to say, though, that for someone who owns only one percent more of the company than I do, you seem to be exceedingly well informed."

Lissa blinked behind the lenses of her trendy specs. "I don't know what you mean, Chaney," she said.

"Well, it seems lately like you've taken on this supervisory role where I'm concerned," she explained. "Instead of us holding meetings as partners in the company, Al sends his message through you, and then you filter it down to me."

"Oh," Lissa said. "Well, you know Laura is really Al's second-in-command in terms of the partnership, but she doesn't really involve herself in the day-to-day operations."

"Yes, she just attends Suzuki violin lessons with the kids, and fucks up everyone's PAL," Chaney declared.

"Chaney, Al's not a fool. He knows how you feel about him, as do I. He knows that you two will never be friends, coming over to his house in Bethesda to shoot pool."

"Yeah, but I believe you told me that there are issues here that are bigger than friendship," Chaney reminded her.

Lissa squirmed in her chair. "Chaney, I know that must've sounded awful when I said that, but it came out wrong," she insisted. "You are my friend. That's why I brought you into the company. At 'Cuse you were like a little sister to me."

"Well, my sistah, sometimes I wonder . . ."

"About what?"

"About what stereotype of your dual heritage you are working right now," Chaney said. "Is it the one concerning the lack of black unity, or the one where money comes before everything else?"

Lissa stared at Chaney for the longest time, and Chaney returned the favor. She imagined what she'd said must've stung deeply. But it had to be said. Chaney sensed that there was no turning back now, that perhaps this was the beginning of her last hoorah at Autodidact.

Finally, Lissa averted her eyes, began picking fuzz that didn't exist off her white blouse. "Well, then," she said. "Cake and pizza start at four. See you in the big conference room."

She got up and left, and Chaney pointedly closed the door behind her. *Good riddance.*

Her mood improved considerably, though, when she sat back down, opened her desk drawer, and took out the bubble envelope. She slipped her finger under a break in the flap and slowly separated the envelope from its adhesive backing. She held the envelope upside down, and a CD jewel case, along with a sliver of paper, fell out. She picked up the paper first. The text, written in the neatest penmanship, read, "For My Old School Seductress."

Chaney let out a holler. *So that's what I am . . .*

Next, she picked up the jewel case and saw a list on the front label under the title *10 Shots to the Heart.* She guessed it was a play on the title of LL's album, *14 Shots to the Dome.*

She read the list in her head; they were all songs he'd burned on a CD for her:

1. I Miss You. AARON HALL
2. Remember the Time. M.J.
3. Thank God I Found You. Joe f/ MARIAH & Nas
4. Around the Way Girl. LL
5. Think of You. USHER

6. All the Things (Your Man Won't Do). JOE
7. Hey Lover. LL f/BOYZ II MEN
8. Georgy Porgy. ERIC BENET f/ FAITH EVANS
9. Somebody for Me. HEAVY D & THE BOYZ
10. I Need Love. LL

Chaney's heart sang. She sat there, shaking her head, her grin a mile wide. *Bruh made me a mix tape.* "This is so sweet!" she cried.

She doubted a selfish bastard like Randy Tyree—or any other age-appropriate brothah, for that matter—would be firing up his Roxio Easy CD Creator to impress her. They were just so above all that.

Chaney put the CD into the holder in her CPU. The Windows Media Player opened, and seconds later, she heard the synthesized opening beats of "I Miss You," then the pure, raw, heartrending emotion of Aaron's gospel-influenced vocals. Chaney closed her eyes and let it all wash over her. She sat and watched the late-afternoon traffic on Rockville Pike, as Aaron bled seamlessly into Michael Jackson, and Nas, then to the others who expressed the emotions he was feeling through the medium Devin loved . . . music. By the time she got to the last track, LL's "I Need Love," she was more sure of her feelings than she could ever remember being. *I love this kid. I really love him.*

The CD stopped. In the silence, everything melted away, all the mental distractions, and Chaney experienced a long-awaited moment of clarity. She took her purse out of her drawer, opened it, and stared at the brown bottle of Fluexa for the last time. Then she got up, left her office, and navigated the winding gray halls of the office, on her way to the ladies' room.

Moments later, after she flushed the Fluexa, she took out her Blackberry and dialed Sean Tolochko to let him know that he, she, and Fluexa were parting company.

Devin finished the final page of the business manager's report and closed the wire-bound document. It was interesting that he would've chosen such a pretty document to tell them, essentially, that they were fucked. With his hand over his mouth, Devin sat across from Didier's impressive oak desk and let it all sink in. "Well, what do you think, Devin?" Didier asked, his gray eyes curious.

"I'm still processing," Devin announced.

"He liked your recommendations for tapping other markets, like the Valu-Pak, and for hiring a publicist to let the community know about our services," Didier summarized.

Despite his shitty mood, Devin smiled. He'd borrowed that suggestion from Chaney. For once, he had a thinking girlfriend who could offer solutions along with the ill nana.

"He also liked our joint suggestion that we establish ourselves as an emergency hospital, staying open twenty-four hours, and that we continue to specialize in surgeries that they do not do or cannot do at the Pet-Thenon," Didier said.

The figures had leapt off the page in the pretty document and were burned indelibly in Devin's brain. "What I didn't like is the price tag," he said. "Where are we supposed to get that kind of money? What bank is going to invest in a business that's about a minute from the red?"

Didier shrugged, that annoying, jaded Gallic shrug that Devin hated from the first day he'd met him. "We're going to have to liquidate, my friend," he said. "Then fuck the bank—we find our own investors, more doctors to buy into our practice."

"I was the calm one when you first came to me with this," Devin laughed bitterly. "Now the shoe is on the other foot."

"Devin, I have lost as much sleep as I can over this thing," Didier said simply. "I remembered why I came to Rosslyn, to set up my practice here. Do not misconstrue. I love my house on King Street and my membership in the country club. But it is not about the money; it never was. I love what I do. I prefer animals to some people that I know. I jump out of bed every morning and come here with a smile on my face. I thought you felt the same way, too."

It came back to him just then . . . why he decided to become a veterinarian, why he risked alienation from his father by not following in KL's and his brothers' footsteps. His passion to help the helpless channeled itself in less smarmier ways than the law. "I love what I do, too, Didier."

Again with the shrug. "Then we will make it work," Didier said. "And part of the immediate solution is us both cutting our salaries in half so we can afford to keep Maria on full time."

Devin laughed. As always, Didier was solution-oriented. For now, he was happy to play Grasshopper to Didier's Zen Master. Plus, Maria was worth more than they were paying her, anyway. "Okay," he relented.

They closed up at five exactly. There were no patients to keep them there. He made a right onto Wilson and headed north to check on KL. He knew this route like the back of his hand. Practically minutes later, he was on Garfield, about to turn into the garage, when he slammed on the brakes. The garage door stood open. Everything, from all of KL's tools, to his black vintage Mercedes-Benz, to the ten-speed bike that Devin had stored over there, was gone. All that was left was an oil spot where KL's Benz had sat. Devin's pulse lunged up his throat to his head, making him dizzy for a moment. Then he looked at the inside garage door that led to the house. *Pop!*

Devin rushed from the still-running Navigator and into the garage. He tried the knob of the door that led to the house; it was unlocked. He threw it open and tore into the house. He went from room to room, looking to see if everything was intact. Then he saw Sadat at the foot of the stairs. "Wuh," Sadat barked, half-assed.

Devin stepped over him and ran up the stairs, inspecting the rooms as he went. "Pop!" he yelled.

Nothing.

"Pop!" he yelled, even louder.

He finally found KL in the old bedroom-turned-study. His father was nodding off in front of the computer. For a second, Devin thought the worst. His heart pounded madly. He shook his father. "Dad!" he cried.

KL started into consciousness, his eyes wide behind his reading specs. Devin sighed, relieved. Then KL looked over at Devin and glared menacingly at him. "What do you want in my house?!" he roared.

Devin jumped back, his turn to be startled. "Dad, it's me," he said, his tone meant to reassure. "Your son . . ."

"You're not Chauncey!" KL yelled. "Get out of my house before I call the police!"

Devin stood back. He bit his lip and blinked back the tears that were burning in his eyes as he stared at his father . . . a true lion in winter.

It was almost twilight when Chaney pulled up in front of the house on North Garfield. She saw Devin on the porch, waiting for her, like that first night they were together. He'd been pissed off then; this time, he looked scared. She got out of the car and rushed up the steps to him. "Hey, sweetie," she said. "What's going on?"

He swallowed her up in one of those hugs that she loved so much and held onto her for dear life. His nose found the pulse point at her throat. "Thanks for coming so quickly," he sighed.

Chaney scoffed. Any excuse to leave that ridiculous pizza-and-cake party, with Al's fake glad-handing of the line staff, and, strangely enough, Randy and Lissa surreptitiously groping each other in the corner of the big conference room. There wasn't enough Fluexa in her system to take that for much longer. "I wasn't doing anything important," she assured him.

Devin let her go. "He left the garage door open," he announced. "Everything's gone. His car, his tools . . . everything!"

Chaney's hands flew to her mouth. "Oh my God!" she exclaimed.

"If I'd done this shit, he would've had my ass in a sling!" he yelled.

Chaney realized, though, that that was fear talking, not anger. She took his hand. "Devin, your dad is seventy," she gently reminded him.

"Oh, so he gets a pass because he's old?"

"Yeah, Dev. He gets a pass 'cause he's old."

Devin sighed, shaking his head. "He scared me to death," he confessed. "When I went inside to check on him, he didn't even know who I was, Chaney."

"Sweetie, people his age forget things, like to close the garage door."

"Chaney, this is different. It was like he didn't even know that I existed. He said he has one son. Chauncey."

She saw the fear on his face morph into pain. Her take-charge side, which she inherited from Anna Lisa, kicked in. "Okay," she said. "Have you called the police?"

He shook his head no. Finally, something she could help with. "Let's do that, then," she said.

Holding hands, they went inside and found KL, seated in a beautifully carved wooden chair that looked Nigerian or Ghanaian. He lay under his blanket with the ever-loyal Sadat at his feet, watching the Channel 7 news with Kathleen Matthews and Maureen Bunyan playing dueling anchors to pundits, speculating whether or not Iraq was next now that the U.S. was done in Afghanistan. She tentatively touched his shoulder, leery of what kind of reaction she was going to get. "Hi, KL," she said.

He looked away from the TV and up at her. His eyes danced with recognition. "Hey, baby girl!" he laughed.

Baby girl. She did remember that her father used to call her that. Her heart immediately warmed to him. She bent down and kissed his face. "Hey, that's a smooth cheek."

"I'm telling you—it's that shaving mousse," he said. "When are we going into business?"

He seemed mentally acute, not that she doubted Devin. She looked over her shoulder at him as he stared at the spectacle in disbelief. "Devin tells me you got robbed."

"Can you believe that?" KL exclaimed. "I have lived in this neighborhood for over forty years with no problems. Times are not changing for the better, that's for sure."

From behind them, Devin asked, "Hey, Dad, where are the insurance papers?"

KL looked tersely over his shoulder. "The office," he snapped. "In the last desk drawer."

They both heard Devin pound up the stairs. KL leaned in toward Chaney. "The boy's upset with me," he sighed.

He was right, but Chaney determined that sometimes, lying was kinder. "He was just worried about you," she said.

"He's a good boy," KL said. "A little fussy, like his mother. She was the best wife. I loved that woman. I always came back to her. I used to joke that she must've buried my drawers in the yard."

Chaney laughed. "That's funny!" she giggled.

"The boy was my last chance to be a good father," KL sighed. "But I messed up. Just like my cousin Norm wrecked his relationship with your sister. When his mother took him clear across the country, and then married that white man, she broke my heart."

Chaney listened in silence. Far from being forgetful, KL seemed to be reliving every mistake he'd ever made in his seventy years. "But he's here with you now," she reminded him. "You can make it right."

They heard Devin pounding down the stairs. He appeared with a manila file in his hands. "Here it is," he announced.

While Devin phoned the police, Chaney sifted through the file and called the insurance company to report the car stolen. Two bored Arlington County cops came and took the perfunctory report, left a copy with Devin for the insurance, then left as quickly as they arrived.

Devin leaned against the front door and sighed. From his vantage point, he stared at his father, who was still under the blanket in the chair. Chaney rubbed a comforting hand along his tummy. "You done good, Devin," she said.

He eyed her, gratitude painfully evident on his face. "Thank you," he said.

She looked him over. She would've done anything for him. She rose on tiptoe and stole a kiss behind KL's back. "You hungry?"

He nodded. "Well, let's get you fed," she said simply.

She kissed him again, then headed to KL in the chair. She touched his shoulder and shook him awake. "KL, you hungry?"

He looked her in the face and smiled. "What you cooking, Anna Lisa?" he asked.

Oh, shit. Chaney stared at KL. Maybe there was something to what Devin had been saying all night.

Chaney and Devin threw together a quick dinner. He grilled some steaks, and Chaney made macaroni and cheese, the spoonable kind, the way Anna Lisa said their mother used to make it. They both collaborated on a salad. Chaney shot the breeze with KL, but she noticed that Devin was uncharacteristically quiet. Even as they cleaned up later, he had very little to say. Chaney let him have his moment. She sensed he'd tell her everything later.

After KL went up to bed, Chaney found Devin seated on the steps of the front porch. She eased down next to him, then nudged him. "Hey," she said.

With his fingers, Devin pinched hair from her forehead, bent his head, and kissed her full on the lips. "Hey," he said against her mouth.

She slipped an arm around his waist, hooking her thumb into one of his belt loops. They sat and stared at the sparse traffic on the street. "What's my dad doing?" Devin asked.

"Gone to sleep," she said.

"This has been the worst day," he explained. "We got the verdict from the business manager. More improvements needed, and no money for them. Then I come here and see that shit in the garage. I think I might've bitten off more than I can chew here." He looked at her with questions in his eyes. "What am I gonna do, baby?"

She shrugged. "You've just got to chew, sweetie," she said simply. "Keep doing what you've been doing . . . rising to the occasion like a man. That's all you can do. No matter what issues you have with your father, tonight you honored him. You're a good son, Devin."

He searched her face with his eyes. "I wish we could go somewhere," he said, then leaned closer and whispered in her ear, "so you could play with the magic stick."

Chaney laughed. She looked down at her watch: *10:30.* "You sweet talker, you," she said. "I really have to get home and feed the dog. It's my turn to ask for a rain check."

"Okay," he said.

Suddenly, she thought about her mix tape. She nudged him. "I really loved my present."

"I love you," he said, then all of a sudden had a shocked expression on his face, like he couldn't believe he'd just said it.

Chaney stared at him, like *did I hear you right?* Her heart lunged against her rib cage. "Okay, let me get this straight," she said, her tone teasing. "Do you love me, or do you love fucking me?"

He laughed, rolling those adorable almond-shaped eyes. "Aw, see?" he cried. "Brothah's trying to bare his soul, and you're ridiculing him."

"I just wanna be sure," she said. "I don't want to get my hopes up, then it turns out that you left out a word, and then I feel like a fool."

He dropped one of his languid, slow kisses on her, where he practically tongued her down, and she felt the familiar rush below the belt. "I love you," he said, this time with conviction.

She stared at him, held a trembling hand to her mouth. "Wow," she breathed.

Then he winked at her. "I also love fucking you, too."

She punched him in the arm. "You play too much!" she mock-whined.

He looked at her, his face full of hope. "So, you gonna leave me hanging?" he asked.

She brushed her mouth against his. *Please, don't leave me like almost everyone in my life has gone and done. Please don't leave me for someone younger, or freakier, or gay. Please don't hurt me . . .* "I love you, Devin," she whispered. "I'm just trying to be a grown-up about all this."

"Why?" he asked. "Just enjoy it. Don't overthink it, or you'll kill it."

Spoken like a twenty-eight-year-old. She laughed, shaking her head. "Easier said than done, but I'll try. For you."

* * *

Devin looked out the window at the grounds of the VA Hospital. In the face of KL's increasingly erratic behavior, he'd made an appointment for his father to have a head CT scan, then he'd called up his brothers for reinforcements.

Devin turned away from the window to look at them. Chauncey, looking heavier and more rumpled than ever, came willingly. To get Eric to come, Devin had to enlist Marlene's help. He'd called the house at a time he knew Eric wouldn't be home. Marlene closed the short conversation by saying, "Devin, we don't see you anymore." He didn't have the heart to tell her why. He blamed the usual culprit— the business. If he'd told her he was seeing someone new, she'd want to talk further, and he didn't trust himself to stay on the phone with her without divulging why he'd been scarce.

Eric, suited down even at the height of August, sat off on his own, thumbing through the clichéd stack of outdated magazines. Every once in a while, his eyes would meet Devin's, and Devin would look away in disgust. Chauncey got up and met Devin by the window. "What's up with you and E?" he asked.

Devin sighed, so tired of being the diplomat. "Why don't you ask 'E'?" he suggested.

"You two are brothers," Chauncey reminded him.

Devin sucked his teeth. "So were Cain and Abel," he said.

Chauncey opened his mouth, prepared to comment further, when a young black man in a white coat entered the room. He headed straight toward them, and they met him halfway. He eyed them quizzically. "You're Kenneth Rhym's sons?" he asked.

All his life, Devin had gotten that same reaction, like, *naw, you guys can't be brothers*. He suspected that folks probably thought KL had adopted them all. "Yes," Chauncey said, speaking for the three of them.

"I'm his doctor, Terry Steele," the doctor announced.

Devin, Eric, and Chauncey chorused their subdued greeting. "Where's Dad?" Devin asked.

"He's in radiology," Dr. Steele announced. "They're getting ready to bring him down to my office. I wanted to meet with you first, as the immediate family."

That didn't sound good. "Why?" Eric questioned. "What's wrong?"

"Well, first, we did the CT scan of his brain," Dr. Steele explained.

"Then we administered some cognitive tests. From both the CT scan and those tests, we were able to make an assessment as to what's wrong with your father."

That sounded even worse to Devin's ears. He knew the technique for softening people up for bad news all too well. The only difference was, in Steele's case, the patients in distress were humans. "What's wrong with Dad?" Devin asked, near demanded.

His delivery was measured, patient. "Your father has Alzheimer's disease," Dr. Steele announced.

Devin felt like he'd been punched in the gut. His father was already a stranger to him because of the tyranny of divorce and geography. Now, KL was actually going to forget him. *This can't be happening . . .*

Eric cut right to the chase. "What's the prognosis? What can we expect?"

Dr. Steele shrugged. "It's very hard to tell," he confessed. "Your father could stay as he is right now for ten years or more. Or he could start going rapidly downhill tomorrow. How has he been behaving at home?"

His brothers' faces drew blank stares. Neither of them had been checking on KL, were busy living their own lives. They looked deferentially to Devin, who finally found his voice. "He vacillates from friendly to mean at the drop of a hat," Devin explained. "He used to be just forgetful. Now, he calls me by one of my brothers' names or he doesn't even remember me being born at all. Sometimes, he forgets to feed the dog. A couple of days ago, he accidentally left the garage door open again and everything got stolen this time."

"That sounds about right," Dr. Steele said. "Bottom line, gentlemen, your father needs your love and patience as he goes through this. It will be a challenge. You'll have to devise a plan to handle what's going to be an uphill battle. It won't be easy, but dealing with the needs of an aging parent never is."

Dr. Steele let his words sink in for the appropriate time. Then he said, "Let's go tell your father, shall we?"

"Okay," Devin, Chauncey, and Eric grimly chorused.

As they followed Dr. Steele through the brightly lit halls, Devin's heart beat with every step he took, filling up with sadness and dread. He swallowed hard against the raging tide of emotion racking his body. He wished he could go back to being the carefree twentysomething, with money in his hands, a bright future, and women of all shapes, colors, and creeds riding his jock. He sure didn't want to be the brothah looking thirty in the eye, with the failing practice, about to ruin his father's life by setting him up to receive this devastating news.

Then his mind kicked into overdrive. He was going to have to put his town house on the market and permanently relocate to the house on North Garfield. And he'd have to call his mother with the news. But most of all, he wanted to call Chaney.

Ten

In the light coming through the drawn blinds, Chaney watched Devin sleep. He looked so tired, like he hadn't slept since KL had been diagnosed. It was only when he was with her, in the safety of her home, that he became his old self again. They did corny couple things, like cooked together, walked Tony, and slow-dragged to cuts from CDs he'd burned especially for her. He showed her his most unguarded self when they made love. It both touched her and frightened her that he would trust her enough to be so open to her, that he could love her so much. *What if I don't measure up? What if I fail you?*

Just then, the phone rang, and she snatched it up before it woke him. "Hello," she whispered.

"Chanes, it me!" Daisy cried, all excited, on the other end.

Chaney looked over at Devin. He'd stirred in his sleep and turned over, exposing his broad back and the crack of his ass from under the covers. "Hey, girl," she said quietly.

"Why are you whispering?"

"I got a man in my bed, and I don't wanna wake him."

"*Pfft!* Yeah, right," Daisy scoffed, like that was so incredible. "Listen, I can't talk long, but I've left ten tickets at the will-call for you. Orchestra seats. The tickets'll have backstage passes in them, but if you run into any trouble, call James at this number."

Chaney grabbed a pen and jotted down the phone number. "Got it," she said.

"Oh God, I can't wait to see you!" Daisy squealed.

"I'm excited, too," Chaney laughed. "There's someone I want you to meet."

They exchanged I love you's, and Chaney hung up. She looked over at Tony, who sat in the doorway to the bedroom, his ears perked up. "Your mommy's coming to see you," Chaney said.

"Wuh!" Tony barked, like he understood exactly what was going on.

Devin turned over and looked sleepily up at her. "Hey," he said, lazily stretching.

"Hey, sweetie," she whispered.

He reached for her, and she slid under the covers next to him. He nuzzled his favorite spot on her neck. "Mmm," he moaned. "You showered."

She giggled. "Yes, and you should hop to it. D and Hiriko'll be here any minute."

He pulled open her robe, buried his head, and encircled her left nipple with his pointed tongue. She shuddered, gasping as he greedily sucked her flesh. Ever since she could remember, that had been the trick to jump-start her. She caressed his dark head. "Maybe we have a little more time," she mused.

Just as he dipped his thumbs into the elastic waistband of her panties, though, the doorbell rang. Immediately, Tony cut and ran down the stairs, raising the alarm. He sighed, pressing his forehead against hers. "Let the circus begin," Chaney laughed.

In Devin's ride, they zoomed along Route 66 West in the H.O.V. lane toward Bristow. Acres and acres of buildings and unspoiled landscape zipped by through the windows. As he drove, Devin surreptitiously locked his fingers through hers. Chaney turned and looked at D and Hiriko, who were also holding hands and staring out the windows as scenes from Northern Virginia passed by. She sensed something odd; they certainly were way more subdued than they were at the wedding. "You two are awfully quiet," she observed.

They both looked mildly startled, like she'd snatched them out of a reverie. "We are?" Hiriko laughed, her voice trembling.

"Just good to be here," D offered. "With civilians."

"So, I finally get to meet my real cousin," Devin laughed, then squeezed Chaney's hand. "As opposed to this fake one here."

"Yeah, you can't fuck me," D laughed.

They all laughed. This was the D that Chaney knew—wildly inappropriate but endearing. "Yeah, I don't think the gay, incestuous thing'll play well here," Devin laughed.

"Hey, we wanted to say thanks for the espresso machine," Hiriko said.

Devin shrugged, like it was no thing. "No problem," he said. "I'm sure it's not the manliest gift I could give, but since you guys didn't have a registry, I had to wing it."

Hiriko scoffed. "Please!" she laughed. "You should see the butchest Marines from D's battalion over at the house, sucking down espressos from those little demitasses. Pinkies up and everything!"

D looked at her and shook his head. Already, they were acting like an old married couple. "Of course, you know, I'm going to have to kill them now that you've told them," he said.

She shrugged, like Gracie Allen to his George Burns. "If you must," she sighed.

"Hey, Devin, how's your dad doing?" D asked innocently. "I was hoping to see him while I'm up this time."

Devin squeezed Chaney's hand hard. She studied his profile, saw his jaw set hard. "He's okay," Devin said. "You know, he's seventy. He has his good days and his bad days."

"Well, we leave on Sunday—day after tomorrow," D announced.

"I'll see if he's up to it," Devin promised.

So much for the moment of levity. Again, they sat in silence as Devin blazed down Route 66.

The police roadblocks signaled that they were close to the pavilion. Uniformed cops waved folks through with fluorescent orange cones, then orange-jacketed staff waved them to the grass dirt parking area. Of course, all the paved spots close to the arena were either reserved for season ticket holders to the pavilion, or they were already taken.

Both couples holding hands, they leisurely made the seemingly endless trek to the pavilion. The night was not a bad one. It was September, and the nights in Virginia were beginning to get cooler. They strolled up wide asphalt pathways among thousands of other concertgoers, until the actual building, a confluence of a triangular ceiling over rows of seats, came into view.

The rest of the party was waiting for them when they got to the box office, a long white building with openings for two-way glass windows. Ticket vendors sat behind the glass, separated from the prospective ticket buyer, with only a sliver of glass at the bottom and a metal disk through which they could communicate. One of these openings had a plain sheet of white paper, with WILL CALL printed on the face with a laser printer.

What will they all think? There was Nathalie, dressed like a pregnant Li'l Kim in pink sunglasses, jeans, high heels, and a crocheted black top that showed off her black bra and the beginnings of a smooth, dark, belly bump. Next to her, Craig, her decidedly more conservatively dressed better half, beamed like a proud papa-to-be. Dani and Sandy were holding hands, looking more like girlfriends than—wink-wink—*girlfriends*. Coco, dressed like she was going to youth camp, not a rock concert in a frilly gingham dress, stood loyally next to her husband, Mike, who looked equally unhip in a dress shirt and black pants. They both looked like poster children for Lens Crafters, with the thick glasses. Miguel looked like the ultimate *sk8er boi*, with the long, baggy jeans, gray hoodie sweatshirt, socks, and sneaks. Juanita was still rocking the Goth look; this being a special occasion and all, Coco finally let her wear the white makeup. She wasn't her usual sullen, preteenaged self. Tonight she looked . . . excited.

Chaney brought D and Hiriko forward and introduced them. D leaned in toward Juanita. "She's my Aunt Chaney, too," he whispered.

Then, the pièce de résistance, she held Devin's hands. "Everyone, this is Devin," she announced, and she knew she was grinning like a fool, but she could've cared less.

Devin held up a hand. "Hi," he said . . . simple and friendly.

Everyone returned the greeting, seemingly genuinely pleased to meet him. Except Nathalie. She removed her sunglasses and sized Devin up. "Uh-huh," she said.

What's that supposed to mean? Aloud, though, Chaney said, "Well, I'll go get the tickets."

Chaney got the tickets and backstage passes from the will call and distributed them to the group. At the entrance to the pavilion, Security searched their bags and purses. Since no one was carrying, the guards let them into the park without incident.

As the sun dipped over the horizon, everyone met up at their seats in Orchestra Two, practically facing the stage. When Daisy did come through, she did it right. With a blindingly bright explosion of deafening pyrotechnics, the rock star appeared on stage amid a flurry of sizzling, rapid-fire guitar licks. The rest of the band, consisting of

Ricky, the bassist in a fly metallic suit, a rhythm guitarist, and zaftig gospel backup singers, added to the mix. The highlight of the show, though, was the girl drummer, who looked like she should be on a Parisian catwalk, not blazing behind a drum kit. She tore it up, wielding sticks every which way. Her image showed up on both of the big screens on either side of the stage, and the crowd went wild.

After the star's blistering two-hour set and an encore, Chaney looked over at Devin. He looked happier than a pig in shit. During the encore, which was the phenomenal radio hit about the power of love, lighters in the place went up, forming a sea of flickering flames in the darkness. Devin stood behind her, wrapped his arms tightly around her waist, and swayed to the music. She felt a confluence of emotions . . . loved, safe, protected, proud that she was the one making him happy right at that moment. He kissed her cheek. She looked up at him. His look on his face said it all. "I know," she said in his ear. "I fucking love you, too!"

After the second and last encore, the lights went up. The crowd took the hint, starting to filter out of the seats. Chaney's group exited stage left toward the entrance to the compound backstage. As they got to the wooden gate, though, it seemed that everyone had the same idea to try to get backstage. Chaney stared, in awe, at scantily clad girl groupies, star-fuckers, and various and sundry potential hangers-on, all hailing the burly men in T-shirts that read SECURITY on the front to let them inside to be with the band. Nathalie and Dani came up to Chaney. "This is crazy," Dani commented.

Chaney reached into her purse and pulled out her Blackberry. She looked for the number of the contact, James, in the database and dialed him up. That was all it took. Minutes later, a thin, wiry guy who looked like an aging Kenny Loggins showed up at the wooden gate and shepherded them in. Daisy, again, to the rescue.

Once inside the compound, James led them inside another building. They followed him down a brick hall, painted gray, to a hospitality room that reminded Chaney of her high-school cafeteria. It was almost as big as one, with industrial-type chairs and tables. "You can wait here for Daisy, folks," James said. "The man of the hour's getting a massage, but after his shower, he'll be seeing people soon."

Chaney's heart raced. She was going to see her sister after so long, and she was about to meet a real, live rock star. She'd been so caught up in the moment that she realized she'd forgotten to pee. She looked around her and saw a sign for a unisex restroom at the back of the room. She squeezed Devin's hand and pointed to the back. "I'll be right back," she assured him.

He nodded. "Okay."

Nathalie and Dani tagged along. Once in the stark, industrial-looking bathroom, they all occupied three of the four stalls. They peed in silence and in unison, then took to washing their hands at the sinks. Finally, Nathalie said, "So, that's Devin."

Chaney felt her face succumb to the shit-eating grin as she soaped her hands. "Yeah," she giggled.

Nathalie stopped washing her hands and turned to Chaney. "I've held my tongue long enough, but I have to ask you if you've lost your mind."

Chaney stared incredulously at her. She didn't even feel the high-tech sensor in the sink stop cascading water over her hands. "What do you mean?"

Nathalie shook her hands on the way to the electronic dryer on the far wall. "I can see you getting caught up," she declared. "You're telling yourself you're in love instead of seeing what this really is."

Chaney felt the heat rise up her neck, up her face, and stop where her scalp began. "What is this: 'The Baby That Made Me Judgmental?' Why don't you tell me what *you* think it is?"

So Nathalie did. "He's your tadpole, you're his cougar," she said. "After the sex haze wears off, you're gonna wake up and realize that you've been sold a wuff ticket."

"What the fuck is a 'wuff ticket?' " Chaney demanded. "Can I have the Bama-to-English translation, please?"

" 'Been sold a bill of goods.' 'Deluded,' " Nathalie explained impatiently. "You and that New York arrogance!"

"I think it's great," Dani stated. "I've never seen Chaney happier."

Nathalie sucked her teeth. "Fucking a twenty-eight-year-old boy would make anyone happy, Dani."

Dani winked at Chaney, and Chaney marveled at how the person she'd been the most leery of was the person who'd been most in her corner lately. "Not me," Dani laughed.

"Dykes don't count."

That rolled off Dani's back. "Oh, you're just trying to spoil everyone's night, aren't you?"

Chaney stared Nathalie up and down. She'd never thought that

Nathalie could be so hurtful, under the guise of friendship. "You and Craig are the only couple allowed to be happy, to procreate, to groove to your own 'jam,' while I'm supposed to be the pathetic single babe you guys keep around for your own sick amusement?" Chaney asked. "Why can't I have love like you? Like Dani?"

"No one's saying you can't have love, Chaney," Nathalie explained. "Just use your head."

How could she explain something so organic as her attraction to Devin? Sometimes, she barely understood it herself. She just knew that she was finding it harder and harder to envision being without him. The tears that filled her eyes were more from frustration than from sadness or joy. "He gives me something I've never had," she said simply. "Whenever I think about him, my heart . . . He makes me feel like he'd die if I wasn't with him. The closeted forty-year-old couldn't give me that, even though he put a fabulous ring on my finger. That age-appropriate pituitary case in Syracuse couldn't give it to me. The forty-six-year-old freak who took me to the swing club couldn't give me that."

Nathalie's perfectly plucked brows furrowed. "Swing club?"

Dani held up a hand, shaking her head. "Later," she said.

Chaney ripped a piece of industrial brown paper from the roll in the dispenser at the far right of the room. She dried her hands, then slam-dunked it into the wastepaper basket. "Me and my New York arrogance are going outside to see my sister and meet a rock star," she declared.

She threw open the door and stormed out of the ladies' room. From the click-clacking of boot heels on the linoleum, she guessed that Nathalie and Dani weren't far behind.

Chaney entered the hospitality suite just in time to see another piece of Anger Theater unfolding before her eyes. When she saw her sister, her heart beat excitedly. Daisy was as beautiful and smoking-hot as ever, with her long, coltish legs in jeans, her full breasts practically bursting out of a midriff-baring T-shirt with the word BROOKLYN emblazoned across her nipples, and her size ten feet in ridiculously clean Tims.

What wasn't so beautiful were the things she was screaming at the top of her lungs at the brothah with the red locks. Chaney recognized him from the pictures Daisy had sent, from seeing him on stage. *Ricky.*

He was trying mightily to stop her from dragging a green duffel that was so huge that Chaney guessed both Miguel and Juanita could fit inside. "I left my whole life in L.A. to come on the road with you!" Daisy shouted, a cry in her voice. "And you repay me by fucking that skanky Cuban skeezer of a groupie in Miami!"

Ricky's light eyes were red and puffy. He looked like he'd been crying. "Baby, please don't go," he begged. "We can talk about this."

Daisy yanked the duffel bag from his tenacious grasp. "I am so gone," she cried. "I'm so gone that the word *gone* is inadequate to describe how absent I will be from your life. You can fuck your way up the eastern seaboard, for all I care."

Ricky wrung those hands that only minutes ago had extracted sweet musical notes from a six-string fretless bass. "Okay," he said, like he was mentally making a compromise. "Okay, baby. I know you need some time to forgive me. Take some time. Be with your sister. But please join me in New York. I'll send your ticket."

"Not if Hillary Rodham-fucking-Clinton was standing in Times Square with an engraved invitation!" she snarled.

Poor Ricky shrank back, and Daisy turned to the audience in the room. Their reactions ran the gamut from embarrassed smiles, to expressions of shock, to averting of eyes. Daisy's eyes found Chaney's. Under all the bravado, and the 'tude, and the rolling of the head, Daisy was cut to the core. Chaney shrugged, flashing her a lopsided smile. "Hey, Daze," she said.

Daisy dragged her monstrous duffel over to her sister. "Please get me out of here, Chanes," she said.

Chaney knew the value of having someone there to provide you with an exit strategy after you'd shown your ass to the world. Chaney took her sister's hand. "Sure, sweetie," she said. "Let's go."

Behind them, Chaney heard Juanita ask her mother, "No rock star, Mommy?"

"No rock star, *querida*," Coco sighed.

Outside the pavilion, where they'd all met up hours earlier, everyone began to scatter to the winds, amid hugs and kisses. Nathalie attempted to hug Chaney, but Chaney turned away. "I'll talk to you later," Nathalie said.

"Not likely," Chaney countered.

Chaney began to really appreciate the value of having men around.

Devin and D dragged Daisy's bag all the way to the parking lot. Hiriko and Chaney flanked Daisy with supportive arms around her waist. "As fine as you are?" Hiriko offered. "He'll be Black History like that."

Hiriko snapped her fingers, her metallic blue nail polish catching the light from overhead. Daisy stared at Hiriko, with her trendy specs, the blond streak in the middle of her forehead, and her flawless make-up. "I love you already!" Daisy laughed.

During the ride back to Chaney's, everyone held their tongues. Chaney herself wondered what to do or say to support her sister, while at the same time being solution-oriented. After all, Daisy was almost three thousand miles away from home, unemployed, with her entire life packed away in storage somewhere in L.A. Mercifully, it wasn't very long before Devin steered into one of the parking spaces in the Suffolk Court lot.

While Devin and D wrestled with the bag, the ladies headed for the house. Chaney unlocked her door and disabled the alarm. By now, Daisy's mood had brightened some. "Where's my baby?" she asked.

Chaney crossed the expanse of the house to the sliding doors and pulled open the blinds. In the deck light, Tony sat in front of the doors, with his ears perked up and his head cocked to one side. Daisy's eyes widened. "There he is!" she cried.

Chaney opened the doors, and Tony froze momentarily, like he couldn't believe that, after six months, it was really her. Daisy knelt. "Come here, boy!" she implored in a high-pitched voice. "Come to Mama!"

Chaney and Hiriko looked on as Tony made a mad dash for her, jumped up on her, and slurped at her face. He barked like a mad dog, howling and whining as Daisy vigorously stroked his coat. Chaney couldn't help but feel a tad jealous. *How could I even compete with that?* Daisy was Tony's mommy, the ultimate alpha dog who'd raised him since he was a puppy. Chaney, on the other hand, was just the facsimile who dog-sat for six months.

Devin and D entered with the bag and closed the front door. "Where should we put this?" D asked.

Chaney looked up from the love fest going on in front of her. "My room," she said.

"Devin, after you," D teased, the implication that Devin had been in her bedroom crystal clear.

Devin just laughed, then looked over at Chaney and winked. He and D proceeded to heft the bag up the stairs.

Tony was still tonguing Daisy down with glee when Devin and D bounded down the stairs. Devin looked down at his watch. "Sweetest, I gotta go," he announced.

Chaney's heart sank. This was definitely not how she'd planned spending the rest of this evening . . . with an angry, lovesick sister and her nephew and his wife, the happy couple. Nonetheless, especially when dealing with Daisy, she'd learned long ago to be flexible and prepared for anything to happen. She sighed. "I'll walk you out."

Everyone took turns hugging Devin good-bye. D was the last. " 'Night, sweetest," D teased. "Don't have our girl outside too late."

"Cousin's got jokes," Devin laughed.

Devin and Chaney walked outside into the crisp, clear September night. She looked up at the dark sky and could see stars and constellations for miles in every direction. "So, that's your family," Devin said. "D's wife looks like me."

Chaney laughed, shaking her head. What an initiation for the guy! "You can run now," she said. "It's not too late. I won't hold it against you."

In response, Devin leaned against the ride and snaked his arms around her waist. She sighed. She'd been waiting to be alone with him all night. "I'm not going anywhere," he declared.

Is this the right time for this? Am I rushing things? Despite the questions running through her head, she dipped into her jeans pocket and took out a single key on a Syracuse Orangeman key chain and a slip of paper. She saw the questions in his eyes and held up a hand. "This is not a marriage proposal—this is a key to my house and the alarm code," she said. "If you feel uncomfortable about this, I can put them away, and we don't have to have this conversation ever again."

He looked down at the offerings in her hand, then back up at her. Just as she thought she'd explode with anticipation, he took them and socked them away in his front pocket. She sighed deeply, able to taste the relief coursing through her. "Unfortunately, I can't give you mine," he said. "The realtor sold my house yesterday. The best I can offer you is my dad's basement."

Chaney smiled, enjoying all her vivid memories of what they'd done in that very same basement. "That's the best offer I've had in a long time," she said.

She eased out of his grasp and leaned against the ride, too. Through the bay kitchen window, she could see Daisy, D, and Hiriko raiding her fridge. *Family.* "Of course, you know the honeymoon's over," she sighed. "No more safe little cocoon."

"That's the test, right?" he asked.

Chaney looked him up and down. Sometimes it surprised her how much wiser than his years he seemed sometimes. He kissed her deeply, and she responded in kind. Moments later, though, Devin was in the ride. Chaney sighed, her heart heavy as she watched the Navigator disappear from the parking lot. She stared out into the darkness long after he was gone. Then she turned and went back inside.

She found Daisy, D, and Hiriko in the kitchen, the kitchen counter littered with Rubbermaid containers they'd taken from the fridge. Tony sat on his haunches and looked up at the activity around him. Food was involved, and anything that dropped on the floor was going to be his.

The culprits looked up at her, like they'd been busted. "We're hungry!" Daisy whined.

Chaney shook her head. "Slobs, every last one of y'all," she said. "Let's hook this up right."

The late-night snack was a hodgepodge of what Chaney had in the fridge that was still good: potato salad, macaroni and cheese, baked chicken from the rotisserie at the Giant, and greens she'd experimented with, using turkey meat instead of pork. They sat around the kitchen table in the bay window and greased, and talked, and laughed. Tony looked up from his spot on the floor next to Daisy, like he was about to join the conversation at any second. The house felt alive, lived-in, right then, like more than just a place to hang her hat.

For dessert, they passed around Chips Ahoys and Oreos straight from the package. "You know your mother'd have a fit if she saw us not doing this," Chaney laughed, picking apart an Oreo to reveal the creamy center. She affected Anna Lisa's prissy tone. " 'Take out what you need, put it in a saucer, and put the rest back in the cupboard.' "

"That's why we won't be telling her," Daisy declared, looking around the table. "Got any soy milk?"

Everyone at the table stared at her. "What?" Daisy asked.

"God, you're so Cali," Chaney laughed.

"That dairy will back you up," said the woman who'd just sucked down three helpings of macaroni and cheese. "Death begins in the colon."

"I know I'm new to the family," Hiriko began, "but could we not talk about colons over the dinner table?"

Everyone laughed. Chaney guessed that Hiriko was going to fit in just fine.

D finished his Oreo, then cleared his throat. "Well, Hiriko and I have something to tell you," he announced.

"What now?" Daisy teased. "A quickie divorce?"

Chaney slapped her sister's bony forearm. "Shush!"

Hiriko and D exchanged glances, then smiled from ear to ear. D slipped a protective arm around her shoulders. "I'm pregnant," Hiriko announced.

Chaney stared at them as they awaited her and Daisy's reaction . . . any reaction. She'd never been so conflicted. First Nathalie, then Hiriko. Even Hershey was pregnant! It was hard to temper her envy at the fact that others were pregnant while she grew fibroids inside her like some twisted orange grove. Hard to accept the switching up of the laws of nature, when the nephew married and reproduced before the aunt.

Daisy was the one brave enough to articulate what both she and Chaney were feeling. "You know, Decameron, you're just fucking up the natural order of things," she declared. "I never thought my nephew'd be married before me . . ." she pointed at Chaney ". . . or even before low man over there. And now a baby!"

Chaney took in how happy D and Hiriko looked. How could it not be right that their love would produce proof as tangible as a baby? She got up and hugged them both. "What my sister is trying to say in her jacked-up, uncensored way, is congratulations, you two," Chaney said. "You make great parents."

Chaney sat down and watched as D and Hiriko kissed again like they were the only two people in the room. *This kid I used to play with is gonna be someone's daddy.* "When are you due?" Chaney asked.

"Next April," Hiriko said.

D lovingly pushed that blond streak from her forehead with his fingers. "I'm trying to get her to move closer up here," he said. "Near you."

"Why?"

D and Hiriko's smiles that were so broad and happy just minutes ago gradually faded. "I got my orders yesterday," he announced. "I'm headed to Kuwait."

Chaney sat in silence, letting it sink in. Seemingly, the warmth left the room, replaced by the cold chill of uncertainty. She wished she didn't know what to expect. Thanks to Norm, they were a military family; she knew the drill. Plus, she'd been watching the news just like everyone else lately. Kuwait was the staging point for a war with Iraq.

Daisy, it seemed, had forgotten the drill. "When?" she asked.

"You know I can't say when, Daisy," he said. "That'd be a security breach."

Chaney sat back in the chair. Suddenly, she didn't feel very well. Her head throbbed, and her stomach roiled. She could feel the beads of sweat pop up in that region just between her nose and her top lip. She felt worse than she did over a decade ago when D had gotten deployed to Turkey during Operation Desert Shield. That time, they'd watched Bush the Prequel on TV, announcing the beginning of Desert Storm.

Again, Daisy articulated what Chaney was feeling. "This is the same shit as '91," she sighed.

Something inside Chaney sensed that this time, it would be much worse. She got up and snatched the phone receiver off the wall. "Enough of this shit, Decameron," she declared, surprising herself at the force of her tone. "You are going to call your mother."

D rolled his eyes, and Chaney prepared for the mother of all arguments with him. But this time, though, it was Hiriko who intervened. "Baby, you and your mother need to squash your psycho Scorpio tempers and come to an understanding," she stated, gently but decisively. "I'm only going to be Monie in the Middle but for so long."

Chaney stared at her, pleasantly surprised. So, she wasn't foul-mouthed and vapid. She actually had a brain in her head. It was most likely her stance that made D take the receiver when Chaney extended it again. "Dial the number," Chaney commanded.

He rolled his eyes and swore like a sailor. But in the end, he did dial the number.

Under the overcast sky, Chaney zipped along the Dulles Toll Road. The only American Airlines direct flights available to Los Angeles that

Sunday were leaving out of Dulles. Through her rearview mirror, Chaney stared at Tony and Daisy. Daisy gazed out at the Northern Virginia mindscape of sprawling office complexes and planned town house ghettoes, not unlike Chaney's. Tony lay with his head resting in Chaney's lap. He had a look on his doggie face, like *Mommy's home!*

It had been a long weekend, which had officially begun with D's phone call to Anna Lisa that Friday night. After D had told Anna Lisa she was going to be a grandmother, she was overjoyed. She'd awakened Norm, who'd been sleeping next to her. D and Norm spent the next few minutes doing the manly glad-handing that came with the knowledge that, yes, Norm had given his son a penis that works, one which will produce an heir for the Hall family. Joy morphed into sorrow, though, the minute D broke the news that he was going to be deployed. Just like she had eleven years ago, Anna Lisa cried a river. It took Chaney, Daisy, Norm, and D hours of long-distance minutes to calm her down.

D and Hiriko had retired to the guest room, while Chaney changed the sheets that she and Devin had made love on. As much as she hated to, she made room for Daisy in her bed. She had childhood nightmares of sharing her bed with her sister. Sleeping with Daisy was like sleeping with a cover-stealing anaconda. Tony lay in the doorway, as usual. Just when the house was quiet, Chaney shot up in bed, completely grossed out. *No, it can't be . . .* D and Hiriko had begun their symphony of fierce rutting across the hall . . . skin slapping skin, the moaning, the groaning, the headboard slamming against the wall. "Baby, I'm gonna come!" Chaney's nephew moaned, his voice muffled by inches of wooden door and drywall. "I'm gonna come, baby! I'm gonna come!"

Finally, Daisy shot up in bed, too. "Well, hurry up and come already!" she screamed. "We're trying to get to sleep!"

"Wuh!" Tony barked, as if to punctuate what his mommy had said.

Chaney and Daisy looked at each other in the semidarkness and burst out laughing, giggling behind their hands like they used to do when they were kids. But then slowly, Daisy lifted her hands from her face. She wasn't laughing anymore; she was crying. "Daisy, what's wrong?" Chaney asked, surprised.

"I miss Ricky!" Daisy wailed.

So, even after her hard-as-nails triumphal exit from the tour, the reality of her situation was slowly sinking in, that she was now in the rebuilding phase after a breakup. Chaney held her sister close and let her sob herself weak. She sighed. *I wish Devin was here . . .*

The next morning, Chaney had barely made it to the bathroom before last night's festive meal came up in chunks. Somewhere in the back of her mind, she remembered Tolochko warning her to wean herself off the Fluexa. She wanted to call him and ask if these side effects were normal, but her pride wouldn't let her be lectured to in his paternalistic tone. She imagined she also felt a pounding in her head. Belatedly, she realized it was the headboard banging against the wall in the guest room. D and Hiriko were at it again.

The pounding continued as Daisy and Chaney made a breakfast that Chaney felt too ill to eat, as Daisy made plane reservations by phone . . . with Chaney's credit card. Daisy covetously eyed the stainless steel bowls that Tony ate and drank from, as well as Tony's harness and retractable leash. "Can I keep these, Chanes?" she asked. "They're nicer than the ones he's got in L.A."

"Why?" Chaney asked innocently.

Then she realized not only was Daisy going, but she was taking Tony home to L.A. with her. "I can't saddle you with him forever, silly!" Daisy laughed.

Chaney looked over at Tony, with his perked-up ears and his huge brown eyes with the adorable blond lashes. She hadn't realized how much she'd grown attached to him until right then. "Of course," she murmured. "He's your dog. Why wouldn't you take him?"

Chaney's sense of loss deepened when she hugged Hiriko, and then D. Tears flowed down her cheeks as she held onto him for dear life. Eventually, though, she let him go and watched, bereft, as he and Hiriko drove off in their Toyota Corolla. They tag-teamed briefly on Route 495, but D hit the 95 South exit, and Chaney continued on 495 toward Dulles. She finally saw a vision of the airport, which looked like something out of the Jetsons.

While the American Airlines ticketing clerk checked Daisy in, Chaney held Tony by his leash, walking him in circles on the tile floor. She'd thought she couldn't wait to get rid of him. Now all she felt at his impending departure was profound sadness. She stooped until she could look him right in the face. She leaned in, lest other travelers milling around nearby think her crazy for talking to a dog. She raised the flap of one ear to reveal healthy pink inside. Cleaning his ears was her last act of pet-sitting. "Thank you, Tony," she whispered. "Thanks for opening me up. Thanks for giving me Devin."

As if in response, Tony licked her cheek. "Wuh!" he said.

"Come on, boy," Daisy said, relieving Chaney of the leash. "This nice lady is going to help you into your crate."

Between the three of them, they got Tony into the same beige crate he'd come in, then deposited him onto the conveyor belt. Chaney and Daisy watched as Tony and the crate disappeared behind a series of black curtain flaps. The transfer was complete.

Chaney couldn't look at her sister. She knew eye contact would've been the end of her. So she handed her a Giant bag, filled with creams, candles, and lip balm. "If you need more, just call," she said.

Daisy clutched her close. Chaney could feel wet drops plopping into her hair. "Thanks for everything," Daisy wept. "Thanks for keeping my dog."

Chaney held on tight, so tight she could feel the fabric of Daisy's sweater pressing into her cheek. She could smell the scent of the tropical cream Daisy had used on her body that morning. "Hey, what's family for if they can't almost kill your dog, get him laid, and make him a father," she sobbed.

"I love you, Chanes."

"I love you, too, Daze."

They parted and brushed the tears from each other's faces. "I gotta go!" Daisy squealed.

Chaney stayed in her spot, watching as Daisy headed into the security line that snaked around poles. She watched as a cute TSA brothah paid her sister extra attention. Then Chaney watched as Daisy's long legs propelled her out of sight into the thick crowd of travelers in the terminal. Just like that, she was gone.

By the time Chaney arrived back at the house, she was fatigued, a combination of too little sleep and too much emotion for two long days. All she wanted was her bed. As she headed up the steps to her front door, though, the De'Ath's front door flew open. Mrs. De'Ath came tumbling out, all excited. "Chaney!" she said.

Chaney, astonished, stared at her. She remembered the last time she'd seen Mrs. De'Ath. *Friendly* wasn't the F-word that reminded her of their last exchange. "Hi, Mrs. De'Ath," Chaney said. "Listen, my sister and I talked about . . ."

Mrs. De'Ath took her hand. Now Chaney was genuinely surprised. Physical contact. *Okay* . . .

Mrs. De'Ath took her inside their home. Chaney glanced around at the English country décor, the watercolors of hearty hunting dogs on the walls, and the cabinets filled with trophies and ribbons that Chaney imagined Hershey had won.

Mrs. De'Ath led her straight to their kitchen. Chaney's breath caught in her throat. Hershey lay in the middle of the tile floor, reclined back like she was the Queen of Sheba. Vying for real estate at her sagging teats was a gaggle of squirming, mewling puppies. They were blind and hairless, navigating the landscape of nipples by touch of their tiny paws and by smell through their little black button noses. "Oh my God!" Chaney laughed, tears coming to her eyes. "Look at them!"

The hardened Mrs. De'Ath was crying, too. "Aren't they beautiful?"

Chaney counted as tiny bodies appeared from the mass of Hershey's breasts. *Four . . . six . . . eight . . .* "Ten?" she asked.

Mrs. De'Ath nodded. "She had them Friday night."

While they were having fun at the concert, Hershey was giving birth.

"Archie and I have discussed it, and after they've been weaned, we want you to have one," Mrs. De'Ath said.

On reflex, Chaney held up a hand. Just when she'd gotten used to Tony, he had to go. "Mrs. De'Ath, I couldn't," she said.

"We insist," she declared, her tone forceful, like that of a *Masterpiece Theatre* headmistress. "We won't take no for an answer."

Chaney looked at the manifestation of new life, right there before her. Maybe it was true, that when one door closed, another opened. Tony was gone, but she could have a piece of him for her very own. Against her better judgment, she found herself nodding. "Okay," she said, in an attempt to convince herself. "Okay."

Only for Dani.

Chaney stared outside the back passenger window of the black Hummer as they moved slowly along rain-washed Georgia Avenue and its complement of liquor stores, takeout joints, scented-oil salesmen, and other fixtures of the 'hood. She figured if Dani could get up out of her bed and rescue her from the wilds of Virginia, she could show her support as Dani promoted *Fast Times at 1600 Pennsylvania Avenue: My Life in the Clinton White House.*

Nathalie was there, too, in the backseat of the car, driven by Chris, Dani's fresh-faced young publicist who'd quit doing PR for the Redskins to strike out on his own. Nathalie was the picture of health. Her smooth, dark skin glowed. Her hair was shinier, her dark eyes brighter. By contrast, Chaney knew she looked like shit. She was tired all the time, from the moment she got up until she passed out in bed at night. She was headachy and nauseated; even right then, she was willing herself not to projectile-vomit all over the ultra-nice interior of the Hummer. She couldn't eat. The only thing she could hold down was soup. Nathalie leaned in and offered her an Altoid, which Chaney took and popped into her mouth. "You don't look so good," she whispered.

Chaney studied her. She was a long ways away from her judgmental self at the concert. "Withdrawal from the antidepressant," Chaney whispered back. "It's like every emotion I'd suppressed for five months came back with a vengeance and is pissed!"

Chris eased up to the curb in front of the Howard University Bookstore, called the HUB, which took up an entire city block. Its blue banners flapped in the soaked wind. Storefront windows, invitingly decorated, showed a sampling of what the HUB had to offer, from popular fiction, to textbooks, to Howard University paraphernalia. Then Chaney saw the familiar green sign. As excitedly as she could manage, she cried, "There's a Starbucks!"

Dani rolled her eyes. "Chaney, focus on me," she said.

Chris gazed panoramically at Dani in the front seat to Nathalie, Chaney, and Sandy in the back. "You go in, ladies," he said. "I'll have to go find parking."

The women got out, and under open umbrellas, rushed the front entrance of the store.

Chaney was already plotting how she could sneak away for her coffee fix at the Starbucks, at the left of the main entrance. She looked around at rows and aisles of books, T-shirts, sweatshirts, Black Greek paraphernalia. She saw the stairs and guessed there was more merchandise up there. Nathalie pointed at the sea of crimson-and-cream Delta Sigma Theta gear on the far wall. "I'm not leaving here without getting me some 'nalia!" she laughed happily.

Dani and Sandy saw the table that was set up for Dani. An 18x24 mounted copy of the cover, with Dani's studio photo in the corner, stood on an easel next to the table, along with a banner heralding the date and time that Dani would be there. Sandy slipped an arm around Dani's waist and lovingly kissed her cheek. Chaney and Nathalie exchanged surprised glances; that was the most affection either of them had displayed in public. "Look at you!" Sandy laughed. "You're beautiful!"

Dani practically beamed. "Thank you, darlin'."

There was a crowd already waiting, too. Some wore press passes from the *Washington Post, BlackCollegeView.com,* Howard's two undergraduate papers, *The Hilltop* and *The District Chronicles,* as well as *The Barrister,* Howard's paper from the law school. "You go get your 'nalia, you go get your coffee," Dani said, then clutched her hands to her chest and fluttered her eyelids. "I must go meet my public."

Chaney and Nathalie laughed as she watched them go.

An hour into the signing, though, Chaney thoroughly regretted having had her favorite, venti white chocolate mocha. The drink pingponged around in her stomach like it wanted out. And the muscles in her esophagus were telling her brain, *there's only so much more of this we're gonna take before we let it out.* Chaney desperately clutched onto Sandy's arm. "You see where the ladies' room is?" she moaned.

Sandy and Nathalie stood leaning against the wall, watching proudly as Dani signed, grinned, and schmoozed her crowd of admirers, which now included a camera crew with a bright light from WHUT. "Upstairs," Sandy answered, distracted.

Chaney rushed away and up the stairs. She barely made it to the blue door that had the universal ladies' room icon on it, barely made it to the stall before reverse peristalsis took over and forced anything she had in her stomach upwards, into the toilet bowl. The force of it made Chaney drop to her knees, clutching the bowl for dear life. Her thought—*Fucking Fluexa!*—drowned in her throat in a sea of vomit. She wished she had a knife so that she could slit a vein and bleed the poisonous chemical out of her body, leach it out of her tissues until she was the same old Chaney . . . argumentative but devoid of the feeling of impending death. She threw up and cried as her stomach muscles were having painful spasms, trying to expel stuff that wasn't inside her anymore. "Oh, God," she groaned. "Oh, God."

Belatedly, she realized that she was crying out to someone she barely even knew, with whom she last had a relationship when she was five. "Oh, God!" she sobbed.

She could see nothing but sparkling blackness in front of her eyes. She surrendered to it, felt her muscles go slack inside her. She slowly dropped to the cold, hard tile and waited patiently until the blackness devoured her whole.

Chaney blinked. The sea of faces hovering over her came into view. *Dani . . . Sandy . . . Nathalie . . .* All of them looked worried. Then she suddenly realized why. She was sitting on the floor in the HUB. Puke drops stained the front of her black V-necked sweater. She held her hands up to her pounding head. "What happened?" she moaned.

"I don't know," Sandy said. "You left an hour ago to go to the ladies' room. We were about to go when we noticed you hadn't come back."

Nathalie slipped a strong arm under Chaney's right armpit. "Can you stand, sweetie?"

Chaney leaned against her, and struggled up on the stacked heels of her boots to stand. Unfortunately, her head was still adjusting to the change in altitude. Chaney wobbled. "Whoa!" she whispered.

Nathalie, Dani, and Sandy grabbed for her before she hit the floor. "That's it, Chaney," Dani said. "You've suffered long enough. We're taking you to the emergency room."

Chaney shook her head . . . and instantly regretted it. The pain seared through her brain like a laser. "No emergency room," she murmured. "Home."

"Yes, emergency room," Dani insisted. "It's right up the street. Chris'll drive us."

"I agree with Dani," Nathalie said. "Whatever this is, it can't be good."

"So, it's settled," Sandy declared. "We're going to the hospital."

Chaney succumbed to the grossly unfair odds of three against one and let them lead her out of the restroom. Chris paced nervously outside. He took one look at Chaney and shook his head, like he knew the day was over. "I'll go get the car," he said.

About three hours later, Chaney was still sitting in the waiting room at Howard University Hospital, with Dani, Nathalie, and Sandy seated in chairs around her. Chaney hugged herself into a small ball as she looked around at the flotsam and jetsam of the area. One man was bleeding profusely from a foot that he had wrapped in a Giant grocery bag. There were people bleeding from beatings, what looked like knife and gunshot wounds in arms, legs, and other minor places that didn't warrant heroic measures just yet. It looked to her like a Saturday night on Flatbush Avenue.

Through the double doors, she could see Chris outside, pacing and talking into a cell phone. The world was trying to go on, and she was holding up production. "Let's go," Chaney said to Nathalie.

Nathalie wasn't having it. "We're staying right here until they call your name."

After another hour, they did. A nurse practitioner in a frightfully ugly floral print smock, white pants, and white orthopedic shoes escorted Chaney and her crew to a room filled with gurneys and drawn curtains. She took the nearest empty bed and handed Chaney a paper gown. "Put this on," she said, with all the warmth of a toilet seat. "The doctor will be with you shortly."

Chaney sat for yet another hour, with her ass hanging out of the inadequate paper gown before a hand pulled open the curtain. Nathalie, Dani, and Sandy looked hopefully at the handsome young brothah in green scrubs who was familiarizing himself with her chart. He looked up suddenly, his eyes traveling from each lady, one by one. "Ms. Braxton," he said.

Chaney slowly sat up and looked quizzically at him, having the wickedest case of déjà vu. Then her eyes widened. *Oh no, this can't be happening.* "Mali?" she asked.

He looked closer, then his eyes lit up. "Chaney!" he laughed.

Nathalie and Sandy exchanged inquiring glances. Dani snapped her fingers. "Aren't you Devin's friend?" she asked. "From that bar in Georgetown. Jamal."

Jamal nodded. "Yes. Jamal Bain."

Dani called the roll, introducing Sandy and Nathalie. She looked down at Chaney, who lay, mortified, trying to clutch the two ends of the robe closed over her ass.

Nathalie laughed. "Oh, Chaney," she sighed. "This means that your boyfriend's best friend gets to grope you and it's all legal."

Jamal grinned. "If it's any consolation, I'll try not to enjoy it," he teased. "Now, it says here you collapsed at the HUB . . . ?"

As much as Chaney hated submitting, Jamal was a good doctor. His tone was even as he took a history. He listened attentively and actively to her present complaint, and he supervised aptly as another nurse practitioner, this one younger, drew blood and asked for a sample of urine. "That wasn't so bad, was it?" Jamal asked, discarding his gloves.

Yes! "I want to go home," Chaney grumbled. "We've been here five hours."

"I'll try not to keep you here any longer than necessary," Jamal promised. "I'll have the lab put a rush on this and be right back."

A "rush" in hospital terms was another hour and a half. By this time, Chris had joined them in the room. *Bless your heart.* "Chris, please . . . go," Chaney insisted. "We can take the metro home."

"I will do no such thing," he declared. "This is the most excitement I've had in years."

The curtain opened, and Jamal reappeared with her chart and a grin a mile wide. "Well, we've gotten the test results," he announced.

Chaney gulped. Then she reasoned, if it were so bad, he wouldn't be grinning like a Cheshire cat. "What is it?" she asked, pinching the gown over her ass.

"Chaney, you're going to be a mommy," he said.

Her hands dropped, and she felt a draft of air hit her bare ass. She narrowed her eyes as she processed his pronouncement in her pounding head. "What?" she croaked.

"You're pregnant," he repeated.

The ladies squealed. "Oh, Chaney's that's wonderful!" Nathalie laughed, clapping her hands. "The two of us! At the same time!"

Dani, Sandy, and Chris joined in the congratulations. All the while, Chaney let it sink in. *I'm pregnant? How could I be . . .* Then she remembered. That morning at Devin's in Georgetown. She could still see the ripped condom hanging in shreds from Devin's penis. But everything that Macca had said . . . her age . . . the fibroids . . . the precipitous drop in the chances of getting spontaneously pregnant . . . all that played in her head as well. And the Fluexa. She'd been taking it religiously for the past five months. What effect could the drug have on a fetus?

"Of course, you need to see your OB/GYN for further care and more information on the exact nature of the pregnancy, but yes, you are expecting a baby," Jamal laughed. "You know it's going to be hard as hell to keep this from my boy, right?"

Oh, shit. Devin. The baby daddy. What was his reaction going to be? "I'm sure when I tell him, you and the rest of his boys will be the first to hear," Chaney said, with a weak laugh.

Nathalie, and Dani, and Sandy hugged her tightly. Even Chris got into the fray. Chaney smiled, but deep inside she was terrified.

Chaney stared at the traffic through her window, at the people who now wore fall jackets for protection against the cool Maryland autumn winds. *I'm pregnant.* It had been over twenty-four hours, and she was still wrestling with the overwhelming fact that she had a life growing inside her.

That morning, at precisely seven o'clock, she was in Macca's office at Arlington Hospital to meet her. Macca was laden down with pastries and bagels for her staff. She looked surprised and happy to see her at the same time. "Chaney!" she laughed, out of breath from toting her load. "What are you doing here?"

Chaney clutched her gloved hands in her pockets to prevent herself from reaching for Macca's throat. "I'm spontaneously pregnant, Macca," she announced. "You led me to believe that the only way that it could happen would be if three wise men showed up at my door!"

Macca looked like she was trying to grasp the news herself. "Come on in," she said.

Once inside, Chaney traded her navy wool suit for yet another paper gown which left her ass hanging out. Macca gave her the full unpleasant examination, and again Chaney had to give up more samples of blood and urine. Macca sat down on the revolving stool, just as Chaney was getting dressed. "Well, it's true," she said. "You're knocked up like a cheerleader."

Chaney glared at her. "This isn't funny, Macca," she declared. "I'm an unwed mother-to-be whose been sucking down an antidepressant for almost six months. That's the trifecta of fucked!"

Macca sighed. "Okay, Chaney, let's deal with your questions about the Fluexa first," she said. "The safety of the drug during pregnancy isn't known definitively yet, but in cases where the benefits to the patient were greater than any possible danger to the baby, doctors have prescribed full doses of it for expectant mothers. With the decreased levels of it in your system, you and the baby should be fine. With you being a pregnant woman over thirty-five, that would be something we could add to the additional monitoring of your condition. Have you told the father?"

The father. Chaney marveled at how suddenly he went from her tadpole to "The Father." "I don't know if we're going to be together long enough to parent a kid, Macca," she sighed. "I don't know if I'm even keeping it."

"That's another option you have open to you," Macca said, her tone subdued. "I want you to think about this, though, Chaney. We're not in our twenties anymore. There's no guarantee you're gonna be Fertile Myrtle. Your chances of getting pregnant still remain slim, regardless of this fluke . . . this miracle."

"What, you're getting all right-to-life on me all of a sudden?"

Macca patted her leg. "No, just giving you the facts, lady. You have a lot to think about. I just want you to have all the information before you decide what to do."

Chaney stared at the traffic as it began to move again. She wondered what her mother's reaction was when she realized Chaney was coming . . . fourteen years after she'd had her first child. When Daisy wanted to be cruel, she would call Chaney "the mistake." Chaney remembered her mother pulling her into her long arms. She could smell Leah Braxton's clean soap scent as she held her close. "My beautiful little mistake," Leah said in her lilting Bahamian accent; then, with her careworn nurse's hands, she would tickle Chaney until she thought she'd pee her pants.

The tears trickled down Chaney's cheeks. She held her hands to her stomach. Over the years, she'd pushed her feelings so deep inside her, so she couldn't get hurt again. But she readily confessed them to herself now. She wanted her mommy.

The knock on Chaney's door sucked her from her thoughts. Hurriedly, she wiped the tears from her cheeks and looked over to see Coco standing in the doorway. "Hey," Coco said. "They're ready for us in the big conference room."

Oh, yeah. They were previewing the first programmed, computer-based lesson for the clients from hell. Chaney hurriedly gathered her notes together. "Coming," she said.

Coco stared at her curiously as they headed toward the conference room. "You okay?" she asked.

She didn't have enough time to relay the events of the past two days to Coco. She'd have to tell her later. "I'm fine, sweetie," she lied.

"Just checking," Coco said.

Chaney's gut roiled reflexively when she entered the conference room. There sat Callie with her superior air, Doug sighing repeatedly like stress was going to send him to an early grave, and Randy, smug as ever in his chair. Lissa sat perched next to him; if she were any closer, she'd have been on his jock. Al, in his rumpled suit, sat on the other side of the table. Laura was joining them for this meeting, too, in her autumn Laura Ashley wear. Chaney felt the tension play around her like a fog. She sensed this wasn't going to be Autodidact's finest hour.

Nonetheless, she fired up the laptop on the table and its adjunct projector. A lit square appeared on the silver screen in front of the room, like magic. " 'Afternoon, all," Chaney said.

Those in the room murmured their response. "Coco'll explain what we're going to see, and then she's going to treat us to the first programmed lesson of the CBT," Chaney said.

Coco took her place behind the laptop. Her fingers flew over the keyboard, and then suddenly, the introductory screen of the *Navy Help Desk Customer Service Computer-Based Training Course (CBT)* displayed on the silver screen, complete with graphics. "This isn't a lesson, really," Coco announced. "This is the section called How to Take This Course. It shows just that . . . the navigational buttons, accessing the glossary . . . all that good stuff."

Chaney dimmed the lights, and Coco let the presentation run. In the semidarkness, Chaney watched their faces. Randy seemed begrudgingly interested, as did Doug. Al and Laura smiled at some of the funny questions that Coco had created, as did Lissa. Callie, by contrast, scribbled furiously every time a screen displayed.

After the last screen, Chaney hit the lights. She and Coco stood proudly before them. "So," Chaney said, her eyes searching the room. "What do you think?"

"Great work, Chaney and Coco," Al said. "But I only own the place."

"Good start," Doug sighed.

Chaney's and Randy's eyes met. *Asshole.* "Randy?" she asked.

"I agree with Doug," he said. "And all the subject matter is on point."

"I agree," Lissa piped up.

Chaney's gaze lit on Callie. Callie was leaned back in her chair, twirling her overused pen between her fingers. "Callie?"

"I think it's a good start," Callie conceded.

Chaney's gaze morphed into one of pleasant surprise. The Client from Hell was pleased. "Great," Chaney concluded. "Since we have a consensus . . ."

Callie held up a finger. "I just want one change," she announced.

Why does that not surprise me? Chaney tried hard to hold the fake smile. "You do?" she said.

"We should rethink the 'Select Next to continue' that allows the learner to advance to the next screen. Why not just 'Click Next to continue?' "

Stay calm . . . "If you remember, Callie, we discussed that during the review of the storyboards," Chaney declared. " 'Select' is Section 508 compliant. You may have learners with disabilities who may not be able to use the mouse, but are able to press the Enter key."

Callie sneered. "I'm familiar with Section 508 of the Rehabilitation Act of 1973, Chaney."

Chaney could feel her blood boil. "Are you familiar with our bill for this project? There was a line item in there, specifically to fund the time needed to make the project Section 508 compliant, and on a six-million-dollar project, we can't exactly argue that compliance would cause an undue financial burden on us."

"Chaney, the section doesn't go that deep into the weeds to address the difference between 'Click' and 'Select.' "

"The word 'Click' is inextricably associated with a mouse, Callie. 'Select' is more versatile."

Chaney looked around her. Al and Laura squirmed uncomfortably in their chairs. Lissa looked away from the exchange altogether. Doug kept sighing. "Maybe Callie has a point," Randy stated.

Chaney stared at him in contempt. Like her, he used to find Callie's little power plays funny. Now he was joining the fray. Callie threw down her pen, and, Chaney imagined, the gauntlet. "I want it changed," she declared.

Who the fuck are you? Fake-smiling began in earnest. "If there's a choice between acquiescing to a subjective aesthetic and adhering to a federal directive, Callie, then I'm going to go with the latter," Chaney fired back.

Callie's face dropped. Doug ran a hand over his shining, bald pate and sighed. "Are you saying you're not going to make the change, Chaney?"

"That would be correct, Doug," Chaney said. "It violates the spirit of the act."

Coco stood up from the laptop. "I agree with Chaney," she said. "We spent a lot of time making sure that we adhered to this and other federal directives, like the Plain Language directive, just to name one."

Chaney met Coco's gaze. *I love you, girl!*

Callie's blond, cool façade had all but evaporated. Her face was rose-petal red. She snatched up her notes and stood. "I'm going back to the office in D.C.," she announced, a crack in her voice. "This is very serious. We need to meet on Monday to discuss how we're going to continue."

Chaney removed her Blackberry from the holster at her waist. "I'm wide open on Monday," she said. "What about you guys?"

Everyone in the room took out either Blackberries or Franklin day planners, checked their availability on Monday, and murmured that it would work. Callie, Doug, and Randy then left the room in silence, closing the door as they left.

Al rocked in his chair, his index fingers under one of his two chins. Chaney could literally see him subtracting six million from the company bottom line in his head. He looked up at her, gray eyes flashing. "You're going to sink a six-million-dollar project over 'Click' versus 'Select?' " he demanded.

Chaney held firm. "Today, it's 'Click' versus 'Select'; tomorrow, it's some other big change that violates a federal directive. I'm not about to pay twenty percent of a fine to the Feds. I don't care how much the client is paying."

Silence. The silence of disagreement and disapproval. Except from Coco. "Again, I think Chaney's right here," she said. "I spent two days in 508 Compliance training. You paid for it. Was that for nothing?"

"I think you're being extreme here, Chaney," said Laura. Chaney realized she actually had vocal cords. "Callie feels you're being resistant to feedback."

Go back to your spoiled brats and fucking up the accounting system. "If it's feedback with merit, I'm all ears," Chaney said. "We've incorporated all of her changes, even changes she asked for, after she'd signed off on the previous deliverable. Here is where I draw the line."

Lissa sighed, à la Doug. "Look, let's keep our cool here," she suggested. "It's Friday. Let's all go home, sleep on this, and revisit the issue again on Monday."

Sleep sounded like a good idea to Chaney. She gathered up her notes. "Sounds like a plan," she said. "See everyone on Monday."

She left the conference room, secure in the knowledge that Al, Laura, and Lissa were going to malign her behind her back the very second she was gone. She could've cared less. Coco followed behind her and shut the conference room door. She and Chaney looked at each other and laughed. "Thank you, Dorothy Boyd," Chaney said.

"*No hay de qué*, Jerry," Coco returned, then headed toward her desk.

Devin stood in the empty waiting room, in front of Maria and the thick glass partition. They both looked up at the TV, turned to Channel 7. Oprah was dispensing feel-good bromides to a studio audience who stared up at her like baby birds with beaks open, waiting for her to puke wisdom down their throats. "So, this is what chicks around the world do at four o'clock, huh?" he asked.

Maria shrugged. "She's my hero," she said simply, her voice muffled by the glass.

The door flew open just then, and anticipation of new patients seized Devin. Surprise replaced anticipation. It was Marlene, glowing in a leather dress, a sable, and high-heeled boots. She looked harried, excited, desperate. Briefly, Devin wondered if she'd found out about Liz. "Marlene!" he cried. "What's up?"

"Devin, we need your help!" she gasped.

She opened the door wider, and KL staggered in. Devin's heart lurched. KL was a mess. Black sooty patches smeared his face, stained his wild salt-and-pepper 'fro. Devin saw tear stains on the blackened cheeks of his father, the ultra-butch Marine. He carried a lump in a dirty pink blanket in his arms. "Devin, please help him!" KL begged.

Devin went closer and pulled back the blanket. He instantly recoiled. It was Sadat. "Oh, boy," Devin sighed, instinctively knowing it was too late.

Sadat's right side, from his ear to the base of his nubby tail, was burnt and hairless. His reddened flesh bubbled, beginning to slough itself off. Sadat moaned, his breathing coming shallow and at longer intervals he took a breath through his blackened nose. Devin looked up at his father with questioning eyes. "How did this happen?"

KL kept shaking his head, as if he couldn't believe it, either. "I fell asleep," he sighed. "Left some soup on the stove. He must've smelled it burning . . . put his paws up on the stove to see." KL looked down at his faithful companion, dying in his arms. "The flames must've caught his fur. His beautiful fur." KL let out a choked sob. "He was making the most awful howling sound, Devin!"

Devin didn't know what hurt more—seeing a beloved pet like Sadat hovering near death or witnessing his father falling apart, acknowledging the fact that he wasn't the master of his domain after all, that the Alzheimer's was rapidly robbing him of all that was familiar.

"Maria, get Didier!" Devin called over his shoulder.

A minute later, Didier appeared in the waiting room, with Maria in tow. Devin's dark eyes met Didier's gray. Didier could tell, too, that Sadat was not long for this world. Maria gently took Sadat from KL's arms. Sadat whimpered meekly. "We're gonna take good care of him, Mr. Rhym," she promised, the one promise they could keep.

"Take him to the treatment room," Didier instructed.

He followed as they disappeared through the doors into the back. KL stared mournfully after him.

Marlene held KL's hands open. "Dad needs to go to the hospital, too," she said.

Devin looked down at KL's hands. They were reddened in some places, badly burned in others. Devin guessed his father must've been in agony. "Pop, we've got to take you to the hospital, okay?" Devin asked.

He searched KL's face with his gaze. His father's moist eyes were vacant. Much to Devin's surprise, he acquiesced. "Okay," he mumbled.

Devin rushed to the back to get his coat. He stopped in the doorway of the treatment room. Didier and Maria looked up at him. Devin immediately knew; Sadat was gone. Devin went in, stared down at him, lying mortally wounded on the metal table. All the good times that Sadat had shared with them as a family over the past ten years flooded Devin's mind. Emotion clutched his chest, releasing a flood of tears down his cheeks. He'd seen so many wounded animals, euthanized so many that he could hardly keep count anymore. But Sadat was like family. This one stung just a bit.

He pushed the tears from his eyes with balled-up fists. "Umm . . . I've got to take Dad to the hospital," he said.

He wanted to drown in the compassion in Maria's warm brown eyes. "Go," she said. "We'll hold things down here."

In the Navigator, Devin followed Marlene's champagne-colored Jaguar to Arlington Hospital. They didn't wait long in the sparsely populated but busy emergency room. Less than an hour after they'd arrived, a nurse took KL back to see a doctor.

Marlene fished out a pack of cinnamon Trident out of her Louis Vuitton purse. She handed Devin one, then put one into her mouth. Devin chewed and paced. His father, the butchest man on the planet, was reduced to a forgetful dog-murderer. "How did this happen?" he asked.

"Your father has Alzheimer's, Devin," Marlene reminded him.

Devin sat plopped down in the seat next to her. "At least he knew to call you."

Marlene shook her head. "I went for a visit. I found him hovering over Sadat, mumbling helplessly." She sighed. "I called Chauncey and Eric. They're going over to look at the kitchen."

Devin sized her up. She was such a wonderful woman. She didn't deserve a shithead like Eric.

She touched his arm. "We hardly see you anymore," she said, a teasing tone to her voice. "It's like you broke up with Liz and us."

"Liz is old news," he declared, more harshly than he'd intended.

"Heard you're seeing Chaney."

He smiled at the mention of the name. "Always had a soft spot for you older women," he laughed, despite his shitty mood.

Marlene swatted his arm. "Bite your tongue!" she cried. "I prefer 'seasoned.'"

" 'Seasoned,' " he grinned. "Chaney's like Cajun, then."

"She's how old?"

"Thirty-six."

Marlene suddenly looked away, staring off into space. "Well, tick tick," she sighed. "Say what you will about Dad, but at least he has children to nurse him when he's sick. Neither of us can say that, right?"

To his surprise, he noticed tears spilling down her smooth cheeks. He was taken aback. *Where's this coming from?* He held her hand. "What's wrong?" he gently asked.

Marlene reached into her bag and took out a gleaming white handkerchief. She dabbed gingerly at her eyes. "Eric's tired of trying to have a baby," she wept. "He says it's putting a strain on our marriage."

Devin stared at her, so heartbroken. "How long have you been trying?" he asked.

"A year," she said.

One year. He wanted to clock Eric squarely in the face. Their jumping the shark coincided with the exact time Eric started fucking Liz. Devin was at a loss for words. All he could do was hug her. She clung to him and silently cried on his shoulder.

She was tired from weeping when the doctor came out. He was young and white, with perfect features and impeccably blow-dried hair, like if a Ken doll had gone to medical school. Like Devin, he wore scrubs and sneakers; he rocked the white coat, though. He looked down at the folder in his hands. "Rhym?" he asked.

He pronounced it right, too, like the other emergency room doctor who'd treated KL the night he'd fallen. Devin and Marlene flew apart, got up, and eagerly met the doctor. Devin noticed that the blue stenciling on his pocket read SCOTT DALEY, M.D. "Yes?" Devin said over his racing heart.

"Your dad burned off a couple of layers of skin from his hands," Dr. Daley said. "When we were examining him, his pressure spiked. He became disoriented. I want to keep him overnight for observation. For a man his age, and with the Alzheimer's, I just want to be sure before I release him."

Marlene dabbed her eyes with a hanky. "Can we see him?"

Dr. Daley showed them behind the heavy metal doors, where KL was being prepared to be admitted. They had him in a hospital gown. He was reclined on a gurney with thick, heavy black wheels. An IV drip hung from a tube, snaking glucose through a tube connected from the bag to the needle in his arm. Devin focused on KL's hands, which were heavily bandaged in white gauze. He looked like a prize-fighter laced up for combat. Devin's heart sank. His father looked so weak and spent, seemingly wearing every one of his seventy years on his face. "Pop," he said.

KL rolled his eyes slowly to see them; Devin guessed he had a sedative in his IV drip. They approached him and the nurses readying him for his trip to a room. Marlene took a comb out of her bag and proceeded to tame KL's wild hair. KL looked up at Devin, his face filled with hope. "Devin, any word on Sadat?" KL asked.

Oh, damn . . . "He didn't make it, Dad," Devin said. "He was too far gone."

KL's face, already rubbery from the sedative, collapsed as he burst into tears that cascaded down his cheeks. Devin swallowed hard over the lump in his throat. He was at a loss as to what to do or say. Especially when KL hugged him. He couldn't even remember KL ever giving him a hug. So he gave in to instinct and hugged his father back.

Devin pulled up on North Garfield and saw Eric's black Beemer and Chauncey's white minivan parked at the curb in front of the house. *Finally, some help . . .*

He found his brothers in the kitchen. His mouth dropped open as he surveyed the damage—the kitchen was practically gutted, the walls and cabinets covered in soot. The yellow paint that Kim-Chin had so proudly applied hung in peeling strips. There was a spent fire extinguisher on the floor, next to an area of smeared, dried blood. Sadat's, Devin guessed. "Damn!" Devin exclaimed.

Chauncey looked around, too. "It's amazing he survived this," he sighed. "What about Sadat?"

Devin shook his head. There were no more words.

Eric threw up his hands in exasperation. "Look at this shit," he spat. "Isn't it obvious now that he can't be by himself?"

"Well, what do you suggest we do, Eric?" Devin asked.

"He needs to be in an assisted-living facility," Eric announced. "Devin, you can watch the house."

"He loves this house," Chauncey reminded him. "He'll never go for that."

"Then we'll have him declared *non compos mentis* and make him go for it," Eric declared.

Heartless motherfucker! Devin stared at him in disgust. "You'd have your own father declared mentally incompetent?"

Eric's light eyes flashed. "I wish you two would stop romanticizing him!" he shouted. "He's a cantankerous old fart. We're only here because he had commitment issues."

Devin would've laughed in his face if he could've mustered the strength. "Says you, in the fucking glass house!"

Chauncey held his hands akimbo in his absence of a waist. "All right, what the fuck's going on between you two?" he demanded.

Devin looked away. Putting it out in the universe meant that it had the potential to touch and hurt people he loved. Like Marlene. "I'll tell him," Eric said. "I'm sick of carrying the burden. Devin caught me fucking Liz at his house. In his bed. Hell, I'm still fucking her."

The sound of silence in the room was like it came from the sound system at the club on a Friday night. All eyes were on Eric. Defiantly, he glared back at them, as if daring them to say something. Finally, Chauncey spoke. "I don't know about you, E," he said, his tone soft, measured. "Something happened to you along the way. I don't know how you could think something like that would be okay. To hurt your baby brother like that. And your wife."

"The world belongs to Big Tort," Devin spat.

Chauncey, the voice of reason, continued. "Even though you deserve Devin's animosity, none of that changes the fact we're brothers. More than ever, Dad needs us to hold it together."

Devin remembered seeing his dad at the hospital. Begrudgingly, he admitted to himself that Chauncey was right. He wasn't going to hold hands and sing "Kumbayah" with Eric. But they were going to need each other to help KL through.

Between the three of them, they cleaned up the kitchen as best as they could. Devin wanted to cry as he scrubbed up Sadat's blood from the linoleum. They peeled off the hanging paint and discarded the fire extinguisher, then took everything out to the trash can in the garage.

Long after Eric and Chauncey left, the silence in the house seemed amplified. Devin stood in the doorway and stared at the charred kitchen. There was so much death and destruction in that house . . . little deaths like that of his parents' marriage, and that of a relationship he'd wanted with his father. The urge to get out of the house was overwhelming.

Devin locked up the house, then got into his ride. Twenty minutes later, he turned into the Suffolk Court lot and parked in the spot right next to the Altima. He looked up at the front of the house. The only light on, it seemed, was the one on the porch.

Tentatively, he put the key in the lock and turned. Instantly, he heard the alarm blipping. He hurriedly got the paper with the code on it from his wallet and punched it in with only seconds to spare. Save for the light over the stove, the house was dark. He inhaled the delicious confluence of scents that was the byproduct of her creams and candles. The house seemed quieter, emptier, without Tony.

He tiptoed up the stairs, heading toward her bedroom. At the top of the stairs, Devin saw her as a sleeping lump under the comforter. He crossed the length to the bed and slid on top of the covers. He pulled back a flap and watched her as she slept deeply. He nuzzled her neck; the cream on her skin smelled like cinnamon sticks. "Chay," he whispered.

She stirred into consciousness, staring at him in the semidarkness through squinted eyes. "Devin," she groaned. "Just when I thought you were in the Boyfriend Protection Program."

He kissed her cheek. He would've inhaled her in if he could've. She made it all go away. "Sorry," he whispered. "Family drama. Let's talk about it tomorrow."

Devin stripped down to his underpants and slid under the comforter. The warmth from both her body and the flannel sheets made him feel cozy. She opened her arms and held him, and he sighed, content. He settled down, his breathing synching up with hers until he finally drifted off into a peaceful sleep.

Eleven

Chaney cradled the phone receiver between her head and neck while she scanned the papers in her hand. She looked at the date on her articles of incorporation. *October 1.* "It all looks good to me," she decreed.

"Excellent," Sandy said from over the other end. "As of yesterday, Three Sisters, Inc. was officially incorporated in the state of Virginia."

Chaney sat down and sighed. She'd done it. She was president and CEO of her own company. Which, of course, consisted solely of oils, shea butter, candles, a mixer, and the miscellaneous contents of the unfinished part of her basement. "Sandy, I love you, girl," she said. "I'll messenger a check over to you for your services."

"Stop it," Sandy laughed. "The first thing you need to do is go to your bank and open a business account. No commingling of personal funds with business funds. You'll have to take all those papers in the envelope with you. After 9/11, they've instituted all of these regulations to make sure terrorists aren't funneling money through our banking system."

Chaney looked up all of a sudden to see Al, in his badly fitting designer suit, standing in her doorway. *What do you want?* "Just a sec," she said to Sandy.

"Hi, Chaney," he said. "Can we see you in the big conference room for a minute?"

We . . . Chaney sensed an ambush. Nonetheless, she smiled sweetly at him. "I'll be down in a minute," she said.

He turned, and through the glass in the door, she saw him lumber down the hall. She returned to her conversation. "Sandy, girl, I gotta go," she announced.

They hung up. Chaney stashed her envelope of crucial papers, then steeled herself as she made her way to the big conference room.

When she entered, she saw the usual suspects: Lissa, who aggressively avoided Chaney's eyes, Laura, this time in a tentlike, funereal black Laura Ashley dress, and Al, seated at the head of the long gray table, next to a fresh box of Kleenex tissues. "Ah, the gang's all here," Chaney said.

Chaney took a seat a few chairs away from Laura and looked around at the crew. "So, what's this all about?" she asked.

Al put his chubby hand on an envelope and shot it Chaney's way. She put a hand out to stop it. "What's this?" she asked, picking it up.

"That's a check for one hundred thousand dollars," Al announced. "Your initial investment in the company. You take that, and we part company. No strings attached."

Chaney studied the envelope in her hands; it was from the Autodidact cream-colored stationery set, complete with the logo in the far left-hand corner. She laughed, shaking her head as it sunk in. *These motherfuckers.* "So, what you're saying by this gesture is you want me to leave the partnership," she announced.

Laura nodded her mousy brown head. "That's what we're saying."

Chaney put the envelope down and leaned forward. Al looked curious as to what she was going to say. Laura seemed tense, leery of the unknown. Lissa still avoided her eyes. "I think I should go, too," Chaney announced.

Surprise registered in Al's twinkling gray eyes. "You do?"

"Yeah, I do," she said. "For quite some time now, I didn't feel like the partnership was working for me. I felt very uncomfortable with the bad client discipline practiced here. It was like we were compromising our integrity as a company and the integrity of my field to score a big payday. I played along for as long as I could, but after Callie's request on Friday, I saw myself being put in an untenable situation."

"She felt you have an attitude," Laura declared. "She said as much in Monday's meeting."

Attitude. White code used to rein in blacks. "So, you did meet on Monday after all," Chaney said. "My invitation to the party must've gotten lost."

Chaney heard sniffling just then and looked across the table to see Lissa weeping. *Oh, bitch, please!* Chaney took the box of Kleenex—which she now realized had been there for her anticipated meltdown—and shot it toward Lissa. "There you go," she said.

Al and Laura looked at Lissa compassionately. Chaney would've laughed if she hadn't been so disgusted by the whole display, by Lissa's performance that smacked of *Look at me—I'm fucking my friend over, but I'm so unhappy about it.*

"So," Al said. "We can do the standard two weeks, if you'd like."

Chaney shook her head, "No, that's okay," she said. "I'll leave today. I actually drove in, so I can pack my stuff into my car."

Al and Laura exchanged a self-satisfied glance. "So, that's it, then," he said.

Chaney slid the check back to him across the table, and in an instant, his smirk was gone. *I'm from Brooklyn; I don't go out like that.* "Not quite, Allison," she said.

His left eye twitched at her use of his most hated girly name. "Umm . . . I don't follow," he croaked.

"Well, Allison," she said, then took a moment to enjoy his corresponding eye twitch, "many developments took place after I joined the company last year. Autodidact benefited from my contacts to secure the six million dollar contract. Also, due in part to my credentials and to my input into our proposal, Autodidact now enjoys the right to bid on OPM contracts for five full years."

Laura perked up. Chaney guessed she was giving her a reason to wear black. "So, what are you saying?" she demanded.

Chaney ignored her, focusing the force of her gaze at Al. "So, Allison," *eye twitch* "I expect that I'll be getting back my initial investment, severance, plus twenty percent of any revenues garnered by Autodidact during my tenure as a partner here."

Al scoffed. "That'll never happen," he declared.

Thought you could play me . . . Chaney got up. "Sure it will, Allison," she said. "You just sleep on it. I'm sure you'll come around to my way of thinking in no time. I'm a patient woman. I can wait."

Chaney left, to the sound of Al's huffing and puffing and Lissa's open weeping. Her exterior was ice cold; inside, she was mad enough to kill.

An hour later, she was in the Altima, with the air on full blast. She didn't know whether to attribute the heat surging through her to her anger at Al and the crew, or to the whole new set of hormones that had set up shop in her body, or to the unseasonable warmth of the day. Heat rays shimmered from the asphalt, reflected off the cars. Adding to her foul mood, she was trapped in a snarl-up on the Maryland side of Georgia Avenue, a snarl-up that was much worse than the typical D.C. area rush-hour traffic that she usually met when driving home through Wheaton.

She blew her horn and cursed at some idiot who'd tried to cut into her lane. "Fuck!" she swore out loud.

Anger morphed into frustration . . . the traffic . . . her occupational troubles . . . her personal trials . . . all galvanized into an all-consuming tidal wave that swallowed her up. She, tough-as-nails Chaney Braxton from Brooklyn, New York, did something she thought she'd never do: she broke down into a flood of tears, into fits of screaming inside her car that panicked her. She pulled over into the parking lot of the Wheaton firehouse and sobbed herself weak. Only one person could make it better. In breaks between her meltdown, she took out her Blackberry and speed-dialed Devin's phone repeatedly. No answer. Each time.

She sat in the lot, following the familiar pattern: Crippling sobbing jags that rocked her to the core. Phone Devin. Still no answer.

After what seemed like forever, she composed herself, took out a hanky from her purse, and dried her swollen, puffy eyes. She cleared tears that had dripped down into her raw throat and sighed. She called Devin again. Again, there was no answer. This time, she left a message in his voice mailbox. "Devin, it's Chaney," she said, trying her hardest not to sound desperate. "Please call me as soon as possible. Love you. 'Bye."

She started the car again and eased back into traffic. The traffic moved in fits and starts, until Chaney was close enough to see what was causing the holdup. At the Shoppers Food Warehouse, where Georgia Avenue met Randolph Road, policemen reined in bystanders while EMTs worked feverishly on someone on the ground. The cars obstructed Chaney's view as she drove by. Immediately, she put her troubles into perspective. Some poor soul was having a far worse day than she could imagine.

Devin screeched into the spot next to Chaney's in the Suffolk Court lot. The digital dashboard clock numbers glowed out 9:30. He knew she needed him; her ten phone calls and two messages on his cell said as much, loudly and clearly. He so hated to triage her, but he was busy getting KL to go voluntarily to the assisted-living facility.

He couldn't help but feel that they'd ganged up on their father. Chauncey fed KL his dinner, as KL still needed help with his bandaged hands. Devin just sat at the table and watched like a tourist as Eric announced, "Dad, we have something we want to discuss with you."

Devin's gut tightened, his heart filling with dread as Eric broached the subject of the assisted-living facility. Predictably, KL was pissed. Unpredictably, he turned to Devin, of all people. "This is your idea, isn't it?" he said, more of a statement than a question. "Because of Sadat. The accident."

Devin's eyes widened. The accusation wounded him at the heart. "No, Dad," he insisted.

"You moved back here so you could spy on me for these two," KL continued, flicking a head in the direction of Eric and Chauncey.

I moved back here so I could get to know you, and now you're going to forget me. Devin stared at his father and sighed. "Dad, we're worried about you, that's all," he explained.

KL stood up, towering over a seated Chauncey and a shorter Eric. "Well, stop it," he commanded.

Chauncey cut to the chase. "Dad, the assisted-living facility's right in Alexandria," he announced. "You need supervision."

KL looked him up and down, like, *the audacity.* "I used to supervise *you,* boy."

"Dad, we're not trying to railroad you," Chauncey assured him.

"Oh no?" KL asked. "*Reis ipsa loquitor,* son. The thing speaks for itself."

"Enough of this shit," Eric declared. "Dad, you go, or we'll make you go. Legally. You're a seventy-year-old man with Alzheimer's. You almost burned down your house and actually killed your dog. No one would contest the request."

Apparently, KL was still agile for a man of seventy. Before Chauncey or Devin could stop him, he clocked Eric in the face, sending him scooting across the wooden floor. Devin shot up out of his chair. "Shit!" he exclaimed.

Chauncey and Devin held their father back as KL hovered over a stunned Eric on the ground. "I will take you out of this world, boy!" KL roared. "Same way I brought you in."

Devin's gaze drifted to KL's right hand. Blood had begun to seep through the gauze. It was back to the emergency room at Arlington Hospital.

I'm so tired. Devin sighed and looked up at Chaney's town house. Lights blazed in the kitchen and in a room—Devin remembered it was Chaney's study—facing the parking lot. He especially needed the oasis now.

Devin turned the key in the lock and entered the anteroom. The alarm chirped twice, acknowledging that a zone had been accessed. "Chay!" he called.

Almost immediately, she came rushing down the stairs. He took a moment to look at her. She wore overalls over a ratty sweater and woolen socks. Far from happy to see him, she looked furious, her eyebrows furrowed, her mouth set in a frown. He'd never seen this side of her. The oasis looked righteously pissed. "Where've you been?" she demanded.

Not you, too. He went into the kitchen; she followed close behind. "I was with my father," he said.

"I've been calling you for hours!" she said. "I could've been hurt or dead somewhere, and you wouldn't even have known."

He looked her up and down, then opened the fridge, looking for something to eat. "Obviously, you're fine, Chaney," he declared, his tone dismissive.

She looked like she was mentally counting to ten, struggling to hold her temper in check, a temper that he didn't deserve leveled at him. "Look," she sighed. "I know you've been going through your share of drama . . . what with your dad and your business. But would it have killed you to return my phone calls? Maybe I could've helped."

Frustration gnawed at him. This home, her . . . it all used to be his sanctuary, where he could retreat from the world that was screaming at him at deafening volume. Now she was ruining it. He slammed the fridge door, and she jumped. "Why are you sweating me with this, Chaney?" he snapped. "My dad needed me."

"Well, I needed you, too, today," she said. "Your time management sucks. And don't accuse me of 'sweating' . . . " she did the air quotes ". . . you. That's bullshit. I've always given you your space."

Begrudgingly, he admitted to himself that she was right. She was the most low-maintenance woman he'd ever been with. That was one of the things he loved about her. But he wasn't in the mood to be conciliatory just then. "I guess there's a line with you older sistahs, and old Dev crossed it," he declared.

Her face betrayed her hurt, which she put into poisonous words. "Oh, and you're the expert on sistahs, you with the Korean mother and that white girl you've been pining for," she spat.

He clenched and unclenched his fist, virulent anger sending his pulse thumping through his head. He could feel that vein in his forehead bulging on the other side of his skin. "You know, sometimes, I really hate your mouth," he declared.

"Oh, really?" she countered. "Is it before, during, or after it's wrapped around your dick?"

He stared at her in disbelief. "Over a couple of missed phone calls. Is this worth it?"

She continued her alternating monologue. "Thank you, Devin," she said. "Thank you for showing me that I really should play with men my own age."

"And who would that be, Chaney?" he questioned. "The gay ex-fiancé? Or the man who wanted to pass you around like a bong at the swing club?"

He was too furious to feel any satisfaction at having pressed her hot button. She pointed at the door. "Get out," she commanded.

He took a deep, cleansing breath. *Okay, Dev. That was a low blow. You deserve this.* "I'll come back when you've calmed the fuck down," he said.

"You know what, Devin? Don't even bother coming back."

What are you saying? Was she ending it right there and then? Their two intense months of companionship, of toe-curling sex—for him, at least—had reached the end of the line? "So, that's it, then?" he concluded.

"That's it," she repeated.

Devin snatched his key ring out of his pocket, located her house key, and, with much difficulty, he wrestled it off the key ring. All he wanted to do was make a dramatic exit, to save face before he folded like a cheap card table when the impact of losing her hit him. He slapped the key down on the counter, gave her one last parting look, and headed for the door.

He felt the air pressure change as the door slammed behind him. From the exiled side of the red door, he could hear the deadbolt snap into place. And he knew better than to try to come back. From what he knew of a proactive sistah like Chaney, he sensed that the alarm code would be changed by the end of the night.

Chaney rested her head on her tear-stained pillow and watched as the sun came up behind the drawn blinds in her room. She lay there for what seemed like hours. After all, she had nowhere to go, especially not to Autodidact. *Yeah, Billy Bad Ass, leave the hundred-thousand-dollar check. Real smart!*

She had no one to get up for. She'd fired Devin before he'd truly become his father, before he'd left her in a crumpled mess for some other woman. *Despite the fact that Devin's very little like his father. Pfft! Yeah, girl, you dodged a bullet!*

She pushed tears from her eyes. *So, to sum up, you're unemployed, alone, and pregnant. And you thought you were better than half those girls you grew up with in Brooklyn. What a joke!*

Chaney covered her head with the soaked pillow. "Shut up!" she commanded her inner voice. "Shut the fuck up!"

The phone rang just then. Chaney took the pillow from her face—she was starting to have trouble breathing anyway—and stared at it. She didn't want to talk to anybody right then. Nonetheless, she picked up the receiver. Nathalie's name and phone number appeared in the caller ID screen. She pressed the TALK button. "Hey, girl," she said.

"Chaney, thank God!" Nathalie cried, seemingly with relief. "I tried your Blackberry. It's been disconnected."

Fucking Al. It didn't take him long to purge her number from the system, to delete her from the Autodidact server so she couldn't remotely access her e-mail. The Blackberry was about as useful to her now as a paperweight. "Al McCulligh and I have parted ways," Chaney announced. "Which is why I'm still home at . . ." she glanced over at the clock and gasped ". . . 11:30 in the morning."

Her pronouncement of her separation from the Shanty Irishman didn't bring the reaction from Nathalie that Chaney had expected. "Girl, turn on CNN," Nathalie said.

Her curiosity peaked like Mt. Everest, Chaney grabbed the remote, flicked on the television, and punched the numbers for CNN into the remote. Almost instantaneously, she saw footage from places she knew, or passed when she drove to the office in Rockville. Only there were cops everywhere, swarming scenes where bodies lay. In a gruesome montage, CNN cut to scenes that looked different, but whose aesthetic was the same . . . murder, mayhem, sorrow. She first saw aerial footage of a lawn mower tipped over on a sidewalk, with a man sprawled out next to it. Then, the montage cut to pumps at a gas station, where a taxicab sat abandoned, broken glass and blood everywhere. Cut to a park bench in a strip mall, where a woman's body was positioned sitting upright. She looked like people Chaney'd seen sleeping at bus stops. Only, from the information she gleaned from the scene, this poor woman would be asleep forever. The last shot showed an empty minivan at another gas station, near the spot where one would vacuum one's car, or put air in one's tires. Lastly, she saw the Shoppers Food Warehouse where she'd been sitting in traffic the previous night, as the sun set. Eerily, the scene played out on TV just as she remembered it in her head, like a morbid snapshot. "What's going on?" she asked.

"They're saying there's a sniper on the loose in Montgomery County," Nathalie cried. "He's killed all these people in a little over two hours this morning, Chaney."

Chaney looked up at photos of the dead, with their names keyed in on the bottom of each picture: Charles "Sonny" Buchanan, 39; Premkumar Walekar, 54; Sarah Ramos, 34; Lori Lewis Rivera, 25.

Then a morbid graphic displayed, showing the path of death that the sniper took: Buchanan, the man mowing the lawn, was shot at 7:41 in the morning in White Flint. Walekar, the taxi driver, was shot just minutes later, at 8:12 in Aspen Hill. Ramos, the poor lady minding her business at the strip mall, was shot in Silver Spring at 8:37. And Lori Lewis Rivera, the last victim for that morning, was vacuuming out her van when she was shot in Kensington at 9:58. They then linked the scene at the Wheaton Shoppers with that morning's shootings and showed a photo of James D. Martin, 55.

Chaney's mind screamed into action. All of these towns were in shooting distance of the Autodidact office on Rockville Pike. Chaney's heart agonizingly squeezed. "Oh my God, Coco!" she gasped.

"Okay, okay," Nathalie said, the calm voice of reason. "You call and check on Coco. I'll see if I can find Dani and Sandy."

Chaney barely heard her. She'd hung up and punched Coco's work number into the phone. Chaney's heartbeats escalated with each ring. After the fourth ring, just when she was about to lose it, Chaney heard her answer, though she did sound agitated. A sigh of relief exploded from Chaney's chest. "Coco, thank God," she said.

"Chaney," she whispered; Chaney could picture her ground-hogging, looking over the top of her cubicle walls to see if the enemy was nearby. "When did you leave?"

She made it sound voluntary. "Last night," she said. "But I'm worried about you. What's going on over there in Maryland?"

"I know," Coco sighed. "It's all over the Web and everything."

"Are you okay?"

"The building's on lockdown," she said. "The management's advised us against leaving. At least until things cool off."

"This is D.C.—they're trained for this sort of thing," Chaney assured her, trying her hardest to sound convincing. "I wouldn't be surprised if they catch this dude by the end of the day."

"I pray that you're right," Coco said. "I'm here, separated from my husband and my babies. My parents, even. And you know, with all this going down, Al and Lissa had the nerve to come to my cube this morning? They were waiting for me, Chaney. Telling me that there may be some litigation on your part and, in essence, I should remember who her friends are."

"The last thing I wanted to do was put you in an awkward position, Coco."

"Don't worry about me, Chaney. This place was getting old anyway. I have plans."

There was a beep on Chaney's end of the line just then. *Call waiting*. She took the phone away from her ear and looked at the green screen. Anna Lisa's name and cell phone number digitally displayed. "That's my sister, Coco," Chaney announced. "I gotta go. You be safe, okay?"

"Okay."

They exchanged I love you's, then Chaney clicked over to the other line. "Anna Lisa," Chaney said.

"Chaney," she sighed, relieved. "You're safe."

The persistence of memory took Chaney back a little over a year ago. Then, she was on the cell phone, trying to track down her sister as she heard about the Twin Towers burning, clinging onto the digital imprint of each other's voices as they jointly heard that the Pentagon had also been hit.

"What's going on down there?" Anna Lisa asked, a cry in her voice. "I'm in the library watching CNN. Something about a sniper?"

Chaney's gaze drifted to the TV. They were replaying the same disturbing images she'd seen moments ago. "You know what I know, Anna Lisa," Chaney said. "This guy's using Montgomery County for target practice."

"Thank God you weren't at work," Anna Lisa said, then paused before the logical progression. "Why aren't you at work?"

Chaney sighed. It was as good a time as any to break her news, as it was better for Anna Lisa to find out sooner than later. "I was released from the partnership yesterday," she announced.

"What does that mean?"

"That means I no longer work at Autodidact."

Over the phone, Chaney could hear Anna Lisa's heels on the concrete floor, hear her descending a flight of stairs. Then Chaney heard the sounds of the city in the background. Anna Lisa had gone outside so she wouldn't lose it in front of her students. "I hope you got back the money you invested," Anna Lisa declared.

So much for the concerned maternal figure who would wrap her in kind words and reassure her that it would all be better. "Not yet," she said.

"Not yet?!" Anna Lisa repeated, her tone rising.

"I'm waiting him out. He owes me more than that initial investment."

Anna Lisa sucked her teeth. "Waiting him out," she again repeated. "Let me ask you something. Do you know how hard it was to make sure that you and Daisy got a piece of our parents' estate? So you'd have it easier than I had it? So you, Chaney, could go through eleven years of university without once having to take out a student loan? So you could have that nice house, and the nice car? I had to practically whore myself out to keep that money safe, and you go and fritter it away like this!"

Recriminations from Anna Lisa stung mercilessly. Even as old as she was, she still cared about her sister's opinion, still sought her approval. Chaney felt tears well up, felt her stomach begin to churn, felt that sweat pop up between her nose and upper lip. "I was trying to secure my future," she protested.

"And what a success that's turned out to be!" Anna Lisa shouted.

Chaney blurted out the first thought to come to her mind, guaranteed for maximum hurtful effect. "What a burden it must be to know it all, Anna Lisa," she commented. "I now understand why D can't stand to be around you, why Daisy went three thousand miles away, why Norm left skidmarks getting away from you. Who the hell wants to be judged 24-7?"

Silence. All Chaney heard over the phone was the sound of Brooklyn going on with life. Her pain deadened the impact of any remorse she might've felt for scoring one on her sister. *Why stop now?* "I guess this is probably the worst time in the world to announce that I'm pregnant," she declared.

"Jesus, Chaney!" Anna Lisa exploded. "Who's the father? Norm's little cousin?"

"Yes," she spat back. "And he's not so little."

"Pregnant with a baby, for a baby," Anna Lisa sighed; Chaney could practically see her shaking her head in her disgust. "How does a woman with a Ph.D. get accidentally pregnant? In 2002?"

"Why don't you tell me, Anna Lisa?" Chaney snapped. "You were the smartest Braxton sister. How'd you get knocked up at nineteen? I guess we've come full circle. Just how pissed Mommy was at you, you're now mad as hell at me."

More silence. This time, over the phone, Chaney could hear Anna Lisa's heels on the concrete, then on tile as she went back inside. When she did speak, her tone was subdued. "Be cruel to me, Chaney, if it helps you feel better about your situation," she finally said. "This is where I get off. Like you say, it's your life. So live it."

Chaney heard a click, then a deafening silence on the other end. Chaney wanted to call her sister back and apologize for all the hurtful things she'd said. However, her body had other plans for her. The familiar waves began to push the contents of her stomach north toward her mouth. The morning sickness that had given her a break was about to make up for lost time. Chaney rushed out of bed and ran to the bathroom.

* * *

The whole crew was there. Chauncey had brought out Renee, who looked plain uncomfortable with the weight in her midsection pressing down on her. This was like a field trip for Jeffrey, Corey, and Chelsea. They happily inspected all the corners of Grampa's huge, new room at the assisted-living facility. Eric and Marlene were at the window, poring over the paperwork needing a signature. Every once in a while, Eric grabbed a hold of his chin and moved his aching mandible from side to side. Evidently, twenty-four hours later, he was still feeling the force of KL's punch.

KL sat on the bed, silently looking at the big-screen color TV on the credenza in front of him. Devin doubted he was watching the programming on Fox Channel 5.

Devin stared at his father from the doorway to the bathroom. For as long as Devin could remember, his father had been larger than life, fearless, oozing personal power . . . especially in the dress blue uniform, with all of his stripes and medals, and the broad shoulders that tapered down to his waist. Even in civilian life, KL epitomized that man who women wanted to fuck and men wanted to emulate. Right then, though, he looked smaller and used up, like an old man in a cardigan, green cords, and comfortable shoes. With his hands still bandaged, he looked like a little boy wearing white winter mittens. He'd lost control of the situation, and his only mode of protest was passive-aggressive . . . churlish silence and deliberate disconnection from his surroundings.

The children plopped down on the bed, next to KL. Devin saw him crack a smile just then. Jeffrey gently took one of KL's bandaged hands. "Daddy says you're gonna like it here, Grampa," the boy said.

"He did?" KL said, shooting Chauncey a venomous look of his own.

Chelsea stared up at her grandfather, with those enormous brown eyes. Devin was convinced she could melt the iciest of hearts. "Are you sad because Sadat went to heaven, Grampa?" she asked, lisping her s's in a way that was more cute than speech impediment.

KL nodded, smiling through his sorrow. "He was Grampa's good friend."

"You're gonna make new friends here, Grampa," Jeffrey assured him.

The brief nanosecond of warmth evaporated. "I doubt it, kiddo," KL declared.

"Hey, you guys, look at this!" Eric called, pointing to the TV.

Like everyone in the room, Devin focused his attention on the news bulletin that had broken through Fox's regular syndicated programming. Eric grabbed the remote and turned up the TV. The imagery was so shocking that even KL knew to turn the children's eyes away. Uniformed D.C. police officers were canvassing a section of road in the District where Georgia Avenue and Kalmia Road met, less than a mile from the border with Maryland, near Silver Spring.

Marlene looked over at Eric. "Doesn't Liz live in Silver Spring, honey?" she innocently asked.

Eric shot a momentary guilty look at Devin, who stared him down. *Asshole.* Eric focused on the TV once more. "Yes, but she's in Chicago, visiting relatives," he murmured.

"Thank God," Marlene sighed.

The cameraman panned the scene. Landmarks, like the Tropicana restaurant and the brightly lit Kentucky Fried Chicken, flashed across the screen. Renee tapped Chauncey on the shoulder. "We used to eat at that KFC, baby," she reminded him.

From the studio anchor's narration, it became clear that Pascal Charlot, a seventy-two-year-old Haitian immigrant, had been waiting to cross the street when he'd been shot down. The anchor took to speculating as to whether or not this shooting was related to those that had occurred earlier in Montgomery County. "Hey, Dev, your friend's a D.C. cop," Chauncey said. "What's his take on this?"

Devin shook his head. "D.C. wasn't getting involved, he said. That brothah in Montgomery County . . . Charles Moose. He's been the one on point."

A nurse entered the room right then. She was short and squat, looked like Madeleine Albright. Her name tag read *Kayla Bloom, R.N.* She clapped her hands. "Okay, everyone, time to say good night to Mr. Rhym," she said.

The kids groaned their disapproval. "You can come back tomorrow," she assured them.

Renee and the kids kissed KL good-bye. She huddled them close and waddled out of the room. When Chauncey bent to kiss his father, KL turned away. Chauncey looked hurt, but he shrugged it off. "What did you used to say, Pop? 'You'll thank me later,' " he said, then joined his family out in the hall.

KL did the same thing when Eric and Marlene took their leave.

Marlene got all the warmth; Eric, the cold shoulder. "Whatever, Pops," Eric murmured.

He handed the paperwork to Nurse Bloom, then he, too, took off. Bloom focused her intense gray stare on Devin. "You, too," she said.

He held up a hand. "In a minute."

She headed for the hall, leaving Devin and KL alone together. Devin sat next to his father on the bed. "What, no hug for me, either?" he asked.

KL did another emotional change-up, right before Devin's eyes. The quickness of it shocked him. KL's eyes were moist. "Please, son, take me home," KL pleaded. "I don't belong here."

Oh God, Pops, don't do this! "Dad, we can't leave you alone in the house," Devin said gently. "We don't want anything to happen to you."

Another change, this one unchecked fury. "You're just like those other two ungrateful bastards," he snapped. "This is your way of getting back at me? For not being there for you? The truth is your mother, that bitch, took you away from me. Who the fuck was she to leave *me*? I never bowed down to anyone, Devin—from when Victor Charlie held a gun at my head in the jungles of the Nam, to when racist commanders wouldn't give me my due. I would've eaten my gun before I got on my knees to beg her to come back."

Just as quickly, the seething resentment he'd felt toward his father, resentment he'd tried to manage for the sake of a relationship, came bubbling to the surface. Devin got up. "Don't you call my mother a bitch," he ordered. "Her family was two seconds away from disowning her for bringing a nigger into the family. She left her family. For you! You're the ingrate."

KL shot up, and he and Devin met eye to eye. Devin knew now what unadulterated anger looked like. He saw it in his father's eyes. "I am your father!" KL shouted. "I should lay your ass out right here!"

"Go ahead, Dad, get it out of your system!" Devin countered. "Then you can explain to me what kind of man sacrifices a relationship with his son to prove something to a wife that *he* did wrong by? What twisted man-logic makes *that* make sense, huh?"

KL looked befuddled. Devin waited for an answer that his father couldn't give him. "You know, Pops, you have a good night," Devin finally said.

He headed for the door. "Devin, don't leave me here, son," KL whimpered.

Devin's heart squeezed. Another perilous dip on the emotional roller coaster that was his life. He stormed past his family in the hall. "Devin!" Marlene called. "Is Dad okay?"

Devin made a beeline for the automatic glass doors, lest he dissolve in front of them, in front of the kids. "He's gonna be fine," he murmured.

He rushed to his ride in the parking lot, jumped in, and locked all the doors. He rocked himself as he sobbed. *I'm twenty-eight, for Christ's sake. Twenty-eight-year-olds don't watch their fathers unravel right before their eyes.*

On reflex, he took the phone out of his pocket and speed-dialed her number. After three rings, he heard Chaney say a sleepy, "Hello."

Then he remembered. *Oh, yeah. We broke up.* He listened as she said hello again, this time more forcefully, more coherently. Pressing the END button felt like he was severing the line to his heart. He took comfort, though, in the fact that, with a madman driving around the area terrorizing people, she was home, safe in bed.

He started the ride and in minutes was driving along Route 1. He soon saw Lockheed Boulevard, the turnoff that led to her house. Bravely, he fought back temptation, went through the green light, and headed toward Arlington.

Twelve

The next day, Friday, was a better day for Chaney. She got up bright and early. She had a shower, brushed her teeth, and dressed in a pair of sweats. She felt clean, alert, and, mostly, free from morning sickness for the time being.

Chaney went downstairs and looked around. Tony had been gone less than a month, and Chaney just now realized how much life he'd brought to her world. Chaney noticed that Daisy hadn't called her to see if she was okay. *Probably under some guy.*

She was searching the pantry for something that she could keep down, or something that wouldn't hurt so much coming up, when the phone rang. Chaney snatched up the cordless from off the wall and looked at the caller ID screen. *Dani.* She was fine, too. Chaney pressed TALK. "Hey, girl," she said.

"Hey, Chaney," Dani returned. This was the kinder, more nurturing Dani that Chaney was getting to know better. "Nathalie told me you left Autodidact. You fine about that?"

Chaney sucked her teeth. The memory of Al and his fake Nuremberg tribunal was playing second fiddle to the shootings in Montgomery County. "Bump Al, can you believe what's going on here?"

"I know," Dani said. "I've lived here for over twenty years. I've lived through Reagan, the crackhead mayor, and gentrification. I never could've imagined some crazy white man would be shooting up the place. You know the cops think he was the one who killed an old man in D.C. last night."

Chaney took the phone into the living room, found the remote, and switched on the TV. The name and age—Pascal Charlot, 72—was keyed under a picture of an older black man. *What the . . . ?* She dropped down onto the couch, her mouth hanging open as she listened to the anchor speculate about the murder. "This is insane, Dani," she said. "That's six people in twenty-four hours."

"I have faith in that brothah in Montgomery County," she said. "That Charles Moose."

"Dani, you live in the District. How are you not scared shitless right about now?"

Dani made the universal scoffing sound—*pfft!* "Girl, I'm a child of God," Dani declared, without equivocation. "I can't be like these people hiding from white vans, because this guy's supposedly driving one. Or cowering behind tarps to pump their gas. How am I gonna worry about something that I can't control?"

The evangelical lesbian. The dichotomy still amazed Chaney.

"Let's deal with something you *can* control," Dani said. "Tell me what happened at Autodidact."

Though she would've given her eye teeth for a cup of French roast café au lait, Chaney made herself a cup of Tazo Passion Infusion herbal tea from Starbucks. *Already this baby's changing my lifestyle.* She told Dani in detail about the meeting, about the check that Al had cut her, with ridiculous strings attached, and about her counteroffer, which he openly disregarded. "It's been two days, and I haven't heard from them," Chaney concluded.

"Waiting for him to cough up any money due to you beyond the initial one hundred thousand is a little naïve, Chaney," Dani declared. "We are talking about Al McCulligh here. You were right for not taking that check, though. If you had, you would've been waiving any claims against the company."

"They're expecting litigation. They even threatened Coco, telling her she should know who her friends are."

"So, give it to them."

"I wouldn't even know where to find someone to handle this sort of thing."

"Chaney, this is D.C.," Dani reminded her. "The guy who collects your trash is probably a lawyer. If you're looking for one of the best, though, you already have an in. You know his brother . . . in the biblical sense, that is."

It took a second to register. "Huh?"

"Eric Rhym. He's a partner at Mackie, Sloane, and Horowitz downtown. He's one of the rising stars of civil litigation. They call him 'Big Tort' . . . you know, 'Tort' being short for 'torturer,' and also because a tort is a civil action."

Chaney's stomach dipped. She didn't know if it was the return of morning sickness or trepidation at interacting with Devin's brother after their breakup. Or even the thought of going head-to-head with Al McCulligh. "I don't know, Dani . . ."

Dani went on, like she hadn't even heard Chaney. "I attended a seminar with him last year, before I gave all that shit up to write the book," she said. "Hold on a sec. I'll get his number for you."

Long after Dani hung up, Chaney stared at the piece of paper with Eric Rhym's number on it. She held the phone in her hands, then put it down repeatedly as her courage ebbed and flowed. Finally, her backbone calcified long enough for her to dial the number.

Day two of life in the assisted-living facility, and KL was still being aggressively passive-aggressive. While Eric made sure that everything worked in the room, Devin took KL to the bathroom and filled up the sink with warm water. Devin looked in his father's shaving kit, and his heart skipped a beat. There, he saw the shaving mousse that Chaney had made for KL, along with the special razors with the wooden handles that she suggested he use. Two days away from her felt like two centuries.

"What's wrong?" KL asked in a moment of uncharacteristic tenderness.

Devin shook his head, then proceeded to wet his father's five o'clock shadow with a damp washcloth. "Nothing," he lied.

"Uh-huh," KL commented. "You're full of shit, son."

Takes one to know one. He didn't dare say it out loud, though. He still had visions of Eric flying across the floor after finding himself on the losing end of KL's left hook.

Dutifully, Devin slathered on the mousse, and they stood head-to-head as he shaved his father in silence. When he was done, he washed

KL's face and patted it dry with a bath towel. "All done, Pop," he announced.

Eric stuck his head in the bathroom. "Well, Virginia's officially now on the asshole's hit list," he announced. "About an hour ago, a woman in Fredericksburg got shot while putting groceries in her car."

KL glared at him, then moved pointedly past Eric and out of the bathroom. Eric laughed, shaking his head. "He's still mad," he said.

Devin hung the damp towels over the shower rod. "You used the law to threaten him. He's probably not going to get over something like that overnight."

Eric looked so proud of himself, like he was the keeper of some delicious news. "You wouldn't guess who called me today."

Devin sighed. "Just tell me who."

"Your cougar," Eric announced, his smile a mile wide.

Devin tried to play it casual, but he sensed he wasn't that good an actor. He felt himself go hot and cold at the same time. "Why would she call you?"

Eric shrugged and sucked his teeth. "She said something about being forced out of her partnership on Wednesday, and how she was thinking of suing the other partners. She wanted me to represent her."

Devin exhaled through puckered lips. *So that's why she needed me.* She didn't just snap on some jealous whim, pissed because he'd made her low man on his very busy totem pole. She was about to lose her livelihood. *And I wasn't there for her.* His actions, which he remembered being justifiable that night, now, through a different lens, seemed self-absorbed, trivializing, juvenile. "What did you tell her?" Devin asked.

"Are you kidding?!" Eric laughed. "I told her no way, that out of loyalty to my little brother, I couldn't represent the woman who'd shit all over him."

"Oh, now you remember to be loyal," Devin said, mocking. "This from the man who was all up in Liz, in my house, while wearing his wedding ring."

"All right, Devin, I've apologized to you for that," Eric stated. "I don't know what else you want me to do to prove how sorry I am."

Devin shrugged. "Simple," he said. "You'll help Chaney. You'll live up to your name, Big Torturer. Or, as much as I love Marlene? She will get a visit from me."

Eric's Adam's apple quivered ever so slightly. Devin was certain he'd gotten his message across.

Chaney sat in front of Eric's oak-and-glass desk. She stared at his view of D.C. and wondered how many people below her were cowering in fear of the sniper, taking great pains to avoid the outdoors, or white box vans. She wondered how many people knew that just that Monday morning, a thirteen-year-old boy headed to school in Bowie, in Maryland's much-maligned Prince George's County—or P.G. County—had been shot while being dropped off at Benjamin Tasker Middle School. When she saw Montgomery Police Chief Charles Moose cry a single tear in his press conference that afternoon as he said, ". . . Shooting a kid, I guess it's really, really personal now," Chaney felt reality hit home. No one was safe from a sniper who didn't seem like he was going to be caught anytime soon.

Eric leaned in toward her from behind the desk. "Are you okay?" he asked.

Chaney looked up at him. He was nothing like she'd imagined. He looked like the brother of Vanessa Williams, not Devin Rhym. He was shorter than Devin and KL. Where Devin was coffee-colored, Eric was a few shades away from passing. His reddish hair barely held a curl, but it offset his large, light eyes, which were striking. He was the smooth attorney in every way. He was impeccably groomed, from his designer single-breasted pinstripe suit, to his shiny black, lace-up shoes. "I'm fine," she assured him. "I'm just surprised that you agreed to see me, after all."

He played with a fancy black Montblanc fountain pen. "In retrospect, I was a bit hasty," he confessed. "I've decided to take your case, pro bono. As a favor to my brother."

Well, that was frank. Nonetheless, she said, "Thank you."

"I want to get some background information on . . ." he looked at his notes " . . . Autodidact. Don't hold anything back. We'll decide on its usefulness later, okay?"

Luckily for Chaney, she wasn't in the mood to hold anything back.

They'd met to lift weights at Gold's Gym in Clarendon: Devin, Mali, and Andre. Jamal had a much-needed day off, and Andre and Devin were playing hooky. It was the stress reliever Devin needed. While punishing his body with weights and hanging with his boys, he could relax and forget about the sniper. At the office, the faithful patients that still patronized them met a waiting room draped in heavy material to shield the glass from someone tempted to pick someone off. He could, for once, think about anything but his father, who vacillated between being furious at being forced into assisted living, and belligerent with the three strangers who came to visit, telling him they were his sons. He could especially keep his mind off Chaney. *Five days and counting . . .*

He thought about her mostly at night, as he lay in the basement of KL's big, empty house, which, thanks to the contractors remodeling the kitchen upstairs, smelled of wood shavings and fresh paint. There were memories of her all around the basement. Everywhere he turned, his mind was flooded with little snapshots of her brushing her teeth naked at the sink, of her letting go and giving in to him in the middle of the room that first night they were together, of the hours they'd spent under the covers of the sofa bed. Finally, on Saturday, he couldn't take it; he moved upstairs to the guest room.

After an hour of intense lifting and spotting each other, Devin and the fellas moved to the showers. Devin let the warm water cascade over him, imagining that all his troubles ran down the drain with the soapy water. Later, they got dressed in the near-empty locker room. Andre was unusually subdued as he slicked his wet hair back with a comb. "Ryan's gonna be *incognegro* while this asshole's shooting up the area," Andre announced. "He said since the shooting on Friday, district commanders have cancelled all leave. He may even get on that cross-jurisdictional task force they got going. Especially since that kid got shot this morning in Bowie."

Jamal shook his head. "That poor kid," he sighed. "A .223 round. That's a nasty bullet to get shot with." He whirled his index fingers over each other in a circle. "It breaks up inside you and the spinning pieces shred anything in their way."

Devin didn't want that imagery in his head. "Thank God I deal with animals."

"Mom and Dad are worried about him," Andre said—Devin guessed he meant Ryan. "I mean, they almost lost one son on September 11. Now this shit."

Andre's eyes misted, and Jamal and Devin exchanged glances. Andre took out a blue hanky and dabbed at his eyes. Devin gave his shoulder a comforting squeeze, which meant, *we're here for you*. Andre looked up at him, then at Jamal and laughed. "Plus, this sniper is seriously fucking up my sex life," he declared. "None of these honeys wanna come out and see 'the Andre naked.' "

Devin laughed at his appropriation of that line from the Slick Rick remix of Al B. Sure's "If I'm Not Your Lover." Jamal chuckled, too. "Yeah, nothing like getting shot at to ruin a hookup," Jamal commented.

"Come on, fellas, let's go out tonight," Andre pleaded. "There's gotta be some honeys out there who aren't spooked by this guy."

Jamal held up a hand. "You're on your own, bruh," he said. "I've got some reading to do, and Devin here's got himself a woman."

So much for forgetting about his situation for a few hours. The old ghosts were back. Devin furiously rubbed his head with one of the gym's generic white towels. "Actually, we're kinda cooling it," he announced, grimacing.

Cooling it? What a joke! He and Chaney were ice cold.

Jamal leaned in, all curious. Andre, too, was all ears. "Excuse me?" Jamal asked. "Since when?"

"Wednesday," Devin said.

Jamal looked like this was as big a shock to him as it had been to Devin. "Why?" he demanded.

Devin stopped rubbing his head, trying to find the words. "I guess it was getting too confining," he said, which he knew was bullshit, but figured it would appeal to two uncommitted guys like Jamal and Andre.

Jamal's expression went from surprise to disgust in seconds flat. He looked at Devin like he was the lowest form of life on the earth. "Huh," he said.

"What's up with you?" Devin demanded.

Without skipping a beat after the news, Andre rubbed his hands together. "See, what better way to get over Old School than to come out with me and score some honeys," he said. "You're back!"

Jamal sucked his teeth. "Yeah, Devin, go out to score honeys with this knucklehead. I never thought I'd see it, but you've become your father. That's what he would do."

Now Devin was pissed. That was the ultimate insult, on every level. "What the fuck are you talking about?"

"Leave your pregnant girlfriend, because the responsibility of fatherhood is . . ." Jamal lent the appropriate amount of scorn here ". . . 'too confining' for you."

Devin stood there as the rest of his words bled away, leaving the only ones that mattered: *pregnant girlfriend.* "What?" he echoed.

"Don't play dumb," Jamal commanded. "You know Chaney's pregnant. She's known for weeks."

Devin's knees buckled, and he dropped down onto the bench in between the lockers. *Chaney's pregnant.*

Andre hovered over him. "I don't know, bruh," he said, looking up at Jamal. "I don't think he's playing."

The blood drained from Jamal's face, like he was wondering how many canons of ethics, starting with doctor-patient privilege, he'd broken. "Oh, shit," he murmured.

The fog slowly began to clear in Devin's head. "Wait!" he said. "How do you know?"

Jamal sheepishly explained what had happened that Friday—how, from what he'd gathered, Chaney had collapsed at the HUB, how her friends brought her to his treatment table at the Howard University Hospital, how blood and urine tests revealed that she was, in fact, pregnant. "I'm sorry, Devin," he said, in conclusion. "She's your woman. I just assumed she'd told you, and you'd rolled out. You know that's my hot button."

Devin remembered that that's how Jamal and his mother ended up in Virginia, how Jamal's father left him and his mother to get a construction job in Bermuda, never to return. But his mind came back to more relevant events unfolding right before him. "How did she seem?" he asked.

"She wasn't overjoyed," Jamal said. "I could tell it wasn't planned. Still, though, I just assumed she would've told you by now."

Maybe she tried to. Devin thought of all of her calls to his cell, calls he'd blown off because understandably, he'd put KL first. "How does he even know the baby's his?" Andre countered. "Maybe that's why she didn't tell him. Maybe she's been tricking."

Devin screwed up his face at the possibility. He couldn't even fathom it—Chaney with another man. "No way," he declared with certainty.

"What, you got her pussy in your back pocket?" Andre asked. "One word: Liz."

"Not this babe, okay?" Devin said. "Not her. She's different."

Jamal was all quiet. Then he said, tentatively, "I hate to say this, Devin, but maybe she didn't tell you because she's not going to have it."

An abortion. Devin sat there with his hand over his mouth. He backtracked in his mind, thought about all the things she'd said, about her inability to parent a child. "Would she really do that?" he asked. Belatedly, he realized he'd done it aloud.

"It's her right," Jamal said. "But Dev, ask yourself what you want. You're twenty-eight. You really wanna be a father right about now?"

"Or worse, have all that baby mama drama," Andre added to the mix. "I know some brothahs who've gotten trapped, and it is ugly."

Devin's inertia gave way to hyperactivity. He stood up and paced. *Think, think.* "I don't know," he said. "But I do know she should've told me. The kid's half mine—this is a decision we should be making together."

"It's her body, her choice," Jamal reminded him. "She doesn't have to discuss anything."

Uncertainty morphed into frustration. "That's bullshit!" Devin cried.

Jamal threw up his hands. "Well, what are you gonna do, Devin?" he demanded. "You're gonna force her to keep it? You're gonna put a ring on her finger? You're gonna force her to make decisions when you're not acting decisively yourself?"

Frustration morphed into anger, anger that fueled Devin. He hurriedly finished dressing in silence. He could feel Jamal and Andre watching him, waiting for his next trick. Finally, as he headed for the stairs, Jamal shouted, "What are you gonna do?"

Devin didn't even turn around. "Act decisively," he declared.

Devin took the stairs two and three at a time and strode out of the gym, until he was squarely on Clarendon Boulevard, watching the traffic whiz by. That sniper was the least of his worries. Forgoing his ride, he whipped out his cell phone and sprinted toward the Clarendon metro. He speed-dialed Chaney's cell phone number; it was disconnected. He then tried her home; the phone rang and rang in his ear. He didn't have any other numbers for her.

By the time he reached the metro, he was pissed, out of breath, and sweating, sweat that the cool October breeze chilled against his skin. *Think, think!* Then he suddenly had a revelation. He speed-dialed Eric.

After running the gauntlet of gatekeepers that kept Eric from his adoring public, he finally got his brother on the other end. "Eric Rhym," Eric said in Devin's ear.

More flies with honey than with vinegar . . . "E, it's Devin," he announced. "So I'm E again," Eric said, levity in his voice. "That's progress."

"I'm looking for Chaney."

"You're in luck—she's here at the office."

He breathed a sigh of relief. "Don't let her leave," he said. "I'm coming over—don't let her know."

Devin could sense Eric's devious lawyer's mind processing in the ensuing silence. "Okay, then."

Anticipation carried Devin down the escalator to the metro. He got a pass and got onto the Orange line train. It was only seven stops, but it seemed like forever before Devin got off at the Farragut North metro. Forgoing the cabs waiting on K Street, Devin ran the five blocks to Eric's office, located on the third floor of one of the neoclassical colossi that marked the landscape of downtown D.C.

The minions in the glass-and-gray offices of Mackie, Sloane, and Horowitz glared at him strangely as he threw open the heavy double doors. He knew he must've looked a sight, too . . . angry and sweating profusely. Only Grace, the receptionist, greeted him like he was an actual person. "He's in his office," she said.

Devin navigated the halls, which bespoke of the hierarchy. The double glass doors with their own lobby and secretary were reserved for Mr. Mackie, Mr. Sloane, and Mr. Horowitz, Esq. Down the hall from them were the decidedly smaller offices of the junior partners. Eric, because he was Big Tort, the partner in closest proximity to the big fish. He and the other junior partners shared a receptionist with blond highlights and a nose ring. She sat in a cubicle outside Eric's office.

Devin ignored her and zoomed in on his quarry. He recognized the back of her head, those curls in the 'fro Devin would thread his fingers through. He saw that she wore a black ribbed turtleneck, saw the end of crossed legs in black slacks and stack-heeled boots. His heart sped up even faster, if that were possible after his haste in getting there . . . so quickly that he got dizzy for a second.

Eric was behind his impressive desk, talking impressively on his phone with many buttons. Then suddenly, he saw Devin striding into the office. He told the other person on the phone good-bye and stood up. "Devin!" he said. "What a nice surprise!"

She turned around in the guest chair, her eyes wide. All the blood, it seemed, had drained from her face. Devin didn't even acknowledge

Eric. He stared holes through Chaney. "We need to talk," he declared. "In private."

"Use the conference room down the hall," Eric suggested.

Devin stormed across the office and snatched Chaney up out of her chair. "Let's go."

She seemed too surprised to protest as he led her by the elbow down to the all-glass conference room, incurring the curious stares of office workers. It was when he slammed the heavy fire door that she let him have it. "Who the fuck do you think you are?" she yelled.

"When were you going to tell me that you're pregnant?" he asked.

She stared at him in shock for about a minute. Then anger replaced her astonishment. "Mali and his huge mouth!" she cried.

"He assumed you already told me, me being your man and all!" Devin returned. "Is it even mine?"

She glared at him, and he sensed he'd crossed the line. *Listening to Andre.* "I'm gonna ignore that, because I know you're hurt, and maybe a little scared," she said. "But keep it up, and I'm gonna cuss you into next week."

He studied her as he took deep breaths that whistled through his nose. She folded her arms across her chest and avoided his eyes. *Calm down, Devin. Back up just a taste.* Finally, he asked, "How pregnant are you?"

"Six weeks."

He remembered what Jamal had said: *Her body, her choice . . .* He swallowed hard. "Are you going to keep it?"

She shrugged. "I don't know. I still have six or seven weeks before I have to think about . . ."

". . . killing it," he concluded.

She grimaced. "Was I wrong in assuming you're pro-choice?"

"It's easy to be pro-choice when you don't have half of you growing in somebody."

Her eyes misted. "I don't need this, Devin."

He lunged toward her; she stepped back. "Well, I don't know the proper way to behave in this situation, Chaney," he said. "I never got anyone pregnant before!"

"Well, I've never been pregnant before!" she cried.

His first instinct was to hold her, so they could make each other's pain disappear. But he kept his distance. Instead, he took off his skull cap, tossed it on the big wooden table, and ran his fingernails along his scalp as he racked his brain for ideas. "I guess we could get married," he threw out there, just to see her reaction.

It wasn't favorable. She raked him with her gaze, then stared at him as if he were a lunatic. "No, we couldn't!" she exclaimed. "We have absolutely nothing to offer each other. I just got released from a partnership. I could lose everything. Your business is on the bubble; every penny you got from the sale of your house, you put into that. You and I are gonna get married and raise our child in KL's basement? Is that the plan?"

He looked at her and saw memories of better times, shared intimacy, physical and emotional closeness. "I love you, Chaney," he said quietly. "We have that."

A sigh trembled out of her chest. She blinked and fat tears plopped down her cheeks. Furiously, she pushed them away. "I love you, too, Devin," she croaked, then cleared her throat. "It scares me sometimes how much I love you. It defies every logical bone in my body. But sometimes, love isn't enough. I look at my sister and Norm. They loved each other, too, but they got married strictly because she was pregnant with D. It took her years to get back to normal after her marriage to the love of her life blew up in her face. Even though they're back together again, she's told me, 'I love him, but I'll never trust him again.' I'm not my sister; I don't have the strength to be the future ex-Mrs. Devin Rhym."

He sat down at the conference room table and stared out into the office. He and Chaney were garnering quite the audience, who'd pass the room and stare in through the glass.

"Plus, you're twenty-eight," she said suddenly. "You want to be a father?"

Jamal had asked him the same thing, and he didn't have an answer. This time, he was prepared. "Dad had Chauncey when he was twenty-five," he told her.

She held up a hand. "Devin, I love KL to death, but let's not mention him, and fatherhood, and marriage in the same conversation."

In spite of his shitty mood, Devin laughed. "You're right," he sighed. "Pops isn't the best witness for the prosecution, is he?"

She pulled up a chair next to him and eased herself down. "I really wish Jamal hadn't said anything," she sighed. "Then I would've known that your marriage proposal was real, instead of some bullshit honor stance you'd felt compelled to take because I'm pregnant."

He wished he could turn back the clock, too. He would've answered her phone calls. He would've been there for her when she needed him. Mostly, he wouldn't have taken that key off his ring and put it on the counter. He looked up at her. "This is how we leave this, Chaney?" he asked.

Chaney buried her head in her hands. "Devin, I can't emotionally multitask right now," she said. "I have to take one thing at a time, and the thing that's most pressing is the fight with my partners. After that, I promise we'll get together and decide what we're going to do."

We. He liked that. At least he was promised a collaborative effort. He looked her up and down. "I'll respect that," he finally said. *For now, anyway.*

He stood up, and she did the same. His first instinct was to hug her close, just like all the other times they'd said good-bye. Again, he defied instinct, instead snatching his cap off the table. Many things he wanted to say to her ran through his head. Unfortunately, they all involved pleas, or apologies, or other appeals to her emotions, which, by her own admission, were taxed to the limit. So, instead he said nothing. He silently moved toward the door, opened it, and walked out into a sea of prying eyes.

Thirteen

Chaney's solution to everything—the sniper crisis, as well as her own personal drama—was to stay in the house. That way, she could avoid shots to the heart from a Bushmaster XM15 E2S rifle—the sniper's weapon of choice—as well as from Devin Rhym. Staying home, too, made it easier to deal with morning sickness that increasingly had begun not to limit itself to the mornings. Just when she thought things in life seemed as unreal as they could, the sniper struck twice by the end of the week. October 9 was a Wednesday. At 8:10 in the evening in Manassas, on the subjective border between Northern Virginia and "Scary Virginia," as Devin called it, Dean Harold Meyers, 53, was shot while pumping gas into his car. Two days later, on Friday, October 11, at precisely 9:28 A.M., Chaney was hugging the bowl, praying for the waves in her stomach to stop, when a bulletin cut in. The WTOP radio announcer said that Kenneth Harold Bridges, 53, of Philadelphia, was shot to death in Massaponax, Virginia. Like Meyers two days before him, Bridges had also been gassing up his car, minutes after talking to his wife on his cellie . . . his "queen," he'd called her. When Chaney heard that, love separated by cruel fate, the tears flowed down her cheeks. She could relate.

By the following Monday, Chaney was empty. Right then, she wished she hadn't stopped taking the Fluexa. The drug would've enabled her to put a positive spin on being pregnant, unmarried, and unemployed. The drug would've enabled her to deal with being at the epicenter of random killings. Instead, the drug was probably almost all gone from her system, and she was paralyzed with fear, unable to leave the house.

Nonetheless, she'd made a pretense of it. She'd showered, changed into jeans and a sweatshirt, and made herself some soup. She was about to comb her hair when there was a knock at the door. *Devin?* Her heart leapt inside her chest, with its ribs sore from heaving her guts out.

She rushed to the door and threw it open. It was Dani, dressed in her usual lesbian togs: jeans, cowboy boots, a hunter-green turtleneck, and a man's bomber jacket to round out the ensemble. "We've come to rescue you," she announced. "Stop you from moping."

Who's we? Chaney looked over Dani's shoulder. Coco and Nathalie waved from the inside of her Range Rover.

Obediently, she put away the soup, slipped on her coat and boots, and joined them.

After a sumptuous dinner, which Chaney watched everybody else but her and Nathalie eat, Dani drove, and they talked shit through three courses. As night fell, they were on Route 7 in Falls Church, heading back toward Alexandria, when Chaney spotted the familiar green sign at the Seven Corners Shopping Center. *Starbucks.* Dani looked over at Chaney from the driver's seat. "Okay," she laughed. "We'll stop."

"Thank God!" Nathalie moaned from the backseat. "I have to pee so bad."

Dani turned off the highway. Minutes later, they were in the warmth of the Starbucks, redolent with the smells of coffee that Chaney could no longer drink. They sat at a round table, away from the plate-glass window that looked out onto the parking lot that was surprisingly full for a Monday night. The clientele varied from older couples, to younger couples with matching nose rings, poring over state-of-the-art laptops . . . all caffeinating. Chaney stared jealously over the top of her white mug filled with decaf vanilla Chai tea. The only thing that made the experience enjoyable was the company of her friends and the good musical sense of one of the baristas to rock "Who is Jill Scott? Words and Sounds Vol 1" on the sound system.

Chaney snapped her fingers to the mellow beat of "A Long Walk," sneaking a gaze over at Nathalie. Gone was the pregnancy glow from weeks ago. Tonight, she looked practically ashen. She hardly touched her vanilla crème Frappuccino. Every once in a while, she'd shift uncomfortably in her chair. "You okay?" Chaney asked.

Nathalie shook her head dismissively. "I fell off a ladder on Friday," she said, with a casual wave of her hand. "Painting at one of the houses."

"*Loca*," Coco said under her breath. "When I was pregnant, I did nothing on purpose. When else are you gonna have that excuse?"

"At least you have Craig to wait on you hand and foot," Chaney said.

Nathalie aggressively changed the subject. She pointed at Chaney. "When we last talked to you, Miss Chaney, you had just gotten a marriage proposal from the father of your baby," she recapped. "A baby you don't know whether or not you are going to keep."

Chaney laughed uncomfortably. "Just as if you were there in the room."

Dani sipped her caffe mocha. "What'd you decide?"

Chaney sighed, trying to find the words. "I don't know if I can bring a child into this horrible world," she declared. "Let's forget about the shit that's going on in my life for a second. This is a world where, you try to raise your child the right way, and he gets shot on his way to school. Or worse, you get the child who ends up driving around in a white van, killing people in the streets."

"Chaney, raising babies is a crap shoot," Coco offered. "It's been that way since we began having kids. I couldn't imagine my life without Miguel and Juanita. Children are a blessing from God."

"This is a gift from a defective condom and very agile sperm," Chaney declared. "Don't get it twisted."

Dani laughed. "You know our friend and God don't really talk on a regular basis."

Nathalie had graduated to hugging herself around the midsection. "Well, my objections to abortion are based on my faith in God," she said, her speech labored. "But Chaney, you were there for my hellish year of in vitro and hormone treatments. People are trying to get pregnant, and you're actually thinking of having an abortion. It just seems karmically unfair."

How can I get you to understand? She threw up her hands in frustration. "I don't know what kind of life this child would have, okay?" she said. "There's that antidepressant that's probably still in my system; Macca can't tell me definitively the effect it'll have on a baby. I'm also facing facts. I don't know how to be someone's mother! Leah Braxton is dead. She died and left me alone. The closest thing I've had to a mother is disappointed in me and upset with me."

"But what about Devin, Chaney?" Coco asked.

"What about Devin?" Chaney countered. "Isn't the world filled with enough baby daddies to last us for generations? Why create another statistic?"

"Sounds like you've made up your mind," Dani said quietly.

They didn't see the look on Devin's face that day in the conference room . . . his eyes pleading, accompanied by his ham-fisted but well-intentioned marriage proposal. For a brief moment, she'd wondered what it would be like to have a family with him, raising their child together, sharing days that added up to a lifetime. She wondered if they'd amassed enough relationship capital on which to build such a foundation. She hadn't made up her mind at all. "Far from it," she murmured.

Nathalie moaned loudly just then, and all eyes shifted away from Chaney and to her. She was near white, and for someone of her complexion, that was jarring enough. And the worrying sounds she was making added to everyone's concern. Chaney leaned in, looking into her dull eyes. "Sweetie, what's wrong?" she asked.

Nathalie again waved that dismissive hand. "It's nothing," she groaned.

The picture window suddenly reflected the flashing lights of what seemed to be police cars and ambulances zipping past, headed toward the other end of the shopping center. Their sirens, en masse, drowned out Jill Scott. "What's that about?" Dani mused.

Coco focused on Nathalie. "You're not all right," she insisted. "Come on. Let's go."

Chaney had one eye on Nathalie and one eye on the door. Both scenarios didn't seem to bode well. Just as Coco was helping Nathalie to her feet, a young woman wearing the trademark orange Home Depot apron ran into the Starbucks, her eyes wide with unadulterated fear. "Someone's just been shot at the Home Depot!" she screamed, a scream that curdled Chaney's blood. "Lock your doors!"

The sniper! It was easier to be further removed when the drama was playing out on TV. Chaney's heart boomed so furiously she could taste the adrenaline it pumped through her body. "Oh, shit, this can't be happening!" Chaney cried.

One of the two baristas, a heavyset woman with short brown hair, rushed for the door just as Coco and Nathalie were headed out, Dani and Chaney following along at a good clip. "Ladies, you should stay inside," the barista cautioned, her voice quavering.

"Our friend's sick," Chaney said. "We gotta go."

The barista gave them a leave-at-your-own-risk look, then let them out. Chaney heard the lock snap into place definitively behind them. If the sniper was out in the cool October night looking for unprotected victims, he'd just found four. Reflexively, she began her relationship with God in earnest. *Oh, Lord, please don't let us die!*

Dani took charge, running to Nathalie's Range Rover, opening the locks by remote. Dani got into the driver's seat; Coco and Chaney piled in the back with Nathalie in the middle. "How are you feeling, sweetie?" Chaney asked.

Nathalie bit down on her bottom lip. "Like I'm having bad cramps," she moaned. "You know, when you're just about to get your period?"

Coco and Chaney exchanged glances over Nathalie's head. Chaney guessed that feeling like you're about to have your period when you're pregnant was universally not good.

Dani started the car and reversed out of her spot. "Don't worry, Nat," she said. "We're gonna get you to the hospital, okay?"

"No hospital," Nathalie moaned.

"You made *me* go," Chaney forced a laugh. "Time for you to wear the assless gown."

Dani sped toward the exit that led to Route 50 . . . and landed smack-dab into a police roadblock. She punched the steering wheel. "Shit!" she spat.

"What?" Chaney asked.

She looked up and gasped. From the height of the Range Rover, she could see that the police had filtered the traffic down to one lane as they searched diligently for the sniper driving the white box van that had been broadcast on every national and local news station. "What?" Nathalie asked.

Coco and Chaney again looked at each other over the top of Nathalie's head. The expression on Coco's face said she agreed with Chaney's assessment that things had officially gotten worse.

Dani switched on WTOP radio and inched along with the rest of the backed-up traffic. The announcer said there had been a shooting at the garage of the Home Depot in Seven Corners. A woman was down. Police had cordoned off Route 50, as well as Interstate 495, in the hope of preventing the sniper from escaping.

They moved slowly in a sea of brake lights, passing police cars with flashing lights every few feet. With every passing minute, Nathalie's moans grew louder and louder, until she was openly weeping, her arms wrapped around her midsection like she could get the cramps to stop through sheer force of will. "Are we almost there?" she sobbed.

Dani and Chaney exchanged a glance that said they weren't even close. Chaney fought back tears. "Any minute now, sweetie," she promised.

Nathalie looked at Coco, then Chaney. "Y'all feel that?" she asked.

Coco furrowed her brows. "Feel what?"

"The seat's wet," Nathalie moaned.

Chaney reached up and turned on the overhead light. She unbuttoned Nathalie's coat. A thick red puddle had begun to pool between Nathalie's legs. Chaney bit down hard on her bottom lip. There was no lying or sugar-coating the truth now. After countless infertility treatments and the initial success, Nathalie was having a miscarriage . . . in the back of her Range Rover . . . in traffic. Chaney took her hand. "Nathalie, you're bleeding," she said, subdued.

Nathalie met her gaze. The look in her eyes told Chaney that she knew what was happening. Open weeping turned to gut-wrenching sobs. "No!" she wailed. "Please, no!"

A trip that usually took thirty minutes, maximum, took two hours that night. At 11:30, Dani sped up to the electric doors to the Arlington Hospital emergency room. Chaney and Coco gently helped Nathalie out of the car. As two nurses greeted them, blood spilled from Nathalie's coat and onto the ground. Chaney knew it was officially over for Baby Phillips.

Nathalie seemed to take it in stride when the emergency room doctor confirmed that she'd indeed miscarried. Chaney, Coco, and Nathalie gathered around her in the bed. Everyone was at a loss as to what to say. Nathalie's eyes displayed unvarnished pain. But she shrugged. "Back to the fertility experts," she sighed with a wan smile.

Then Craig came, and her heroic stance evaporated. It was like he gave her permission to show her grief. He came in, acknowledging the ladies with a nod. Then he looked at the love of his life, his soul mate. Chaney's heart ached as she watched him fall into her arms. He clutched onto her, sobbing like he'd split in two. She quietly wept. "It's okay, baby," she whispered. "We'll try again."

Glimpsing into their agony made Chaney feel like a voyeur. She opened the curtain and left; Dani and Coco were close behind her. She rushed outside, into the waiting room. There, others watched the TV, tuned to CNN, as they showed a photograph of a woman. Keyed under the picture were the words, LINDA FRANKLIN, 47. The anchor said that she was an FBI analyst and cancer survivor, out buying supplies with her husband for a home they'd just bought.

Nathalie was right. Sometimes, life could be so karmically unfair. Which was why she wondered how, when some people had to use heroic measures to make or sustain life, it was just her dumb luck that one sperm would meet one egg—unassisted—and be able to live in her hostile uterus. Why was she so special? Then she realized that Macca had not used hyperbole when she'd talked about pregnancy being a miracle. She, Chaney Braxton, was the recipient of a miracle.

Eric and Chaney sat in the big conference room at Autodidact. Eric tapped his Montblanc pen on his legal notepad. Chaney wondered if it was the pregnancy or being back at Autodidact that brought on the waves of nausea. She guessed it was probably her imagination, but she supposed she could still smell the pizza and cake from the last party she'd attended there to celebrate the OPM contract.

Right then, the usual suspects entered the conference room: Lissa, who still aggressively avoided Chaney's eyes; Laura, this time in an unflattering tent of a blue sweater-dress; and Al, in his badly fitting designer threads. He shot a twinkly gray glance at Chaney, then at Eric. "Good morning," he said.

Asshole. Chaney glared back at Al and said nothing. That was what Eric was for. "No opposing counsel?" Eric asked.

Al shrugged. "This is just a preliminary meeting, right? Why would I need a lawyer?"

"That's entirely your call," Eric said. "As the attorney of record for Dr. Braxton, I'll go first—if you don't mind, that is."

"Not at all," Al said.

Lissa rolled her eyes behind her trendy specs. "Can we get to it, please?" she said impatiently.

"Of course—I'll cut to the chase, then," Eric declared. "Dr. Braxton and I put in writing her contingencies under which she'll leave the partnership. We were both curious as to when we would have a decision made regarding them."

"Her contingencies are grossly unfair," Al declared. "We're more than amenable to returning Dr. Braxton's initial investment of $100,000. And if she cashes that check, she is enjoined from suing the company for further monies."

Eric laughed, taking copious notes. " 'Enjoined,' " he laughed, then pointed his index finger at Al. "You sure you've never been to law school? You got the jargon down pat."

"Not a day," Al declared. "But I know what's fair."

Eric looked like he was chewing on that statement for a good, long while. "Okay," he said, then went into his file and extracted a document. "Let's take another approach here," he said. "That's your partnership agreement with Dr. Braxton. Can you read the highlighted portion, please?"

He slid the document Al's way. Al took his time perusing it, then looked up. "And?"

"It says that Dr. Braxton, as a twenty-percent partner, is entitled to twenty percent of the profits of projects garnered while she is a partner in the company," Eric refreshed him. "While Dr. Braxton was here, you went from pulling $750,000 dollars in revenues, in 2000, to over two million dollars this year alone, due to her contacts in the industry. I also spoke to a contact over at OPM. She said that even though your proposal was quite exceptional, the solidifying factor was that you had a PhD in the field of instructional design on your staff. So, since you know what's fair, would it be fair to say that one can draw a causal relationship between Dr. Braxton's presence here and your increased revenue stream?"

Chaney watched, in awe, as Al went rose-petal pink. "Of course, one could make that uneducated assumption," Al said. "But the increased revenue could also be explained by other variables and vagaries of the market."

"Ah," said Eric. Chaney came to see that that particular exclamation preceded a smackdown. "Actually, my firm did a survey of government agencies and their trends in granting contracts. The survey showed that such big awards, like the six-million-dollar award you got, were atypical. I can get you a copy if you'd like. My question is, why would you want to force a partner like Dr. Braxton out when she's proven to be good for the company?"

"She didn't meet company standards," Laura finally spoke.

What a joke! Chaney's fury spiked. So, unfortunately, did the morning sickness. The waves in her stomach began to undulate ever so slowly, and Chaney dreaded what was about to come.

"Come on now," Eric said. "What are these company standards? Defying federal directives at the request of an ill-informed client? Taking the hit from another vindictive client who took her to a sex club—unbeknownst to her—and became miffed when she wouldn't put out? Because I think we know what's at play here: if you ditch the partner most concerned about product standards instead of money, then you keep these clients with nefarious agendas happy."

Lissa stared at Chaney, her mouth open. So, Randy had introduced her to Club Pendulum, too. Chaney wondered if she went in the back room with him and indulged him in a threesome.

Al's previously petal-pink face went beet-red. He suddenly turned to Chaney. In all the time she'd known him, she'd never seen him this upset. "You have nothing to say about all the trouble you're causing," he commented.

Trouble I'm *causing?* She would've laughed if she felt comfortable opening her mouth that wide. "No, because unlike you, I availed myself of counsel," she declared.

She stood up and covered her mouth. The waves were coming fast and furious. She had to make her escape before her scant breakfast resurfaced. " 'Scuse me," she murmured.

Al stood up and blocked her way. "You're not going to destroy everything we built here with your frivolous lawsuit," he declared.

"Is this necessary?" Eric asked, brows furrowed and tone strenuously argumentative. "Let her pass."

"Just take the check and be done with it," Al commanded.

The waves roiled in her stomach were coming like a freight train. "Excuse me!" Chaney cried.

"Sit down," Al commanded. "We're not through!"

I asked you nicely. Chaney opened her mouth and lurched as the vomit sprayed all over the front of Al's slacks and shoes. He leapt back in abject horror as he watched the regurgitated food settle into the fabric of his clothing. He turned three shades of pale. "Ugggh!" he groaned.

Lissa and Laura screamed. Laura, the dutiful wife, took a hand-kerchief and tried in vain to help him clean up.

Chaney retched until the waves stopped. The end result was a puddle of stomach contents on the big conference room carpet, vomit spray on Al, and a smell that permeated the room. Eric stood up, not even batting an eye. "Now, I think we're through," he declared.

Later, Chaney and Eric sat across from each other at the Starbucks in Federal Plaza, on Rockville Pike. She sipped her decaf Chai, the taste of it clashing with the minty feel of her freshly brushed mouth. Everything, right down to the taste of the Chai, took her back to the horror of her last visit to the Starbucks at Seven Corners. *Poor Nathalie . . . Poor Linda Franklin . . .* She shook her head. "The sniper killed another person, practically up the street from here, this morning," Chaney told him. "This brother who drove a Metro Line bus. Conrad Johnson. Thirty-five years old! When is this shit gonna stop?"

Eric shrugged. Clearly, he wasn't one of those people "in the grip of terror," as the national news described folks in the D.C. area, who, in reality, were trying to go on with their lives in the face of being stalked by a madman. "He'll make a mistake, Chaney," Eric said. "That's how these guys eventually get caught."

She changed the subject, lest she let it overcome her. "So, how did you think we did with Al?"

Eric laughed. He seemed genuine. "Well, I wouldn't have recommended throwing up on him, but after a minute in the room with him, I sure could understand the inclination," he said, with a devious grin.

Chaney relived the sight of Al going from alpha male to positively humiliated, at her hands. "He should've moved," she said simply.

Eric leaned in, uncharacteristic warmth in his light eyes. "My office is small, and people talk," he said. "You're pregnant, aren't you?"

There was no turning back now. She sipped her Chai. "Yes," she confessed.

"Devin's the father."

She nodded. Eric sighed. "Well," he said, "my brother and I have always had issues. Which were magnified when he moved back here last year. But he's a good guy, generous to a fault. You don't have to worry about him doing right by you."

Whatever that was. She and Devin had yet to discuss what "doing right by her" actually meant.

Eric's cell phone rang just then; it sounded like an actual analog phone ringing. He retrieved it from his breast pocket. "Hello," he said, then he turned white. "I'll be right there."

"It's Dad," he announced after he hung up. "He's had a mild heart attack. I've got to go."

Fear suffused Chaney, fear at yet another loss. "I'll go with you," she said.

Chaney and Eric tentatively entered what looked like the hospital wing of the assisted-living facility. Devin, who'd been talking to a doctor outside one of the powder-blue doors, looked up at the two of them. Chaney's heart leapt at the sight of him. He smiled wearily at her as she and Eric approached him. "Hey," he said.

"How is he?" Eric asked.

"Come and see for yourself," Devin said.

He opened the door. KL lay in his hospital bed, with an IV drip in his left arm. He was far from death's door. In fact, even infirm, he was putting the moves on the pretty young Latina nurse who tended to him. She giggled coquettishly. "Mr. Rhym, you are old enough to be my grandfather," she said, with a strategic batting of her long lashes.

KL chuckled deviously. "One word for you," he said. "Viagra."

"Jeez, Pops, throw in an Eskimo and a Samoan sistah, and you would've had the full set," Devin laughed.

KL looked up. "Baby boys!" he greeted Devin enthusiastically, then touched the nurse's arm. "These are my sons."

The nurse looked up from the IV to give Devin and Eric the once-over. Her gaze lingered on Devin a little too long for Chaney's comfort. "Handsome devils," she finally decreed.

KL looked Chaney straight in the eye. "And who's your lady friend?" he asked.

Chaney's face dropped. There it was—another tangible sign that Devin wasn't crazy, that KL actually had Alzheimer's. He was going to forget every moment of the fabulous life he'd led. He was going to forget his sons, his ex-wives, her and her sisters. Chaney imagined it was a horrible way to go, to be robbed of the experiences that gave one the wisdom of age.

Slowly, Chaney approached the bed. "Look closer," she said.

He did, squinting as he tried hard to remember. Then his eyes lit up. "Chaney!" he exclaimed. "How are you doing, Baby Girl?"

Chaney slowly wrapped him in a hug, taking care not to dislodge his IV. She pressed her face against his smooth cheek. He smelled like aftershave and hair pomade, just like a black dad would. She closed her eyes and inhaled his scent. "You've got people thinking you're sick," she laughed. "You better stop Denzelling."

KL giggled wildly, surprising her. She looked up at the nurse. She nodded knowingly. "A sedative," she explained. "We're taking him for an angiogram."

As if on cue, two black orderlies who looked like they'd occupied the Skins' defensive line came through. "All right, Mr. Rhym," one of them said, rubbing his hands together.

"Uh-oh!" KL laughed giddily. "Time to pop smoke!"

Chaney ran a hand lovingly over KL's wild hair. "See you soon," she assured him.

KL didn't hear her; he was going deeper into his sedative buzz. The nurse accompanied the orderlies as they wheeled him out of the room. Devin pointed at the caravan. "I'd better . . ."

"No," Eric said. "You stay and talk. *I'll* go."

Stunned, Devin stared at his brother as he and the crew wheeled KL through flapping gray doors. "Did he pick up a heart on the way over here or something?" he asked.

Chaney laughed. "Maybe he's turning over a new leaf."

Devin scoffed. "He's a lawyer, Chaney."

The typical awkward silence permeated the moment. Chaney wondered what to do, or what to say, or if she should do or say anything at all. After what seemed like forever, he spoke. "How are you feeling?"

She smiled a lopsided smile. She assumed that this was the type of thing that couples who'd planned their babies talked about. "Sick every waking hour of the day," she said. "Morning sickness—what a misnomer!"

"Can I help?"

His face was curious, open. *You're sweet!* "You could carry the kid for me," she laughed.

She could see tons of questions in that open face, but one trumped all others. *Are you going to keep the baby?* She didn't want to go into that now. All she wanted was to curl up in her bed where it was warm and safe. "Could you give me a ride home?" she asked. "I don't know how safe it is waiting for the Fairfax Connector."

He smiled. "Sure," he said. "Let's go."

The ride up Route 1 to her house was quiet, save for some go-go cut that was playing on WPGC. Chaney imagined they were both still ruminating on the revelations of their last conversation at Eric's office. Once at the house, they hurried in. Chaney disabled the alarm, and he shut the door securely. "Safe for another day," he said.

Memories of him occupying this space hit her full force . . . all the times he'd stood in this house when they were friends—after, when they'd become lovers. She smiled sheepishly. "Thanks," she said.

He nodded. "You're welcome."

"You were right," she said. "We should talk."

"About what?"

She closed her eyes and sighed. *Here goes everything* . . . "I'm keeping the baby, Devin," she announced.

There. She'd said it. There was no turning back. She opened her eyes, searched his face. His expression was one of bewildered surprise. "Wow," he breathed.

The understated word actually said it all. "Wow," she giggled.

Like lightning, he was in front of her. Before she could fathom what was happening, his mouth was on hers, a kiss she eagerly returned. Tongues met and dueled. Hands explored faces, bodies. Nerves in her whole body rose up in response, and she knew that there was no Fluexa to separate her from feeling him, so purely, so naturally, like he was kissing her for the very first time.

They parted, breathing heavily. Their eyes met and held. He pointed at the door. "Umm . . ." he said, seemingly struggling to find his thoughts, "let me go get my father settled, and then we'll talk, okay?"

She nodded. "Okay."

He backed away slowly toward the front door. "I mean it," he promised. "This time, I'll call."

I believe you. Suddenly, though, she thought about Harold Bridges . . . one minute, talking to his "queen," the next minute dead from the sniper's gunshot. "Please, baby, be careful."

"I will," he said. "I love you."

"I love you, too."

Chaney watched him go. *Please, dear God, let him come back safe* . . .

Devin, Maria, and Didier stayed late, purposely to watch the press conference aired live on TV at 8:00 P.M. He had Jamal and Andre on a three-way call on his cell phone. They were watching, too, as Charles Moose and the entire task force announced to the press that they had caught the snipers, confirming news reports from earlier in the day. The TV cameras panned all the players at the mike on the dais. Just then, Devin saw a familiar face, looking all serious in uniform, behind D.C. Police Chief Charles Ramsey. "That's Ryan!" he exclaimed.

"That's my nigga!" Andre whooped loudly over the phone.

"Nothing like all these folks dead, countless wounded, and a city scared shitless to guarantee career advancement," Jamal commented wryly. "I never would've thought there were two snipers. And brothahs at that! And that brothah, Malvo. Do they have to keep saying he's Jamaican? Like we need any more negative press. It's the same shit when Colin Ferguson shot up that train in Long Island. Or remember Ben Johnson? When he was winning, he was Canadian. When he got busted for doping, he suddenly became 'Ben Johnson, that steroid-using Jamaican!'"

Nothing could dampen Devin's sense of euphoria. He just laughed. "Mali, chill, man."

He heard a beep just then, over the phone. *Call waiting.* "Hold on, fellas," he said.

He pressed TALK to click over and greeted the person on the other line. "Dr. Rhym?" the man asked, his tone too somber to be delivering good news.

Devin was immediately curious. "Yes?"

"This is Dr. Griffin, over here at Helping Hands, the assisted-living facility," he said. "I'm afraid we need you to come over immediately."

Pop. Devin swallowed hard over the heartbeat traveling up his throat. "I'll be right there," he said.

Dr. Griffin and the Latina nurse were waiting for Devin in the lobby when he arrived. "My dad," he said, his voice a hoarse whisper.

Dr. Griffin shook his head. "Some time after he'd had dinner, he arrested," he announced in that calm voice Devin imagined they taught them to use in med school to deliver bad news. "We tried to revive him, but there was nothing we could do. He died before we could transport him to the hospital."

Devin covered his hands with his mouth, listened to his breathing, rocked back and forth on his heels as he wondered how someone as mighty as KL could be dead. And so suddenly. They'd spent the previous night together. They had dinner, and Devin helped with his physical therapy for his still-scarred hands. Devin gave him a shave, and they'd watched TV. He'd even told him that he and Chaney were going to have a baby, which made him grin from ear to ear. "I knew you had it in you, boy," KL laughed. "You're a Rhym man!"

KL's mind was clearer than Devin had ever remembered it being that night. They'd talked until the Nurse From Hell evicted him, saying that KL needed his rest. Devin tucked him in under the blankets and kissed his forehead. KL smiled up at him, and Devin felt he'd finally bonded with his father. "Matthew 3:17," KL murmured, between sleep and wakefulness.

Not you, quoting the Bible. His father had seen so much shit that he'd long ago doubted the existence of God, long ago abandoned the teachings of the Baptist church. "What's that say, Pop?" Devin asked.

KL had softly touched his cheek. "'This is my son, the Beloved, with whom I am well pleased,'" he'd said.

Devin met Dr. Griffin's expectant gaze. "I want to see him."

In the sterile light of the room, Devin stared down at his father on the ice cold steel gurney, covered up to the neck in a white sheet. KL looked like he was sleeping, like he'd just passed out in his Ghanaian chair in the living room. The only thing missing was his tiny reading glasses. Devin had come from this man, had spent his entire life in the pursuit of his approval. And now, he was gone. *What am I gonna do now?*

Fourteen

Devin took off the jacket to his black suit, loosened his black tie, and eased wearily down into KL's African chair. He looked around the living room, as if he could see it the way KL used to, and let the silence of the house wash over him. From the chair, he stared up at the fireplace mantel, at the 8x10 photograph of his father Renee had found, framed, and put up to establish KL's presence in the house. No need. Devin could feel KL's presence. So he talked to him.

You had an amazing funeral, Pops!

KL had arranged everything at Arlington Cemetery before he'd passed. All Devin had to do was make a call. Kim-Chin had helped Devin find KL's dress blues, complete with his sword and scabbard. Kim-Chin laughed, shaking her head. "You father, he was officer in charge of Marine Guard at U.S. embassy in Seoul," she said. "First time I see him in this at a party, I fell in love."

KL lay in the chapel at Fort Myer in Arlington for viewing. The following Wednesday, he was carried by horse-drawn caisson from the chapel to his grave at Arlington Cemetery, on a hill, overlooking D.C., in listening distance to the bells from the Netherlands Carillon.

I knew you didn't want this overthought eulogy; that would've embarrassed you.

Over the casket, in the crisp October breeze, Devin began to say what he could about a father he'd only just gotten to know over the past year. "Today we lay to rest Kenneth Leon Rhym, son of Leon and Sara Rhym of Crewe, Virginia. Father to Chauncey, Eric, and Devin. Grandfather to Jeffrey, Corey, and Chelsea," Devin sighed, and his voice caught. But he pressed on, lauding his father's accomplishments, and letting the world know just how much he was loved, even when it wasn't easy. It was the end that got him. He could feel his throat closing, feel the wetness coming in his eyes, but still, he pressed on. "So, now, dear father, always faithful warrior, there are no more battles for you to fight. You're at peace now."

The tears defied him. They spilled out onto his reddened, contorted face. Just as he felt more vulnerable and exposed than he'd ever wanted to feel, with hundreds of eyes focused on him, he felt a soft hand press a hanky into his. He dabbed his eyes, looked down, and saw Chaney's face. His heart filled with love for her. He slipped an arm around her waist and clung to her for both physical and moral support. Then he placed his hand on the casket, inside which KL rested. "You are home," he wept.

Sobs and wails filled the gray sky, as a lone bugler played "Taps." Devin clutched onto Chaney for dear life, burying his head in her shoulder at the awfully loud but ceremonial twenty-one-gun salute. He remembered how fake it looked on TV, when people would jump at the sound of the bullets cracking off. But it was so loud that he did jump, especially, too, since the entire area had been sensitized to the sound of gunfire, courtesy of the snipers, John Muhammad and Lee Boyd Malvo.

The casket team slowly folded Old Glory into a neat, tight triangle. The team leader then passed it to the chaplain. The chaplain turned and saluted the Marine Corps' military representative, a grizzled white officer with a veritable quilt of stripes on his chest. The representative turned and paused, looking quizzically at KL's motley family of three ex-wives of different colors, sons who also looked radically different, one black and one white daughter-in-law, and one girlfriend.

Per custom, as Devin was in position at the left front seat graveside, the representative presented the flag to Devin. Devin hugged the flag to his chest and looked up into the representative's steely gray eyes, surprisingly finding comfort there as the Marine said quietly, "On behalf of the President of the United States, a grateful nation, and a proud Corps, this flag is presented as a token of our appreciation for the honorable and faithful service rendered by your loved one to his country and to the United States Marine Corps."

The party here was crazy, Dad!

Kim-Chin and Beverly, First Wife, had done all the cooking: a mixture of Far East meets Old South. Daphne supervised and got as drunk as she possibly could without passing out, much to Eric's extreme embarrassment. She'd sidled up to Jamal. "And what's your name, honey?" she slurred. " 'Cause, I like the big, black snake, if you know what I mean."

Jamal looked horrified as Eric took his mother away like she was a naughty child.

People approached Devin all day to sing KL's praises. Older men would say, "Hey, I fought with your dad in Korea," or "I served with KL in 'Nam," or "I worked with your father at the Pentagon." Younger men took Devin aside to say, "M.P.s caught me fucking an officer's wife, and your dad got me out of a court martial," or "I was caught holding a dime bag, and your pops flipped it and actually convinced the JAG court that I didn't mean to buy chronic, that I thought I was buying oregano! Your pops was the man!"

And I know you didn't care for Bill, but he was respectful to your memory.

Bill even took the extraordinary step of booking a suite for himself and Kim-Chin at the J.W. Marriot on Fourteenth Street, despite the fact that Devin insisted they stay with him at the house. "This was your father's home, Devin," Bill said simply. "I'm not going to interfere with that."

Bill occupied a space in the background, supportive to his wife and stepson, but never demanding any attention. Devin admired how he blended so seamlessly into the family that was Diversity Central. He'd even sought Bill's counsel about the practice, about what they should do. "Sometimes, you've got to walk into the belly of the beast, Devin," he said, his voice indicative of quiet wisdom. "If you can't beat them, then you have to figure out a way to join them. Survival is key."

Devin marinated on that one.

You should've seen Kimmy, Pops! I saved her!

Kimmy came through, and she looked like he'd remembered her in high school, with the sun shining through her. She was happy again, and as blond as he'd remembered her. She was also very New York, from the chic black dress and shoes, to the cultured way she spoke. And the boys . . . Dante was taking baby steps. And Denis was the man. His hair was cut. He looked like he was eating properly, and he was taller, too. In a moment on the porch, when Devin had snuck away to lose it, Denis had come up next to him and touched his shoulder. "Don't cry, Uncle Devin," he said. "It's gonna be okay."

Devin smiled through his tears, setting the boy on his lap. "I know."

And Chaney . . .

When he'd called her to give her the news that KL had died, she was over at the house in minutes. "What can I do to help?" she'd asked.

Typically, she'd given him his space. But he knew she was there, in the background making sure that things ran smoothly in the foreground. She'd even won over his mother. When Devin introduced her, haltingly, she said, "*Annyong ha se yo.*" He was surprised. She'd asked him casually how to say hello in Korean; he'd told her and had forgotten about it. Until right then. Kim-Chin smiled and hugged her, the woman who was carrying Kim-Chin's grandchild. "*Annyong, na ddar,*" Kim-Chin returned. *Hello, my daughter . . .*

She'd brought D and Hiriko, made sure that Devin finally got to meet the infamous cousin Norm, and her sister Anna Lisa. She held him close as they all left. He clung to her and buried his nose in her fresh 'fro. "We were supposed to talk," he lamented.

She patted his back. "No rush, sweetie," she said. "When you're done here, we'll talk."

Pops . . .

Devin got up out of the chair, approached the mantel, and picked up his father's photograph. With his finger, he traced the lines and shadows of his father's face, the frame glass smooth underneath his fingertip. "I love you, Pop," he sighed. "I just wish we'd had more time."

Chaney's heart was heavy as she stood on the sidewalk, watching the men pack up the rental Mercury Mountaineer as Anna Lisa and Hiriko supervised. Again, the house was going to be empty. D and Hiriko were going back to Quantico, and Anna Lisa and Norm were going with them.

Anna Lisa took a break from the task and joined Chaney on the sidewalk. They'd suspended their hostilities, in the wake of KL's death.

Between the two of them, they'd been busy preparing to arrive, preparing for the funeral. There had been little chance to talk. Chaney assumed that now was when they were supposed to make up for that lost time. "Let me backtrack," Chaney teased. "First I was the quisling who didn't tell you about D's wedding, then I was the squanderer of inheritances, and then I was the reproductively careless. Have I gotten us caught up to the last conversation we had before you came?"

Anna Lisa grinned sheepishly. "Okay, okay," she said. "So I overreacted a bit."

"Yeah, like Chernobyl overreacted," Chaney laughed.

"You forget, Chaney, that sometimes, I look at you, and I still see the little baby I named," Anna Lisa said.

"I'm about to have a baby of my own, Anna Lisa," Chaney reminded her.

"Then you'll see what I mean," Anna Lisa said. To Chaney, it sounded like a veiled threat. "It's not easy to shut that instinct off." They both stared at D, stuffing bags into the hatch. "That's where three-quarters of my problem with him stems from."

Chaney looked at her sister. Poor woman, she couldn't help herself. Chaney slipped an arm around her sister's shoulders. Anna Lisa looked up at her and smiled. "You raised us," Chaney reminded her. "We're gonna be just fine."

Just then, Chaney saw the black Navigator pulling into the parking lot. Her heart skipped a beat. *Could it be . . . ?*

The car parked next to Anna Lisa's rental, and Devin, in a black suit and matching coat, jumped out. "Oooh, look who's here," Anna Lisa teased.

Chaney playfully punched her in the arm. Anna Lisa gave her the evil eye that used to work when she was a kid. "Don't make me take my shoe off, girl," she cautioned.

Chaney and Anna Lisa watched as Devin hugged D, and then Norm, and then Hiriko. "If he's anything like his father, then he's a good man, Chaney," Anna Lisa said. "I just want you to be happy, my sistah."

"Me, too, Anna Lisa," she said. "I think I've earned it."

Devin looked over at them and flashed Chaney a brilliant smile. She went hot and cold all over. Given everything he'd experienced recently, he still had a bit of joy in his heart. *You're wonderful . . .*

Devin approached them on the sidewalk. He hugged Anna Lisa first. "You're leaving so soon?" he asked.

Anna Lisa nodded. "Yes, going to spend some quality time with my son before he goes off to fight George W. Bush's senseless war," she said, then twisted up her mouth like she'd just tasted bitters.

Chaney poked her. "Now, you promised you were going to ease up on that."

Anna Lisa sighed. "I'm gonna remember all of this stuff you're telling me and laugh out loud when you have your own," she declared.

Devin focused on her, and it was like everything around her melted away. He slowly embraced her. "Hey," he said, his deep voice vibrating through to her heart.

"Hey," she returned.

Anna Lisa cleared her throat. "Well, that's our cue to leave," she said. "You be good. And just promise me one thing. Keep an eye on your friend Nathalie. I enjoyed all the dinners over at her house, and seeing the places she's rehabbing, but I think she's trying to keep busy to forget about the miscarriage."

Chaney nodded. "I'm already on it," she promised.

Chaney and Devin said good-bye to Anna Lisa, Norm, Hiriko, and D, staring long after the Mountaineer rolled out of the parking lot.

Her eyes met Devin's. They were alone together. Again. "How are you holding up?" she asked.

The pulse at his jaw throbbed. He shrugged, but Chaney could tell his loss was just as fresh as when he'd called her on Thursday night with the news. "What's that old cliché: as well as can be expected?" he laughed awkwardly.

She grabbed his elbow. "Come on. Let's go in. I'm freezing!"

Once inside, Chaney took his coat and hung it up. "Want some coffee? Tea? Something?" she said.

He gave her an appreciative once-over. Even though she felt self-conscious in her ripped jeans and ratty green cardigan, she could sense what was first on his mind. She looked away, and laughed. He laughed, too. "Am I that transparent?" he said.

She shoved her hands into her pockets. "Yeah, you are."

"To be honest, though, I am a little hungry," he confessed.

He was in luck. She broke out everything that Anna Lisa cooked since she arrived, all packed neatly away in Gladware: baked turkey, stuffing, greens, peas and rice, macaroni and cheese, cole slaw, potato salad. They sat at the kitchen table and feasted. When he was done, he rubbed his belly contentedly, stretched his legs under the table, and leaned back.

She started to clear the table. He helped, coming up behind her with the rest. "What are you doing tomorrow?" he asked casually, putting the dishes in the sink.

She elbowed him. "Marlene's having a baby shower for Renee. Somehow, she heard that I make these shea butter products and wants me to show 'em to her."

He smiled, a devious twinkle in his eye. "I'm gonna do the Shaggy," he said. "Wuddn't me."

"Only he stole it from Eddie Murphy."

He laughed, fishing in his pants pocket. He handed her a white envelope. "I found this on Dad's dresser. I think he meant to give it to you before all the stuff happened with Sadat and everything."

Chaney wiped her hands on the nearest tea towel and took the envelope from Devin. Her name, in block letters, was written on the front. She slipped her finger underneath the glue side, tore it open, and pulled out a folded piece of yellow legal paper. She unfolded it, and her heart lurched. Inside, addressed to her at the PAY TO THE ORDER OF line, was a bank draft for fifty thousand dollars. Wordlessly, she handed it to Devin. "Shit!" he exclaimed. "What's this for?"

Chaney read out loud the contents of the letter, written in KL's neat, cursive penmanship:

Baby Girl,
Here is something to start you up in your pursuit of happiness. When I first met you, you were a happy little girl, in spite of the shit hand God dealt you. You sat in my lap and shared your candy with me. Now, thanks to Devin, you're back in my life. You shared your immense gift with me. I want you to share that with the world.
KL

Chaney looked up at Devin, handing the letter to him so that he could read it, too. "What a sweet man!" she sobbed. "I don't deserve this!"

Devin set the letter and the check down on the counter and pulled her into his arms. She surrendered as he held her close, rocked her gently. "Who knew with Pops?" he said. "He believed in you. He literally put his money where his mouth was."

She buried her face into his chest and sobbed until she was empty, her weeping evolving from tiny earthquakes of emotion and tears, to a deep sigh. She moved away from him and wiped her wet cheeks with the backs of her hands. She laughed, embarrassed by his close scrutiny. "Damn, girl, what'd you put in that shaving mousse?" he teased.

"Love," she said.

She picked up the check and looked at it, shaking her head in utter disbelief that KL would do something like that for her. *Miracle Number Two* . . .

She looked up at Devin. "Thanks . . . for the hug," she said sheepishly. "You were always a great hugger."

Devin moved in closer. He dried her damp cheeks with his long thumbs. "What kind of kisser was I?" he teased.

Chaney stared longingly at his full pink mouth, with the top lip ever so slightly larger than the bottom one. *Go for it!* She tiptoed and brushed her mouth against his. Just from his touch, shock waves rumbled through her. She leaned her forehead against his and laughed softly. "Excellent kisser," she decreed.

He kissed her again and again. "How'd I put it down?" he asked, again with the teasing tone.

She cocked her head to one side. Her turn to tease. "You know, I can't remember," she said. "It's the strangest thing. You're probably gonna have to refresh my memory."

He sighed with mock exasperation. "I guess a man's gotta do what a man's gotta do."

She took his hand and led him toward the stairs.

Once upstairs in her room, they leaned into each other for what seemed like hours. He smelled like cologne and laundry detergent and his own special scent. She greedily inhaled it in. She pressed herself closer to him, so she could feel the hardness of him against her. She leaned her head against his chest and sighed. "I missed you."

He slid his fingers underneath her sweater, his long fingers kneading the flesh at the base of her spine. "I'm not going anywhere, baby."

She pushed him to the foot of the bed, and he laughed as he

plopped down on the mattress. He gazed up at her with hooded, dark eyes as she began discarding clothing, from the cardigan, to the confining bra. Then she worked the button and zipper of her jeans and pushed them to the floor. She stood in front of him in nothing but black bikini underwear, as if inviting him to finish the job.

He reached for her, clutching her by the thighs and pulling her close. To her ultimate surprise, he pressed his ear against her stomach. "He's in there," he said in awe.

Chaney stroked his dark head. "Or she," she giggled.

He kissed her tummy, once, twice. He stuck the tip of his tongue in her navel, and she gasped. Thanks to his eager fingers, the black bikinis went south, too, and so did his mouth. He took her leg and draped it over his shoulder. That long, pointed tongue darted between her legs, tasting, circling, invading her. She shuddered, grabbing his head and urging him further.

He stopped suddenly, and she ached for more. He stood up in front of her, and she watched, anticipation mounting as he tossed off layers of clothing to reveal that delicious, long, taut body that she knew every inch of. She looked down, and he was standing straight up at attention, pointing directly at her. He pulled her into one of his world-class hugs. His mouth found hers, and they kissed lazily, like they had all the time in the world and no particular place to be. Hands stroked soft, bare skin, fingers interlaced with fingers, limbs intertwined with limbs. "Chaney," he whispered. "I love you, girl."

"I love you, too, baby," she whispered back.

They crab-walked to the bed, laughing at their awkward progress, and she slid in under the covers. She opened eager arms to him, and he languidly slipped on top of her, propping himself up with his elbows. She opened her legs, and with one long motion, he was inside her. He threw back his head and moaned. She arched her back to meet him. They were completely naked with each other, no rubber, no pretense, no Fluexa to dull the sensation of his skin against her skin.

He felt new again, harder, longer, stronger. She clung to him, drove her pelvis against his, trying to get him deeper and deeper inside. He moaned, she groaned. He sucked at her mouth, she thrust her tongue deep into his. Their breathing came shallower and harder as the moment intensified. That neurological tremor that had eluded her for so long became an all-out release, and every muscle in her body rose up to comply. She screamed, she cried, and she howled as an orgasm rocked her from the tips of her toes to every follicle on her scalp. In the background of her cries, she heard him moan loudly, felt him twitching on top of her as he filled her up.

He laughed wearily, kissing her mouth over and over. She laughed, too, tasting his salty sweat. "Finally, that's what you sound like," he said. "I wanna hear more of that."

She wrapped her arms around him, and he lay against her, until their breathing slowly returned to normal, and eyelids flickered, allowing peaceful sleep to come.

Devin sat on the edge of the bed, watching her sleep. It finally started to sink in. She was the mother of his child. The thought of it intrigued him more than it frightened him. He knew he wanted to spend the rest of his life with her; that was a given. But children . . . *What kind of father would I be?*

For now, though, the answer to that question would have to wait. He was going to go handle his business. He shifted, and she stirred awake. He wanted to stare at that face every morning. "Hey," he whispered.

She stretched. The covers gave way, and he got an eyeful of breasts with hard, pink nipples. *Focus, Devin.* "Hey," she yawned. "Where are you going?"

He shrugged. "Work," he said. "I'll meet you over at Marlene's later, okay?"

She nodded. Already, her eyes were closing again as she drifted back to sleep. "I love you," she said, her voice hoarse from sleep.

I love you, too. "You're just saying that 'cause I whipped it on you," he laughed.

A smile played at the corners of her mouth. With an index finger, he drew a heart over her left breast, kissed the finger, and pressed it in the middle of the heart. Then he went to find his clothes.

Sometimes, you've got to walk into the belly of the beast . . . If you can't beat them, then you have to figure out a way to join them. Survival is key.

Bill's words echoed in Devin's head as he entered the glass doors of the Pet-Thenon. He marveled at the shelves and shelves of pet food for every species of animal imaginable. He stared down the spacious aisles, where customers strolled with pets on leashes or in plastic carriers. The piped-in Muzak was the soundtrack to the activity that swirled around him. He hadn't felt so small and insignificant since he was a child.

Devin entered the gateway that separated the store from the animal hospital. A round, navy-blue admissions desk was packed with harried women in powder-blue scrubs. The waiting room was stacked with pet parents, with animals in varying stages of distress. In the waiting room alone, he saw the Levinsohns, Fluffy's owners, the Johnsons with Fifi, their Bichon Frisee, and the Powells with their cat, Pete, in his signature blue carrier.

Devin tried hard to maintain his composure. Michelle Powell, the ten-year-old daughter with a face full of freckles, recognized him and waved. "Hi, Dr. Rhym!" she called.

Devin waved back. Her mother, seated right next to her, pretended not to see him.

One of the women behind the rotunda looked up and smiled. "May I help you, sir?" she asked.

You could close up shop and leave town! He knew that would never happen. "I have an appointment to see Dr. Steffes," he announced.

"And you are . . . ?"

"Devin Rhym," he announced.

"Just a sec," she said, then a page for Dr. Steffes went through the entire animal hospital.

Devin waited for ten long minutes, staring at patients in the room and hazarding guesses at diagnoses. Just when he started thinking that Bill and his advice were wack, the door to the back room opened—Devin guessed that was where they performed their limited surgeries—and a bewildered, middle-aged white guy, complete with blue scrubs and a white coat, came barreling out. "Dr. Rhym?" he questioned, looking around the room.

Of course, the man wouldn't have known him from Adam. He'd only spoken to him on the phone. Devin stood. "That's me."

Dr. Steffes sighed. "I'm sorry I kept you waiting," he said. "I should've had my head examined, telling you to meet me on a Saturday. It's crazy today, and I'm the only one here. You wanna reschedule?"

Devin recognized opportunity when it came knocking. "I could give you a hand if you'd like," he offered.

Steffes paused briefly, like he was tempted, then shook his head. "Nah!" he said. "I couldn't ask you to give up your Saturday."

Devin shook his head. "I'm already here, and I'm dressed," he laughed. "Really, it's no problem."

Steffes sighed, deep from the soul. He vigorously pumped Devin's hand, squeezing his elbow. "Bless your heart," he said gratefully, then pointed to the girl who'd helped him previously. "Danielle over there will get you sorted out. Just do what you do best!"

Danielle threw up her hands. "Let's get you a coat," she suggested.

Devin nodded, then watched as Steffes rushed away. *You're gonna owe me big for this . . .*

Chaney was horrified. She stared at Renee, seated in the white wicker chair reserved for the mother-to-be. Renee looked like she'd swallowed a basketball. She wore a black woolen muumuu, woolen trouser socks, and black mules over feet so swollen that Renee looked like she had elephantiasis. Gamely, Renee submitted as the evil, thin, nonpregnant women made her a hat out of the remnants of gift wrapping paper and made her wear it. In short, she looked like she was ready to blow at any second. Chaney looked down at her tummy, still mercifully flat, as flat as it could be with ten finger sandwiches and shower cake in it could be. *Is that gonna be me nine months from now?*

Marlene, the consummate hostess, began passing out the gift baskets that Chaney had made the day before. Chaney's heart pitter-pattered. With a wave of her free hand, she indicated Chaney, who sat with a gaggle of sistahs—Chaney learned from conversation that they were legal-aid lawyers—three seats away from Renee. "Chaney made these baskets for us to sample," Marlene announced. "Inside, there are scented shea butter creams, shaving mousses, wood-handled razors, and scented candles."

"This is how I got pregnant, ladies!" Renee laughed, and naughty cackles followed in response.

"Who's Chaney?" asked a white girl in the far corner of the expansive living room, next to the pile of expensive gifts.

Chaney raised a hand, and Marlene pointed her out. "There she is," Marlene said. "She's Devin's girlfriend."

So, she needed Devin to legitimize her. Devin's girlfriend. Another title added to the growing list. One of the sistahs she was with stared at her quizzically. "Little Devin?" she asked.

Chaney got the none-too-subtle hint. She used the same response she'd leveled at her sister. "He's not that little," she declared.

The other women hooted and hollered, and the offending sistah wore the gas face. "I know das right," Chaney heard from one of the women in the room.

Renee looked down at the offending sistah from her white wicker perch. "Serve you right, witcha big mouth," she laughed.

Devin stared at Chaney, handling herself with the crowd of busy-bodies. And he appreciated the ringing endorsement. He cleared his throat and came into the room. "Why are my ears burning?" he laughed.

Chaney's eyes met his, and her heart leapt. He looked so hand-some, all suited down in hunter green. *Please rescue me!*

The women teasingly singsonged their greetings to him, which he graciously returned. Then he crossed the room and planted a wet one right on Chaney's open mouth. If these women could see the depth of his feelings for her in his heart, they wouldn't question his right to be with her. "How's it going?"

Chaney shook at his touch. He'd proven to her that she didn't need chemicals to achieve physical and emotional fulfillment. She especially loved the physical fulfillment part. She looked away briefly, catching glimpses of all the women in the room staring at them. "Good," she said quietly.

He'd wanted to be alone with her all day, to tell her about his triumph. He cast a panoramic gaze at the ladies in the room. "Can I steal my honey for a bit?" he asked.

Marlene looked like she'd just found her voice. "Of course," she said. "We were just finishing up."

Chaney and Devin each thanked Marlene, wished Renee luck, and thanked the ladies for trying the products. "They're really great," Devin assured them. "I use them myself."

"Bring her back, Devin, when you're through," Marlene called after them. "Each guest gets a miniature dieffenbachia!"

Chaney sensed that no plants, no pets, no men was officially Black history. She laughed out loud as they headed for the car. He loved her laugh; it sounded like she was happy all over. "What?" he asked.

What he didn't know would hurt him. "Nothing," she said.

In the ride, he headed for the Dunn Loring metro station, on the Orange Line. Chaney looked over at him as he drove. He looked too happy; something must be up. "Where are we going?" she asked.

"I wanna go visit Pop," Devin said.

He felt if he was contemplating fatherhood and, possibly, commitment, he should be in the aura of someone who knew both intimately.

Devin parked, and they got on the train. Chancy remembered that night they rode the metro together. She giggled as visions of him break dancing played in her head. "What are you gonna beatbox this time?" she teased.

Devin, you corny motherfucker! It still amazed him that she found that so charming. "Aww, man," he moaned. "I would've done anything to impress you that night."

Holding hands, they took the train all the way to Rosslyn. On the escalator ride up to the surface, she held on tight to his hand. Their eyes met. *I can't keep my hands off you!* Chaney thought. She tiptoed and kissed his mouth. He closed his eyes and returned the favor. *You taste so good,* he thought.

They strolled through Rosslyn to Arlington Cemetery, then got on a bus to take them to the gravesites. Chaney could feel the mood turn somber. While tourists got off to see the graves of JFK and Jackie Onassis, and Robert Kennedy, and other luminaries who'd gone before, they continued on until they arrived at the turned earth where KL had been buried just days before. "It doesn't seem official yet," Devin mused. "I guess the marker will help."

Chaney watched as Devin bent, grabbed a fistful of the dirt, and then let it sprinkle through his fingers. Her eyes misted. That vibrant man who'd saved her—twice—was under this very plot of ground. "It hardly seems real."

He stood up and clapped his hands together, expelling the loose dirt. He turned and got a look at the city laid out in front of him. He studied her profile as she looked out at D.C. "I wanna marry you," he said, then breathed heavily, then played the declaration back in his mind. He'd put it out there in the universe.

Chaney stared at him. "I'm having the wickedest case of déjà vu."

"I mean it this time," he declared. "I love you. I want to be with you for the rest of my life. I have something to offer now. Today, I helped save my practice by agreeing to work with the Pet-Thenon to secure referrals and new patients."

"I didn't get into this for a ring, Devin. I especially didn't get pregnant to force you to marry me."

He held up a hand. This was shaping up to be a replay of the scene at Eric's office. He sighed. *Don't force it.* "I can put a ring on your fin-

ger, or we could shack up, if you want," he said. "I don't care. I just
want to be with you. Be a father to our child."

Why are you resisting so hard? Then it hit her. Fear of change. Fear of
disappointment. Fear of loss. Warty, all-consuming, ugly-as-sin fear.
"Can I think about it?" she asked sheepishly.

He shrugged, trying to play it off, but her refusal hurt. "Okay.
Think about it."

The sun started to dip, and the wind began to kick up. "We should
get going," he said, subdued.

Chaney nodded, then leaned down. Devin was sweating a marker.
At least his father had a gravesite that Devin could visit. " 'Bye, KL,"
she singsonged. "Be back soon."

They retraced their steps in silence, back to the Rosslyn metro.
There were no playful kisses this time as they rode the escalator and
made their way to the platform. She knew he was pissed, but how could
she explain that even though she loved him, that what he wanted scared
her to death? She couldn't understand it herself.

She took his arm and put it around her shoulders. She nudged
him, curled up in that special hollow of his throat. He looked down at
her, and even though he felt rejected, he smiled down at her. *Don't
give up so easily, Dev.*

Just then, they felt the breeze down the tunnel and saw the flashing
lights that signaled the arrival of the approaching train. He snapped
his fingers. "Okay," he said. "We can either take the Blue train to you
in Alexandria, or the Orange train to my house in Clarendon."

"What are you saying, boy?" she laughed.

"Simple," he said louder over the noise on the platform. "If it's
Blue, I'll ease up off you, but if it's Orange, we're going to my house.
Our house."

They both turned to look at the electronic sign on the platform. It
read—in glowing block capital letters—BLUE LINE TRAIN TO FRANCONIA-
SPRINGFIELD ARRIVING.

Devin sucked his teeth. "Fuck," he said.

Let go! Chaney hugged him close. The plan was ingenious. She
stared up into his face, with the hangdog look of disappointment
firmly plastered there. "Well, I've got to go home," she said, then she
nudged him. "After all, if I'm going to your house, I'll need to get
some clothes."

Devin's heart raced. He grinned from ear to ear, raising and lowering his eyebrows suggestively. "No, you don't," he laughed suggestively.

The train eased to a stop, and about a minute later, the doors slid open. Hand in hand, they got onto the train.

Epilogue

Everyone gathered at the house on North Garfield Street to celebrate Thanksgiving 2003, which coincided with the first-year anniversary of the grand opening of Three Sisters, Inc., Chaney's line of natural beauty products. An 18x24 lithograph of the logo—a line drawing of Chaney, Daisy, and Anna Lisa—graced the anteroom of the home.

Chaney looked around her and reflected on the past year. KL's initial investment, along with the settlement that Eric had secured for her from Autodidact, provided the start-up capital for her business. She hired herself a small staff—which included Coco—and leased office and factory space in the Torpedo Factory in trendy Old Town Alexandria, just on the Potomac. Devin's restructured business plan also worked well for the Rosslyn Veterinary Hospital. The referrals from the Pet-Thenon, as Devin had predicted, provided a constant and necessary revenue stream. The practice grew to add new partners.

Christmas of 2002, D was deployed to Kuwait, so Chaney was far from astonished when, on March 19, she'd heard over the car radio that Operation Iraqi Freedom had begun. As D had requested, Hiriko relocated up to Alexandria. Chaney enjoyed having her close. She and Hiriko shared pregnancy stories, strange cravings, and unconditional love for the lives growing inside them. Only Chaney's body seemed to be growing like John Hurt's in *Alien*. After an ultrasound, Macca later revealed that Chaney was actually pregnant with twins, one of which was definitely a boy. "I saw nuts on the sonogram," Devin laughed proudly with his boys.

Hiriko gave birth to Sachiko Anna Lisa on April Fools' Day at the VA Hospital on Irving Street in northwest D.C. Anna Lisa cried more over her first grandchild than D had when he saw his daughter via streaming video web cam at the house. They watched as his fellow Marines handed out pink cigars somewhere in Iraq.

As fighting intensified, D learned that the usual six-month tour of a Marine would be extended indefinitely. Then Hiriko got The Call on April 14. The day before, D's battalion took casualties as U.S. forces stormed Tikrit, Saddam Hussein's birthplace. D was wounded in action; many in the battalion were killed, including the sweet, fresh-faced Lance Corporal Richardson, who'd tried to step to Chaney at D's wedding. Anna Lisa was headed down from New York again.

Seventy-two hours later, D had arrived at Bethesda Naval Hospital. Heavy and uncomfortable, Chaney stood for hours until he finally arrived via ambulance from Andrews Air Force Base. Every inch of him was bandaged, except for his eyes. D took Chaney's hand and squeezed it. Chaney struggled valiantly to hold it together. "See, I promised you. No Walter Reed," she laughed mid-sobs. "No addadicktomy for you."

Just as they wheeled D away, Chaney felt a whoosh, then a torrent of moisture between her legs, like she'd wet herself in public. Devin, eyes wide, looked down at the puddle she was standing in. "Sweetest, I think your water just broke," he announced.

D was coming out of delicate neurosurgery as Chaney, after ten hours of labor, delivered Leon Devin and Regine Kim-Chin into the world. Anna Lisa finally decided to retire from the New York City public school system and moved in with Hiriko and D. As did Daisy, who pulled up stakes, left California, and moved back East.

Chaney watched as Anna Lisa fussed over D, who was still shaky from his brain injury. He didn't complain, and just allowed his mother to feed him more turkey. Norm and Hiriko looked on and smiled. Renee allowed her latest, little Kenneth Leon, to suckle her while she and Chauncey talked to Daisy about their legal-aid office in southeast D.C. Jeffrey, Chelsea, and Corey ran through the house, laughing as they chased Kimchi, a Labrador retriever of a curious gray color from

Tony and Hershey's litter. Chaney shook her head, watching Eric and Marlene, sitting on the couch like distant spectators. Chaney sensed their marriage was not long for this world. Chaney felt hands slide suggestively around her waist and smiled.

Devin nuzzled his second-favorite spot on her body; tonight, she smelled like fruits. Andre had told him that, after a year, he was going to want to chew off a leg to get out of his relationship. Devin knew from kindergarten not to listen to Andre. He loved her more then than he did that day on the train, when she said she'd be with him. Every day, his family made him happier than he'd ever imagined he could be. "Come here," he whispered. "I wanna show you something."

He took her hand and led her up the stairs, the stairs he used to zip up and down when he was a kid. Now his kids were going to do the same. He showed her to the room that used to be his room, then KL's study. It was now a nursery, complete with a massive crib, changing table, two rocking chairs, and Afrocentric lithographs that she'd picked out.

Chaney's heart squeezed. In the crib, Satch and Rae slept snuggled together, like she and D used to when they were younger. They'd come full circle.

Lee was wide awake. His little head, with the shock of curly hair, not unlike KL's darted from his mother, to his father, then back to his mother. Chaney still couldn't believe that she was someone's mother. Times two. Tolochko has asked her when last she'd experienced joy. Finally, she had flesh and blood answers.

Devin grinned broadly. "I've taught my son a trick," he said, his tone loaded with suspense.

Chaney was leery. "I'm waiting," she said.

Devin looked down at his beautiful little boy who brought him hours of joy. "Go on, Lee," he urged. "Show Omma your new trick."

Lee extended a chubby little fist Chaney's way. "Ah!" he cried.

As much as she loved her son, Chaney was unmoved. "He does that when he's giving me spitty Cheerios," she said.

"He's a little slow on the basic motor skill," Devin apologized, then to Lee, "Let Daddy help."

With gentle fingers, Devin pried opened Lee's tiny fist. This time, Chaney gasped. She was beyond moved. In her son's soft little hand was an emerald-cut golden engagement ring. "Ah!" he said again, as if to say, See, *Mommy?*

Devin savored the expression on her face. He wanted to remember that forever. "So," Devin concluded, "we've got the house and the businesses. We've got the illegitimate half-Cablanasian children. Are we ever going to make this official?"

Chaney looked over at him and felt a complete absence of fear, a vacuum filled to the brim with love for him, and their children, and their family. She pressed a kiss on his delicious pink mouth. Devin's heart sang. "What the fuck?" she giggled. "Let's get married!"

Devin saw out of the corner of his eye as Lee took the ring and flung it across the room with surprising strength for a seven-month-old baby. "Oh no!" he cried.

He dropped to his knees, and so did Chaney. Like two tigers, they stalked the hardwood floors, looking for anything that sparkled. "We should just live in sin," she laughed.

"Not after I just spent two months' salary," he chuckled.

Chaney rolled over on her back and watched as he frantically searched. "Hey," she said.

"What?" he said.

"Come here."

He did as he was told. She wrapped her arms around him, and tongue-kissing began in earnest. After all this time, the ring could wait . . . for a little while longer, anyway.

WHAT YOU WON'T DO FOR LOVE
WENDY COAKLEY-THOMPSON

ABOUT THIS GUIDE

The following questions are designed to facilitate discussion in and among reader groups.

DISCUSSION QUESTIONS

1. What would you speculate is the reason for the recent emergence of "reverse" May–December relationships (i.e., older woman, younger man)?

2. How would you explain Chaney's attraction to Devin, and Devin's attraction to Chaney?

3. Is Devin's family unique, or are such multicultural families becoming the norm?

4. Contrast Chaney's relationship with her sisters with Devin's relationship with his brothers.

5. Do you think the relationships between KL and Devin is typical of that of a son trying to find an identity separate and apart from that of his father?

6. About clinical depression, Macca states that if more Blacks " . . . were open to accepting the diagnosis, instead of thinking that we can just 'walk it off' or 'seek Jesus,' then we'd have less misery in our community." What are your thoughts concerning depression among Blacks? Are they in concert with or diametrically opposed to Macca's views?

7. Do you feel the Fluexa helped or harmed Chaney in her dealings with the Autodidact partners and clients?

8. Would you characterize Chaney's fear of marriage, children, and abandonment as irrational or well founded?

9. After which episode (e.g., the destructive behavior, the drug overdose, etc.) would your patience with "Tony Braxton" have been exhausted?

10. Why do you think Nathalie was more tolerant of Dani's lesbian relationship with Sandy than she was of Chaney's May–December relationship with Devin?

11. When John Muhammad and Lee Boyd Malvo launched a twenty-three-day killing spree throughout the Washington, D.C., area, the news media portrayed the region as "in the grip of terror," or characterizations to that effect. Does this story effectively lend another perspective of that particular moment in time?

12. What do you think the future holds for Chaney and Devin? For your favorite character(s) from the story?